GIM NIGMA

THE SEARCH FOR GIM NIGMA

Written Story and Illustrations
BY DAVID ABRAHMOV

Copyright © 2017 David Abrahmov
All rights reserved
First Edition

PAGE PUBLISHING, INC.
Conneaut Lake, PA

First originally published by Page Publishing 2017

ISBN 978-1-68348-675-6 (pbk)
ISBN 978-1-68348-676-3 (digital)

Printed in the United States of America

Gratitude to God

I dedicate this book with Love & Honor to my dear parents

Josian Hadas Abrahmov & Benyamin Biko Abrahmov

To my mother that lived a challenged life and still carried on with a heart full of generosity, kindness, innocence and unlimited love, she was a selfless woman who always wanted to help those in need, I thank you mother for your love, care and devotion, may your sweet smile shine upon us all
Until we all meet again
I forever love you

To my father that worked hard all his life to provide and take care
of his family, he was a kind, generous, sweet and selfless man,
a simple knight, his sword was a hammer, with it he build and
created, I thank you father for your devotion, love, care and your
own special wisdom that continues to guide me and others in life
Until we all meet again
I love you my father

The book is inspired
With their wisdom, kindness, simplicity,
love and genuine care for others

I love you and I hope I will make you both proud

David

Special dedication to my beloved wonderful sister

Leah Abrahmov

You are a true champion and a loving woman, you are a
gift in my life and to others as well, I am proud of you and
thanking you for encouraging and supporting me,
I will always be there for you I cherish you and I love you forever
You are an amazing sister

Special dedication to my beloved wife and my best friend

Laurie Bergstein-Abrahmov

I have waited a long time for a special someone like
you, and I am grateful to have you in my life, you are
a beautiful, sweet, smart and strong woman,
I thank you for being so genuine and loving
I cherish you and I love you

Special dedication

To my family and all my dear friends

Special thanks to Orli Santo
for translating the book with deep devotion and care, your
artistic touch is greatly appreciated. Thank you Orli.

David

Special dedication with Love and Honor

Itzik Mordechai
Miri Shimoni
Ronit Nechushtan
Tziporah Sylivia Bergstein
Odile & Pierre Guedj
Grandfather David
Grandmother Tziporah Deda
Grandfather Eliyaho
Grandmother Leah Rosie
Igal Shasho
Zina Zilpa Mordechai
Elkazar Mordechai
Malka Sheindel
Ivy & Ronny Seigle
Baroukh Abadi
Ben Yochanan
Deborah Bernstein
Marian Sergi
Jack & Esther Goldblatt
Viviane Aboudi Mizrahi
Norman Naftaly Bergstein
Tamar & Avrahm Pili
Levi and Natella Abrahmov
Yasha Abrahmov
Bagi
Mania & Zvi Brier
Yoram Nir Hod
Miriam Gitel and Moshe Yosef Melzer
Gyongyi & Armin Kaufman
Sara bat Yehoshua
Chaim Zvi ben shalom
Oshrat Viner
Ruth Geula Suliman
Shulamit Meshulam
Uri Vaknin
Abie Cohen
Isaac Meger
Chaim Yechiel Miller
Edward David Attia
Ami Shmuel Amitzur Heller
Lorenzo DeVito
Abraham Ben Issac Weber
Sally Avivi

This book is also dedicated as a triumph to the Jessi Cohen
kid and to all the passionate dreamers out there
Never give up on your dreams, fight and make them come true
Go out there and make the world better

Love

David Abrahmov

Chapter One

Earth, the year 2050. The beautiful, lively planet, once brightly colored in blue, green, brown, and white, is now darkened, the colors faded, faded to nothing. The ground is burned and black; the sky is dull gray. The bright moon, subject of such romantic yearnings in the previous centuries, disappeared behind a thick dark veil of fog that fills the sky. The year is 2050, thirty years after the war that destroyed everything, every hope. Every dream, every love, every blooming flower, and every tree.

Russia, the former century's most powerful empire, was disintegrating. Its government was controlled by the mafia, who secretly obtained the codes for the country's nuclear heads. Then the Russian crime lords forged an alliance with the other major crime organizations all over the world: Italy, America, Germany, and South Africa's chief criminals came together to create the world's largest international terror organization and forge a diabolic plan for complete world domination.

Vaskov, head of the Russian mob, was assigned control over Asia, Japan, and Australia. Head of the Italian mob, Bartholomew, got south Europe; Bammark received authority over north Europe and the North Pole. Drakkar, head of all mob heads, took control over the continent of Africa and the entire land of America.

Bartholomew, Bammark, Vaskov, and Drakkar joined; and the result of this evil merge brought to the destruction of the world. At the year 2020, the organization nuked Australia, wiping millions of lives away without a warning. That was their strategy: everything on the ground of Australia suddenly obliterated, all bodies to ashes, birds, ants, kids, or just people living their lives.

The empire was the source, the core, and the center of all evil, the sum of all crime. This evil force had the world in the palm of their hands. Since the year 2020, the tactic was to wipe entire nations of the Earth if they resisted, if they refused to surrender their property. Land, freedom, and yes, even their honor to the empire. The price of resistance was utter extinction.

One by one, having no other choice, governments bowed to the powerful organization, surrendering their armies to the ever-growing army of the empire, which became undefeatable over the last thirty years. Humans everywhere were transformed into a race of slaves. Every child born into this era of enslavement, destruction, and suffering, is told by the story of a land once called Australia, where in a single second, tens of millions were wiped off the planet's face. And that is why people gave up their honor and property to this organization of evil; sorrow and pain was everywhere

That is why even the meaning of the word "honor" was forgotten by the world, and why little children no longer go to school. Why the whole human civilization is nothing but the power of the negative over the weak. The weapons are in evil hands, the world's saviors, knights in glowing armors are all gone, all extinct.

The armies of the world have been thoroughly corrupted. Whoever refused to join the empire's huge army was killed on the spot or sent to one of the many work camps scattered in every city in the world.

Life has lost its color, the night rules over the daylight, and despair is stamped in the people's faces. Tiny underground resistances try uselessly to harm the empire, and when captured, the rebels are taken to the city walls, where the soldiers hang them by their feet and behead them. With the blood gushing from the open necks, the soldiers paint a message on the wall: "So will be done to those who dare defy the empire."

It is the era of utter destruction, when women are raped daily, as casually as a person may eat breakfast, when tradition and culture or freedom are words erased from the man's daily life. It's the year 2050, thirty years to the murder of the human spirit.

Chapter Two

The year is 2050, thirty years after the great destruction. Bartholomew, one of the empire's leaders, is asleep is in his bed, sweating profusely—that embarrassing physical attribute that made him a laughingstock among his peers.

"No... no... no," he moans in his sleep, tossing in the pool of his own sweat. "No!" he cries out. His eyes are shut, but his body is twitching. For the first time in many years, Bartholomew, the man who is himself a nightmare to the whole of humanity, is having a nightmare. In his sleep, there is no escape. He sees images that terrify his soul; he sees himself and his friends, raping a pack of crying, screaming women. Their struggle is useless; they are helpless. He laughs, but as he laughs, the Earth cracks open beneath him and from it bursts, with a terrible screech, a huge glowing orb of light. That screech can mean only death, a horrible death. He watches helplessly as his friends, reaching out to him, crumble to ashes. Their screams make no sound; they are nothing but small piles of ashes on the black floor. He is alone, alone facing the glowing globe and its deafening scream. "No!" he cries, but to his shock, no voice comes out. Blood trickles slowly from his eyes as they see the shining orb take on a the shape of a man... he rises suddenly, bursting out of his sleep like a small fish escaping from a predator fish in the deep dark water. He runs through the bases corridors, his cries echoing behind him. A group of black-clad guards lets him by, surprised to see one of their leaders whimpering and running like a child escaping a gang of bullies.

"Drakkar! Drakkar!" he calls as he bursts through the heavy metal doors of his leader's chamber.

"Why the hell are you yelling? What happened to you?" Drakkar turns to him angrily. "I thought it's past your bedtime."

"Drakkar, gather all the comrades," stammers Bartholomew.

"What? A meeting? Now?! Are you mad?" Drakkar turns toward the huge windows framing his room, the highest one in the base. "Go molest some girl. You'll feel better," he mutters.

"I dreamt something horrifying," Bartholomew persists, his voice choked. "I dreamt…"

A moment of hesitation takes over him. He flops into a huge couch covered in black leopard skin and considers. Should he really embarrass himself by going on? As it is, he's already known as a coward among the ruthless rulers of this miserable planet.

"You dreamt? You dreamt what?" Drakkar interrupts his thoughts, pacing with hands crossed behind his back. "I didn't know you're the dreamer type."

Bartholomew wipes the sweat trickling down his pudgy cheeks. The two watch each other for a long, silent moment. Finally, Bartholomew whispers, "I dreamt our end, Drakkar…"

With sudden rage, Drakkar grabs Bartholomew by his collar, lifting him from his seat.

"We will never have an end, never! Again you come to me with your nonsense. The drugs twisted your whole thinking." As abruptly as he grabbed him, the dark leader powerfully slams Bartholomew down into his chair. As he rearranges himself on the black couch Drakkar continues, "Maybe you're too weak for this business, ha? Perhaps Bammark and Vaskov should split your cut among themselves? You know I can easily be rid of you and your foolish dreams… my end. Ha!" Drakkar roars in laughter, but the chubby leader meekly persists.

"But I saw it so clearly… it was—"

"Enough!" With a powerful blow to the face, Drakkar silences his cowardly companion. "I will hear no more about it, you fool."

The large doors open again, and two large figures step lazily into the room. "What's all this noise about?" asks the tall, broad-shouldered one. "I can't concentrate on selecting the women for my nightly party," continues the man with the oiled, tightly pulled back golden hair. It is Bammark, the German Aryan. With a wicked smile he adds, "It's a task that requires great concentration."

"Our comrade Bartholomew is bugging me again with his silly dreams," Drakkar answers dryly.

"And what have you seen this time?" asks Vaskov mockingly. He blows his nose on a red handkerchief and signals one of the guards to hold it for him. "Hidden treasures? Or how our empire grows and takes over other worlds?"

"No… no…" answers Bartholomew, catching his breath. "I saw our, our end… it was so real, the whole empire, an army of a hundred million soldiers… demolished."

"Haha!" thunders Bammark's laugh. "Is that even possible?"

"One man," continues Bartholomew rapidly. "It will be the work of one man, one figure. I tell you, I saw it!"

"Go back to sleep and don't snort any more of that purple stuff I brought you from Canada," smirks Vaskov, hands in his wide pockets.

"You don't believe me, but I'm not faking it," complains Bartholomew.

"That's enough!" cries Drakkar, exasperated. "Return to your quarters, Bartholomew. I'm not in the mood for this dream babble, is that clear? Instead why don't you think of how to deal with the rebels in the north, that's more important," the leader of the empire concludes.

Bartholomew walks away gloomily, leaving his mocking companions behind. His anger rises with every step he takes down the corridors. He rides the fast elevator down to his car and instructs his chauffer to drive toward a high building near the empire's great castle. The vehicle gathers speed, the long windows are locked with black shields, and a pair of black wings emerges from the car's sides as it accelerates and takes off toward the tall, red structure.

Chapter Three

The slopes of the Alps: dust clouds cover the terrain; on the horizon appear tiny black figures, figures that at a closer look turn to armored vehicles and hovercrafts filled with soldiers in black uniforms. Everywhere are the long, slanted barrels of laser guns, grenades, and bombs.

The racket of the procession wakes little Farel. His eyes open slowly, and suddenly, he leaps from his bed and cries, "Mama! Mama!" Yolanda, Farel's mother, quickly gets out of bed, as her husband Alfred buries his head under the pillow and mutters for her to come back. Mother and son rush to each other in the corridor. "What is it, Farel? What happened?" asks the startled women. The nine-year-old child looks at her with eyes full of fear. She lifts her gaze, and in the window behind him, she sees the last horror she will ever see: green and black hovercrafts gliding over the village of Battry-Nyle. Within seconds, Alfred is out of bed, shouting to his neighbors to run, but it's too late, there is nowhere left to run to.

On a green hill in a red hovercraft—red, the vehicle color for captains of the demolition units—Commander Passon lights a thick, brown cigar. A young, blond soldier, her tight uniform generously revealing her curves, is slowly caressing his leg.

"What have they done, sir?" she asks.

Passon blows smoke through his mouth impassively and lay his heavy palm on the young women's thigh

"Them…? Nothing, only Drakkar ordered General Kraus to practice some live war maneuvers with the hovercrafts."

"So these slaves are the targets?" asks the girl innocently.

"Yes," answers the man with the cigar dryly. As he speaks, loud explosions begin, accompanied with the high-pitched whistles of laser guns. Its early morning, and the bird's chirping is swallowed in a cloud of thick black smoke, drowned out by the shrieks of children as they scatter everywhere looking for their parents, who are already dead.

Passon smiles at the girl, ignoring the sordid scene happening less than a mile from his hovercraft. His soldiers shoot down anything moving, black figures bringing death with them. Strong men try to fight back, but it's useless—where's the honor of true battle? Where's the decency? Gone, they no longer exist, long lost somewhere in the pages of the human history. The girl's legs spread open over Passon's thighs, her lips kiss his, in front of them the terror commences at the feet of the beautiful Alps, as if the mountains are trying to hinder the massacre; but they remain still. One by one, the voices of the villagers cease. Twelve hundred people lived in that village—work groups of slaves that built a special tunnel for the transfer of metals used for the construction of new weapons that would guarantee the empire's future reign. Their work was finished, so their lives were also finished. In the allies of the village, a few people are still trying to escape to the nearby forest. This is a generation condemned to terrible suffering, starvation, and death. Born to live as slaves and die abruptly and unjustly.

Passon finished his business with the young soldier. She puts her black, tight uniform back on. She sensually passes her hand through her short blond hair, applies red lipstick to her lips, and gets behind the wheel. "Shall we move on, sir?"

"In a moment, honey." Passon watches a woman carrying her infant daughter, she is running, her heart is beating hard and fast, a tender smile of hope on her face. The forest is not far now. Step by step she is getting closer; she and her daughter may still survive this. Passon draws a long pistol from the holster on his thigh; he aims through his green round glasses, gently squeezes the trigger, and smiles to his companion. "You see? My soldiers missed that female." A blue laser beam slices the Alpine view, pierces the woman's heart and tears her body open. Spurts of blood splash on her baby girl's face, who's wailing loudly, not understanding why all this is happening. The devil Passon squeezes the trigger again with an evil joy. The crying stops.

"Now we can go," calls the man with the green round glasses. The young woman pulls back two gear shifts and presses a glowing red button. Jets of fire flare up behind the hovercraft and it swiftly fly's toward the empire's palace. Practice is over—everybody can go home now. The soldiers in black uniforms and black helmets board their tanks and again the procession is raising thick dust clouds. Behind them they leave twelve hundred mutilated bodies, silently seeping innocent blood—blood of children and infants that could have been on the top of the world, doctors, writers, scientists, diplomats, and poets, but no. The empire selected them to be nothing but canon flesh to practice on. No survivors… the empire leaves no survivors."

Chapter Four

Tears of blood from eyes of silent mothers
Girls playing with their dolls
Are now running down the corridors of heaven
Mischievous children no longer cheer as they play
For today their hearts are still
- It was not nature that cut the ebb of life.
I will remember this day… remember forever
—Adam Swandon

Adam Swandon is standing on a mountaintop and staring at the bright blue sky, tears ceaselessly flowing from his eyes. His face is tightly grasped in his hands; he is squeezing his head in an eruption of anger and frustration.

"Why?" a whisper escapes his mouth. "Why?! Why…" the whisper turns into a great, heart-rending cry: "WHY!"

No answer, no response. His hawk eyes scan the bleeding village; he rages and shouts at the creator. "Why?! Why, God? They are so tiny and helpless, why can't I do anything, I'm just one man, I've got nothing, I'm just… I… oh, God." The angry sobs don't cease. He rises slowly and gazes over the Alpine landscape. The sun is about to disappear behind the mountains. Suddenly thunder roars; the noise is so loud that Adam freezes in his tracks. Through his tears, he sees the white, glowing lightning shoot through the sky, then silence returns. Adam nearly faints from the shock of the sight. Very weird—the sky is bright and clear, not a cloud in it, and yet he heard this mighty thunder, and after it, the lightning that split the sky, as if cracking open the endless heaven. Adam stepped back, nearly stumbling, hesitantly asking himself, "Could God have answered me? Is he angry at me for speaking my heart?"

He quickly climbs down the mountain slopes toward a small wooden cabin. He steps into the room and suddenly his small house seems like a hostile and dangerous place. A strange anxiety grips his heart; he feels the anxiety tearing through his chest. He runs quickly through the his small room and grabs the backpack his father gave him for his twentieth birthday, an old green army pack, large enough to carry some necessary clothing items. He opens his little refrigerator and presses the little computer his friends smuggled for him; small drawers pop out, and he takes from them food packages and shoves them in his bag. He made up his mind—this place is dangerous, it's time to leave. Adam takes a last glance at his house. At the pictures of his friends and family. He is reminded of that day he had to leave to find food for the villagers, and since then, he couldn't find them again. He leaves his house on the mountain flank. The sunset's golden glow softly enveloped the pastoral view. Adam fixes his eyes on the smoldering village for a moment then gazes toward his source of food, the tiny garden that yielded fruits and vegetables for him through those four years he lived here alone, and now he is leaving it all behind. "I'm nobody's slave. I won't accept this fate. I believe in God, the great creator, after all," says Adam to himself, and in spite of the grief and fear that the soldiers will come and kill him too, he's suddenly uplifted with a powerful feeling of victory from hearing his own words.

With his small laser pocket blade, he sets the house on fire, watches as the flames climb over the wooden walls. He steps back slowly, toward the nearby forest. Finally, Adam Swandon leaves his house out of view and is swallowed in the dark green wood. The sun is gone; the night conquered the silent landscape.

Chapter Five

The fierce cold almost cut through Adam's thoughts like a knife as he was walking among the thick tree trunks. A thin layer of ice covers the ground; small patches of green moth are struggling to grow through it. Adam wraps his hands around his body, pacing quickly, wary of hungry animals that might attack him. He doesn't let the thought disturb him. In his heart, lava of fierce rage is boiling; he gives himself no rest. Suddenly he's grasped by the realization that his cozy little house is gone, now he is alone and far from everything. He's taking an immense risk by leaving his safe shelter. His eyes focus only on the natural path in front of him. His familiar pack hangs down his back. He convinces himself that it's not that cold; he's determined to walk on, but his body simply won't allow it. "It's the middle of the night and I'm alone in the forest. I've never been so late in the forest alone." It's so cold. His steps down slow to a halt. With his wide palms, he rubs his arms from the bitter cold, standing in a small clearing in the forest. He convinces himself that this place is safe enough, no need to fear. He gathers a few sticks and piles them together in a tight cluster. As he bends to light the fire, he feels his muscles cramp from the cold; a fierce gust of wind blows through the trees and scatters some of the firewood, but he tells himself he will get this fire going no matter what. He pulls out his trusty pocket laser blade; with a push on the small red button, a short red laser beam shoots out. He uses it to light the firewood, which smolders slowly, then little red tongues start devouring it. Shortly, there is a tiny, warm flickering glow lighting the clearing, and Adam Swandon is no longer cold, a little smile on his face, his one-day beard barely seen as a result from the bright light the campfire produced. He takes from his pack one container of packed food and one loaf of bread that smuggler friends got for him. As he eats, sights of the carnage in the village Batteri-Nyle flash in front of his eyes, but he manages to finish his meal without a tear. As he repacks his knapsack, he prays to God to look over him so he may wake tomorrow unharmed. The heat of the campfire and his own exhaustion lull him to sleep, and then the dreams come…

Blue, the whole dream is washed blue, like the ocean. Adam is walking in a desert, which sands are blue and the sky above is a deep, mysterious shade of blue. Four huge figures are rapidly approaching him from the four cardinal directions—dark, terrible figures, accompanied by terrible howls and screams. The hope drains from him as they draw near, a heavy scent of death hangs in the air. Adam screams, but his voice is muted, and at the moment, the huge figures raised their long arms to grab him, a beam of light envelops Adam and he disappears into it. Adam relaxes in his sleep, his breathing returns deep and calm, and a shade of a smile settles on his face. He sleeps calmly as dawn breaks with a loud chirping of birds.

A bright beam of light breaks through the trees and blinds Adam momentarily. He sits up, rubbing his eyes, and checks there are no hungry animals around about to jump on him. He's relieved to find his green pack with all his belongings right next to him where he left it. The campfire died before dawn, and it seems that the snow and ice have retreated a little. Adam rises and goes searching for fresh water; he sees a little brook that small forest creatures were drinking from. They watch him from afar, as if showing him the way. He washes his face and drinks from the clear, cold water.

"I must reach the closest town, but I must go carefully. The empire's army is everywhere." The idea of being caught terrifies him, but the feeling that a higher force is protecting him, guiding him toward an unknown goal, comforts him, he started marching forward.

Yellow beams of light glow through the foliage of the tall elms. Adam is walking down a wild path, untouched by human feet. "I'm pretty far from my valley… I must be getting closer to the town," he says to himself, when he hears a noise behind him.

"What are you doing?" asks a loud voice. A man covered in furs steps through the tree and appears suddenly behind him. Adam is startled. He didn't think there was another human in the forest.

"What do you think you're doing?" asks the stranger, louder. Adam prepares himself for anything.

"What do you mean, sir?" replies Adam politely.

"I mean it's sheer madness to run around like this in broad daylight, while the empire's hovercrafts are scouting the area, and every free man they find is arrested and sent to the work camps," answers the strange man.

After a moments of silence, Adam says, "Don't worry, they're not around. The sky is clear, it's a beautiful, sunny day."

The man slowly pulls an old rifle from under his furs. "Don't worry, I'm not gonna shoot you," he assures Adam. "It's only for hunting." He sits on a rock and gestures to Adam. "Sit down, let's eat something. I'm Peter by the way."

"Adam, Adam Swandon," smiles Adam as they shake hands.

Peter passes a portion to Adam, and they feast on hard farmer's bread with white goat cheese. "The cheese tastes great," Adam remarks.

"Ya." Peter smiles proudly. "The thanks goes to wife, Dorina." His smile widens as he thinks of his wife, a big strong mountain lass, which Peter is still madly in love with. "Maybe you should come to my house, it's really nearby."

"How is it that you're not suspicious of me?" asks Adam, astonished by the open friendliness of this patchy-looking man with the wild, red beard. "How come you don't even suspect I'm from the empire's army?"

"Well," asks Peter after a moment of consideration, "why don't you suspect me of the same thing?" They regard each other silently for a minute then burst out laughing.

"Come," says Peter, "its already noon, come to my house, I like you, come and meet my wife. It's been ages since another person reached us so deep in the forest. You are coming with me." Peter hoists his old hunting rifle on his shoulder and they both start marching into the thickets. Adam accepts the stubborn invitation kindly and follows deep into the forest, his wariness and curiosity trailing him as he is following behind his new friend.

The faint sound of leaves crunching underfoot mingles with the forest bird's chirping. It seems as if this place is untouched by the horrors of the empire, as if it's a scene taken from an ancient twentieth-century film. Adam feels a warmth rising in his chest, a sense of nostalgia. He sees pictures from his past, his family, his kid sister, his loyal dog called Hawk; these warm thoughts are followed by memories of the empire's takeover, like a thick, dark cloud over humanity. The fear, the enslavement… he recalls his grandfather's stories, when he was just a toddler, about a similar war that happened in the forties of the twentieth century…

"What's on your mind?" asks Peter, interrupting his grim thoughts.

"I'm… ha," stammers Adam and sighs, "I don't know what to tell you, Peter, I really don't know… but I've got this crazy belief in my heart, that somehow I'll find a way to save us humans, all of us, from this evil rule." Peter stares at Adam intently and walks on silently, his eyes on the ground.

"What's the matter, Peter?" asks Adam. Peter just paces on, muttering through clenched teeth, "I had that dream too. I guess dreams come true only in one's sleep."

"No, Peter, you must not think that way. I know the situation seems hopeless, but I keep hope in my heart. My grandfather, peace be with him, once told me a saying I remember to today: as long as there is air in my lungs, there is hope. There is always hope," said Adam.

Peter turned to Adam sharply and changed the subject by pointing at a beautiful wooden cottage surrounded by forest trees. "Look, there's my house. Let's go in, Adam, and rest for a while." Peter knocked on the door and seconds later his wife Dorina appeared in the portal, greeting them both with a wide smile. Peter hugs her warmly and kisses her round cheeks. "Dorina, meet Adam. He'll be having lunch with us." Dorina shakes Adam's hand, who is showing some signs of awkwardness. "Peter has an excellent eye for people, Adam. I'm not worried at all," she says, shooting a sidewise glance at her husband "welcome to our home." Peter lights himself a pipe.

After a few moments, Dorina called from the kitchen, "Lunch is ready!" Mesmerized by the smell of delicious food, they all sit around the wooden table, and Peter thanks the creator for the food.

Chapter Six

Drakkar, the dark leader of the empire, is sitting in his big, black armchair, and his eyes are scanning the transparent sheets reviewing the results of Passon's recent mission with the combined units—the demolition of a village on it's entire population, women, children, and men. Seeing the results gave him a taste of the feeling he enjoyed most—the sensation of utter and complete control. He locks eyes with the portrait on the wall, the portrait of the twentieth century greatest mass murderer, Adolf Hitler. He deeply admires the man and his work. He too believed that the human race should be governed by a selected few. He proudly pumps out his chest as he stares at the eyes of the figure, proud of his great achievement, enslaving the whole human kind to his empire. He lays the information sheets on the table as sleepiness washes over him in a slow wave. His eyelids are getting heavier. He surrenders to sleep and immediately slips into a dream. He sees himself in his big bed surrounded by adoring women who are feeding him delicacies from the palms of their hands. As his pleasure mounts, he suddenly hears a sharp whisper. He turns around but sees no one. He understands he alone is hearing the disturbing, eerie whisper. The women circling him began to dance around the bed; the whisper grows louder, he rises from his bed and cries for silence but the noise grows ever louder. It's now a scream, a horrible screeching sound; the women are spinning round him, ignoring his plight. He draws his laser gun and shoots in all directions; the women he hit keep on dancing and smiling at him, unaffected. He wishes to wake but the dream holds him captive, a cold hand grasps his shoulder, a form clad in black. The figure wants him to follow but he cringes and steps back. His sleeping body is now covered in cold sweat, twisting and turning in his bed, but the dream is relentless. The black figure calls him to follow, but he refuses; he turns and runs up the staircase. His confidence floods back the moment he is with his comrades—Bammark, Vaskov, and Bartholomew. They are torturing a group of people together. Near them he notices a deep, flaming abyss—he orders his friends to throw the people into the fire. He doesn't blink at the bitter cries of women, children, and men. His friends, standing behind him, laugh delightedly at the sight of bodies falling. Suddenly a blinding light engulfs them all; they cover their faces to protect their eyes from going blind, through the shafts of light they see the figure, in its arms it carries the people thrown to the abyss safely back to the ground, it is approaching them now, the figure moves ever closer to the petrified leaders, then the terrible scream sounds again, and with a gasp, Drakkar wakes.

"What's this cursed dream?" Drakkar asks himself as he calms down. "It's all damned Bartholomew's fault, his ridiculous nonsense infected my mind." He considers going back too sleep but rules against it. "Il go to *her*," he decides. "*She* will know the meaning of this."

He starts walking down the long, twisting corridor, winding ever lower, to the lowest level of the base. There dwells the old witch Irma, who chose to live far from the luxuries of the empire's rulers. Irma is a scheming old hag, known and respected by all for her great mystic powers, like reading palms, seeing through distance and time, and reading minds.

The two guards at her gate notice their great leader approaching and hastily stand up, saluting. Drakkar shoots them a mocking glance and gestures to open the doors. He walks into the room and calls, "Dear Irma, Irma! How is my favorite witch with the magical powers?" He walks toward her, arms open to embrace her, but with her back turned to him, she raises her left hand and blocks him with her powers.

"Spare me your sugar coated flattery," she says dryly.

"I merely wanted to hug you and ask how you are," answers Drakkar meekly as he understands he cannot struggle against her will, which was keeping him pinned to the spot.

"You come to visit me in my cellar only when you need something from me, and you don't need your witch as much as you used too. I'm growing older, my powers weaken as I age," complains the old witch, who still did not even turn to look at Drakkar. She lifts the purple tinted crystal bowl from the table and gathers her black robes around her.

"Nonsense, Irma, you are young and strong," protests Drakkar, trying to win a little bit of sympathy.

"Tell me why you're here," answers Irma coldly. Drakkar unfolds his dream to her. As he nears the end, the crystal bowl slips from her fingers and crashes loudly to the floor, scattering into thousands of tiny purple shards. Drakkar's eyes open wide with astonishment. Only then does Irma turn to him, releasing him from her magical grasp. She faces him with a grave expression.

"It has begun, then." Drakkar sits on the rim of a red velvet seat

"What began? What are you talking about?" he asks.

Irma does not answer him. Instead, she turns to the dust-coated library, sifting through the ancient books like a beggar searching for food in a heap of garbage. Suddenly she stops and pulls a heavy volume off the shelf. On the front cover, there is an etching of a sun, with golden rays coming out of the center of the circle.

Drakkar starts thinking to himself, *Why am I here? Why should one simple nightmare disturb me so?* Irma's wicked eye's trap his gaze. "It's not merely a nightmare, my dear," she cackles. Drakkar is taken aback that she managed to read his thoughts—the witch being known nationwide as a mind reader, he has been guarding his thoughts well.

"The day is near, great leader," she continues.

"What day is that, Irma?"

"The day is near when you must face the son of light, who will challenge your rule on this Earth," she replies, slowly leafing through the book in her lap. "This is the prophecy, Drakkar, inscribed by a being not of this world. Only two of these books exist, and one of them is here in my hand." Drakkar notices her expression darkening and asks urgently, "But how is this relevant to me and my nightmare?"

"Oh, it *is* relevant, relevant and so!" calls Irma heatedly. "Listen, Drakkar, this book is very old. My late Grandmother Trudy, who served the dark forces loyally a centaury ago, gave it to me and swore me to continue her service and assist the next dark leader in his evil reign over humanity. She foretold that I will serve the leader that will finally enslave the entire human race and drive them mercilessly—since people are weak, easily tempted by their own greed, and should be used only to serve a means. So I used them well, leader of the empire, and I stand by your side to see that our reign of power continues. But that dream you had disturbs me deeply."

Exhausted from her long speech Irma drops into a black leather seat and continues in a low voice, "By the signs foretold in this book, now is the time when the son of light should be coming to Earth." She turns a few pages and focuses on a certain passage. "You were thinking of Bartholomew… why?"

"He told me of a dream of his, in which my empire is destroyed by some mysterious higher force…" His voice trails off and he regards the old woman for a long, silent moment. Then suddenly he stands up and shouts, "I don't believe this mystic nonsense and I never did, do you understand, you old hag?"

Irma protests, "A prophecy cannot be escaped! All the events foretold in this book came true. Your arrogance will destroy you, Drakkar, if you don't act correctly you will lose."

Drakkar wishes to reply but the old witch swiftly continues, "This dream comes from the center of the universe, from the endless, all-powerful source, and it came to instruct you to prepare for your fall from power." Drakkar's face was livid with rage. "Foolery, insane nonsense, Irma! What are you talking about? The center of the universe? Legends, prophecies? I don't believe in all this gibberish, I think you and Bartholomew are plotting to drive me mad together. My rule was created through my own superior planning, it wasn't handed to me by anyone. I alone managed to do what no other leader ever succeeded with to efficiently take hold of the entire mankind. They brought on their own downfall by inventing the all-powerful atom bomb. They handed themselves over to me on a silver tray. Now I am the supreme ruler of the world, I and my three partners, so I will tolerate no more 'center of the universe' mumbling, no 'endless force' talk! I am the only force to reckon with here!"

Quietly he continues, "I was wrong to come to you. You are here to serve as an advisor to the empire's rulers, Irma, not as a superstitious gypsy fool telling me of my empire's fall." Drakkar storms angrily toward the exit as the old women shrinks fearfully into her seat. He turns to her again before he leaves. "It was a meaningless, random dream. I will continue to rule with no mercy. Like you said yourself, people are fools, they are good for only two things: the first is to work hard and produce energy for my empire, and the second is to die as they are doing it. The real reasons for this nightmare are the tales of the coward Bartholomew—his words put the images in my head." The leader nodded casually to Irma and left the room.

"Perhaps you are worthy of your fate…" whispers Irma, but quickly changes her line of thought. "I must check the book again for the prophecy Grandma Trudy told me of." As she pours through the pages, her face grows more alarmed.

"I must get through to Drakkar somehow, before it's too late…"

Chapter Seven

The sun has already disappeared behind the snowy peaks. Peter and Adam are sitting on the wooden terrace after a satisfying meal, listening to Dorina singing from the kitchen. "Ho, where are those days, when my lover brought me roses red, to weave a crown around my head." A small smile shows through Peter's tangled beard as he savors his wife's clear voice.

"She sings beautifully," Adam remarks.

"Yes, my friend. My beloved sings from her heart—about missing those good days, the days of freedom, the days before the empire came to power," says Peter. Adam is deeply touched by the love of this couple, and by their kindness. It seems wondrous that in this time of tyranny and terror such humanity may survive.

It's nighttime; the constant little noises that rose from the forest during the day have now ceased, leaving only the voice of crickets echoing through the tall, snow-covered treetops. In this frozen landscape, one dot of light glows warmly—the house of Peter and Dorina. Adam looks up at the starry skies and a silent wave of joy moves through him.

Peter inhales deeply from the ancient pipe—a gift from his grandfather big Arkio—and starts a fresh conversation.

"What are you planning to do, Adam?"

While still gazing at the sky, Adam replies, "Believe me, Peter, after meeting you and Dorina, I hate to leave this wonderful place. There is a special feeling here, a feeling of peace, of safety. Yet—"

"Yet what?" asks Peter immediately.

"Yet as we sit here, snuggly hidden in the depth of the forest where the hovercrafts and the patrol vehicles do not come, not too far from us tens of thousands are enslaved. After what I saw in the valley, the entire village of Battery-Nile massacred in front of my eyes, and I could do nothing… The images are truly carved into my mind." Tears quickly form in Adam's eyes. He turns his face to hide them. Peter takes a deep drought from his pipe, and after a few moments, a long trail of smoke billows from his mouth.

"I understand how you feel, Adam. I know what you're talking about. I was a member in one of the underground resistances fighting in the area three years ago. After all our friends were killed, I promised Dorina we won't go back to the city—here in the forest we have our freedom. It's true that we are cut off from the rest of humanity, but we survive here. The forest fills all our needs. Dorina's parents died in a work camp less than thirty miles from here, so we have no one left to care for but each other, do you understand?"

Sitting silently in her chair, Dorina reaches out to her husband and takes his hand. The two exchange glances, as if they have a silent language that only the two of them can understand. Peter lifts her hand to his lips and kisses it warmly. Adam is slightly embarrassed by this; the couple sense that, and Dorina abruptly turns to the men and asks, "So who wants some hot chocolate and cookies?"

"I do, what about you, Adam?" Peter cooperates. "You haven't tasted Dorina's delicious cookies yet, have you?" he exclaims cheerfully.

Adam rises from his chair and looks down at the loving couple. "Peter, Dorina, I have to tell you it has been a very long time since I met people so kind and loving as you two. You help my heart understand that there truly is hope. That's why I must leave. I must continue in my way. I must find a way. I don't know how but in my heart there is a strong faith. There's nothing left to lose." When he finishes his sentence, Dorina steps into the house, and Peter draws near him.

"Adam, I'd love it if you'd stay and live here with us, but if in your heart you have the faith and the will to change the way things are, I can only wish you luck, from the bottom of my heart. My father taught me that we are all born with a destiny, and with a little luck, we can fulfill it. It makes no difference if you feel your destiny is to be a shoemaker or to be a president. If you truly believe in it, just do it."

Adam is a little surprised by Peter's words, but his heart agrees with them. He lays his hand on Peter's shoulder. "Thank you for those words, Peter. I won't forget you and your wife Dorina. You showed me that despite the destruction, despite the terrorism trying to crush us, there is a love that sparks all that is positive in the universe, and that spark is worth fighting for."

At that moment, Dorina comes out of the house with a jug of hot chocolate, and with a lively smile, she serves the two friends a plate of hot cookies.

Chapter Eight

A messenger knocks on the door of the empire's leader. The door opens; with shaking hands, the young lad presents his leader with a small disk, gleaming in the lights of the room. Drakkar signals the youth to vanish and the guards close the doors behind him. The leader inserts the disk into a computer, and on the flat screen standing on his desk appears Irma's image. The man responds indifferently yet continues to watch and listen. "Ho, great leader, I discovered some very important facts in the book, and it is of great importance that you summon the rest of your friends. You must listen to me, I have only you and your dominion's interests in mind. We must meet, and fast."

The broadcast is over. The leader runs his hand through his thick beard. He stares at the elongated mirror decorated with the empire's symbols: snakes and scorpions, black and gold, entwined in each other.

"Perhaps I should listen to what the old hag has to say. Perhaps with her magic powers, she could tell me where are the Hawks of the New Dawn Resistance. They have been giving me some trouble lately."

Drakkar presses a button on his desk, summoning one of his guards. Within moments, a tall soldier appears and immediately salutes his leader.

"Summon the people," says Drakkar, and hands the soldier a thin, silver plate. "You have all the information here. Do it now."

The soldier salutes again and quickly leaves the room of the empire's ruler.

In Argma, the empire's palace, a figure wrapped in a black cloak is making its way up the passage leading to the main hall—a vast, round room, large enough to contain more than a thousand men. One by one, the guards and soldiers draw back from the mysterious figure as it glides slowly toward the round hall, where it was told that Drakkar and the rest of the empire's rulers are awaiting it. The figure stops in front of two huge doors, guarded by two strong, tall men, but as it returns their gaze, their faces pale and they quickly slink away, some evil force almost paralyzing them.

At the entrance to the hall, with the slight aid of her magic powers, Irma slowly opens the heavy portals without ever touching them and paces through them toward the group clustered in the center of the hall.

"Welcome, Irma," calls Drakkar to the old woman. Irma notices he has calmed down since their last meeting, and she nods to him, signaling she accepts his words, and she appreciates the fact that he understands she must have had a grave reason for this very special meeting. It is truly a rare occasion for Irma to leave her dark quarters in the bowels of the palace's cellars.

As the old hag draws near the group of men, Bammark steps back and mutters through his teeth, "What a stench rises from this old woman!"

Suddenly, with no warning, Bammark finds himself glued to the high red ceiling. "Hey, release me at once!" he shouts angrily. Irma's narrow eyes turned blood red. The rest of the men step back, fearing they might get hurt; only Drakkar dares to come close and asks, "Irma, let him go. I'm sure he apologizes for what he said."

Irma slowly lowers Bammark down, and a few feet from the ground, she suddenly releases her magic grasp so that Bammark falls and hits the floor with a thud.

"Damn!" he shouts in pain, and Irma giggles lightly.

"That goes to whoever speaks badly to old Irma," says the witch.

"And now let us deal with matters of importance," calls Drakkar to her. "Why did you summon us with such urgency? My guards informed me you have sensational news."

Irma burrows into her cloak, and to Drakkar's dismay, she pulls out the ancient book from her library. She points at the etching of the golden sun and starts to speak, "This is the book that my late grandmother gave me when I was a child, a book that was passed down to her from her grandmother." The husky men exchange glimpses, as if waiting for the bottom line. Irma catches their thoughts and quickly continues, "This book was written by the warlocks who dwelt in South America, and the rumors are they transcribed it from the original one, created by the strangers, who live in worlds far from here."

Vaskov comes close to his friend Drakkar. "How far will you let her go with this talk, Drakkar? Our empire is stronger and mightier then it has been in years."

Irma responds casually and continues in a low whisper, "I am only here to warn you. The ancient words were written long before I was born. By my calculations, this book is two hundred years old. It tells of the son of light that comes from afar, not from the planet called Earth, but from the other world."

39

"What are the chances that this is the truth, Irma?" asks Drakkar in a hushed tone. The witch glares at the leader with a mocking smile. "Ho, my dear, when you came to my room under the Argma palace, where I live my gray life, when you told me of your dream, when you mentioned Bartholomew's dream. I knew it is time to read the book my grandmother gave me again, all the signs show this."

"I knew it! I knew it! You dreamt a similar dream that can mean only one thing—this is real, and we must prepare ourselves for—"

Bartholomew's sentence is cut short by a sharp blow to his face, coming from Bammark's angry fist.

"I won't tolerate such bunk, you invertebrate!" Bammark turns furiously to Drakkar. "Listen to me, Drakkar, I won't hear foolish tales from an old hag reading to me a book of children's fairy tales. Bartholomew's stupid dream affected you, my friend. I don't know you to be one swayed by prophecies and gibberish. Pull yourself together. You are the leader of an empire, the man who rules the world. You mustn't listen to such talk," says Bammark angrily. He turns to the exit, rubbing his fist against the palm of his hand, throws Bartholomew a threatening glance, and steps out.

Thoughts start racing through the ruler's head. "Perhaps Bammark is right, Bartholomew and Irma, those fools, they've influenced me."

Irma comes toward him in little steps. "Listen to me, you stubborn man, listen before it's too late! The prophecies always proved themselves to be true!"

Drakkar turns on the old witch with an unprecedented outburst, "Bammark is right, Irma!" he yells. "Prophecies can come true only we give them meaning, so I don't believe in that book or its contents, do you hear me? From now on, you will not disturb me with any more of this talk. Return to your place Irma, continue with your work." The leader is confused, his thoughts colliding; a part of him believes in the witch's words and the book in her parcel, while another part wishes to remain logical and rational. Bammark has left the room long ago, leaving his peers behind. Vaskov is leaning on one of the massive, round pillars, decorated with etchings of historical leaders. Bartholomew, still on the floor, starts crawling toward Irma's feet. "I believe you, Irma, my dreams… you say that they're actually describing our end?"

Irma extends her thin, pale arm to him and helps him to his feet. "No, Bartholomew dear, the dreams may be interpreted in many different ways—that is what I'm trying to explain to your stubborn friend. The dreams come to warn us."

Bartholomew wipes a tear with his sleeve, the tear that came from Bammark's blow. "What should we do, Irma? Tell us."

In a flaming rage, Drakkar leaps at Bartholomew, a long, golden sword in his hand; he lays the sharp blade against Bartholomew's throat, and with a raspy cry, he mutters through clenched teeth, "If I hear your voice one more time proclaiming the empire's weakness, this blade will bathe in your cowardly blood, do you understand that, Bartholomew?"

The weight of Drakkar's body crushing down on him made Bartholomew's stammered answer even more mangled. "Y-yes, yes… glorious leader."

Drakkar straightens up, retrieves the golden sword to its sheath, adjusts his jacket, and comes near Irma. "No more, Irma, no more," he whispers to her.

Irma's narrow eyes stare at him coldly, but she keeps her mouth shut. The trembling Bartholomew grabs his throat and finds a thin line of blood where Drakkar's golden blade was pressed. Again silent tears roll down his cheeks, as his eyes follow Drakkar's figure leaving the room. Vaskov paces silently behind him. Vaskov always agreed with Drakkar, never once in all these years did he speak against him, but this time, for some reason, his heart goes with the words of the old woman.

Chapter Nine

Peter opens his eyes to the morning light that's washing over the forest and all the animals in it. He turns to his wife and kisses her full cheeks, and she replies with a warm smile. Through the window, he sees his new friend standing outside and staring at the clouds moving across the sky. After washing and dressing, Peter steps out and walks toward Adam, who is feeling as if time has stopped moving. Peter hesitates to interrupt Adam, who is obviously savoring the beauty of creation, but Adam notices him first and turns to face him. "Peter—"

"I know, Adam, that you're leaving," replies Peter quietly before Adam finished his sentence. "I have these weird feelings in me. On one hand, I'm sad that your leaving, and the sadness is made worse by what my heart is telling me that you won't come back here again." Adam is touched; he is trying not to get carried away by Peter's heart breaking words.

"Peter, I…" Adam tries to speak, and Peter lays a heavy arm on his shoulder.

"No, Adam. It's all right, because my heart is also encouraging me like it never did before, it's sending me a powerful positive feeling—that the road in front of you is great and full of light, and not me nor anyone else can move you from that path. My dear father taught me that in most cases, the heart doesn't lie, and we should take what it tells us seriously."

By now, gentle tears are falling from Adam's brown eyes. "Peter, I have no reason to live, unless I'm walking that road your heart has told you about. Because of that I must keep on walking and searching for a solution for all the evil and suffering in this world, I will try with all my might, I must!" Adam calls in exhilaration. A special friendship has grown between these two in a short time. The two men are standing on a glorious, bright morning at the feet of the Alps, knowing that they are about to part. Dorina steps out to them with a bag full of her fine delicacies and hands it to Adam, who's wiping his tears with his sleeve. He takes her hand and kisses the smooth palm, thanking her for her kindness. She gently lays a hand on Adam's cheek, understanding him completely. The hearts were conversing between these three figures.

Peter approaches Adam; they look in each other's eyes, and without further words, they embrace powerfully and briefly. Only Dorina dared speak one blessed sentence, filled with warmth. "Good luck, Adam. The supreme power is, was, and will always be with you. It will guide you along with your pure thoughts, and your heart's senses will steer you even through the dark." Adam receives with love all that this special couple had to give him, especially the hope, hope that will remain in his heart forever. His thoughts are now lit by a never fading blaze of hope.

Adam starts pacing toward the forest, holding a map Peter gave him that will direct him to the nearest city. As he walks away, he says to himself quietly. "I hope your father is right, Peter, and your heart indeed speaks the truth."

Two hours pass since Adam parted with Peter and Dorina, and now he must hasten to follow the map and reach the city quickly, before the empire's hovercrafts start patrolling the area in search of rebels. The sky, which was blue just a few hours ago, is now covered by black clouds, as if trying to warn Adam hurry up, trouble is on its way, and indeed at that same moment, as Adam takes from his bag one the sandwiches Dorina made for him, the racket of machines freezes him on the spot. The sandwich slips from his hands. For a moment, he feels sorrow over the food as he remembers Dorina's warmth of heart, and how much she loved preparing her delicious treats; he raises his eyes and sees a huge, black hovercraft sailing slowly above the forest.

"They didn't see me, it's hard to recognize a single human figure through the forest," thinks Adam, but the huge hovercraft is slowing down, as if it really did spot Adam through the dense tree trunks. Adam feels his heart pounding fiercely, twice as fast as before. He tries to calm himself. "The hovercraft must have heat detectors, they saw me, I must elude them. Being captured by the empire's forces can lead to only to two things: work camps or death. I'm not interested in experiencing either," he says to himself. By now, the hovercraft has stopped directly over Adam's location.

"No time to waste. They're on to me," he says to himself silently. Suddenly he remembers a trick his father taught him when he was a child; his hawk eyes spot a small pool by a nearby clump of vegetation. "The water must be freezing, but there's no choice," he thinks to himself. He lays his green backpack on a rock by the pool, says a short blessing, and leaps into the freezing water. A short, shocked cry escapes him, even though he tried his best to prevent it. His body trembles, his skin pales. "I hope they leave soon, because I'm about to freeze," he tries to encourage himself.

Inside the big hovercraft, Commander Gra is yelling at his soldiers, "What do you mean, you lost the life signal you got seconds ago!" one of the soldiers, sitting in front of a control panel with lighted, multicolored buttons, answers his superior, "It was there a second ago—now it's not. Perhaps it was a large forest animal, and it somehow slipped away?"

Gra swiftly approaches the soldier, who begins trembling. "You fool, quit babbling—do another search, and if you find nothing, move on," says Gra in an impatient tone.

Adam understands his deception worked; his body temperature indeed dropped due to the water's fierce cold. He also understands that if he doesn't get out in the next few seconds, he won't live for long. A gasp of relief leaves his trembling body when he sees the hovercraft move away.

"I'm saved," Adam exclaims to himself. He looks at the sky and thanks his father for the lessons of years ago. He steps out of the water. He gets a campfire going to get his body heat back to normal, occasionally leaping from tree to tree to check if anybody is following him. Adam feels the day pass with every step he takes through the forest.

"According to the map, I'm nearing the town... yes, I can smell the machinery, I'm getting close," Adam says to himself, and the town appears in front of him. He remembers that when he was a child, his father would bring him here to help carrying the groceries they couldn't get in their own village in the valley. The loud mechanic noises stop his thoughts of his father, the noise of hovercrafts taking off and inspecting the city streets. People aren't walking, they are quickly scurrying to their houses before the curfew begins; the empire doesn't allow people to wander free in the streets after work, fearing that in time they may gather and act against it. The empire is everywhere—almost everywhere, because Adam Swandon is free, and his spirit is free, and his heart rebels against all his eyes see.

As the horizon darkens into night, Adam is cautious to blend into the rushing crowd. He turns to an elderly man pacing with the hastening procession. "Pardon me, sir, is there a hotel or a tavern here?" the man, who looks around fifty years old, tanned and bald, turns his gaze to Adam. "What? In this place? Are you a secret agent for the empire?"

Adam is amazed at the bald man's question. "What? No, of course not, I escaped from the valley. I used to live there on a mountain range above the village that was massacred not long ago."

The man slows down at the news; apparently, the city people knew nothing of the carnage. After a few seconds, he picks up his pace again.

"You must walk faster, sir," he says to Adam, who immediately speeds up.

"So do you know where I can find a place to sleep?" Adam repeats his question. All around them, men and women are rushing; the curfew is close, and they must swiftly get home.

"The blue house," the man blurts out after a long silence.

"The blue house...?" replies Adam with a question.

"Yes, the blue house, if you are careful you can break free of this group, next corner take a sharp right, walk fast, after about two hundred meters you will see a house painted blue, you will find a place to sleep there, but know that the place is swarming with empire agents, seeking out the underground coven members." The man looks straight ahead as he speaks, not turning to Adam in fear that the inspectors in the hovercrafts above will notice a suspicious movement.

"Thank you, sir, I thank you greatly," says Adam warmly.

Now the man does turn his head, as if touched by Adam's thanks, and with a little smile, he replies, "May the great powers be with you."

Adam advances toward the blue house. The place is silent, as if it empty of any living soul, as if it is disconnected from the world, from the threat of the empire, from the hovercrafts and everything else going on. A strange calm engulfs Adam; he feels his hunger nagging at him. As he approaches the door, he hears a distant, heartbreaking violin tune. He opens the door and the music playing in the background takes his heart, a melody from a distant place, far from the entire humanity. Gazes sweep over Adam from all directions, coming from the elderly people sitting by the thick, rounded wooden tables. The picture in front of him seems to Adam like an ancient image, something from a hundred years back at least. In the center of the wall to his left, there is a fireplace, with a golden light emitting smoke and heat in it. The older people look at the young, strong figure standing in the doorway, and the music keeps on playing. An old man with a long, white hair and beard is performing wonders on the violin, plucking from it the most beautiful tunes.

"Welcome to the blue motel, stranger," a young, pretty woman approaches Adam, staring with large blue eyes directly into Adam's hawk eyes.

"Did anybody follow you here?" she continues.

Almost trapped in her gaze, Adam replies quietly, "No, I'm here alone."

She reaches out to Adam and takes his hand. "Come, you must be hungry. Enriko made a great vegetable soup today. Do you have money?" asks the pretty girl as she leads Adam toward a thick, round wooden table.

"I have money, what's your name?" asks Adam. The gazes of the people by the tables turn back to their own business, games of cards and checkers.

The lass introduces herself, "Heralda. My name is Heralda." She is a beautiful girl, with a curved, womanly body, and from under the purple bonnet on her head, black curls flow everywhere. It seems to Adam she is the youngest person in the motel lobby. The old man stops playing, and several elders turn to him, clapping their hands. Heralda seats him by Adam then returns in a minute with two clay bowls filled with hot vegetable stew. "Eat carefully, it's very hot," says the pretty young woman, throwing Adam a glance and a smile as she returns to the kitchen.

"She likes you," says the old man, while looking for his spoon.

"Who likes me?" asks Adam, surprised by the old man's remark.

"Who? My granny! Who? I'm talking of sweet Heralda. She likes you. If only I were fifty years younger…"

Adam looks curiously at the old man, who started sipping from the hot soup.

"I'm Adam Swandon," says Adam and extends his hand to the elderly man.

The man watches the hand for a few seconds then offers Adam his own old hand. "I'm Joshua." Adam shakes his hand gently so not to hurt him but is surprised to discover that the handshake is firm and strong like one of a young lumberjack. Without further words, Adam turns to hungrily gulp down his soup. Suddenly the aroma of the soup, and the smell of other cooked food in the room, brings up sights from the past; he remembers the soup his dear mother made him and the rest of the family when he was a child.

"Where are you wandering, my boy?" The old man's question pierces Adam's thoughts

"What do you mean, Joshua?" Adam asks. The old man is staring into Adam's eyes as if he is reading his entire history since birth, and that sensation sends cold chills down Adam's spine.

"Your eyes reveal everything. You remembered somebody very dear to you." Adam is astonished by the old man's power to see what's in his heart "How?" But Joshua already retuned to his soup. "First we eat, dear boy, then we talk." Heralda comes back, all smiles, especially in Adam's direction.

"How's the soup, guys?" asks the pretty lass.

And Joshua replies immediately with a smile showing through his thick white beard, "Wonderful, just wonderful, my complements to Enriko—and when you serve it, it is simply perfect." Heralda giggles bashfully. Now Adam is smiling at her too, suddenly the two smiles turn into laughter, carrying all three of them into a long, hearty burst of laughter. Adam feels better in the company of these two.

• •

Down the narrow corridor of the blue hotel, Heralda guides the tired and full Adam to his room, gently clasping his arm. "Come, I prepared a nice bed for you," says Heralda.

Adam is feeling extremely sleepy, he can't stop yawning. "I'm so tired, Heralda. What did you put in my soup? I feel…" Adam's vision begins to blur, the sight of Heralda watching him clouds over, and in his confusion, he senses other figures joining Heralda. He feels other hands squeezing him, pulling him into a dark room. His body no longer responds to him; he cannot keep his balance. He drops unconscious on the floor in the room.

CHAPTER TEN

Irma's dark room is filled with the scent of lemon and peach incense, a sweet aroma she likes to wrap herself in before she falls to sleep. With her narrow, almond-shaped eyes, she is looking at the book of prophecies and thinking to herself, "Who will believe me and the book's prophecies? People today are more materialistic then ever. No one is interested in spirits and dreams these days, only in the tangible. The spirit is of no importance anymore." Her thoughts are interrupted by a light knock on her thick door. Irma already knows who it is; her powers still exist. She senses the presence behind the door.

"Come in, Bartholomew," she calls loudly. The door is pushed open by Irma's magic powers, and through it walks no other then Bartholomew, one of the evil empire's leaders.

Bartholomew is thinking to himself, "Yes, she can read thoughts. She knew it was me before I announced myself, think good of her, think good of her." Sweat is already trickling down his broad forehead from tension and fear of the weird woman.

"Stop exerting yourself, Bartholomew, you'll end up drowning in your own sweat. Calm down and tell me, what do you want from me at this late hour?"

After Irma's words, a certain relaxation showed on Bartholomew's face, who was mopping the sweat off with a silk handkerchief.

"Irma, I wanted to tell you, I believe in you and your book. Do you really think my dream foretells the end of our grand empire?" asks Bartholomew.

Irma stares at the couch, and with her telekinetic powers, she manages to offer Bartholomew a seat. "Sit down, Bartholomew, and listen to me. The prophecy is connected to yours and Drakkar's dream. They come from the core of the universe, from its center, where everything has already occurred and is still occurring. When we open a small window in our subconscious to fears and worries, energy from the universe's center pours into our minds, translating into a dream that explains our own fears to us. All that is left to us is to interpret it as we wish. There is always the opportunity to change the outcome, fate is a changeable thing, that is what I'm trying to explain to stubborn Drakkar."

Bartholomew is more then a little confused, yet he tries to follow Irma's words. "You are trying to explain to him that…?" asks Bartholomew briefly, and Irma continues, "That there is indeed a prophecy in the ancient writings, foretelling of the coming of the son of light to our world, to drive away the darkness and drain the power of our great empire, and our part is to understand that this is a tangible possibility."

Bartholomew pales with Irma's last few sentences. He draws close to her, closer than ever before to this strange woman. "Tell me, Irma, what can we do? How can we stop the prophecy written in this ancient volume you are holding?"

Irma sinks into a prolonged silence. She knows that Bartholomew, though the coward in the bunch, is quite a manipulator. She already understands he is trying to weave a plan without Drakkar, the empire's undisputed leader, knowing of it. "Tell me, Bartholomew, what do you wish to do?"

Bartholomew approaches the library, decorated by a considerable amount of cobwebs and pulls out the book. "I suggest you and I study this book and learn what is written, and if you say the son of light can be prevented from coming here and confronting us in order to break our rule over the world, let us join forces and do this," says Bartholomew, and a diabolical smile spreads on his face.

"And what of Drakkar?" asks Irma. "He doesn't need to know anything of this. I have all you may need. In manpower, weapons, and any other thing you may choose to use in order to stop our rule from falling."

Irma takes the book from Bartholomew's hands and sits on her red couch.

"So be it. We will join in an effort to save Drakkar's rule, without him knowing of it, since he does not believe in prophecies, and because of that shortcoming, he may lose everything. But know, Bartholomew, that I trust no one—and if you try to act behind my back, I will know, and before you know that I know, I will fill your bowels with fire."

Beads of sweat again start rolling down Bartholomew's forehead. "I wouldn't dare do that, Irma."

The two take hold of the book. Bartholomew complains there is not enough light in the room, and Irma picks up a few scraps of brown fabric and lays them on the table by the bowl of incense, where a bright flame immediately sprigs from them, casting some light into the rooms space. "Better?" asks Irma, watching Bartholomew pointedly.

The two focus on the book. Irma speaks certain words, and to Bartholomew's amazement, rays of colorful light break out of the weird letters, gathering in the center of the room, forming there into a fuzzy figure.

Seeing this, Bartholomew grabs his pistol. "What in the devil's name is this?" cries the chubby leader. Irma shows no excitement whatsoever< she approaches the blurred figure and speaks a few sentences to it in an incomprehensible mumble, and the figure slowly takes on a clearer form.

"It's my Grandmother Trudy. Don't panic, you fool, it's a recorded message from the past. Only by cracking certain codes can the information hidden in the book be released."

Bartholomew relaxes and lays down his gun. "Interesting," he says, "and what does your Grandmother Trudy's say?"

Irma spreads out her scrawny arms and begins chanting incomprehensible sentences. Bartholomew refrains from thinking, fearing the old woman might read his thoughts and tries, instead, to concentrate on the occurring in the room.

Grandma Trudy's image becomes active and a quivering voice echoes through the room, "At the third decade to the era of the black sky, a trail of fire will blaze from the blue planet to the planet of land, and destroy the four evil spirits." Hearing these few words Bartholomew begins to tremble. Irma kept listening intently to Grandma Trudy's words. "One heart, unique and pure, will dare challenge the four kings ruling the Earth planet." Suddenly, the radiant figure of Grandmother Trudy freezes in silence.

"What happened?" Bartholomew inquires timidly. Irma lowers her hands, looking a little dizzy.

"Ow, the communication through the ancient writings drains a lot of energy from me, and to unlock the rest of the prophecy, I must first study the rest of its codes." The disappointed Bartholomew throws himself on the red couch and says, "Then we have a lot of work ahead of us, is it not so, my dear Irma?"

Chapter Eleven

"Trails of brown and golden leaves cover the avenues of the amazing city of New York. The trees are all clad in gold and brown. A heartbreaking autumn breeze is caressing me and my beloved, both of us in gray coats, our hearts united with the nature surrounding us. My sweetness gazes at me with eternal love, tears of joy and love falling from our eyes, embraced, under the large trees that are shading us, as if shielding us from this war that started twenty years ago. Oh, how I miss being twenty-one, when my beloved was alive and in my arms. Evil snatched her from me; I remain alone.

I am standing on an avenue coated with brown and gold leaves, alone in my dark gray coat. Alone, I was twenty-one when I traveled through the USA, a year away still from the empire's takeover. My beloved was on the ferry returning from Staten Island, and that's that. I am alone, the lingering scent of her perfume pierces my heart with a sweet pain; this trip was an escape from everything, an escape from facing what was happening in the world. I always dreamt to live in America, but the empire changed my plans… now I am leaving to search for a cure to all the pain in this world. I have nothing left to live for. I am willing to give my life for a remedy, to bring salvation from all this slavery…"

The voice in Adam's head now mingle with voices surrounding him with feverous questions: "Who are you? Where do you come from?"

He wakes in a room, circled by men and woman, all of them staring at him. Joshua's elderly face comes near him. "Speak, my lad, if you tell the truth I promise nothing will happen to you. Speak."

Adam understands now that he has been drugged; thoughts race through his head, he comprehends the situation. "I see, you're thinking that I'm from the empire, right? Well, I'm not, my name is Adam Swandon. Till not long ago I was living on a mountain cleft above where the village of Battery-Nile used to be. Untie me!"

A young man in his twenties comes near Adam and presses the barrel of his laser gun to Adam's cheek.

"What do you mean where Battery-Nile used to be?" asks the youngster in a mocking tone. Joshua lays his heavy hand on the youth's tense arm. "Enough, Kley. Calm down, there's no need for this," says Joshua calmly to the young man. The three men and three women are circling Adam, watching him suspiciously.

"Just check the mark, see if he has it he's one of them," calls one of the girls, her eyes ablaze.

Adam doesn't understand what she's talking about; Heralda nears him from behind, and in one movement, tears open his shirt, from the collar down.

"Well, anything there?" Kley asks curiously.

Heralda's suspicious expression lifts. "Come see for yourself." The entire group gathers behind Adam's back. "I knew it," Joshua exclaims. "He's not with the empire." Old Joshua stands by Adam and gestures the third man to untie him. "What mark are you talking about? Do empire agents have a mark on their back?" asks Adam as he rubs the area sore from the rope.

"They have a symbol tattooed from their napes their mid-back. It's a drawing of a scorpion with the head of a snake, all in red," says the girl who suggested that Adam be checked. Kley leans to old Joshua and whispers in his ear. "We must hurry, sir, the weapon shipment is due any moment." Joshua raises his hand, signaling Kley to relax. "I know, I know." He turns to Adam with the rest of the group at his back

"Listen, Adam. As you already gathered, we are opposing to the empire, and the small group behind me is made of young, brave sons of freedom, underground warriors, crying 'no more' to the empire's destructive universal rule. We are called the New Dawn Hawks, and there are more groups like us, scattered through the world, carrying different names. We are active mainly in southern Europe, and we all have a common denominator: we refuse to live in a show of fear." The man speaks with growing passion and fervor. When he finishes, Adam's gaze passes over the figures in front of him, seeing them now tall and powerful, as if surrounded by an aura.

"I see now, you are an underground militia, and you thought earlier that I'm an empire spy because of the curfew coming, you thought I was sent to infiltrate you."

"They did that before," replies Heralda immediately, watching Adam's hawk eyes. She comes near and exposes her left shoulder, and he sees the deep scar of a laser beam that ripped through her young body no more then a year ago. "Like you see, we can trust no one," she says. Kley approaches Joshua again, this time not whispering but speaking loud and clear, "Sir! We must reach the children's complex now. That is the appointed rendezvous point."

Interrupting Kley, Adam asks, "Can I help with anything?"

Kley regards him disdainfully. "First of all, change that shirt."

Adam smiles lightly as he turns to Heralda. "Do you think that instead of hot soup laced with drugs, you could give me a shirt?"

To Kley's annoyance, Heralda answers with a wide smile. "I'll see what I can do for you."

Joshua smirks, and the rest of the group is carried into laughter within seconds. "You see Adam, at least you learned that every worrisome and scary situation in life can be laughed at," summed Joshua. A second later, Adam joined the rest of the room in their laughter.

This is how Adam was first acquainted with the New Dawn Hawks Underground Resistance.

Chapter Twelve

It was late. The New Dawn Hawks, with Adam among them, clustered by a wide structure functioning as an orphanage—a hundred yielding children growing up in an era of slavery, maturing there under a heavy guard of empire soldiers, just so they can be sent to work when they are grown enough, another generation of slaves on its way.

Adam wore a black shirt with short sleeves that clung tightly to his biceps, slowly growing accustomed to his new friends. Joshua asked for his assistance in the mission. "Let him just watch us, so he won't get in the way," requested Kley.

"They're supposed to be right here, this is the set place and time," said Kley, looking around nervously,

"Well, where are they?" Joshua remarked.

Heralda started to express her fears. "I have a bad feeling about all this." Adam watched the New Dawn Hawks and said nothing. Suddenly a wide smile broke on Kley's lips. "Hey, here they are, Jetto and the rest." Three figures, clad in gray cloak, were coming their way, their heads covered by hoods.

"Why did it take so long?" Kley asked. Jetto looked at the team and his eyes fixed on Adam. "Who is this?" They all looked at Adam, who understood he must answer back immediately. "I'm Adam Swandon, and I am not an empire agent."

Jetto drew near him. He was a heavily built man, almost two meters tall, so big Adam had to tilt his head up to look directly into the hulk's eyes. "We'll see about that," said Jetto with a threat in his voice. Joshua came between the two men, trying to ease the tension. "We better calm down, all of us. It's late and we have to stay quite." With the old man in between them, a eerie silence fell on the street. The New Dawn Hawks huddled tightly on the street corner by the large orphanage.

Heralda clung to Adam, tightly clutching his muscular arm. "I have a bad feeling," she whispered in his ear.

He pats her delicate hand and looked at her questioningly. "What do you mean, Heralda?"

Just as he was finishing his questions, Heralda's eyes widened with fear and a startled scream escaped her lips. Adam, bewildered, turned around and his hawk eyes managed to catch the sight of Jetto shooting at Kley and the rest of the bunch. Without thinking, Adam leaps at Jetto, holding the laser weapon that shot down Kley and his friends. Heralda ran over to Joshua, who was hit in his shoulder. "He betrayed us, Heralda. He crossed over to the dark side of humanity," groaned Joshua, twisting in pain. Heralda gently stroked his face.

Adam was wrestling Jetto, trying to fend him off Heralda and the injured Joshua. Jetto, though large and strong, was cumbersome compared to Adam; he tries to shake Adam off, uselessly. Adam held on relentlessly to Jetto's massive arm, and with his other hand, grappled the arm holding the laser gun that kept on shooting deadly beams into the black skies. Adam quickly understood why Jetto continued ceaselessly shooting; above them in the dark sky appeared suddenly a flock of hovercrafts, like black ravens, rapidly drawing near. Adam understood he must act fast. Flinging his left leg, he hit Jetto squarely between the legs. Jetto doubled over in pain. Heralda swiftly pulled out a small pistol and shoots Jetto over and over again, until the clip was empty, and Jetto took his final breath. But the beams shot from Jetto's gun already alerted the empire's hovercrafts that weapons are being smuggled. Jetto betrayed his friends and paid for it with his life, his large form lay on the floor, punctured by numerous shots.

Joshua mumbled something inaudible. Adam kneeled by him. "Can you walk?" he asked. His mouth near Adam's ear, the old man whispered, "We must get out of here before it's too late."

"What do you mean?" asked Adam.

Heralda kneeled by them both. "He means that the empire isn't satisfied with this. They'll 'clean' the whole area. The hovercrafts above us will start bombing any second now," she replied, tears forming in the corners of her eyes.

"What?!" cried Adam, enraged. "What about all this people here in their houses? We must warn them!" Heralda pointed, turning Adam's gaze to the buildings down the dark street he sees men and women swiftly passing through the doorways running as far as possible from the center of the incident.

"They got lucky—not like the poor orphans," Heralda said, her voice heavy with sorrow.

Kneeling on one knee only, Adam's body straightened, his muscles powerfully convulsed. Suddenly he looked so strong. "The orphans?" He gasped, shocked.

"Yes." Heralda's tearful eyes were empty of hope. "A hundred of them, children and teenagers, living in this building," she replied in a broken voice.

"Unbelievable," said Adam in a mounting rage. "We have to get them out of there."

Joshua's old hand touched Adam's side. "It's too late," said the old man in a pained whisper, as he lay on the ground oozing life, his white beard painted red by his own blood.

"Look, Adam." Joshua points at a group of hovercrafts that started shooting red laser bursts at the entire area. "We must leave now, we failed our mission, everybody's dead, that lowlife Jetto sold us out," said Heralda, her voice choked with pain and anger.

She stood and looked down at Joshua, sprawled on the floor, and Adam kneeling by him, trying to stop the bleeding. "She's right, leave me here, run for your lives," gasped Joshua, convulsing in pain.

"We are not leaving you here, my friend, and I'm going to take all of the kids out of that building," said Adam in a resonant voice.

Heralda hit his broad shoulder with her right hand, and over the blast of guns and the racket of hovercrafts, she yelled, "You're crazy, Adam, you'll get killed!"

At that same moment, a row of empty buildings caved in on itself, torn down by the ceaseless bombing. Adam rose from his place and lifted Joshua with him, as Heralda helped him from the other side. Supported by the two young people, the old man was dragged to a drainpipe.

"Do what you can to stop the bleeding," said Adam, and Heralda nodded in agreement. "And what will you do?" she asked. Adam stood above the drain hole, looking down at them with fierce eyes. "I am going to save the children," he said decisively.

After hiding them in the sewer, Adam understood now he must do what was right. His heart was pounding wildly, nearly splitting his chest, but he could not let his fears and doubt suffocate him. He decided he will save the kids, and that's what he was going to do.

Heralda and Joshua watched from under the sewer lid as the sturdy figure moved away from them, toward the burning fire.

In the black windows stood the children, crying, screaming, begging for help and deliverance. The hovercrafts continued blasting away, in order to "clean" the area—and actually, who would stop them? No one, the world has no custodian left; human life is casually disregarded.

Adam placed himself by an old fire hydrant and looked around. He must act quickly. He picked up an iron rod, hot from the fire, but through his rage he felt no pain. With his muscular arm, he began slamming the rod powerfully into the hydrant, again and again, the madness rising in him with each swing. After a number of strikes, the old hydrant broke, and a burst of cold water powerfully gushed out into the burning world. Adam soaked himself from head to toe, and after a few seconds, when he was thoroughly wet, he began running madly toward the burning flames, while protecting his face from burns. Driven by madness and determination he began yelling as he plowed his way through the burning beams falling all around him. Through the hiss of fire burning, he heard the muffled voices of children, crying for help. The voices were coming from above him. He carried on in that direction, taking care that the stairs don't break under his weight.

"Kids! Kids! After me," he cried to them. Suddenly, out of the thick black smoke, burst dozens of children. They ran to him, clustering around the figure bringing them hope.

"Don't scatter, kids, stay close to me!" Adam called. Sobs and screams of boys and girls mixed with the fearsome hissing of the yellow and red monster, the fire threatened to devour them all, but hope and determination burn mightily in Adam. Though he was burnt a little, his clothes singed, Adam led the children out into the open air. He chose two grown adolescents of about fourteen to help him; they immediately accepted his command, trusting this special man who saved them from certain death. They stood outside and led the dozens of kids escaping for their lives toward Heralda and the injured Joshua, who signaled them to come.

The soldiers on the hovercrafts were shocked by the sight. The shock quickly changed into anger. They began aiming their guns toward the savior, Adam Swandon. After a few minutes of frantic activity, Adam managed to secure all the kids.

The hovercraft commander screamed at his soldiers. "Destroy that insolent!" The soldier responsible for weapon control shakily followed his commander's instructions. He couldn't miss; the sensors lock on Adam's running figure through the flames. A terrible dread swept over Adam. His back was to the hovercrafts and he was running toward the kids bunched around the spot where Joshua and Heralda were located.

"Adam, run faster. They're aiming at you, run!" Adam heard Heralda's cries and ran on madly.

The wounded Joshua tugged weakly on Heralda's shirt, pulled her closer, and whispered, exhausted, "Tell him to run in loops… loops…" Through the noise and confusion, Heralda grasped his words, and called out to Adam, "Run in curves, Adam, run in loops!"

Heralda remembered from her fighting lessons that the hovercrafts can't hit targets moving in loops, the weapon control system being based on straight lines and squares. Adam began running in loops and the blasts shot at him missed time after time. Adam felt exhaustion slowly take over him and understood he must come up with a fast solution to the shooting. He ran with all his might toward a cluster of tall buildings, with narrow passages running between them. Thus, he managed to draw the hovercrafts away from Heralda and the kids; they pursue him to shoot him down. They take up high, above the tall buildings, but the sensors still clearly show Adam's image, running among the high buildings. Adam was panting, his heart threatened to burst through his chest for those extreme efforts. He said to himself, "They will lose me here, and I managed to get them away from the kids." Suddenly he saw a local power spot, and by it, used to regulate the electricity flow, some high-pressure gas cylinders. An idea came to his mind.

The hovercrafts slowed down, waiting for Adam to make a mistake. Tense, nervous expressions hover on the soldiers' faces, as they all look at their commander, whose eyes are locked on the radar screen, trying to see Adam's running figure. "Patience," he whispered nervously. "In a moment he will show up on screen—and then we will wipe him off the face of the Earth," said the commander to his soldiers.

Adam carefully but swiftly took apart one of the pipes connected to the cylinder, while making sure that the safety pin in still locked. In one hand, he held the pipe he disassembled, and with the other, he dragged the cylinder to a dark crossroad, where he laid the cylinder on its mouth, making sure that the safety is still in place. The balloon stood in the center of the crossroad, between four tall buildings. Adam's eyes are constantly focused on the safety, making sure it doesn't move, saving the soldiers some work. In his hand, he still held the metal pipe he took from the cylinder, a meter in length. He watched the hovercrafts, waiting tensely. When the first hovercraft slowly glided above him, he jumped out from his hiding place, shouting and waving his arms, as in his heart he said a prayer, "May this work."

One of the soldiers, a wicked grin on his face, called the commander, "Here's that rodent, sir, I can see him on my screen!"

The commander answered with a terrifying cry, "then what are you waiting for, idiot, shoot him! Shoot!" the commander slammed the steering wheel powerfully. "Kill him!" The hovercraft inched closer to secure its target.

When it's almost fifty meters away from him, directly over the gas cylinder, Adam's blood began to gush in his veins. "I have one chance only, I can't miss," he whispered to himself.

The soldiers flipped on the switch for his laser mechanism.

"He's directly in range," the soldier shouted excitedly. The commander's eyes are nearly popping from their holes; on his face spread a diabolical smile. "Come on come on!"

On the ground, Adam shut his eyes and prayed silently for a moment. Then he swung his right arm, holding the metal pipe, and threw the pipe toward the cylinder's safety, and at the exact moment that they fire at him, the pipe, like a javelin, hit the safety and the cylinder flew like a rocket directly into the underside of the hovercraft, smashing into it with an immense fiery explosion that shook the entire area. The blast shot at Adam hit the ground only a few meters away from him, hurling him into the wall of a building. Suddenly a strange voice echoed through his head: "The time will come… the time will come." Stunned, Adam lost his consciousness.

On the other hovercrafts, the rest of the soldiers could not believe their eyes. "Where is he!" yelled the fat commander in the hovercraft near the one that exploded. "Find him fast!" He continued yelling, and after a long, anxious moment of checking all the systems, his soldiers informed him, "He's gone, sir. He must have been wiped out by that laser blast from the hovercraft, before it exploded. The fat officer rose from his seat and approached the soldiers in charge of steering. "Turn the fleet to Argma. We must give a full report of what happened here."

"Sir?" asked the soldier on the steering wheel, expressing his surprise. The fat chief brought his round, sweaty head near the poor soldier and screamed with unprecedented fury, "Turn the hovercrafts to Argma now, do you hear me!?"

Heralda and Joshua stood staring, stunned, at the retreating hovercrafts, already far from the area, and only Heralda said, in tears, "Ho, great creator, Adam, where is Adam?"

Chapter Thirteen

A soft, tender light began spreading through the sky, which was turning light blue with sunrise. It was the break of dawn. Heralda and the kid's faint cries echoed from afar, they were looking for the daring man, their hearts heavy with the fear that he is no longer alive.

Adam himself lay tossed like a ragdoll, his body bruised and wounded. He wasn't conscious but his heart was still beating. From between the old, charred carton crates came a low sound—a small, hesitant form slowly draws near Adam. The shadows withdraw from the little form, the dawning light reveals the identity of the mysterious figure; a small puppy with gray fur is checking the strange man who seems harmless, for the moment. It is said that dogs are a species with a high level of sensitivity; they immediately recognize positive energy. The tiny dog comes nearer and nearer with miniature steps. He whimpered at the weird man but got no answer. He laid his small right paw on Adam's thigh, sniffing, checking for signs of life. He notices the blood pouring from Adam's open wounds and starts licking Adam's face, who still does not respond at all. Suddenly the dog's ears perk up; he heard far away voices. Walking away from Adam, he oriented himself with tiny steps toward the feeble voices. When he noticed that the voices are moving away, growing weaker, he began barking ceaselessly.

The voices of children ring out louder, "Over there, come, we hear a dog barking!" Heralda followed the barks of the pup and started running in that direction. With every step, the barks grew louder and clearer. She could already see the rascal pup barking and pouncing, coming close and withdrawing, barking ceaselessly, coming close and withdrawing, as if trying to say, "Follow me!"

Excitement gripped Heralda as she saw something that lifted her heart; she saw Adam, slumped against a building wall. He is not moving; anxiety crept over her, but she didn't lose hope. She came near the man, sprawled motionless on the floor and feels to see if there is still a breath of life in him. A joyous grin dawned on her pretty face when she saw Adam is alive, unconscious but alive. She saw his open wounds, saw that he lost quite an amount of blood, and knew that time is short. She signals the two kids with her to help her carry him. She undid the purple handkerchief tied around her narrow waist, tore it through the middle into two pieces, and with a professional dexterity, she dressed the two wounds, which she thought were in first priority to be treated, the one on Adam's left forearm and the one near his left knee.

The small pup was watching the young woman's movements curiously. He came near and barked softly, as if thanking her for treating the wounded man. She noticed him and smiled, patting his little head with gentle hands. "Thank you, kind puppy, you helped us a lot, but now we have to vanish from here." She lifted Adam's heavy form, laying his left arm on her shoulder, while on the other side one of the children supported his right arm. His head rolled forward, a sight that scared the kids, who were thinking he might already be dead. Heralda comforted them with words of hope. "It's fine, kids, he simply passed out." And she continued immediately, "Come, we must make an effort to reach the hiding place where Joshua and the rest of the kids are." They all started moving away slowly; only the gray pup stayed behind.

Chapter Fourteen

In Argma's huge lower corridor, an assembly of three army personnel were walking. In front the fat hovercraft commander, his face pale. Behind him march the two soldiers who were with him in the hunt after Adam. They watch each other in silence; only the fat commander keeps on muttering inaudible words. He didn't know how he would inform his superior about this incident, how a simple man managed to escape a whole unit of the great empire's hovercrafts, managing on top of that to blow up one of the hovercrafts. Such a thing never happened before. A deep apprehension burdened his breathing. The three reached a moving walkway. They stood on the silicon strip moving slowly toward the superior commander of the hovercraft fleet.

The fat commander pulled out a white handkerchief and mopped the sweat off his high forehead. His head is nearly bald and the little hair he had left is smoothed back. He turned to his soldiers. "You wait outside. When I go in, it won't be easy breaking this news to the top commander." He turned his back to them again, and the two soldiers exchanged glances, secretly gloating at their commander's trouble since he constantly bullied them, but beyond a shade of a smile on their lips, they showed nothing. Nodding lightly, they stood to attention behind their fat superior.

At the sides of the long corridor, first rays of morning sun filtered through the immense dark windows, painting the moving silicon carpet in a weak light. The routine activity of empire soldiers, passing on either sides of the moving sidewalk, filled the hallway with the undecipherable chatter of talking.

The fat commander with his two soldiers have reached the office of Kraus, the captain of the hovercraft fleet. Two oversized scowling guards moved aside at the site of the fat hovercraft officer and his two soldiers, who took their place at the right of Kraus's big office door. One of the guards opened the large door. The fat commander took a deep breath and stepped into the office.

The room of Kraus, captain of the hovercraft fleet, was large and wide. An old classical tune, two hundred years or older, was playing softly. Kraus was sitting on a bulbous leather purple couch. He has a slim, wiry body. His narrow, pale face was burrowed in the young hands of his favorite hussy. Her long, auburn hair covered his shoulders. She was sitting in his lap like a naughty child. The fat commander was momentarily distracted by this attractive girl, a slight tension was felt in the air. It was broken when Commander Kraus noticed how the fat commander was exploring the redhead's trim body and cleared his throat. The fat man understood the hint immediately and turned his gaze to the large windows, while the young girl rose and stood by the large windows, and lit a long, slender cigarette. Kraus turned to face the chubby commander, whose hands were crossed behind his back and was tensely waiting for permission to speak.

"Commander Petrov, you don't look too well," Kraus remarked casually. "Are you sick, Petrov?" asked the captain of the hovercraft fleet. His fingertips were stretched and touching each other as if he is about to clap, his posture upright and symmetrical, his elbows rested on his knees and he was gazing down at Petrov through narrow eyes.

"No, sir, I feel fine," stammered Petrov.

"Your face is showing some anxiety... what do you have to tell me?" asked Kraus.

The young girl was enjoying the show in front of her. She giggled lightly and drew gently on her slim cigarette, which was growing shorter.

"My supreme captain, sir," commander Petrov started speaking again, his face taking on a serious, professional expression, while in his heart he strived to impress the giggling, luscious young woman.

"A few hours ago, we left on a demolition mission to eliminate the underground militia called the New Dawn Hawks, while they were making a gun smuggling deal, which was supposed to harm us."

Kraus nods calmly, with a hum. "Hmmm?"

"Well, sir, one of their own members, who was paid to spy for us, let us in on what's about to happen. After receiving his signal, we attacked, eliminated all involved, and as customary, began to clean the area. Suddenly a mysterious man burst through our laser blasts into the orphanage in the vicinity."

Kraus was still sitting in the same posture, and with the same unaffected expression, he asked, "Well?"

Petrov continued, "He rescued all the children from the flames. When we found that, we locked in on him, aiming to destroy him, but he was moving so fast, our shooting systems just couldn't hit him..."

At that moment, Kraus rose from his comfortable seat and stood in front of the fat Petrov, who looked like a small round jug compared to his tall and slender superior commander. Petrov glanced fearfully at Kraus but continued speaking in a lower tone. "He disappeared among the high buildings in the center of the city, our sensors had difficulties locating him... then when number one hovercraft came close, leading the structure, he sent a missile at the hovercraft from ground level... I... I..." mumbled Petrov. "I think it was a gas cylinder, he improvised something in field conditions... he blew hovercraft number one to shreds, I immediately fired back, and we demolished him."

Kraus didn't move. A silence settled on the empty room. Suddenly, with no warning, a blood-curdling scream broke through Kraus's lips, followed by a ringing slap to Petrov's round face. "Idiooooot!"

The slim, tall figure was bent over the commander's stout form as if about to swallow it. The redhead was no longer smiling. She understood the situation is about to change, and she should leave, quickly. "Kraus, sweetie, I have to go now," said the ginger girl with a squeaky voice.

Still looking directly at Petrov's face, Kraus turned his left arm and pointed at the young vixen. "You're not going anywhere, Trisha," he said in a threatening tone and continued in a whisper, "You will leave when I want you to, do you understand, dear?"

Trisha froze in her tracks, knowing that it will be unwise to disobey the high commander of the hovercraft fleet. "Yes, Kraus dear. I'll wait right here," said Trisha. She noticed her cigarette was finished and turned her eyes to the view portrayed through the tall windows, distracting herself with the flight of the aircrafts outside.

Petrov was silent; the wallop he just received from his commander sent him back to his childhood, when his father used to beat him for his misdeeds. Kraus took up a new direction. "Tell me, Petrov, do you know that the man is dead?"

The fat officer, as if woken from a deep sleep, answers with a stammer: "I... I..."

"You what?" asked Kraus mockingly. Petrov could no longer impress the young girl; he was praying silently that she would leave the room and won't witness his humiliation, but that didn't happen. "Sir, do you mean did we find his body? Well... no, we didn't, I recommended retuning immediately to Argma to deliver this report," he said.

Kraus stepped toward his desk made of flat, black marble. He gently caressed the smooth surface of the desk. "So he must still be alive, not so…?" said Kraus in a whisper and continued immediately without giving Petrov a chance to answer. "I want you to arrange a special search unit, go back to that place, and retrieve the man's body in ice," concluded Kraus.

Petrov was cursing his bad luck, but he answered his superior affirmatively, saluted, and left the room, his soldiers trailing behind him. In his exit, he feels no better then he did entering.

Trisha drew near Kraus and caressed his thin neck. "Come, let me make you feel good," said the ginger girl. He fixed her with a disdainful look. "Not now, I must speak to our leader and report what happened. Go have a bubble bath in the meantime, and I'll see you later, with the rest of your lady friends." He pushed her off him lightly. She left the room blowing him a kiss from afar. Kraus pressed the communication button in his desk—a short sound rang through the room, then Bammark's voice came through: "What's the matter, Kraus?" The commander of the fleet related all he heard from Petrov. Bammark's reply was not long: "I'll pass it on to Drakkar. In the meantime, take care of this small matter." The connection was severed. With a typical indifference, Kraus sat on his overblown couch, lit a thick cigar, and resumed listening to the classical tune that filled the room.

Chapter Fifteen

Two hours only from the return of the hovercraft structure to Argma, the great round conference hall was in an upheaval. All the empire's leaders were present, raging and foaming over information of the recent events. It has been years since such a thing happened, one simple person—from the underground, from a population of slaves, from the bottom of the barrel, managed in his impudence to blow up an empire hovercraft, carrying officers and soldiers. "How can it be?" they asked themselves. They spoke of their fears with an openness legitimized by the severity of the occasion. They were wary of this event setting a precedent, resonating through the little underground militias spread all over the world. Rumors spread fast.

Bartholomew was standing at old Irma's side; the two are ignoring the angry gathering of leaders and whispering among themselves, "Irma, this is the time to tell Drakkar and the rest of our recent discoveries."

Irma stared at Bartholomew with a puzzled expression. "Our latest discoveries, Bartholomew?"

Bartholomew was taken aback. "Well, we are working on this together, no?" asked Bartholomew. Suddenly Bammark approached the two, cutting their conversation short. "What are you talking about, scoundrels? Maybe you should share it with the rest of us."

Irma looked at the leader as if waiting for his permission. Drakkar understood her gaze, and asked that she tell the gathering all she knows.

"Well, gentlemen, a short time ago, I stood here and told you about the ancient prophecies. You expressed serious doubts about what I had to say." Drakkar folded one hand and with the other stroked his beard, and Irma continued, "Now the pieces are beginning to fall into place: first your dreams, Drakkar, and Bartholomew's, and this surprising event, with a mysterious man that single handedly brought down an entire empire hovercraft."

Bammark, with his typical doubtful attitude, cut her short. "We are always dreaming some kind of weird and mysterious dreams. It means nothing in real life. It's all nonsense, Irma!" He waved his hands dismissively and turned his back to Bartholomew and Irma.

Vaskov turned to look at Drakkar. "My friend, how important do you think this matter is? Do you believe there is truth in the old hag's words?"

The leader looked at his partner and replied with a hard, sealed expression, "I already had the captain of the hovercraft fleet take care of this business. He began pacing toward the large doors of the great hall, still speaking, "I'm getting a steady report from my people." He stopped and stood before the great doors then turned his head to the group of people he left behind. "This matter is being taken care of. It's insignificant. We shouldn't be disturbed by it. It's a minor success of a small, local underground group. In a few days, we are having a grand banquet for all the top brass. Get ready for it." Without further words, the massive man exits the room, leaving behind Irma and the rest of his comrades with perplexed expressions.

"He is as stubborn as a mule, I knew it, that's his worst flaw," said Irma to the rest of the band. Bammark got annoyed again. "You come here with the coward Bartholomew, trying to shoot us down with tales of prophecies and dreams—cease, old woman! The world is ours, the world is in the grip of the empire, and no little scoundrel can uproot such a huge empire."

Irma didn't speak, hoping that Bartholomew will reply, then she remembers that she can't actually rely on him, so she directs a piercing gaze from her narrow eyes directly into Bammark's, who was indeed startled for a moment by it.

"Listen to me well, listen all of you. I've done my part, now you deal with it the way you know. I will leave now, but remember, you know where to find me if you want me." Irma finished the sentence and turned toward the exit, but before leaving, she turned again to the group huddled in the center of the hall. "Look, the prophecy isn't speaking of an irrefutable fact. It's here just to warn us. It's not I that wrote it, but someone much wiser than all of us, many years ago." She took one last look at all of them and paced toward the doors again, the usually withdrawn Vaskov broke his habit and spoke to his two friends.

"Perhaps we should check this thing a little more thoroughly then just sending a patrol unit to find the man and kill him?" Bammark didn't reply but looked closely at his usually reserved friend. He knew that if Vaskov takes the time to say something, it usually has some sense in it.

Bartholomew pulled on his long red coattails that were sweeping the floor and said, "We are the rulers of Earth, Bammark, and that is why we must always defend our rule, by not allowing something marginal to grow and turn into something major."

Bammark was surprised by the logic in the words of the man they usually all mocked, and replied, "We will see what happens with the patrol unit when it finds the culprit that blew up our hovercraft. In the meantime, we must concentrate on managing the rest of the world," concluded Bammark and signaled his departure, letting them all know that this meeting is now over.

Chapter Sixteen

The school yard, little Adam is running with fear in his heart, the other children vowed to beat him after class. He is thinking, *I'll slip away and make it home fast*, but no, behind him appears the group of boys and girls. The place he comes from and his poverty marked him as an outcast, an outsider. He feels the dread choking him; boys and girls shamelessly line up to cast him out from among them. He doesn't remember even what brought on this occurrence, his heart was pounding, he understood his survival depends on his legs and how fast they can run. *Why is this my fate?* he asks himself. He had no concept of God yet. He was an eleven-year-old child that felt nobody understood him at all, not at home and not in school. He began running like the wind, faster and faster; it seemed his feet didn't even touch the ground. He felt the other kids running behind him in a crowd, shouting, "Out! Out! We want Adam out!"

Some of them closed in on him and managed to smack him. Tears of pain and anguish filled the hawk eyes of the young boy. The indifference of bystanders was painfully noticeable on this day. "Oh, its just some rowdy kids." That's what they were thinking, never realizing what their eyes witnessed—a customary pattern of humanity. The persecution of the different, the outcasting, the mental and physical ruin of the weak, the weird, humanity didn't change, not then, not now. Again the solitary and different is chased down by the crowd, apparently this how the creator wanted things to be, it happened in the past, and it is happening again today. Adam manages to make it home. The door locks behind him, the pain on the outside stays on the outside; after the door is closed starts the pain from within.

Heralda lays another moist towel on Adam's hot forehead. He is still unconscious. She smiled to him, seeming as if she is waiting for him to smile back. Her eyes fill with tears.

She took a seat by Adam's side. He was laid out on a soft, white bed, his head resting on a white, yielding pillow. He was covered with a gray blanket, not too heavy, yet warm enough.

Heralda took Adam's hand. He didn't move. She began whispering to him softly, "I've never seen a man as brave as you. You must hear me, Adam, you must get better." She was alone with Adam in the big room lit only by a table lamp. She keeps on talking to him, believing in her heart that somehow, he hears her. "Joshua is already feeling better. He's healing himself quickly with the meditations he does. Among us, he's the only one familiar with these methods of healing. When he feels better, he will heal you too, I hope you're not in pain, oh, Adam… what you did there that night will be remembered for generations, as long as I live and as long as the those lucky children that you saved that miserable night live. The entire city is talking about it, even other resistances heard of it. Oh, Adam, if only I could know where you really are right now, where is your spirit. Can you hear me?"

The images change. Adam's heart is stolen by the beauty of the richest girl in class. His heart is stung; he is thirteen, a kid held in the throngs of a one-sided love. He stares at her in class. She returns his gaze and he feels his heart sinking in an ocean of sweet pain. The fog takes over again. "Am I dreaming?" Adam asks himself. He can't feel his body, but he hears a voice, a soft voice speaking directly into his thoughts. He knows the voice: "Heralda, that's the voice of pretty Heralda, but why can't I talk to her? Why can't I sense her hand on mine?" With his mind's eyes, Adam sees himself lying motionless in the bed, and again everything disappears. Adam suddenly feels himself surrounded by a blue light. He is overwhelmed by the beauty of it, a soft blue light enveloping him all around, and through the light Adam sees an indistinct face. Even though he can't recognize the features of the mysterious character, the hazy visage radiates a good energy that brings Adam to a state of special tranquility. He sensed that the mysterious face is smiling at him and he felt himself filled with joy by what the face emanates to him. The hazy figure started to speak to him, "Don't worry now, Adam, don't worry. Rest now and heal, to the man whose road is hidden from him, rest now, the time will come."

The figure softly dissolved into the blue light until it vanished completely. Again, the fog gathered and covered everything.

Joshua entered the room holding two hot tea mugs. He was feeling better; his wounds were nearly healed.

"Heralda dear, it's time you rested. I'm strong enough now, I can take care of him myself," said Joshua as he handed her one of the scalding mugs. She held the cup, and noticing that it was very hot, placed it on the dresser by Adam's bed. Joshua sipped gingerly from his tea and looked questioningly at Heralda. "Were there any changes?"

Heralda crossed her arms and said, "No, Joshua. He hasn't moved at all. Three days have passed without any sign of him recuperating."

Joshua laid his hand on the young woman's shoulder, and with his other hand, he gently moved the blanket covering Adam. He turned the young woman's attention to Adam. "Look, Heralda, your bandages and devoted treatment have stopped the bleeding, and the words you put in his mind are making him stronger. People don't believe this, but words spoken with honesty and love do indeed reach the person's subconscious, curing him through his own self. The words help him focus his energy, and thus it goes on."

Heralda rises from her seat and takes her tea with her. "I'll leave you alone with Adam now, so you can use your abilities to speed his recovery." She kissed the old man on his cheek and adds, "It's good to have you back, Joshua." Joshua smiles back at her. He remains alone in the room with Adam.

"Now, my boy, where does your consciousness lie? I know you hear me. My voice will guide your healing powers to speed your recovery. Focus on my voice, it will guide you."

As Joshua takes a seat on the chair by Adam's bed, Adam sees someone familiar through the thick fog in his mind, and he is deeply touched. He sees a small boy, about eight years old, standing on the edge of a high hill. A warm wind is caressing the child's face. Beneath the hill is a green valley, full of rocks and a variety of trees. The child turns his gaze to the sky and his eyes are filled with tears. He opens his mouth and asks the Almighty God for the strength to change and heal the world, to be someone big and succeed.

The boy turns to Adam. "Remember our promise," he says to Adam. "We cannot forget our dream." Adam feels a shiver run through his entire body. "But we are only the two of us," he replies. "We can't do this alone, the forces of evil are so immense and we are so tiny, and here I am, sprawled on the bed and incapable of doing anything at all, and who are you, child?"

"I am you," answered the child. You and I that have been suffering for years, I am you, we wanted to be something our entire life, to change, to heal, to fix, but we never believed we can actually succeed in doing it. I am here because it is time," said the little boy.

"Time for what?" asks Adam. "Time to believe in ourselves and go against all conventions, against all odds, one soul can change an entire world." Suddenly Adam saw a huge book in front of him, and the huge pages started to turn until the place where the words were written: "One soul can change an entire world."

"But what should I do? I'm badly injured, my body isn't responding to me." Adam saw the child is drifting away. "Hey, kid, where are you going?" The fog returned; the hill and the child on it disappeared. Suddenly Joshua's voice resounded powerfully. "Adam, listen to me, from moment to moment you grow stronger. Your body and your soul rejoin. You are becoming yourself again. Adam, listen to me, don't give up, you can and you will come back, come back Adam, come back."

Again, the blue light flooded around him. A sense of relief and well-being enfolded Adam, and Joshua's voice became clearer and clearer. "Adam, come out from the darkness into the light. Don't let the gloom take over you. Concentrate on your healing powers, cause your body to heal rapidly, all the wounds are quickly healing."

Joshua's voice rang like thunder in Adam's ears. In his mind, he sees the light coming closer and closer. The fog vanishes. Adam's breathing returns to normal. Joshua breaks into a wide smile.

Adam woke up…

In the living room of the small house where the members of the resistance lived, there was quite a commotion. Joy and excitement overtook all the people present; the man that rescued the hundred orphans was conscious again. The parlor was full of light and cheerful faces. Heralda was in the room with Adam, helping him to get dressed. Adam was staring at the large mirror at the right of the bed. Then he turned to Heralda. "How long was I unconscious, Heralda?"

Heralda didn't rush to answer him. She busied herself organizing the shoes and clothes that people brought him. "Three days, Adam. You were unconscious for three days, and Joshua managed to bring you back to life. I'm so glad."

"Three days, are you sure? Look at my wounds. They are nearly healed, as if it's been a month or more."

The pretty girl stopped folding and turned to look at the curious man. "Joshua masters ancient healing techniques that have something to do with hypnosis and tapping into the unconscious mind. It's beyond my own understanding, but I'm sure Joshua could answer all your questions," said Heralda. She noticed Adam still had some difficulties with getting dressed. It's hard for him, she thinks, he is still not completely healed, but what Joshua did is truly astonishing. Adam recovered almost completely…

She assisted him to finish dressing, as he kept staring, dazed, at his image in the mirror. With Heralda's help, he was finally attired in black army pants, made from a special fabric, resilient but light, and on his torso, he wore a black, tight linen shirt, with long sleeves that reached up to his forearms. The shoes were black army shoes that custom tailored themselves to the movements of the feet they were on. Adam felt good in this new outfit. Heralda caught his eye with her smile. "Come, Adam, some people want to meet you and make your acquaintance."

The strapping young man looked at her questioningly. "My acquaintance?" asks Adam, bewildered. She didn't answer him, merely taking his arm and led him to the parlor.

On a long table, many delicacies were laid out—meat, poultries, and broiled vegetables. The smell of fresh bread hung in the air of the living room. The orphans were already engulfed in the task of eating, enjoying themselves immensely. Old Joshua was the first to draw near. "Let me see him—come here, lad." He embraced Adam warmly, and the rest of the people crowded around him. "It's outstanding what you did there, lad, simply outstanding," said one of the men as he shook Adam's hand with reverence. Another woman drew near with her friend and they both embraced him warmly. "Way to go, Adam. It's been years since humanity has seen such courage."

Adam was staggered by all the commotion around him, and he sought out Joshua to shield him somewhat. People started drinking. Cheerful music played in the background. Joshua led his friend toward two padded chairs, and they sat down. Adam was still feeling pain in certain parts of his body. Joshua noticed that and remarked, "Don't worry, Adam, it will pass faster than you think."

A small boy came near Adam, and with an awkward smile offered him a cold drink. "Take it from him, Adam, that's the little he can do for you," said Joshua.

"What do you mean?" asked Adam, and the old man replied immediately, "He knows that it's you that saved him from the infernal in the orphanage that night."

Adam, deeply moved, smiled to the silent little boy, took the beverage from him, and stroked his head affectionately. The child turned on his heels, quietly gloating, and returned to his friends playing on the parlor floor.

"It's hard to believe. I was nearly dead. Joshua, how did you manage to cure me so quickly?" Adam asked the old man.

Joshua looked at Adam and said, "Drink and rejoice, Adam, for today you were returned to us alive. We will have time to talk later."

Chapter Seventeen

A hum, growing louder and louder, distracted all present in the parlor. Heralda came near a rectangular screen attached to one of the walls. She pushed two buttons on the control board to the left of the elongated screen. "Password?" Heralda demanded. An image of a young man appeared on the monitor. "After the night the dawn will rise," the man replied.

Heralda confirmed, "Tarrio, why are you contacting us? You know that we have been attacked by empire forces a few days back, and dear members were killed, and the empire spies must be monitoring the underground's communication channels."

Tarrio looked at Heralda through the screen and noticed Adam and Joshua; a few more people standing behind Tarrio crowded the screen.

"My condolences, members of the New Dawn Hawks militia. The entire team of the resistance would like to express its grief for this incident."

Joshua stepped into the center of view. "That's nice of you, Tarrio... I'd like to introduce you. This is Adam."

Joshua pulled Adam to himself, presenting him to Tarrio and his people. "So this is the man all the undergrounds around are buzzing about. It's a great honor, sir," said the man on the monitor.

"I... I..." replied Adam with a stutter, as Tarrio carried on, "Sir, everybody is talking about what you did, how you rescued all those kids from the flaming building—" Joshua decided to interfere.

"That's enough, Tarrio! Now tell me why have you contacted us so urgently?"

"It's like this, sir, our people from the east sent us a hot trail. The empire is bent on finding and destroying the man that blew up its hovercraft in the center of town a few days ago. We also understand that they are guided by the empire's satellite communication, and that a whole unit of Storm hovercrafts already left base, heavily armed."

Joshua coughed and looked at Adam and the people surrounding him. "Well, rumors travel fast, that's why we have no choice. That hovercraft unit has an address, and, Adam, you are it. We have to get you out of the city, you have to move on."

Heralda burst into his sentence. "That's ridiculous, Joshua! We can protect him here, we still have enough ammo and we're well hidden, and besides, he still isn't well enough." Joshua stopped Heralda from going on. "Even though, we must smuggle Adam away from here. He is in great danger here." More people in the room mumbled their agreement, that if the empire finds his location, it will quickly pin him down, and if it will pin him down, he will die."

Tarrio's communication was over. The people in the parlor, by old Joshua's command, have all scattered. The young woman and the wounded man paced slowly down an underground corridor belonging to the militia. Adam was telling Joshua about what occurred in his latest dreams, about the little boy and the other things he witnessed. Joshua stopped them all in their tracks, his face suddenly lighted with hopefulness.

"Adam, I'm no great scholar of dreams, but going by what I learned as a young psychology student in the National University of Italy, based on the wisdom of my teacher and mentor the Great Altoro Pikola, you are facing a great turn in your life—and apparently, your entire life led up to this purpose."

Adam was confused by Joshua's words, yet he tried to find some logic in them. "What are you trying to tell me, Joshua? That I'm some kind of messiah? Some kind of savior? That's ridiculous! I'm just a simple man. I know that a moment ago I was looking for ways to uproot the empire, but let's be serious for a moment… I'm just one man, the empire has an army of millions of soldiers, all over the world… no, Joshua, you are wrong. I'm not who you think I am."

Adam stepped away from them, waving his arms. Heralda moved to run after him, but the old man stopped her. "Let him go, Heralda. If he's meant in some way to be the savior of us all, he can't avoid recognizing his true destiny,"

Heralda looked questioningly at old Joshua, "Do you really think he is that out of the ordinary?"

The old man sighed. "Heralda dear, there is something you must understand, every man is unique in the way he views his own life. A man's dreams show him what it is that he truly wants in life, and his life seems to be taking on the form of a crucial calling."

Heralda continued listening intently to the words of the old man, and he continued, "You saw for yourself what happened a few days ago that night, no man has ever managed to take down an empire hovercraft till that day, with only his empty hands."

Heralda's expression began to change as she accepted Joshua's words, and his thoughts became a part of her, yet she says to him, "But Adam is still wounded. Even with the progress in his healing, he's not ready for a journey."

Joshua began walking back in the direction of the parlor, holding Heralda's narrow waist with one hand. "I know you developed feelings for him."

Heralda was startled by the old man's words. "How did you…?"

"These old eyes saw many things in this world, and they can recognize when someone's in love." The young woman raised her hand and stretched out her finger, asking Joshua not to mention a word of it to Adam. Joshua promised the youngster he would not mention a thing to Adam, and they proceeded to the common room in silence.

With a slight limp, Adam paces through the narrow corridor until he feels a gentle breeze and understands that he reached the exit. He took pleasure in the light wind caressing his face. His entire body felt exhausted. His mind was troubled over what Joshua hinted, and he began to ask himself disturbing questions—is he some messiah figure? Is he the savior of humanity? He snickered awkwardly at the exaggerated questions he was asking himself.

He watched the nearly full moon surrounded by a reddish halo. It occurred to him at that moment that even the moon is bleeding as a result of the era of the empire's evil rule. He sat down on a rounded cement construct. He checks his pocket and finds his trusty little laser blade. He felt a warmth of exhilaration flood his chest as he remembered the day he received the blade from his father. The wind began to blow harder, and the branches of the trees around him bent in surrender to the sway of the wind. Leaves began falling all around; he remembers that day on the mountain's face, watching the horrible massacre in valley below him, a few miles from the place that was once his home. He remembered the burning resolve to bring a great change, to seek a cure for all this sorrow that humanity's drowning in.

He began to feel himself growing excited from the direction of his thoughts, and the more focused his thoughts became, that he must continue his strange journey after the solution, after the cure to the evil existing everywhere in the world—the stronger blew the winds accompanying his thoughts. He felt odd but reassured, as if the wind was encouraging him in his line of thought, encouraging him to think and focus on rising and doing something. Suddenly Adam noticed his aches were no longer existent. He looked at his wounds, and to his amazement, he sees they are gone. Barely a shade of a scar could be seen. He was deeply thrilled, and he looked around him at that moment for someone to share this experience with, but he was alone, with himself and with the red tinted moon, and the strong winds whistling ceaselessly, as if saying to Adam, "Go on, Adam, go on with the journey and don't stop. Find the true solution to all this suffering."

He felt as if he is hallucinating, yet he was sharply aware to all that surrounded him. Adam rose from his seat and gazed at the moon that began receding behind the black clouds of this special night. He focused his thoughts on the decision to push on. It was weird that minutes ago, he sneered at the thought that he's a messiah figure, that he as a single person could bring on a change. He ignored his doubts for this moment and came to a decision.

"Yes, I will go on. I have nothing to lose, and I promised him." He remembered his promise to Peter and Dorina. He was very excited; the strong winds blew and blew, their gait sounded like a scream, and in that single moment, when Adam resolved in his heart that he will continue his search after a solution and he won't give up until it's found, the winds instantly stopped blowing. Everything around him grew silent, then the moon broke through the black clouds with its shining glow, as if it defeated them, pushed them off. The black clouds slowly receded, and the sky was once again lit by moonlight.

The wind died out. Silence. The branches of the green trees stretched upright. Once again. Adam felt like he did the day he stood on the mountain cliff and saw that special sign of the lightning, soundlessly splitting the horizon. He turned his gaze back to the parlor, toward old Joshua, Heralda, and the rest of the New Hawk's underground. His hawk eyes reflected utter determination. He tells himself to be brave and push on and not to give up; he took on himself a tremendous responsibility, and he felt there is nothing left for him but to do it. He decided to turn to Joshua, to seek his advice and guidance. He felt he was getting back on the track of the journey to find a cure to the world's evil. Perhaps the old man knows something, the slightest hint of a trail.

He began pacing toward the center of the commotion, determined to go on. He approached the group of people that immediately turned at the sight of the strong young man, gasping at the sight of his swift recovery. They can see that all his wounds vanished. A vast murmur passed through the crowd: "How? How?" But no one had an answer.

Heralda, stunned, draws near Adam and asks about his health. He nods, smiling, signaling he's okay. Old Joshua, who has seen many things in his life, has never seen this before. He knows that even though he hastened Adam's recovery with his healing techniques of speaking to the subconscious, aiding the healing of his body with the help of the spirit, such a swift recovery is impossible, and on such a level that the injury didn't even leave a sign. He knows now, more than ever, that Adam was meant for greatness, that he is special, and he himself in his old age must do whatever it takes to help Adam fulfill his destiny that is tied to humanity's destiny.

The old man approached the young one and said, "Your face says you have reached a decision… what is it?"

The young man looked at Joshua with his hawk eyes and said, "I understand that this is something I must do, I must make an effort to solve all this evil in our world, I know I must try, but I don't know how I would do it. Only the idea burns in me."

Heralda listened quietly, then the old man spoke, "Listen to me, Adam. When I was a child many years ago, my grandfather told me a tale, passed on to him by his grandfather for many generations. It's a story that we all treated as a legend, but like the old saying goes: where there is smoke there is fire, meaning that there is something behind this legend."

Adam showed his curiosity, he asked Joshua to tell him more about it, so the old man with the long white beard carried on: "The legend tells of a mysterious force, buried in our world thousands of years ago, by powers from other worlds. Not much is known of this legend, but there is a trail—they tell of someone who knows of the truth in that legend more then anyone else, a weird and mysterious person, who lives alone, deep in the heart of the African deserts."

Adam's and Heralda's faces reflect skepticism, and Joshua noticed that. He felt a little embarrassed for mentioning the idea of a children's tale that he heard when he was just a kid, but then Adam surprised him by calling out the question: "Where can he be found?"

Joshua laid his hand on Adam's shoulder. "Sorry, boy, that's all I know, but in our age, when everything seems to be lost, every spark of hope must be taken seriously, even if it's something out of a fairy-tale. I still think the matter should be checked." The young man considered this for a few seconds then surprised with the question: "And why did no one ever try to find this man in the desert, and see if there is some truth to this legend?"

The old man smiled and said, "That's a very smart question, Adam. Truth is, very few people knew of this tale, but many years ago, there were some who tried. A few were treated as mad men on a fool's errant, others never came back, and others gave up on the idea. Besides, people don't believe in fables and stories. It's easier to get accustomed to the harsh reality then to go on far-fetched journeys, or so most people believe."

Adam answered at once, "Well, I'm not like most people. I believe in hope, and I refuse to accept the reality the empire forced upon our world, and I also believe this legend should be explored, to verify if there is any truth in it or not. We must at least try."

Adam's words deeply impressed Joshua. "All right, Adam, I think you are on the right path, at least in the way you think, so I'm going to do everything I can to help you fulfill your quest. We have friends all over the world and they too will help you."

Adam felt reassured by these words. It was late; Joshua suggested that tomorrow they will move on, and everyone should sleep now and gather their strength for tomorrow.

Chapter Eighteen

In one of the officer quarters inside Argma palace sat Kardo Fonson, commander of the Parakees unit, cleaning and checking his weapon, a photon laser gun. "This gun has a history," mused Kardo. He cut short many lives with this gun. He caressed the black shiny weapon while waiting in his room for Petrov's call to the debriefing, before they leave for the assignment. He will have to reunite with his old friends now: Chickon, Asan, and Baltimore—the four warriors that always fought the empire's fights. They were the ones to locate the heads of the underground militias, hidden in all kinds of secret burrows all over south Europe then trap and annihilate them. The Parakees were known for there excessive cruelty.

He stroked his cheeks thoughtfully with both his hands. A long scar, bulging from the center of his left cheek down to his chin, reminded him of old scenes from the days he fought the empire's opponents; he remembered the underground warrior that leaped at him, utterly crazed, who with one swipe of his sharp sword ripped open Kardo's face. He remembered as he gripped his old faithful gun tightly how in those critical moments the gun helped him drive the assailant back with brutal shots. The stubble on his cheeks skipped over the thick scar.

He heard rumors of the new mission that he and his friends were going to head out west and locate the mysterious man that managed to blow up an empire's assault hovercraft.

"Now that's something that doesn't happen every day... I wonder who is the man who dared do such a thing?" Kardo pondered. He rose from the corner of the bed he was sitting on and came up to a metal cabinet attached to the right of his bed; he pressed a small plate and a small drawer popped out, and from the drawer, a flat monitor flipped open and rose slowly to an angle of forty-five degrees.

The monitor displayed four colored circles, green, red, yellow, and blue. He sighed quietly and pressed the yellow circle, and from a thin slot under the drawer, two yellow pills dropped directly into Kardo's rough hand. He sat back on his padded bed and stared at the two yellow pills. There was a time when he wanted to quit those drugs, but he gave up that idea long ago. It started from the empire's victory celebrations, in which the regime encouraged plunder and depravity.

The drugs where scattered in all directions, whenever they wanted them, as much as they wanted; he felt the thirst for the active material in the pill, a sudden desire overtook him, and in an instant he shoved the two yellow tablets down his throat. He tightened his eyelids in one long, strong blink; he seemed to be suffering from the burn of the drug in the back of his throat, and after a few seconds, he felt better, younger. He sensed his energy coming back to him. A slight shame enfolded him with the knowledge that this is merely a temporary sensation and it's all artificial; he was fifty-five, and he believed the way to stay fit for his post was in taking these substances.

A long buzz suddenly broke into his thoughts, followed by a human voice: "Kardo Fonson, arrive at the debriefing room." It was time.

He checked himself in the mirror, inhaled a long, deep breath through his teeth, and said out loud, "Let's go and find this mysterious guy, bring his head to our four leaders, and gather the fat award we deserve."

He smirked at his reflection, left his room, and went to the debriefing hall. His friends were there already, dressed in reinforced black uniforms, armed from head to toe. They greet each other with wide smiles. It's been a long time since they saw each other. They all sat on metal chairs and two young, pretty girls in black uniforms served them drinks as the lot replied with smiles and grins. The hall door opened suddenly and Petrov, captain of the hovercraft unit, stepped in. The four rose to their feet and saluted him. Petrov described the events of that accursed night to them, and the battle scarred old gang kept on smirking at the hovercraft commander's helplessness and incompetent reactions. The fat commander didn't like their behavior one bit; still he went with the flow. He knew who they were. He knew that a conflict with them was a bad idea if he wanted to get something from them.

He handed out thin plates with the details of the incident and the estimated location of the mystery man who blew up the hovercraft. The four Parakees soldiers gave up shaving long ago; their shabby looks bothered Petrov. *What a lack of discipline*, he thought to himself. If they were under his command, things would be different. Though they worked for the empire, they were, to his regret, free from all army regulations, so he said nothing.

Petrov drew near the group of the Parakees warriors and said, "Try to bring him back alive, but I won't be sorry if you bring me his body either." He flashed a wicked smile at their direction, and Kardo replies with a smile no less evil. "We usually don't bring our targets back alive, if you get my drift, Petrov?"

The Parakees gang with Petrov among them burst suddenly into loud laughter. The Parakees saluted Petrov again and went on their way; their mission was to capture the man that slighted the empire. They came to a docking station of hovercrafts and armored war vehicles, where their special war craft was awaiting them: the warship of the four—"the Parakees hell-monster." It was the battleship the four had from their first days of fighting in the empire's ranks. It was a war machine heavily armed with laser canons, guided missiles, and old millennium shotguns.

"The Parakees" was a heavy, massive vessel that was capable of hovering high over the ground; it was one of the newly innovated vessels called "hydro-amphibian," that in the last ten years was developed in different places over the world.

The Parakees is capable of soaring like a hovercraft, sailing on water, hurtling on six monstrous wheels; it's a state-of-the-art warship that can function in any terrain: air, water, land. It's unstoppable, and now it's being manned to chase down and capture one man. They harnessed themselves to the seats. Kardo and Asan grabbed the steering wheels, Baltimore took on the computerized control system, Chickon manned the weapons system, Kardo gave the signal, and they were on their way.

Chapter Nineteen

In her dark, cold room, foggy with smoke and incense, old Irma was poring over the book lying open in front of her on a thick wooden table. With a laser-guided cruiser, she follows what the book told her—Grandma Trudy is here, inside the words, and when she stumbled on a certain combination of words, she managed to crack another code, a hologram of the ancient prophet glows up from the book and reveals a few more details of what is about to happen in this time.

Bartholomew has become the witch's co-worker. He serves her black, hot tea; he sets the cup down near her quietly, trying not to disturb her with her work. He believes in his dreams; he believes in what the witch is trying to prevent he doesn't want to die. He doesn't want his empire to collapse and crumble through this prophecy. He remembers from his talks with Irma that she told him that there is always a way to change the face of destiny. He roots for the regime of fear that took over humanity for the last thirty years. He has read books and watched old films from the former century—and he worshiped the Nazis, who in such a short time managed to take over half the globe. He pondered Hitler's mistakes in trying to do this on his own. He compared himself and the three other leaders to the structure of the Nazi rule from the last century, and he boasted that the way he and his friends seized rule was more subtle and practical, stealing the codes for the nuclear weapons of the world's powers and turning that against them as a clean cut blackmail. The existing government had to utterly surrender to the new evil rule, to hand over the keys of authority without resistance—and so it was.

He was very proud of his own actions and his friends in power; in the last thirty years, they forged the most powerful organization that ever existed on the planet's face. He received report, some time ago, of the dispatching of the Parakees, the famous "locating" unit that used to operate for the empire in the past. He remembered that gang of fifty-year-old men whom he did not particularly like, but he thought to himself that the main thing is that they'll get the job done and locate the mystery man.

Bartholomew decided to stop troubling himself over all these matters. It doesn't matter to him what happens with the man they catch. *What does matter*, thought Bartholomew to himself, *is to figure the truth behind the prophecy using Irma the witch and to neutralize the possibility of it ever coming true.* A chill ran down his entire body when he thought for a moment of what Drakkar would do to him if he knew of his deeds with Irma. He immediately changed his line of thought, sipped carefully from the hot tea, and sat down on the sofa by Irma. The old hag was engulfed in her work; she mumbled indistinct words to Bartholomew, and he dared to speak back. "Irma, is there any progress?"

Following Bartholomew's question, Irma turned a cold, dark stare toward the stout leader, who froze for a moment in his spot. "I'm still looking for the way to decipher the rest of her codes, so we can get more information from my late grandmother Trudy," said Irma in a hoarse voice.

Bartholomew sipped his tea and didn't say another word. His eyes swept over the walls of the witch's strange room, and lingered upon the collection of snakeheads concentrated on the black wall to the left. He wondered to himself, *Why does she keep the snakeheads?* He noticed the snakes were all of the same kinds, cobras and vipers.

Irma is still standing silently, facing the ancient book. In her mind, thoughts are racing, of how determined she was to unravel her grandmother's words; she imagined how the empire's leader will reward her for saving his dominion from collapsing. Irma sensed her body weakening from the effort of using up her magical powers on breaking the additional codes still needed to release Trudy's recordings. Bartholomew eased himself on to the couch, holding up the mug of black tea, when Irma suddenly uttered a deafening scream.

At that moment, Bartholomew's teacup slips from his fingers, the crystal chalice smashes to tiny bits on the floor of the room. His eyes watch with Irma's as the holographic rays burst out from the center of the book. Irma stepped back, nearly stumbling, Bartholomew immediately rose toward her, and despite his heavy weight and clumsy body, managed to grab hold of Irma just before she fell to the ground. The both stand a few feet away from the image glowing through the beams of light radiating from the book. Grandmother Trudy, in all her glory, was standing in front of them. Irma has managed to break the codes, and now Trudy will uncover for them the rest of the hidden secrets of the prophecy threatening to put an end to the dark dominion.

Chapter Twenty

Morning broke over the city that began once again with its bustle and commotion. Soldiers of the empire's platoons led large groups of people to another day of slavery, only in one small house on a street corner, far from the noisy streets. Joshua drew near the couch Adam was lying on and gently woke him. "It's time, my boy. We must get you to the train station. From there you will go on to the seaport, where more friends will be waiting for you, and they will help you to go on with your journey," said old Joshua in a whisper.

Adam rubbed his eyes and rose heavily off the sofa. "I'm ready, Joshua, I'm ready to move on," said Adam. Looking into the old man's eyes, he could feel the hope Joshua had for him; for a moment, he wanted to tell the old man not to expect too much, since no matter what his intentions were he doesn't know where he will end up, but he kept these things to himself. He joined the old man, who took him to another room in the house that was now empty of the people that filled it last night.

Heralda was waiting for the two men in the kitchen, a warm breakfast laid out on the table. Heralda looked at Adam and smiled. "Sit and eat. I made fresh rolls," she said warmly.

Joshua kissed the youngster's silky cheek. "Just from the incredible smell of the rolls, I am full," said the old man with a smile as he sat at the table to eat.

Adam stared at the feast in front of him. "Thank you, Heralda, the food looks tasty."

"Well, are you just going to watch it, or will you sit down and eat?" asked Heralda with a smile. The young man sat by the table and began eating quietly, wondering when again would he encounter such warmth and kindness in people, then he remembered the higher force, and said to himself in his heart, *Trust in the higher force, Adam, trust in the good creator.*

A few hours later a group of people left the small house, a group consisting of five people draped in cloaks. The sun was already in mid-sky. The group included Adam, Joshua, Heralda, and two more members of the New Dawn Hawks underground that escorted Adam to the railroad station. The group mingled with the great crowd filling the station, armed empire soldiers were walking around, inspecting person after person with their threatening gazes. The voice of metal chafing against metal drowned out the noise of the crowd, a long silver train stopped on the tracks and waited for the slaves heading to the work camps.

Joshua saw this was the proper opportunity; he turned to Adam and whispered in his ear. "As soon as the train doors open, jump in with the rest of the people."

Adam nodded in agreement; as he did that, the hood covering his head fell back a little, partially exposing his face. One of the empire's soldiers, standing far away from Joshua's group, noticed them, and his suspicion caused him to call out to them to stop. At once, the group paced faster toward the train standing on the track. The soldier pulled out a long metal whistle from his black uniform pocket, and blew a long whistle, instantly drawing the attention of the rest of the soldiers in the place. The soldier continued with the whistles, and a great panic swept over the crowd. People began running in all directions so not to get hurt; the silver train doors opened automatically and people poured in. The soldiers started running toward Adam and the band of underground members, but the frantic people running everywhere blocked them from reaching Adam and his friends.

"Quick, boy, you must be quick, step into the train," Joshua rushed Adam.

Heralda was looking at Adam, and he looked back at her. Through the noise and havoc around them, Adam managed to speak, "I will never forget all of you. I'll keep on this path no matter what." He gently drew near Heralda, his lips brushing against her cheek and kissed her softly. He could notice that her eyes were brimmed with tears, but he said nothing. The empire soldiers began shooting toward the escaping group, who clung to the silver train; despite his old age, Joshua swiftly pushed Adam into the train, calling out fervently, "We will meet again, Adam!" The soldiers aimed their rifles and glowing laser bands were shot from their barrels, but for nothing. The train had automatically shut its doors and moved with a jet-like speed toward the horizon. The frustrated soldiers tried to find Joshua, Heralda, and the rest of the suspects, but they failed, luckily for the group the tumult of the crowd around covered their escape. They blended into the masses; the soldiers had no choice but to report the events to their commanders. It didn't occur to them for a moment that they actually missed the man who slighted the empire that the man wanted by the reign of terror had just managed to escape on the silver train making it's way quickly to several work camps. There was no driver on these trains, everything was automated.

Adam began to breathe easy. He watched the people around him that were still alarmed from the commotion that occurred on the stop before. In a few minutes, they would stop in another station, and in will come the people who were once free to work against their will in work camps controlled by the empire. As the train hurtles ahead on the tracks at tremendous speed, Adam thinks of his friends that were left behind, of old Joshua and the beautiful Heralda, and he asks God to help him not disappoint them.

Chapter Twenty-One

Kardo sat quietly in the Parakees, watching his computer monitor, his eyes following the last report received from Argma. The report related the latest incident that occurred on a train platform. His hand rubbed the stubble on his chin. After a few seconds, he instructed Chickon to steer the Parakees toward a coordinate showing on the computer screen.

"Listen to me, people, in this spot, we meet with empire spies. They have photos taken on the train platform. Apparently, the suspects that escaped may very well be the underground members affiliated with the mystery man that hit the empire hovercraft. By these pictures, we can identify and locate that son of a devil and bring his body to the empire's leader. Then we can celebrate like in the old days, on booze and females." The entire group of men burst into a thundering laughter. The Parakees started her engines and departed toward the meeting point.

After an hour of traveling, the Parakees stopped heavily in front of a road tavern in some removed area. The four men entered the nearly empty tavern, who most of its occupants were thoroughly drunk, some of them slumped over square wooden tables. The tavern owner approached them carefully. "Hello, gentlemen, welcome to the Ivory Tower Tavern, what can I get you?"

Asan opened his mouth and roared, "Bring us ale, and a lot of it!"

Kardo looked at Asan and anger showed on his face. "We didn't come to drink, Asan, we're here on business, we'll drink when we're done," said Kardo.

Asan didn't reply. He walked in and sat near one of the tables, over which a drunken man was bent. He shoved the man to floor with a merciless kick. The tavern owner was startled; he understood these were dangerous people. He moved away and stepped into the kitchen, a terrified look on his face; he smiled at them, but he smiled out of fear.

A few seconds after the four Parakees men sat by their table, two thin and tall people in black uniforms covered by black long coats approached near them. "Are you the Parakees people?" asked one of them, who was wearing rounded, purple tinted glasses.

Baltimore stared at the two. "And who's asking?" asked Baltimore with a mocking jeer. The skinny man with the purple glasses sat down and right after that so did his colleague. Their faces were pale and harsh.

"We are secret agents for his highness, the leader of the empire," said the man with purple glasses.

Asan sneered. "Wow, what an honor," and Kardo intervened, "Well, gentlemen, I understand you have important information for us, certain pictures, ain't it so?"

"Indeed," replied the man with glasses, and he drew a few sheets from the pocket of his long, black coat. Kardo took the pictures in his hands, and after a few seconds, he said, "I can hardly see anything in these pictures, whoever took them was blind." The empire agent cleared his throat and answered with a certain awkwardness. "You must understand that taking specific pictures of the suspect wasn't planned. The photos come from an automatic camera, such as exists in every train station controlled by the empire."

Kardo rose from his chair, standing with legs slightly astride, he rearranged his belt and fleetingly stroked his gun. "Well, gentleman, you did your part. Could you at least point us in the way the suspect escaped?"

The emaciated man sitting by the owner of the purple glasses took out a map from the inner pocket in his coat and said, "This is where the train is heading." He traced a dotted line with his finger, leading to a seaport. The man continued, "We know the train has a three-hour track, and the last stop is the harbor. We estimate the suspect is trying to get on a ship."

"Oh really…? You think? Well, thank you so much for that information. You're dismissed, as far as I'm concerned, leave," said Kardo disdainfully.

The two men in uniform were filled with rage at Kardo's degrading behavior to them. Kardo noticed that. "So? You want to do something about it?" he said with a smile, grasping the shoulder of the man with the purple glasses with one hand, and in the other lightly holding the gun barrel.

The two men in uniform kept their silence. They looked at each other and signaled they should leave. At their retreat, the four men began laughing mockingly. As they approached the door, the owner of the purple glasses whispered to his colleague, "Barbarians, animals. I really hope they get killed on the way." Asan looked at Kardo with an anxious smile.

"Well? Now, can we drink?" Kardo looked at his friend with amusement and called loudly for the barkeeper to load the table with ale. The barkeeper did as the guests commanded, and the four men commenced in drinking until night came.

Chapter Twenty-Two

The screech of the train wheels woke Adam from his daze. It's been a few hours since he parted with Joshua, Heralda, and the rest of the New Dawn Hawks. A strong light flared through the windows of the silver train. Again, the doors split open automatically, and an amazing view of green-blue water was revealed to Adam. He inhaled the ocean air and was filled with joy. Only a few people, dock workers, remained on the train. A few empire soldiers mulled around, smoking cigarettes and talking.

As Adam made his way out of the train car, the wind touched his face with a loving caress, the scent of the ocean mingled with the brackish smell of fish being sold on moist wooden counters. The sky was almost free of clouds and the sun was celebrating in the blue. Adam blessed the wonderful sight revealed to him. He looked around and a few empire soldiers were making their way toward him; in an instant, his heart was beating fast and a dread filled him. He hurriedly covered his face with the hood, the soldiers where only a few feet away when suddenly a long arm grabbed Adam and pulled him toward a fish stand stacked with large, silvery fish. "Sir, fresh and savory fish, heaved from the sea today, for you—in an incredible price!" a young man called out at toward the baffled Adam.

At that same moment, the soldiers passed right by him, engulfed in their own conversation. "Relax, they're gone. It's okay," said the young man to Adam and immediately added, "Pretend you are interested in buying fish." The young man continued to occupy himself in wrapping the wet fish with old newspapers, while sending brief smiles in all directions, all this time talking to Adam, who still didn't know what was happening but felt a relief at the soldiers' departure.

When they left, he dared ask, "Who are you, please?"

The youngster stopped his work and drew closer to Adam; he answered him with a low voice that swallowed in the shouts of the other fish hawkers. "I'm not exactly a fish vendor, I'm Jeremiah, and you must be Adam Swandon, right?"

Adam replied with a smile when he understood the man must be one of Joshua's friends that has come to his aid. "Yes, I'm Adam Swandon, and you…"

Jeremiah continued, "I'm a friend of old Joshua. Let me introduce you to my captain." The two made their way to a small wooden cabin standing on the pier, removed from the fish stands. It was decades old, the wooden plaques were breaking off, one could see the erosion of the structure. Jeremiah opened the cabin door, checked behind him to see no empire soldier has trailed them, then entered, and Adam came after him. The sight in front of him seemed like an ancient oil painting; the cabin was actually a single large room, a stove was on in the corner, and in front of the stove, on the floor, lay a rather large wolf.

The wolf raised his head toward the two men entering the room. Adam was surprised to see a patch on one of the wolf's eyes. The large animal noticed Adam's curious stare and gave out a slightly irritated growl, followed by one powerful bark, when suddenly a thunderous voice echoed through the large room. "Quiet, Arak! He is a friend of Joshua's, so behave respectfully." Adam turned his gaze to the man who spoke to the large wolf. He was sitting by a thick wooden table, smoking a pipe. Ribbons of smoke curled out from it and decorated the room, until they faded into air. The man was wearing an old navy captain uniform, reminding Adam of pictures he saw when he was child; it was a Second World War uniform. Jeremiah nudged Adam closer to the man, whose face was adorned with a short, white beard.

"Adam, Meet Captain Damtry Nelson, chief of the great sailboat, the *Oracle*." Adam could sense the bearded man's strong presence. He reached out his hand; the captain of the *Oracle* reached out in return, and they shook hands.

"Nice to meet you, sir, I'm Adam Swandon," said Adam.

"Sit down, lad, and please, call me Nelson," replied the man wearing a captain's cap from the last century. "You must be hungry, no?" he continued.

The men took a seat around the table, and Jeremiah served Adam bread, cheese and a little fish from an earthen plate. Adam looked at his plate longingly and turned to Nelson who kept on smoking unhurriedly: "Sir… I mean Nelson, I would like to thank you for helping me, and…"

The captain silenced Adam and answered in a soft voice, "Don't worry, lad, everything in its own good time. Right now, you eat, drink, relax. Later we will talk some more."

Adam replied with a smile, feeling the captain knew just how hungry he was. Arak the one-eyed wolf drew near and sat down by Adam's feet as he began eating, to Adam's surprise.

"It's a rare thing that Arak comes near someone new. He trusts you, you must be made from good stuff," the captain concluded his words with a quiet laughter. Adam, his mouth full of food, looked cautiously at the wolf sitting near him and smiled a careful smile, and the wolf answered him with a mirthful bark. Adam felt like he is safe among friends again.

The roar of the Parakees's motors scared off the seagulls that crowded the harbor, and they took to the air. The heavy vehicle plunged ahead with little regard for people passing by. The empire soldiers recognized the Parakees and let her through with no interruption; the merchants in the fish stands quickly moved aside, expressing their anger as the Parakees passed.

It was late afternoon; a few stands were toppled over by the rowdy gang's inconsiderate driving. Inside the armored vehicle, the four were laughing incessantly at the way the poor people scurried away; they were still a little intoxicated from their night of drinking. They were all complaining of their headaches and how they wanted to go on sleeping, but they had a mission to fulfill. They had to trap or kill the mystery man who slighted the empire. The cries of people escaping the place reached the sensitive ears of Arak the one-eyed wolf, and he began barking ceaselessly, announcing that something isn't right.

The captain rose from his seat, looked out the window, and spit out a curse, "Damn them to the devil!" Jeremiah and Adam jumped up and came to the window. Arak continued barking, and before the two asked their question, the captain told them, "No choice, friends, we have to move to the ship, right now."

Jeremiah cracked the door open and Arak squirmed out, seemingly checking that passage is safe. The cabin was fairly removed from fish stands and from the Parakees, which was parked on the other side of the harbor. Nelson spoke to the two men and the wolf, "Luckily we're pretty far from the crowded pier, but the ship is halfway there, so we must move fast and draw no attention, is that clear?" Adam and Jeremiah nodded in agreement. The captain drew a two-way radio from the inner pocket in his coat and called, "Be ready, we're coming."

From the other side of the connection came a voice: "We are ready for boarding, the team is ready to cover you if needed."

"Very well, guys, and may God be with us." The three men advanced slowly on the wooden pier toward a large sailboat with blue sails, which was waiting two hundred feet from the old wooden cabin. They moved leisurely, following Arak, who took the lead with quiet movements. On the other side of the pier, the empire soldiers were scolding the fish stand owners, who were complaining of the disruption of their work by the presence of the Parakees. In the meantime, the Parakees crew climbed out one by one from the armored vehicle to the pier's plaza, scanning the terrain. In the dock were a few military ships of the empire and a few trading ships under the empire's protection. "Keep your eyes open, fellows. By what the spies told us, the guy should be around here."

Just as he was finishing his sentence, a cry came from one of the soldiers. "Underground men! Underground men!" the soldier cried incessantly. Immediately the Parakees crew turned to Adam and his new friends, laser guns drawn in their hands.

"Damn it, they're on to us!" cried Nelson and began running toward the ship. On his way, he shouted to Adam and Jeremiah, "Run, guys, run!" Arak darted into the ship, and from the *Oracle*'s ramparts appeared the rest of crew, guns in their hands, and to Nelson's instructions, they opened fire, covering the three fugitives.

The Parakees squad began shooting at the three, but their shots were lousy, the group was still intoxicated, the alcohol still running through their veins ruined their aim. The empire soldiers also opened fire, but it was useless; the *Oracle*'s crew was shooting relentlessly, and it managed to cover Nelson, Jeremiah, and Adam as with the help of a few sailors they quickly boarded the ship unharmed. That made the Parakees team livid with anger. Kardo was furious with himself and the rest of his crew for drinking too much last night. He called his friends to arm the Parakees and bomb the *Oracle*.

Captain Nelson took command over his ship and ordered the ship navigator to proceed quickly into the open sea, but as the navigator was doing his bid, Jeremiah called, startled, "Look! That huge vehicle is aiming missiles at us!" Nelson didn't flinch for a moment, but ordered one of his seamen to engage the *Oracle* special combat system.

Within seconds, Adam was amazed by an astounding sight; the ancient sailboat extended two huge doors, opening from both sides of the ship and halting in a position of forty-five degrees; on the inner side of the doors was revealed a system. Of laser canons, which began immediately shooting colorful laser blasts toward the surprised Parakees. The joy of the *Oracle* crew was halted, however, when three black empire hovercrafts blocked out the sky. The hovercrafts aimed their weapons at the *Oracle*; the captain understood it's too much, and he must do something before the *Oracle* takes a hit from one of the hovercrafts. Adam saw the concern on the captain's face. He felt a deep appreciation for the immense efforts of the *Oracle* crewmen to protect him, even though they didn't even know whom he was. All these things summed up to a single conclusion in his mind; he must do something. He approached Jeremiah quickly, an idea coming to his head: "Jeremiah, my friend, do you have little lifeboats on board?" asked Adam excitedly.

"Of course, they're called jetties, and they are really fast, but why do you ask?" replied Jeremiah quickly.

Adam laid a hand on Jeremiah's shoulder and smiled. "Come with me, I've got an idea," said Adam, and the two got into on of the little jetties on the ship, some of the crewmen were shooting at the hovercrafts, which maneuvered in between their shots, and some were shooting at the Parakees, which was trying to hit the *Oracle*. The captain noticed Adam and Jeremiah and cried to them, "What are you doing?!"

Adam replied, "Don't worry, Captain, I can't sit here aimlessly while good people are doing all they can to protect me. I've got to do something." He urged Jeremiah to go down to the water with the jetty, and within seconds, the jetty touched the blue seawater.

"What can we do with this little jetty, Adam?" asked Jeremiah curiously.

Adam replied heatedly, "I can't drive a jetty, but I'll be with you because I know you can. Maneuver between the shots, and at the same time, we'll fire at the hovercrafts, drawing their attention."

Jeremiah's face lit up. "Got it, Adam," he said with a smile. He immediately mobilized the jetty, and at the same time shot short laser bursts toward one of the hovercrafts, which instantly turned its weapons to the small, agile jet boat. The hovercraft pilots were thrown off balance when confronted with another factor: the two hovercrafts decided to open chase after the tiny jetty, which annoyed them as a fly might bother a large rhinoceros. The two hovercrafts began accelerating their pursuit after the jetty. Jeremiah was stressed by the situation but Adam continued reinforcing him, telling him he is doing a great job.

Adam's own heart was pounding fiercely, but he decided to continue. The two Hovercrafts sped up and began shooting heavy blasts that came extremely close to the body of the fast little ship. Jeremiah looked at Adam as if wishing to retreat, but Adam insisted, "Go on, Jeremiah, don't be afraid, just go on toward the third hovercraft shooting at the *Oracle*." Thinking for a minute that Adam must have lost his mind, Jeremiah kept on driving fast toward the third hovercraft that had its back to the jetty and behind them, coming up fast, the two hovercrafts continually shooting. From afar, Nelson, commander of the *Oracle*, noticed the two black hovercrafts approaching him rapidly and also managed to see the small jetty leading them swiftly toward the *Oracle*.

"What in hell are they doing?" he asked himself. Then he sees, right in front of his eyes, how the little jetty, with Adam and Jeremiah in it, is about to crash into the back of the empire hovercraft. At that moment, Adam suddenly shouts to Jeremiah loudly, "Now, Jeremiah, Now! Turn left, left!" Jeremiah instantly carries out Adam's order, and just as the jetty breaks left the hovercraft crewmen notice their rapid advance toward the third hovercraft, but it's too late; the three 'hovercrafts smashed together in an unavoidable collision, creating a violent explosion in the sky overhanging the sea. All the faces watching froze in utter astonishment.

"You did it, Adam," cheered Jeremiah.

"No, Jeremiah, we did it," replied Adam. The flaming remains of the hovercrafts came falling down from the sky and were swallowed in the blue water. All the soldiers on the pier fell silent for a moment; even the Parakees crew couldn't believe that such a thing could happen. In one second, three of the empire's great hovercrafts were pulverized, and all because of one little jetty and the two people on it. The captain smiled to himself and thought, "Joshua apparently knows what he's talking about." The *Oracle* retrieved the huge folding doors and the weapon systems were tucked in, hidden from human eyes. The little jetty was hauled on board and the crewmen ran toward the two brave lads, cheering them, but Captain Nelson called, "The party's not over, look over there!"

Everyone watched the Parakees eased itself into the water and moved toward the *Oracle* as it aimed its missiles at it. Adam looked apprehensively at his new friends and his gaze stopped on the captain, who was looking back at him. Instead of expressing anxiety, the practiced captain was smiling. Suddenly he called, "Engage turbo engines!" A few moments later, at the bottom of the ship from behind, appeared two elongated, silvery engines. Nelson came close to Adam. "Don't worry, my friend, the turbo engines are only operative for a very short time, but they haven't let us down yet. Look!" as Nelson gave the order, one of the sailors pressed a button, and trails of fire erupted powerfully from the long, silvery, metal cylinders. The *Oracle* moved with jet-speed, disappearing in a blink into the horizon, to the amazement of the Parakees and the empire soldiers, who were left gaping on the pier.

Chapter Twenty-Three

In the little house at the end of the street, the place where the underground of the New Dawn Hawk's gathered, a meeting was adjourned. Old Joshua was running the meeting, and all the youngsters were sitting around him, listening to him. He complemented the work of the men, and unfolded the plan for them. He told them of the officers' ball for the empire's top brass, about to happen in one day. He said they must go on a mission, disrupting the ball, showing the empire's heads that the underground is still alive and kicking, and they will not surrender to the enslaving rule of the empire. He called in front of all present that humans are born to freedom, and they all have a right to exist with honor. Everyone agreed with his words; only Heralda was thinking of Adam, and where he is, and if he's okay.

Joshua noticed her distant gaze and came to her, "Don't worry, dear, I believe our friend Captain Nelson and the rest of the *Oracle*'s crew will help him get safely to where he needs to go. But we must do our part. We must do our best to bring people their freedom. Ours is not a small responsibility. We must be focused on our mission," said Joshua.

The young woman looked at him like a student, intent on her teacher's words. She stood up. "You are right. We must do our best," she replied.

Joshua assembled a task force for the officers' ball, where they would try to hit the top-rank empire officers. The old man conveyed the mission details to his people; the task force would include him,

Heralda, and three more young guys, doing their best for humanity. After they all went over the mission details, the old man summed, "Friends, we leave for the operation tonight at sunset."

Chapter Twenty-Four

The *Oracle*'s blue sails cooperated with the good wind, who was lovingly pressing the great ship on, away from the hostile port, that threatened not long ago to demolish the *Oracle* and its crew. The loyal sailors were busy with the upkeep of the ship; they were all good, decent people, deeply respective of their noble captain, and Nelson himself was grateful to his loyal and dedicated crew. They were far from trouble, for now.

The captain wandered the ship's deck with the wolf, looking for Adam. He found him leaning over the rail, staring far toward the place where the blue water merged with the endless horizon. The captain drew near the man and opened a conversation. "What's with you, lad? Why does your face look so worried?"

Adam began to tell Captain Nelson all that befell him since that day he watched the terrible massacre in Battery-Nile from the cliff's face. The captain listened to every word, deeply impressed by the incident on the mountain cliff, and by Adam's fierce desire to bring an end to humanity's suffering. He remembered that when he spoke to Joshua earlier, the old man told him of Adam's brave acts in saving the orphans from the burning building. Nelson sensed immediately that there was something special about this man standing in front of him.

"What you did there amazed my entire crew. You've got a lot of guts, Adam," said Captain Nelson. Adam turned his gaze back to the endless ocean. "Captain Nelson, I did nothing. It's Jeremiah who drove the Jetty, Jeremiah shooting and maneuvering, he's the one who made the hovercrafts collide."

Adam stopped talking, he noticed the captain wanted to say something, and indeed the captain began to speak, "Well... listen to me, dear Adam, I'll tell you a little tale I heard many years ago, and this is story for life, so listen closely." The veteran captain inhaled deeply; the wind blew lightly, accompanying Nelson words, lifting them one by one to Adam's ears.

"The tale is about the biggest, strongest ship in the world. This ship had the best crew. A fortune in equipment and weapons, the queen gave her blessing to its departure. This ship was awarded the best captain in the royal navy and huge, majestic sails. The time came when the ship was supposed to finally leave on its famous cruise. The ropes were severed from the dock. A crew of strong, muscular sailors toiled and worked to launch the ship to sea, but with all that, the ship did not budge. The crew waited for hours, and finally, they selected one sailor to represent them in front of the captain who was standing alone at the nose of the ship, watching the horizon. The sailor came near his captain respectfully, and asked, 'Sir, the entire crew wishes to know: why aren't we moving?'

"The captain didn't reply and didn't even look at the sailor, and the sailor carried on, 'Sir, how is it we are standing on the grandest ship in the world, with the best sailors on it, and you are the best captain in the world, and we have the best weapons and terrific equipment, and yet we aren't moving, why?' The smart captain turned his eyes to the questioning sailor, then turned his gaze to the ship's large sails, and pointing at the sails, he answered, 'We're not moving because there is no wind.'"

The captain concluded his story and noticed the questioning expression on Adam's face. "Well, Adam, you say that Jeremiah is the one who acted perfectly and managed to neutralize the hovercraft's dangerous attack. But who urged Jeremiah and encouraged him to bravely continue? Who was the strong wind at Jeremiah's back? You, Adam, you, understand, it was you that guided our Jeremiah to act like that. It's your spirit of leadership that did it, and the creator was with you the entire time, it was his will."

Adam was greatly surprised by the captain's words. He didn't picture the events like Nelson defined them. The captain laid a muscular arm on Adam's shoulder and said, "Remember, Adam, you have the potential. The doubts will always try to suffocate you, but you must understand that only you, in your determination to fulfill your will, can banish the doubts and win. Believe, Adam, believe."

The captain turned on his heels, whistled to Arak, and the two left Adam, to digest the words just said. Adam remained alone by the railing. The ship chopped the waves vigorously. He felt the stares of the curious crewmen on him; they still didn't recuperate from the sights of the recent events, but they obeyed Captain Nelson's instructions to leave Adam alone for now and let him slowly get used to the crew. The captain told them briefly that they are assisting this man because he helped the underground greatly, and Joshua thinks he is crucial in the struggle against the empire's reign of terror.

Chapter Twenty-Five

Trumpets rang out as the top officers of the empire made their way down a blood-red carpet, which led into the great banquet hall of Argma, the empire's palace, belonging to the empire's leaders. Hundreds of soldiers stood to attention and saluted the procession of superior officers. The four empire leaders were the guests of honor, they were preparing to enter the hall, but suddenly one soldier ran to the empire's leader and put a small, transparent plaque in his hands; it was an urgent call related to the ball's security. Drakkar left the procession of leaders that continued marching into the hall that was filled with the noise of music and conversation. The leader was told the message is from the witch, Irma, sitting in her dark room at the bottom of the palace. Drakkar asked himself what she might want, the old hag, and promised himself that if she again mentions the nonsense about the prophecy of this book in her hands; he will get very, very mad. He entered a small, dark room, and through a monitor, Irma's image appeared.

"Oh, my great leader, listen to me please, I sense with my magic powers that foreign forces infiltrated the palace."

The leader sat on a black couch that was in the little room and began speaking in an irritated tone, "Irma, I warn you, if this has anything to do with the book of prophecies—"

The leader didn't finish his sentence as Irma interrupted him. "Listen to me, please, I sense the powers of light, they are here!" She turned to her crystal ball and asked the leader to pay attention to the special sights unraveling in its depth.

Drakkar focused his eyes on the ball, which now filled the entire screen, and really, he could now discern the characters moving in a single file, their guns in their hands. Those were old Joshua, Heralda, and the rest of the New Dawn Hawks members. The leader's expression gradually hardened, and his hand curled in a tight fist. "It must be the underground people… How did they penetrate the palace area? I will hang the soldiers responsible for guarding that section," said Drakkar furiously.

The large screen went back to the image of Irma. "You see? I'm not wrong, my powers warned me of this. They want to harm the officer's event, you must stop them!"

Drakkar rose from the couch and called toward the witch, "Irma, you did a good job, I'll command my soldiers to get the infiltrators this instant. Continue following them with your powers, which serve the empire loyally."

Irma could sense the effort in his voice as Drakkar complemented her services; she knew he doesn't mean his tributes seriously, but she said nothing, just smiled at him a smile that accentuated every wrinkle engraved in her scrawny face, took a little bow, and her image disappeared off the screen.

The leader called one of the soldiers standing in the hallway and ordered him to arrange a force that would detain the palace infiltrators. Heralda paced slowly behind old Joshua. She was feeling a kind of nervousness in the pit of her stomach that caused her discomfort; she understood her intuition was warning her that something is wrong. She couldn't hold it in any longer; she wanted to tell Joshua about it. The underground unit was preparing to make a showy explosion that would show the empire that hope still exists, and the underground will not confirm to the empire's reign of terror over humanity. Heralda laid her hand on old Joshua's shoulder, and just when she was about to speak her mind a blast of fire tore through her thoughts. Heralda and Joshua fell instantly to the floor for cover; the three men tried to counter fire, but too late, the shots discharged from the soldiers guns overtook hit them. They collapsed to the floor, lifeless. As one of the soldiers was about to shoot Heralda and Joshua, who were laying on the floor that began to take the color of the underground's members blood, a shrill voice came from one of the two-way radios that were on the soldiers. "Don't kill them, bring them to me!" the soldiers stopped their activity, grabbed the two captives violently, and dragged them to the dungeons.

Joshua and Heralda looked at each other helplessly, hurting together for the loss of their friends, their partners in the struggle for freedom. The leader returned to his diabolical friends, who were holding two women each. The women weren't smiling. When Bammark asked Drakkar what was so important that he left them in the entrance to the hall, Drakkar smiled cruelly. "Nothing very important, just a small, miserable assembly of underground people, that our men wiped out before they could do anything. They just don't understand that no one can take on our empire," said Drakkar, and the smile on his lips turned into a strangled laughter, full of malice, that spread to the rest of his friends, except Bartholomew, who was thinking in his heart of the prophecy about the coming of the son of light, he felt the danger of the prophesy coming true in the fact that the underground even dared try entering the empire palace to carry out their plans. Something is going on. He thought, *Where do the undergrounds draw such courage to go on a mission like this?* He thought that Drakkar must be hiding many things from the rest of them, but fearing the reaction of the cruel leader, he chose to remain quiet.

The officer's banquet ended with a speech of the empire's superior leader, telling with pride and arrogance that the empire's arms have a firm, hard grip over humanity, and the slaves are toiling well.

He commended his officers and gave them a free hand to treat the opposition to their rule as cruelly as they like. Thousands of officers applauded the dark leader and his friends, the rulers of Earth. After a while, the banquet was over and everybody turned to their business, Drakkar went back to his quarters, seeking to communicate with the old witch; he wanted to know what became the fate of the old man and girl that were captured earlier. Irma asked him to interrogate them in her own way, so she may draw from them any important information they had about the empire's homeland security. The leader agreed, saying he himself won't bother which such trifles; he left the matters of interrogating captives to the old witch, and she was very happy with that: she wanted to know if they where related to the mystery man who slighted the empire, the same man wanted now dead. She wanted to see if there is truth in the prophecy, and if the underground members know anything of it.

Drakkar's peace of mind was disturbed by the annoying reports of another escape of the mystery man from the empire forces, and the failure of the Parakees crew to wipe him out. The reports that reached told of the man being smuggled on a special sailboat, which brought destruction on three hovercrafts of the mighty empire's army. A rage burned in the dark ruler over the rumors that the Parakees crew were drunk at the time of battle. He decided to take this matter much more seriously; he asked to call the other three leaders for a special gathering, and in addition, he also summoned the top officers of all the empire's fleets. He received confirmation from them all. For a moment, the thought crossed his mind of Irma's ambiguous words of the prophecy, but he put the thought aside and focused on the special gathering he was orchestrating.

In a short while, the leader's quarters filled up with high commanders of the empire's army; all the chairs were taken, but everyone rose to their feet when the four leaders entered the room. Everyone bowed respectfully to the four. A few female soldiers, in tight black leather uniforms on their shapely bodies, served drinks in long purple crystal goblets. Everyone returned to their seat, on edge to know why did Drakkar summon them all only one day after the great banquette; what was so urgent?

Drakkar looked at all his peers then stood up in front of his men, passed a hand over his coiled black beard, and began speaking, "Gentlemen, I gathered you here today because apparently we have a small problem that needs solving. And I see fit to ask for your strategies in this matter." The leader related the latest events to all present, and after they heard, they all agreed this man who insulted the empire's rule must be killed, him and the people that helped him escape. The large doors of the room swung open. And the four Parakees men marched in. they felt the furious gazes of the army's top ranked resting on them, and the piercing stares of the four leaders burrowing into their eyes. They felt a certain awkwardness, yet they quickly regained their balance and their confidence when they were offered to stand in the head of any scenario of the operation that may be, and they convinced the people around them that this time they will follow the job through, this time they will bring the top ranks the head of the bastard that slighted the honor of the realm. Kraus, top commander of the hovercraft fleet, suggested a large-scale attack of commando hovercrafts that would blow the ship out of the water. Another commander objected, saying that idea was already tried, and it failed miserably. Vaskov surprised all of them by suddenly taking the stand. "This time, the attack is in open sea, so I suggest we use one of our deadly submarines for the demolition operation of this bloody ship." A silence settled over the great room, and then Drakkar said, "That's it, that's what we'll do, I don't want us wasting any more time on this stupid business, I want one of our submarines to leave now to destroy this insolent man in his puny ship."

The dark leader tapped Vaskov on his shoulder, who was smiling proudly for offering an idea Drakkar accepted so swiftly. Drakkar was impatient with the entire thing; he wanted to finish as soon as possible with the matter of this man and his ship. He wanted to turn his full attention to more important things. He couldn't believe this little issue turned into something he had to summon all the top ranks for. He approved for the commander of the submarine fleet to immediately launch the huge, lethal submarine called the *Black Octopus* on the *Oracle*'s demolition mission.

All the remaining officers drifted away, each one to his own activities. The four leaders parted. Drakkar asked the submarine fleet commander to keep him updated on the progress of the attack and its results, and Bartholomew turned to the cellars of Argma. He goes to her, to Irma; he must know more about the book of prophesies in her hands. The further he came to her room, deep down in the bowels of the palace, the more cold he felt all over his body, as if he is standing in a graveyard on a winter day. The darkness around makes him feel gloomy. When he reached the wired witch's abode, the doors opened by themselves, as if they were waiting for him to enter. The stout leader noticed the witch was moving restlessly from one section of the house to another, entirely disregarding Bartholomew's presence.

The man couldn't hold back, and he began speaking to her, "Irma, I wanted to ask you a few things."

Irma sensed the fear in the stout leader's voice, but she didn't answer him. She carried on moving as if she was looking for something she lost. Bartholomew tried again to make her speak. "Irma dear, witch with the cosmic powers, did you find anything new and interesting in your book of prophesies?" said Bartholomew in a flattering tone.

As the man mentioned the book, Irma stopped her fussing and turned to him. "Why do you ask that, Bartholomew?"

The chubby leader recoiled, fearing the old woman with her magic powers. She repeated her question. "Why do you want to know if I discovered more things in the book of prophecies, your great leader has tossed the mere idea of a prophecy aside, he mocks it, he mocks me for trying to do my duty and maintain the rule of darkness and fear over the human race forever." The chubby leader took a seat on the couch and crossed his hands over his round belly. "You have nothing more to worry about the prophecy, dear Irma, or more correctly, that this man harming the empire hovercrafts has something to do with the prophecy, since our empire is heading out to destroy him as we speak," said the man, smiling contently, but Irma demanded more information.

"You mean the empire is out to demolish the mystery man?" asked Irma excitedly.

Bartholomew leaned to her and said, "I mean that probably, in the bottom of his heart, Drakkar did hear your words, even though he doesn't want to admit that. Just by the fact that he summoned all the top commanders of the empire army, that he is doing something about this threat. Today he approved the launching of the *Black Octopus* submarine to sink the ship the mystery man is boarding."

Irma kept silent for a moment then said, "Well, I see our glorified, cruel leader does have a little sense." She smiled a tiny diabolical smile and looked pleased at the news, but the smile faded as fast as it appeared. "I hope Drakkar doesn't belittle this subject, because sometimes, when you trivialize one little mouse running through the house, you discover later that the entire kitchen has been destroyed," said the witch.

In a dark prison cell, its walls dank and cold, darkness enveloped the room; only a delicate ray of light penetrated through the small porthole in the heavy iron door separating between Joshua and Heralda and the liberty and sunlight outside. The two are imprisoned deep in the dungeons of the empire's palace. Even in this dreadful situation, the spirit of the old man didn't break. He encouraged the beautiful girl, keeping her from despair: "Remember, Heralda dear, just a tiny bit of light drives out a lot of the darkness."

The youngster found some comfort in the old man's words, but she feared their fate. She wasn't afraid of getting hurt or dying on the battlefield, but to be a prisoner of humanity's enemies is something she never imagined she could face. The elderly man held her hands and rubbed her arms vigorously to keep the chill away from her, so she won't get a cold. She clung to him and he embraced her, like a grandfather holding his granddaughter. The two were silent for a while, until the quiet was broken by the sound of footsteps slowly approaching. The steps came near the cell of the two; Joshua could sense the presence of a concentrated evil force. He felt how the presence of this evil makes his throat tighten, and Joshua began suffocating.

Heralda noticed this and called in fright, "Joshua, what's going on?!"

The old man couldn't speak; he was struggling to breathe properly. The footsteps halted, the pacing figure stopped in front of the iron door, silent as the heavy iron door slowly opened. Joshua began breathing normally, to Heralda's relief. Their eyes, accustomed to the gloom of the cell, could not discern the figure standing in the open portal, the lights from the hall glowing behind it.

"Is the room we accommodated you in comfortable?" asked the figure mockingly as it entered the space of the room. "We prepared the best lodgings for you," continued the approaching figure."

Joshua shielded Heralda, who was actually trying to protect the old man. "Who are you?" asked the old man in an aggressive tone. The figure raised one arm toward the entrance and the iron door slammed loudly with the thud of metal hitting metal. The meek ray of light dimly revealed the face of an old woman, with narrow, wicked eyes.

"I am Irma the witch, a third generation servant to the forces of darkness that govern the puny humans. I am here because I want some answers from you," said Irma in a threatening tone. Heralda advanced a few steps toward the figure and called out bravely, "We will tell you nothing, old witch, leave us in peace," the old woman said nothing. She began walking slowly in small, shuffling steps toward Joshua, passing Heralda and smiling at her. She stopped less than a foot away from the old man. Joshua understood the woman was here to interrogate them and draw information about the underground's activities, then suddenly, with no warning, Joshua was flung in the air by Irma's powers, she pinned the old man to the wall. Seeing this, Heralda leapt at the witch with a war cry, but with a wave of her hand, the witch blocked the youngster, who fell frozen to the floor, unable to move.

The wicked old woman drew very near to Joshua, who was pinned to the wall; he could feel her powers reaching into his mind, trying to rummage through his thoughts. Irma was astonished to find that the elderly man knew how to block her. She put more effort in the attempt to brutally penetrate Joshua's thoughts, but the man knew the telepathic techniques and he managed with a tremendous mental effort to block her every attempt. The more she tried to telepathically ransack his mind, the more she encountered the man's mental force, blocking her from the possibility to draw information from his mind. The exertion caused the old man a stabbing headache; he began crying out and squirming in pain. The old woman also felt her power dwindling; she didn't imagine the man had knowledge and powers of his own. The struggle between the two continued for a few long seconds more, Joshua struggling with an immense effort to block the witch's negative powers from breaking into his mind and discovering information about the resistance, and about Adam and his goal, and the witch, simultaneously with her telepathic efforts, interrogated the old man with questions.

"I want to know, is this mystery man related to the ancient prophecy?"

Besides his muffled cries of pain, Joshua gave no answer to Irma, who didn't cease from her effort to break into his mind and pressed on with more questions. "Is he going to lead a struggle against the empire rule?" A rage rose in the old witch, and she yelled, "Answer me, you stupid old man, answer my questions now!"

The old man's eyes grew wide as they gazed penetratingly into the hag's evil eyes, and a bitter cry broke from his lips, "Nooooooo!"

Irma felt her powers diminish, and in one moment, she uttered a terrible screech and tossed her hands up in the air. She stepped back from Joshua who immediately fell to the ground and released her grasp of the old man slumped against the wall, holding his hurting head. The hag was breathing heavily; the effort has drained her powers. She was frustrated she couldn't penetrate the old man's mind to discover what she wanted to know. Heralda was also released from the witch's magic grasp, and without delay, she turned to Joshua to check on him. "Oh, Joshua, are you okay?"

The witch backed away from them toward the iron door and said, "Well, you know how to block my powers. I don't know where you learned to do that, but don't worry. The mystery man you helped escape is as good as dead." The old hag smiled wickedly. Heralda rose from the floor and stood up, facing the witch. "What do you mean?" she demanded. The old woman used her hands to open the iron portal, her magic powers depleted from the effort. She turned to the two and with the same diabolical smile she replied, "Well... the four leaders of this vast empire sent a submarine toward your foolish friend and his ship, and this deadly submarine will blow him off the face of the water blow him to little bits." The hag locked the iron door heavily. Her evil laughter echoed through all the prison corridors, slowly receding until it faded completely. Heralda burst into tears. "Oh no, Joshua, they're going to kill our Adam, did you hear? They're going to send a submarine to sink the *Oracle* and drown him." The old man recovered a little, and he lifted the weeping youngster's head. "Listen to me, Heralda," he said in a calm voice. "In the life of every man or living creature there are always certain occurrences threatening to diminish the spirit of life and give the darkness an eternal hold. But if you look at the sky and see it covered with black clouds, concealing the light of the sun from Earth, you must always remember that behind those dark, foreboding clouds there is a strong and wonderful sun. Optimism must always be in your heart, and when the situation seems so ominous and sad, we must always remember that just like the good wind blows the clouds aside and helps the sun to light up the Earth again, so must we pray persistently, to make our own spirit gust so powerfully it will blow the threat away, and conquer it."

The youngster looked at him curiously and asked, "What are you actually saying, Joshua? That we should pray for Adam?"

The old man answered with a tiny smile peeking through his thick white beard. "Exactly. We won't despair, we will sit together you and I, and together we will focus our powers in a meditation. With absolute faith and pure intent, we will send out a telepathic message to Adam, somewhere far out there, and warn him of the danger approaching him and our friends, the men of the *Oracle*."

The young woman was thrilled by his words. They sat crossed legged, facing each other, their palms pressed against each other, and began repeating again and again, "Dear Adam, we are sending your mind this message: warn Captain Nelson of an empire assault." The two focused entirely in the words they were repeating with a full faith that wherever he is, Adam will receive their message.

Chapter Twenty-Six

In her typical small, shuffling steps, Irma made her way down the shadowy prison corridors of Argma, the empire's fortress. She couldn't stop thinking of how the old man managed to prevent her from penetrating his mind and reading his thoughts, prevent her of discovering the vital information of the resistance's actions and the mystery man's intentions, and is he really the man from the prophecy? All these questions disturbed her mind, the immense effort she spent on reading the old man's mind left her exhausted. She was flooded by a lust for revenge; she wanted to hurt the old man and the young woman, and she was thinking of how she would do it.

As Irma reached her lonely dark room in the cellars of the fortress an idea came to her mind, that she would have Bartholomew send the two captives to slave in one of the empire's work camps, on the Mediterranean island of Sardinia, where the work camps were especially harsh. She wanted to punish the old man for not giving in to her interrogation. She would ask that he be given the hardest tasks; she wanted him to die in agony. These cruel thoughts recharged the negative powers of sorcery in her body. She sat on her sofa, rubbing her hands together. Then with one hand, she drew back a piece black fabric covering a black keyboard. She tapped on a few keys and Bartholomew appeared on a small screen in front of her.

"Bartholomew, I want you to do something for me," said Irma to the figure flickering on the screen.

"Of course, dear witch, what is your request?" answered Bartholomew with a question.

Irma asked him to receive her computer communication, which states the details of her request. The chubby leader read it as the witch waited, and after a few seconds, she said, "I hope you can do this for me, Bartholomew."

Bartholomew pressed his plump face closer to the screen, a mean smile drawn on it. "With pleasure, dear witch," he said. Irma was content with his answer. She bid him farewell and finished the exchange with him. Then she leaned back in her seat and said out loud, "Now, you miserable old man, we will see if this man you worked so hard to save will come to save you."

Chapter Twenty-Seven

Not much time passed before the iron door to Heralda and Joshua's cell opened again, and in the entrance stood sturdy soldiers with mean smiles on their faces. They grabbed the old man and the girl violently, and when Heralda tried resisting, one of the soldiers slapped her face powerfully. Joshua was restrained; he could do nothing. He just called out to her and asked her not to resist, to go with the flow for now. The old man looked at one of soldiers leading them out and asked, "Where are you taking us?"

The soldiers all laughed, and one answered mockingly, "We're taking you to a vacation resort." The soldiers' laughter roared down the corridors. The two understood they're probably being taken to a work camp. Joshua recalled the pictures he saw when he was a kid, of people from the century before that were also taken to work camps of the Nazi regime, from which they did not leave alive. He remembered the pictures of young women and strong men and whose freedom was taken, how the Nazis broke the back of innocent people, how, with unbelievable cruelty, they slaughtered millions of people. He prayed to the sky above that history will not repeat itself. He thought of young Adam and his fierce will to save the world from the empire's rule, and as he thought of it, the idea seemed hopeless.

It all seemed lost, but no, he refused to brake. As long his spirit is still in his body, hope is eternal, that can't take that away from an old man who's seen so much in his life. He decided he will not give up hope no matter how grim the situation seems.

An hour later, Joshua and Heralda found themselves with a bunch of other people whose hands and feet were bound; they were all loaded onto a ferry heading to Sardinia, toward the work camp where Irma intended the old man to brake and die from hard work. Heralda and Joshua did their best to lift the spirits of the people sharing the ferry with them, telling them there is hope, there will be a salvation, but regardless of the two's efforts, the people's faces remained downcast. They knew they were heading to the harsh work camps where they will be slaves till they breathe their last breath. Joshua began telling the people of Adam and his deeds, and of his faith in the young man. Some of the people disregarded his words, but some clung to Joshua's tales, because they wanted to hold on to their hope for redemption.

Chapter Twenty-Eight

The sun warmed the faces of the sturdy sailors, who worked in harmony to navigate the *Oracle*. Captain Damtry Nelson commands over the navigation with extreme accuracy and Adam, working along with the team, learns the sailors work well. The captain and crew grew very fond of him; he has become one of them. The one-eyed wolf, Arak, was by Adam's feet most of the time, and between the two, a warm friendly bond came to be. As he was working on the deck, a strange sensation overtook Adam. He felt something like a soft voice echoing through his mind, warning him of an imminent danger. Short flashes of old Joshua's face accompanied the voice. At first Adam tried to ignore this, but the weird voice didn't leave him be. He decided to go to the *Oracle*'s captain and tell him of this. "Nelson, I hear a strange voice in my head, the voice doesn't stop, it gives me a feeling that I'm being warned somehow of an approaching danger." Adam noticed the captain showed no surprise; it seemed he understood what was happening.

"Besides this weird voice warning you of danger, do you see anything?"

"Yes," replied Adam immediately. "I see these flashes of Joshua's face."

The weathered captain looked at Adam with a serious face and said, "Adam, my friend, apparently our old friend Joshua is using a telepathic meditation to warn us of a looming danger. He is very gifted with it. He must know something, so he is trying to contact you to warn us."

Surprised, Adam asked Nelson, "Is that actually possible? That Joshua is communicating with me through a telepathic meditation?"

The captain replied, "Yes, it's possible, and we must get ready for whatever danger approaches." Captain Nelson took a stand with Adam at his side. "Friends, listen to me," called Damtry to his crew, who all as one turned and looked at their beloved commander. "I just learned through Adam that empire forces are nearby, and they will try to harm him." A murmur passed through the crowd of sailors. The captain stopped for a moment and gazed at Adam standing at his side and laid a heavy hand on the young man's muscular shoulder. "And we will not give them that pleasure, right friends?" he said loudly, smiling and winking at Adam.

The entire crew cheered loudly for their commander, for his willingness and determination in protecting Adam and the *Oracle* from any harm. Arak the one-eyed wolf joined the cheers with happy barks. Adam stroked his head with warmth and said, "If you agree with Captain Nelson, Arak, then I have nothing to worry about."

Arak the wolf laid his right paw on Adam's thigh, signaling in a bark that he agrees. The entire crew of the *Oracle* decided that whatever may come, they will prevail. Suddenly a horrible crash came from the right side of the ship, in a moment wiping away the men's high spirits. At once all the crew, with Adam and Captain Nelson, ran to the railing to look at the sea surface to see what caused the crash, and they all saw an astounding sight—a young blue whale trapped in a metal mesh, that tightened around him the more he tried to break free of it. "Damn!" called Nelson. "Poor animal."

Adam looked with great pain on his face and turned around to his friends. "I'm not a seasoned sailor like you, but I have no doubt we must do something for this suffering creature." Jeremiah came near Adam and the captain. "Yes, we should do something to help this whale, but his parents may be around and they can be downright deadly. They always swim in packs," said Jeremiah, and just as he finished his sentence, another sailor shouted from another side of the deck. "Look over there, here they are, his parents!" He pointed toward a pair of enormous whales, each one of them the size of the *Oracle*. Adam was overcome by awe; it was the first time in his life he saw whales. "Dear God, they're amazing!" he called.

The rest of the crew showed no special interest in the giant sea creatures. Captain Nelson wanted to take no chances; he ordered the navigator to do whatever necessary to back away from the area. Adam understood this by the sudden movement of the ship. "Nelson, what are you doing? We have to help this poor creature, if I remember correctly whales need to breath too, and he must be trapped in the damn net for a while now," said Adam.

Captain Nelson answered his friend, "Well, they're these wretched hunters in this area, that abuse and kill these beautiful animals for money, but I'm sorry, Adam, there is nothing we can do for them."

Adam didn't seem to agree with that. Nelson could understand that, and he explained his unwillingness to act. "Listen to me, Adam. We are doing our best to help you reach the place you want to go. Maybe you've really been chosen by God to save humanity, we don't know if that's true or not, Joshua believes it is, and after what I've heard of you and saw with my own eyes I too believe in your will, but, Adam, I can't risk anyone from my crew and you neither, because if we get near this young whale his parents will smash the *Oracle* to pieces."

Adam saw the logic in the captain's words, but just then, a heartbreaking cry came from the little whale, trying in vain to break free; that cry penetrated the man's heart and he knew he must do something. Without warning, Adam Swandon leapt into the cold blue ocean.

"No, Adam, don't do it, you'll get yourself killed!" shouted Nelson in Adam's direction. The entire crew crowded around Nelson, showing their concern for their friend in the water. Nelson yelled at the man again, "Get out of the water right now, that's an order!"

Adam grinned and called to the men on the ship, "Don't worry, Captain, I'm fine, I can't see an animal suffer, I have to help it."

Nelson didn't answer. He looked around him at his crew and then cried out, "Friends, what are you doing, standing around like this? Help Adam in any possible way!"

One sailor bent toward Adam. "What do you need? Tell us and we'll do it."

Adam called out to them cheerfully, "Throw me a rope to tie around myself, and if anything happens, just pull me back to the ship." Adam thought to himself that it's a risky plan, but he will make it anyway; the rope was tossed to him, within a few seconds he had the rope fastened around him. He threw a glance back at the ship, where his friends were looking over him with great concern; three muscular sailors held tight to the rope, making sure they could pull Adam out at any moment, and Captain Nelson oversaw the proceedings carefully, praying quietly that God be with this brave lad.

Adam began swimming cautiously toward the marine creature, acquainting himself to the size and might of the beautiful mammal. "Don't worry, friend, I'm here to set you free," said Adam, struggling through the great swells of water created by the young whale's desperate movements. The great mammal's eyes met the hawk eyes of Adam Swandon. Adam felt a shiver run down his entire body. A strange sensation of heat flooded him; he could sense the whale calm down, as if he spoke telepathically into Adam's mind, "I trust you, help me." The young whale's gaze strengthened Adam and his resolve to save the young mammal grew. The whale's enormous parents began circling Adam and their child in wide rounds, which caused Captain Nelson much worry, but he relaxed at once when his sailors pointed his gaze toward the large whales and their actions. A wide smile spread on the bearded captain's face. He understood what they were doing; they were merely protecting their child. He forced himself to trust Adam more but still asked one sailor to be ready for anything that may come.

Adam was focused on his efforts to rescue the large mammal. He noticed the wounds along the whale's body, created by the friction of the metal net against the smooth skin of the young creature. After a few minutes filled with great effort, Adam found the latches holding the net closed and began his frantic labors to release the latches, five in number. The great mammal had exhausted himself completely. Adam noticed this and doubled his speed, a great elation took over him, and as the last latch broke open he felt as if time was standing still, then the entire crew, including Captain Nelson, burst into victorious cheers for Adam and for the young whale, who with his last strength erupted out of the net; seconds ago, it's future grave, and it's immense, wounded body flowed again into the blue open sea. The other whales, his parents, drew near him; it seemed to Adam that they were expressing a great joy, just like humans do when they're reunited with their loved ones. Tears of joy rolled out of Adam Swandon's eyes; he didn't sense the cold or the danger anymore. He understood this is what he had to do, and the good creator came to his aid. He thought to himself that every living creature should be able to live free in the wonderful nature that God created. In his heart, he thought that no one has the right to disturb the freedom of another living being; he felt honored to do what he did. Suddenly he felt his entire body pulled back. It was his friends from the *Oracle*, dragging their companion back to the safety of the ship. The cheers of the sailors mixed with the mysterious calls of the whales, slowly withdrawing from the ship with the blue sails. Adam, soaking wet, vigorously shook his friend's hands. He was staring far into the horizon at the departing family of whales. The heavy hand of Captain

Nelson on his shoulder, accompanied by a smile that turned swiftly into a roaring laughter, retrieved Adam's wandering mind to the ship.

"Damn, Adam, you're totally crazy, but in heavens name. You have the guts of a true sailor," said the captain of the *Oracle*. Two other sailors wrapped Adam with a big blue towel; he began drying himself, catching his breath again.

"Come, friends, it's time to enjoy a good meal and relax from all these events," called the ship's cook with a smile to his crew, and they unanimously agreed that is the best thing to do right now.

Chapter Twenty-Nine

In the work camp on the shore of the island of Sardinia, the cries of slaves ring out—slaves who years ago were free men, men who could follow their dreams. Old Joshua can barely stand on his feet under the load of hard work. Heralda tries to keep an eye on him from afar; she sees how the world today treats an elderly man. There's no more honor; honor is crushed. She prays for Adam's well-being. In her heart, she hopes that this special man indeed managed to receive their message. Joshua, with several other men, is pulling carts loaded with coal. She sees the soldiers towering over the toiling men, deadly weapons in their hands and the devil's smile on their face.

Many years ago, similar expressions were seen on the faces of Nazi soldiers, who almost wiped out an entire nation. Her blood boiled in her veins; suddenly, the bitter lash of a whip across her back broke though her thoughts. Her cry of pain sounded too far away, Joshua noticed it and cried in his heart.

"God in heaven, please, let salvation come to us, let these suffering humans go free, please God, I believe, I believe," prayed Joshua to the sky. Barbed wire fences surrounded the camp. Guards and soldiers were everywhere. The barrels of laser guns were always aimed at the slaves to stifle any attempt of escape or mutiny. Every now and then, the crack of a whip would sound, followed by a horrid shriek of pain ringing through the air. The dull eyes of people whose freedom was taken away could occasionally comfort themselves in the breathtaking view of the stunning blue ocean. The salty scent hanging in the air embodied a kind of liberty. As soon as they arrived, Joshua spread the word of Adam and his ambition among all the people. He wanted to encourage them, that he may very well be the hope for humanity. He asked the men around him to pray for Adam and his mission. Most people had lost their hope already, but not him, not old Joshua. Saturated with knowledge and experience, he had lived long enough to know there is always hope, one must never give up.

His thoughts were cut short; the old man's eyes saw something—something that justified his encouraging thoughts. A smile of calmness and hope broke under his white beard; all the coal stains on his wrinkled face were overshadowed by the wide smile that breathed new life into Joshua. The sight of blue sails, the blue sails of the *Oracle*, far out in the distance, revived his spirit, and he spoke the words out loud to the air. "Adam, bless the Lord."

Chapter Thirty

Drakkar took a seat by the rest of the members of the empire's leadership. With them, he waited anxiously to a word from the field. They were seated around a blood red table; to the right of the leader Drakkar sat Bammark and Vaskov. Only Bartholomew sat to the left of his leader, without making a sound. Drakkar's eyes were fixed on the communication radio in front of him. In a few minutes, the deadly empire submarine will reach the marine sector where the sailboat the *Oracle* was located.

Irma, the old witch, is hidden somewhere underground in her dark room; she is mumbling at the crystal ball she inherited from her grandmother, the ancient book of prophecies lays open in front of her. Her face is worried; she sensed a large unexpected threat to the submarine's mission to destroy Adam and the *Oracle*. She concentrates and gathers all her powers to penetrate the thoughts of the empire's leader. After a long, strained minute, she manages to break through.

"Drakkar," her chilling voice echoed in Drakkar's mind. The leader of the empire froze in his tracks. "What the hell?!" cried Drakkar. His friends threw a weird glance at him but said nothing. "Drakkar, listen to me, you must warn the *Black Octopus*." In an instant, Drakkar realized Irma was following the situation from her dark room at the bottom of the palace. He did not want his men to know of this, so he replied to Irma with his thoughts, "Leave me alone, Irma, we're in the middle of the mission to destroy the ship the mystery man is on."

Irma did not let Drakkar go but went on with her deeds. "Don't let your arrogance and pride destroy your rule! I sense with my powers that something dangerous may happen to your deadly submarine. Command your men to start shooting now. Now, Drakkar!"

The leader toughened his position. "Irma, leave me alone, no one can match the forces of my empire. Are you trying to weaken me? Your words will weaken my soldiers. I will decide when we shoot, mind yourself and don't meddle. I'm the leader of the empire, nobody else." Drakkar turned his thoughts to the radio as it gave off a short, sharp squeak; the submarine was making contact and reporting its status.

Irma was offended by Drakkar's words. To herself she said, "You, Drakkar, you alone with your pride and arrogance will bring on your own demise. My powers don't lie to me. I sense a threat to the mission, there is something in the mystery man that Joshua would not talk about. I feel the pureness of his heart in the air around us. Grandmother Trudy, remember, I did my part." Irma returned to the thick wooden table with the large crystal ball on it. The ball filled with thick, yellow smoke; the witch raised her scrawny arms in the air and began waving them around in weird patterns, on her face a wicked smile.

Inside the crystal, a picture began forming, of the Island of Sardinia in the middle of the Mediterranean Sea. A mumble of pride broke from the witch's lips over the fact she could still, in her advanced age, master her magic powers. She sensed this is the crucial time when the empire must destroy the mystery man, the man who dared slight the empire, the man who dared challenge the great army. Irma was treating the matter in the way of Grandma Trudy, who passed on to her the duty to help Drakkar to protect the dark empire and continue the reign of horror over the human race. She continued moving her hands around her crystal ball with odd gestures. The effort showed on the pale, wrinkled face of the old witch, but she wouldn't stop; she knew that Drakkar was striving to keep his thoughts blocked from her, but she decided to keep her telepathic channels open, and she was now engulfed in what her eyes were seeing.

Inside the *Black Octopus* submarine, the Parakees men were gathered in front of a huge screen. Kardo, the leader of the group, turned to his friends and to the empire soldiers with them who's job was to steer the submarine to its destiny—the *Oracle*.

"Men. We are close to the target. Here is the sailboat the *Oracle*. We must obliterate the bastard that escaped us at the pier. This man, and the crew of the *Oracle*, insulted and undermined your leader's reign. As you know, we, the Parakees men, will lead this assault. You are all subordinate to us and our orders." His tone became increasingly mean. "Is that clear to all of you?" yelled Kardo loudly.

The empire soldiers had no love for the Parakees men. Everybody despised their arrogance and self-importance, yet the soldiers feared them terribly. The Parakees were known for their barbarism, so not one of the empire soldiers allowed himself to disobey. Asan stood with his friend Kardo, pointing at the large screen where the *Oracle* could be seen in the distance. "Here's the ship, Kardo, we can shoot it down from here, two torpedoes and we blow this scrap of wood out of the water, and we can go back to Argma fortress and collect our money," said Asan to his friend with a smile.

Kardo gazed at the rest of his friends, manning different positions and whispered, "Yes… but first we must drown the mystery man." On another monitor to the right of the giant screen appeared the digital image of the *Oracle*, and on it a pair of crossed lines.

The shout of Allator, the sailor on duty at the head of the mast, startled the entire crew that set down to eat a few minutes ago. Still chewing the piece of chicken that was in his mouth, Captain Damtry Nelson called out to Allator, "What the hell is wrong, Allator?" The other crewmen stepped out, some of them still holding their food, and before the frightened Allator answered his commander, a fierce explosion appeared merely a few feet to the left of the sailboat, a great eruption of fire and water gushing in all directions. A great swell, formed by the explosion, pushed the *Oracle*, tossing some of the crewmen against the other rim of the ship. "Hold on, men!" shouted the captain to his men. "We're being attacked by underwater torpedoes!" the captain pointed at two strong sailors. "You two, take the wheel immediately and balance the ship! Adam, come here."

Adam ran to the deck and stopped by the captain. "Captain, what's happening?" asked Adam, breathing heavily.

The captain spotted the submarine from afar. "Look there, Adam, Joshua, and Heralda's telepathic warning came to be." Nelson pointed toward a black dot, only a few miles apart from the *Oracle*. "It's a deadly slayer submarine, an empire submarine, and they came here to destroy you and us, but you know what? We won't let them do that after all."

The captain's words sparked a flare of hope in Adam's heart. "Tell me what to do, Nelson, I want to help," called Adam eagerly.

"First we organize a weapon for all men to hold," said Nelson. The *Oracle*'s sailors were frightened, yet still listened to their loyal commander. Arak the one-eyed wolf was in the back of the ship; he began barking loudly toward Captain Nelson. By that time, Adam already grabbed an old laser gun and was waiting with the rest of the crew for Captain Nelson's order to shoot. Arak's incessant barking disturbed Adam; he asked himself, *Why is Arak barking like that? And why is he so far from the bow, way back in the stern?* Nelson eyes were locked on the menacing black dot slowly closing in on his beloved ship. "This is a time for courage, men!" cried Nelson heatedly to his crew.

"Fire!" shouted Captain Nelson, and at that same moment, all the rifles began firing beautifully colored laser blasts, but because of the still great distance the shooting didn't cause the submarine any damage at all. Adam was shooting with the rest of his friends, but he was more interested in the persistent barking of Arak, the large one-eyed wolf. "Captain Nelson, why is Arak barking like that?" called Adam to the ship's commander, who could barely hear Adam over the shriek of the laser beams being shot ceaselessly at the approaching submarine.

"Arak is a brave wolf, he never runs from the battlefield," Captain Damtry expressed his bewilderment and continued commanding his people to shoot and create a defensive wall between them and the deadly submarine, but deep inside Damtry Nelson knew that these simple guns couldn't overcome the fortified steel of the great empire submarine.

Inside the *Black Octopus*, the environment was one of both confidence and disregard to their opponent, the *Oracle*. Seeing the weak laser shots coming from the ship's men, Kardo burst into a roaring laughter with his friends, and with the rest of the empire soldiers, who for the first time joined in the Parakees men laughter. Chickon was the only one not laughing; he was very serious as he loaded the next missile, hoping that this time it won't miss. Adam Swandon looked to the stern, trying to see why Arak kept on barking. His curiosity caused him to leave his place among the *Oracle* men, who kept on shooting toward the approaching submarine. He jumped over the ropes and barrels that rolled across the deck because of the impact of the torpedo they narrowly missed before. He came near Arak, who jumped with joy when he saw Adam come to him.

"At what are you barking like that?" called Adam as he hastily pat the wolf, as Arak turned wildly, pleading with Adam to turn his attention to the sea. Adam understood by now that Arak the one-eyed wolf is a special wolf, and all the faithful wolf was asking for was to show him the wonder he has witnessed with his one eye.

In the meantime, Chickon aimed the torpedo gun at the *Oracle*, and a great blast resonated when Chickon, with a mean smile on his face, pressed the detonation button. The torpedo missile burst its way toward its target to blow up. Nelson's face contorted in fear as he watched the trail of water crossing the placid ocean face with extreme speed, heading toward the sailboat. There wasn't anything left to do, the captain called to his men in a broken voice. "Take cover, friends! Prepare for impact!"

Just as he finished speaking, the torpedo missile crashed into the left side of the *Oracle*'s bow. The ship's men held on tight to anything possible, taking cover in time, thus keeping the damage light. Fire and smoke erupted where the missile hit, from the impact Adam Swandon and Arak the wolf were tossed overboard. Captain Nelson, desperate, understood that nothing more can be done, the

Oracle was a sitting duck; their time was running out; for a moment, he considered opening the side doors of the *Oracle*, but because the torpedo hit that was now impossible. Captain Nelson's was taken by even a greater fear when he saw the figures of Arak and Adam floating immobile in the water. Some of the crew ran to the stern to help Adam and the wolf, but their eyes grew wide at the amazing sight unraveling in front of them; Arak and Adam were lifted from the water upon the head of a huge whale that burst from the blue ocean toward the flaming *Oracle*. At that moment, Adam and Arak regained consciousness; they couldn't believe their eyes, they were on the back of an enormous whale, saving them from drowning. The entire crew, including Captain Nelson, was staggered, still trying to grasp the astonishing vision of a huge whale floating by the burning *Oracle* with Adam and Arak standing on its head. Nelson figured it was the father of the young whale, returning Adam the favor for saving his son from certain death just a few hours ago. The whole crew cheered, their faces washed with joy. Adam caressed the face of the whale his rescuer, thanking him, and Arak accompanied him with happy barks. At that moment, Adam grasped the special connection of all living creatures; he understood the harmony between them all. He understood that this is what Arak meant to tell him with his barking, the barks marking their salvation, shaped as a flock of whales surrounding the *Oracle*, determined on protecting it.

Inside the black submarine, Kardo furiously slammed his fist into the radar boards. He couldn't believe his eyes. His friends the Parakees crew exchange astonished looks.

"What the hell is going on here? Where did all these damn whales come from?" Chickon asked Kardo furiously. The empire soldiers where poised to carry out any order of the Parakees crew; the next moment, without any warning, Kardo let out a shout, "Fire! Shoot them, exterminate those damn animals!" The two empire soldiers clutched the laser canon control rods, a shudder ran through their body but they obeyed Kardo's orders and commenced shooting at the whales.

The laser blasts tore mercilessly at the whales defensive line. Adam stared at the atrocity unfolding in front of his eyes and the eyes of all surrounding him. To his back, the *Oracle* burning from the missile hit and to his front the wounded whales, their cries of pain breaking Adam's heart, a great fury screaming from within it.

Not far away from there, the empire soldiers were ordered to herd all the slaves toward the island's shore, so the slaves may see their hope for salvation defeated. The slaves are shoved along one after the other, still holding tools in their hand, their tired bodies awash with sweat from the hard labor. The mocking laughter of the empire soldiers rang through the air, holding their guns and watching the confrontation way out in the sea. An old man stands among all the people, his eyes flowing with tears of fury, his body weak but his spirit calls out in a whispered prayer. Old Joshua was whispering words of unbreakable positive force, that were carried from his lips on the good wind directly into Adam Swandon's desperate mind. "Ho, God, help Adam, give him strength, help him fight, help him fulfill himself," Joshua intoned quietly.

One of the soldiers noticed and called to him, "Hey, old man, shut up over there, just look to the sea and watch your hope fade in front of your old eyes."

Joshua turned a courageous look into the soldier's eyes, who for a moment felt the old man penetrating into his miserable soul, and was compelled to turn his eyes away. The old man continued with the whispered prayer, pure and full of positive intentions. "Adam, hear my voice. Don't surrender, don't let the doubt overcome you, rise and fight, think positive, think positive and act with pure faith that you will win, fight, Adam, and win."

Through all the chaos around Adam sensed a voice echoing within his thoughts; he grasped what was happening, and said with a smile, "Joshua." The young man gripped the fin of his ally the whale and turned his gaze to Captain Nelson, who without a word understood that Adam was determined not to give up. Adam instructed Arak to leap back on the *Oracle* and the loyal wolf obeyed. Adam felt that he and whale became one. The whale rose up high so Adam may see all the *Oracle*'s crewmen from above; he called to Jeremiah, "Jeremiah, throw me the grenade you're holding!"

The stunned Jeremiah didn't think twice, but with full trust tossed the last grenade in his hand to Adam, that swiftly caught it in one hand. A mad fury took hold of Adam Swandon, man and whale as one shot forward toward the deadly submarine. Adam and the whale burst through the flames and all the wounded whales, Adam grabbing the great mammal's fin in one hand and in the other holding the only grenade remaining. The whale uttered strange shrieks, echoing over a great distance. Within seconds, dolphins emerged all around them, swimming vigorously to assist the great mammals, their brothers.

Adam looked around him and was amazed at what his eyes saw. He couldn't believe that the dolphins too, are coming to his aid. He felt a powerful elation, but didn't let the excitement distract him and kept on pushing forward, nothing could divert him. From afar, he heard the excited calls of the *Oracle* sailors. Captain Nelson was dumbfounded at the sight of a whale carrying a human on its back. He recognized how important it was to help animals in distress, We are all living creatures, all deserve the chance and the right to live, these thoughts transformed into a heartfelt prayer that this brave man, making his way through the blue ocean with a single hand grenade will succeed in destroying the deadly threat of the *Black Octopus*, that was shooting an endless stream of laser blasts toward the whale rapidly swimming toward it.

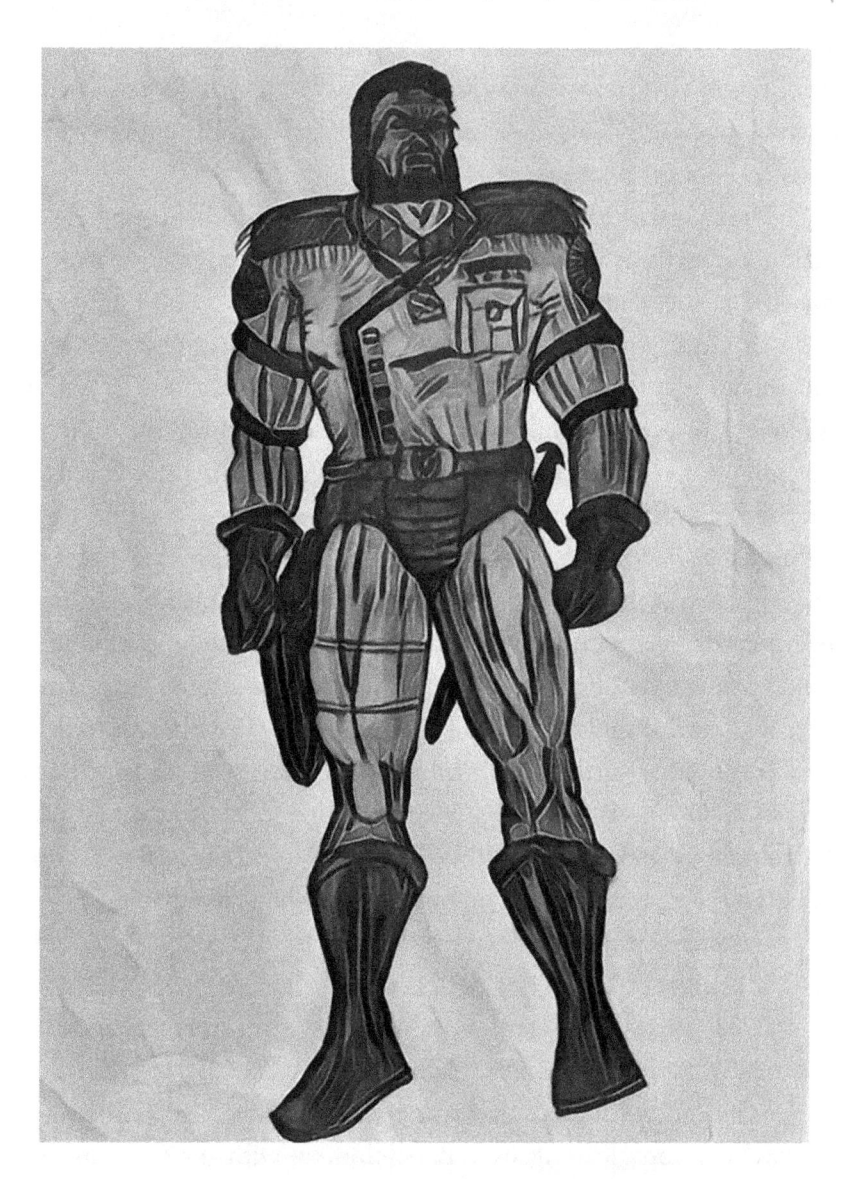

In the palace of Argma, there is a great commotion; apparently word spread of the great battle in the middle of the ocean, and all empire soldiers, from the top brass to the lowliest maintenance worker were glued to the television screens, hearing the amazing developments from the anchor of the empire's official channel. Everyone hears of the mystery man that the empire has targeted for destruction, and now this man is riding through the ocean on the back of a whale, heedlessly making his way toward the empire's submarine, bent on destroying it.

Drakkar slammed his fist into the table. "I can't believe what I'm seeing, look at this man, riding a whale, heading impudently toward my submarine, damn, and my people can't manage to hit him!"

Vaskov, trying to calm him, laid his hand on the leader's shoulder, but the leader of the empire pushed him away angrily. Bartholomew watched the large screen, the satellite broadcast showed the mysterious man whom the empire disregarded from the first moment, and the empire's great leader mocked this man; he mocked the prophecy, he mocked the warnings of Irma the witch, and now everyone can see how truly dangerous it was to disregard this man that right now became a serious threat to the entire empire. Bartholomew couldn't hold back, he turned to Drakkar carefully and said, "You see... Irma was apparently right. He does belong to the prophecy she told us about." Drakkar turned his burning eyes to the stout leader, he felt his blood boil in his veins with anger, and in one second, he pounced Bartholomew and was pounding his fists viciously into the chubby man, who deeply regretted that last sentence he spoke.

Bammark leaped to break the two apart, Vaskov did the same but didn't put too much of an effort in it.

"Relax, Drakkar, leave him alone, we must reconvene, we mustn't fight among ourselves," called Bammark to his peers. Drakkar halted, his face sweaty, his hair and beard wild. He raised himself up heavily, his body leaning over Bartholomew with his face gushing blood. Breathing heavily, Drakkar held on to Bammark and rose to the table, looking again to the big screen in front of them. The screen continued to relay the satellite images of the occurrence in mid sea. Drakkar thought in his heart, "It can't be that Irma is right. It can't be that the stupid prophecy is true."

The slaves standing on the shore looked at the amazing sights, small smiles appearing on their tired faces. The scattered soldiers felt confused, torn between guarding the slaves and observing the battle unfolding far in sea.

Irma sees it all in her crystal ball; she whispers to herself, "I knew it, my dear Grandma Trudy, you told us to beware of the man who challenged the four kings of the dark empire, that fool Drakkar must be seeing this on his satellite screens now, he shouldn't have slighted my words."

"Go, my dear whale, go," whispered Adam to the whale, holding on to its fin so not to fall off. Suddenly a blue light engulfed the man and the whale, and both together hear a voice whisper clearly: "The whisper that becomes a scream." Adam looked around him to see who was speaking, but beside the foam spraying off the whale's course and the dolphins cruising hastily beside him, he sees nothing. The hawk eyes of the young man focused on the submarine with a fierceness he never knew before in his life; his fist is closed tightly around the last grenade of the freedom fighters. Adam felt a peculiar confidence, coming from the blue light surrounding him. The continuous laser blasts emanating from the submarine again and again missed the man and the whale, now closer then ever to the fearsome *Black Octopus*. Suddenly in his mind, Adam saw the people of Battery Nile village, massacred by empire soldiers, his mouth opened wide and a bitter cry breaks from the mystery man's throat. "This is for you, villagers! I avenge you!" With a furious throw, Adam hurls the last grenade at the front of the submarine, the whale dove in with Adam on his back, and at that exact moment, a tremendous explosion put an end to the laser screeches of the damaged submarine. Adam and the whale were nowhere to be seen. Suddenly with lightning speed all the dolphins closed in on the submarine, which began burning like a fireball on the blue water, the dolphins surrounded the submarine and began wildly slamming all the laser barrels, over and over they thumped them until all the laser barrels bent and broke, and the submarine was rendered helpless.

The entire crew of the *Black Octopus* was gripped by panic, the unbelievable just happened; one man on a whale and one simple hand grenade overpowered a deadly war craft. The ball of flames began slowly sinking into deep water. The Parakees team began hurling the empire soldiers in all directions as those cried for help and tried to escape; Kardo shot the soldiers standing in his way and led his three friends to a small escape pod. All four entered the pod, and within seconds, the small escape submarine was making its way through the ocean, far away from the burning, slowly sinking submarine that carried the rest of empire soldiers to certain death.

Nelson was utterly bewildered by all his eyes just witnessed. But the violent explosion occurred very close to his friend Adam Swandon; the heart of the veteran captain was racing in his chest as he called the sailors to make an effort and scan the water well to find the daring man. The burning submarine was swallowed entirely in the great ocean. No trace remained of the war craft that just a moment ago posed a true threat to the fate of the *Oracle* crew. Just as suddenly as they appeared from nowhere, the dolphins were all gone. The entire team was calling in Adam's name, searching with growing worry for the special man and his uncanny companion, the great whale.

Arak's single eye was sharper than a human eye, and suddenly, his face lit up and he began barking with great excitement. Jeremiah was the first after Arak to notice the great whale as he broke out of the water with a spectacular splash, the brave Adam on his back, shouting loudly to his friends on the *Oracle* with a face awash with joy, "We did it! We did it!" Damtry Nelson helped Adam climb on board and embraced him so warmly and tightly Adam practically couldn't breathe. The rest of the ship's crew was jumping with joy, yelling and cheering for their brave friend. Arak the one-eyed wolf leapt on Adam, toppling him over, and licked his face happily.

The captain calmed down a little, looked around the ship, and saw where there was a fierce struggle moments ago there was now only silence, except for the voices of the wounded whales, who defended the ship with their own bodies. "Poor things," said Nelson, turning to his men. "Friends, we must do our best to help these brave whales." A big smile was spread on Adam's face, completely agreeing with the captain's words. He rose immediately and called his friends.

"Let's bind their wounds!" after the spirits calmed a little, the crew went to the assistance of their new friends the wounded whales. In the meantime, a small group of muscular sailors turned to quench the fire caused by the missile hit. After caring swiftly and devotedly for the whales, the *Oracle* men waved their odd new friends good-bye and watched them slowly drift away from them, far into the horizon connecting between the peaceful ocean faces to the sinking sun.

"This was an especially rough day," said Nelson to Adam. "We must find a hiding place quickly, because after what happened today, I have no doubt that the empire heads will engage themselves in a more serious offense. We must be prepared for anything." As the captain went on, Adam said nothing, listening very attentively to the words of the veteran fighter. "Not far from here there is a small hidden island, where there are many people who oppose the rule of terror of the damn empire. There we can rest, recuperate, and of course fix the ship. Luckily it isn't far away."

The sun had set completely, and a starry night decorated the horizon hanging above the sea, sheltering the *Oracle* that sailed slowly and carefully to the island of shelter.

Very far from there, on the island Sardinia, a great happiness filled the hearts of the slaves in the work camp. Tears of joy and hope fell from tired, old eyes. Joshua looked up at the black starry sky and thanked God for his benevolence. From moment to moment, he knew that something big is about to happen in the near future that will affect all humanity, something very positive, but he couldn't ignore the difficulties this special man will face; this man who chose to go on a journey in search for a true solution to the evil in this world. He was very tired. Confused soldiers ordered all the people to return to the camp, enter their lodgings, and go to sleep, and to prepare for another grueling workday tomorrow morning.

Joshua met Heralda, who also witnessed the miraculous occurrence far out in the ocean. The two smiled and hope lit their tired faces, happiness filling their hearts. The soldiers led everyone to their shacks and ordered an immediate curfew. It was quiet on this night at the work camp and Joshua fell asleep with a smile and a revived hope in his heart.

A few miles away from the island, on a dark night with only the starlight shining delicately on the water, the little escape pod of the Parakees crew pops out the deep and floats on the surface of the water. A small portal opens and four angry figures squeeze out and breathe the air in deeply. Kardo grabs his transmitter and begins calling the empire's rescue forces for help. "This is Kardo speaking, send us a rescue crew immediately!"

On the other side they could hear a broken voice, confirming that a rescue crew will be sent to pick up the Parakees from the place they were stranded. The four men exchange glances, how can it be that such a thing happened, one man on a whale destroyed a large, fully armed submarine of the empire that rules the world? They didn't speak and just waited to be rescued.

Chapter Thirty-One

A small medical team entered the office of the empire leadership and began treating the bleeding Bartholomew. Vaskov peered into his companion's wounded face. "Oh, Bartholomew, you fool! Look what you did to yourself. Can't you keep your mouth shut for a while?"

The wounded leader made no effort to answer. He gladly accepted the help of the medical team's head, who decided to move him to the infirmary for further treatment. Bartholomew's eyes expressed pain and suffering, but also hate and fury toward the empire's leader. As he was led away by the medical team he noticed Bammark's smile, who seemed to be gloating. He decided he would not forget that.

Not far from there, at the bottom of the empire's fortress, the witch Irma sensed Bartholomew's furious thoughts, and greatly feared a crumbling of the leadership. She was very upset with Drakkar's stubbornness and stupidity, refusing to listen to her when she warned him earlier not to make light of the prophecy. She sat on her couch and sighed deeply. "Poor Bartholomew." She regretted the stout leader's injury but agreed immediately that better him then her. She held the ancient book of prophecy, and she asked herself a question that surprised her: Where is the second book of prophecy? By Grandma Trudy's words, another book like this exists, the actual original; she knew that the book in her hand was a copy of it, transcribed by Grandma Trudy herself. The question began to greatly unsettle her. She decided to reach Bartholomew without Drakkar knowing of it and discuss this new insight with him. She recognized that Bartholomew can cooperate with her, at least he understands, he was the only one taking her and the ancient prophecy seriously. Drakkar had a dream that came from the center of the universe, Bartholomew had a similar dream. An evil expression spread on Irma's face. She rose from her couch heavily and moved to a wall hung with stuffed snakeheads. She stared at a particular snake and said to herself, "The old man and that young woman displayed great courage earlier when I interrogated them, they have a connection to this mystery man who may be related to the prophecy. I need to know his name, and where he came from, the empire secret agents say that they smuggled him from somewhere… so the agents will be the key." A diabolical smile spread on the old woman's face, as a wicked thought weaved itself in her evil mind.

The corridors of the empire's fortress were in turmoil. The rumor of the mystery man who destroyed the deadly empire submarine spread quickly, everyone saw and heard the satellite broadcasts of the battle between the *Oracle* and the *Black Octopus*, everyone knew that a new force exists, threatening the empire more than ever before. For the first time ever, the empire's men expressed fear and worry, the people that built their lives by using other people, by turning free men to slaves and abusing the weak were terrified. The empire's leader knew this and following the recent events he decided to call in an emergency meeting.

Chapter Thirty-Two

The blue sails of the *Oracle* stretched forward, filled by the good wind, blowing especially strong this day. Captain Damtry

Nelson was smiling; he was satisfied by the way things were playing themselves out. He was very proud of his crew, fighting so fiercely against the empire forces, and though he feared the threat of the empire would be much more serious from now on he didn't let these thoughts erase the peaceful smile lighting his bearded face. The team, united as one, worked together with Adam, each one doing his particular thing to keep the damaged ship afloat, sailing as fast as possible to the hidden island that will harbor the *Oracle* and her men, at least for a while.

The ship sliced through the waves, moving briskly toward its destination, where the bearded captain meant to fix his ship and feed and rest his crew. He was also very interested to know the latest news of the resistance members, who continued their struggles against the vast army of the corrupt empire. He patted the faithful Arak as he gazed up to the bird's nest, waiting for confirmation of land ahead. Indeed after a few minutes, Allator shouted merrily toward his commander, "Sir, land ahoy!"

The entire crew ran to the bow of the ship, and big smiles spread across all faces. Damtry embraced Adam with his arm and said, "You see, my friend, God above came to our aid, here in front of us are the refuge islands of Esperanza." Adam's eyes gazed at the group of dark dots on the horizon line, it was the small group of islands occupied by refugees, people who chose to be free and fight the evil rule in any possible way.

As the sun turned to a flaming orange ball that sunk slowly in the sea, a small dingy escorted the sailboat that entered a small bay, full with vegetation that immediately hid the *Oracle* from any suspicious eyes. The group of sailors busied itself with docking the large vessel, while Adam, Jeremiah, and Captain Nelson went down to the shore accompanied by Arak the wolf. A silence hung in the air; everybody was alert and tense, prepared for anything that may come. Usually many people crowded the shore to receive the veteran captain, who was practically familiar in this place. Damtry Nelson laid one hand on the handle of the laser gun in his belt and said to his peers, "Usually my friend Simon comes to greet me with the rest of his men. It's very strange no one is here."

Adam advanced and looked around him. "Perhaps something happened here?"

The captain kneeled and examined the sand. "I doubt it, no signs of struggle," said Nelson. Suddenly they heard in the background a strange howl, similar to the howl of a jackal; to everyone's amazement, Captain Nelson replies with a similar howl. After a moment, a sound of laughter burst from the green bushes, a bunch of laughing figures appeared and hastened toward the group that came off the ship. The group's eldest spread out his arms and called, "Welcome, you old sea wolf!"

The captain replied with a hoarse laughter, hugging the man, "Simon, you rascal, its been three years since I've seen your ugly face!"

The two embraced, laughing without stop. Adam enjoyed seeing such vigorous laughter in a place far removed from the fear of the empire. It looked like a small heaven full of bright green and soft white sand under his feet. Adam exhaled a sigh of relief. He felt safe in his new location.

Captain Nelson ordered a small group of sailors to stay on board to guard the *Oracle* and commence in repairing the ship, Simon signaled a few men to join the *Oracle* men and help them. Nelson called Adam to join him, and the three began walking barefoot on the seashore by the *Oracle*, which was docked nearby. Nelson introduced Adam to Simon and told him of his adventures so far. Simon's face became serious and his rumbling laughter disappeared. He approached the young man and looked at him without saying a word, then suddenly he laid his right hand on Adam's shoulder and said, "You have to meet Paola Katarina." After these words, Adam felt Simon's hold on his shoulder tighten, and the matured man added, "It takes a lot of courage and fierceness to do what you did, and if what my old friend says is true, only Paola Katarina can help you know the truth of yourself and your unique resolve to free humanity from the enslaving dictatorship of the empire."

Simon let go of Adam and his gaze dwelt long on the ship, whose sailors just lowered its blue sails. "I see you've been through quite an adventure. The ship is badly damaged. It's a great luck you didn't sink. The good Lord must be with you," said Simon.

Adam turned to Simon and asked curiously, "Who is Paola Katarina?"

This time, the bearded captain spoke, "Ho, Paola Katarina, she is a unique woman, an offspring to a famous family of gypsies who has the ability to foretell the future—"

Adam interrupted him. "A fortune-teller?"

The captain felt the tone of disdain in Adam's voice. "She's not any fortune-teller. She has the power to know things. No one can explain her abilities, but she is a good, kind woman, and just as my friend Simon suggested she may help you, it won't hurt to try." Captain Nelson said.

Adam nodded his agreement, though he doubted a human's power to predict someone else's future. Simon sensed his doubt and said, "Listen to me, young man. Did you expect a whale to come to your help, or dolphins to endanger themselves to protect you and the *Oracle?*" Simon's aggressive questions made Adam understand that there are a lot of things in the world that are unknown, sometimes the human mind has difficulties understanding and accepting certain things. A gentle smile spread on Adam Swandon's face. "All right, friends, let's go meet Paola Katarina," he said.

Simon's laughter returned, and he fondly slapped Adam's back. "Now you're talking, boy. Yes, we shall go to her, but now, to receive my dear friend Nelson, we will have a feast—because no matter how great the threat of the empire is, it won't stop us from living a full life." Simon's words greatly cheered Adam and the captain.

The sky turned dark already, little waves gently broke against the well-hidden ship, and all the people around prepared for the celebration. Further up the shore, in the inhabited area, kids played and ran around, men and women were busy preparing the food. Tables were laid out; the entire place was lit by colorful lanterns, some green, some red and yellow. From moment to moment, the festive feeling rose toward the party about to happen late at night. Merry music played from guitar strings and flutes. The air filled with joy and festivity. The *Oracle* men together with the people of Esperanza sat beside the long tables, celebrating their last victory over the empire submarine. The cups filled with fine red wine, and the eyes of the people filled with happiness as they cheered Adam for his resourcefulness and courage in confronting the danger and overcoming it. Captain Damtry Nelson sat by his old friend Nelson and the two exchanged tales of old adventures and new discoveries about the struggles of the underground group of the New Dawn Hawks with the empire soldiers. Adam looked around him and saw all the joy filling the air, but his heart was touched by sadness as he remembered Heralda's gentle face, and Joshua's kind features. He remembered that as he sat here, safe on a hidden island in the heart of the sea, surrounded by happy people celebrating life; they are out there with millions of others, suffering hard enslavement and the fear of the wicked empire. His heart began sinking into a depth of sadness. He deeply missed the people that helped him and saved him, from moment to moment a strange unquiet grew in him. He realized he must do something to save his dear friends, and as he was pondering this, a woman of about fifty sat down at his side. With her brown skin tone, glistening eyes, and colorful clothing, it seemed she didn't belong to this place. She smiled at Adam, and two dimples appeared in her round face. Her skin gleamed softly in the light of the small campfires lighting the festive dinner. Adam stared at her as if snared by some peculiar spell. The woman turned to him and asked, "Why is your face expressing sadness?"

For a moment, Adam did not hear her question, feeling a certain magic in the air, but then he asked, "I'm sorry, what did you say?"

The woman took a cluster of reddish grapes in her hand and repeated her question: "Why is your face expressing sadness?"

Her brown eyes simmered with the light of the burning fire not far from them; she continued speaking, "Look, everyone is celebrating, happy about friends coming from overseas. Why aren't you happy?"

Adam looked at the fire burning in front of him, his hawk eyes focused on the flickering flames. "I cannot be happy when I know dear friends of mine are suffering, not far from here, and I sit here doing nothing," answered Adam, returning his gaze to the woman, a delicate smile taking place on her full lips.

"I see you care deeply for your friends. I sense you have a special sensitivity and a rare compassion to other humans," said the woman. Adam felt a chill running through his body at the words of the woman with the mysterious brown eyes, and before he could answer she carried on, "I heard much about you, I heard how you rescued orphaned children from a sure death by fire, I heard how you dared face the empire hovercrafts and fight them, I also heard the empire is hunting you down for offending their authority, and above all I have heard that you're looking for the solution for all the evil filling our world."

Adam was slightly bewildered at the mysterious woman's vast knowledge of all that befell him until today, but he realized that apparently the rumors of him spread wide and far. "Excuse me, but who are you, lady?" Adam asked quietly.

The woman turned to Adam completely and suddenly he saw how beautiful she was; the firelight revealed a pretty face full of charm. "I'm Paola Katarina," answered the woman with a face full of light.

The celebration went on. Children played around the campfires, the music continued painting the night with joyous chords, and Paola Katarina carried on, "I feel you carry a great pain, years of pain." The strange woman closed her eyes and seemed to suddenly shiver. Adam felt a little awkward but waited to see what would happen. The woman opened her eyes, seeming calmer, an odd tranquility in her face. "You carry within you a deep pain of many years." The woman took hold of Adam's hand and caressed it with hers. "Do you believe in reincarnation?" the woman asked Adam.

He thought to himself that the woman seemed very nice, but now she will probably start with all the gipsy mutters of reincarnation and witchcraft. He smiled to her and ignored her question. "Look, I respect every person, but I don't really believe in those things." As soon as he finished speaking, Paola Katarina laid her hand on Adam's forehead; Adam felt how soft her hand was and sensed a unique peace settle over him. "I know you are a rational man and you find it difficult to believe in such things, but I'm not offering you spells and superstitious ideas. I come, indeed, from the gipsy people, but my vision is universal—and you have been feeling this pain not from today." Adam pulled back and asked at once.

"What do you mean?" She rested her hands on her knees and answered him with a question in her gentle voice. "Tell me, Adam, don't you feel as if you have been carrying the pain of the world for centuries?" At this question, Adam froze on the spot, mouth wide open. How does this woman know of his years of pain? How does she know he feels exactly like she described in her question? How did she discern things hidden so deep in his soul?

"I know sometimes you feel like a very old man, tired of witnessing the suffering of men, animals, nature, and as if for your entire life you have been trying to deliver the world from its agony."

Adam found it hard to believe how accurately she described how he has been feeling his entire life. She smiled at him again and said, "Everything in life has its own time."

Adam regained his composure and repeated the woman's words: "Everything in life has its own time?"

Paola Katarina rose from her seat and gave Adam her hand, asking him to walk with her a little, and he accepted.

From a distance, Damtry Nelson and his old friend Simon watched Adam and Paola Katarina leave the place. The captain raised his beer mug and asked his friend, "Do you think he is the man?"

Simon sipped from his beer and answered, "You were with him these last few days, you saw what he's capable of, and as for me it's been years since I heard of someone so brave as to openly confront the empire. From what you told me, my friend, this man is very special—but time will tell…"

Paola Katarina and Adam walked barefoot on the soft sand of the beach, now cooled by the night. The sky was full of twinkling stars, and the soft murmur of the ocean waves laid a pleasant calm on Adam. They walked together, and the woman's pleasant voice filled the atmosphere. "Adam, what are you searching for? What do you seek in this life?" The questions of the woman in the colorful clothes caused Adam to halt.

He looked at the sky and spoke, "I want to help people, all those who suffer. I want to bring a positive change to this world, I wish I could be granted with some special force to save humans all over the world from the agony of slavery, to tell them that they can better their lives, to choose a path of a life full of light, to help them fix their lives, to heal this pain that has plagues this world for hundreds of years now, that is what I would ask of myself in this life, Paola Katarina. That is what I want."

Small teardrops gently fell from Adam Swandon's hawk eyes, and suddenly he covered his face and wept. "I have no point in this life unless I can change the world, and once and for all abolish the evil force from God's creation. People were not meant to be slaves, children were not meant to be beat, women weren't meant to be raped, animals are not meant to die in order to function as a decoration for humans. My dear father taught me that every living creature deserves a life of freedom, even the tiniest ant that crawls the Earth."

Adam dropped on his knees and his sobs tore through the silence of the night. Paola Katarina reached out to him and softly wiped the tears off his cheek. He rose back to his feet and saw that the kind woman's pretty eyes were also filled with tears, rolling down her full cheeks. She looked at him warmly, he felt as if it was his mother looking at him and was deeply touched. Her eyes met his and she told him in her soft voice, "You are a special man, I feel your heart is pure. I feel your unique intentions and how important this dream is to you. We must open the ancient scrolls of the ancestors and read of the dynasty of your soul. Give me your hand, Adam, and trust in me a little. But above all, trust in yourself and in your dream. Come." Adam composed himself and decided to follow this kind woman who brought him to confess his dream. He felt he should count on his instincts that told him to follow Paola Katarina. The two walked toward a wooden cabin, decked in colorful flowers. Adam's heart pounded strong; he couldn't believe how far he had gotten, and his confidence grew with each step he took after this special woman.

Chapter Thirty-Three

Outside the fortress of Argma, a great mayhem was unfolding. Processions of different vehicles, on land and in flight, were making their way to the empire's palace gates; head hunters, summoned from all over the world, since the leader of the great empire, Drakkar, has offered an enormous sum of money for trapping the mystery man. He no longer has faith in the Parakees team, which despite their latest failure also arrived in their special vehicle. The men of the fortress were excited by the sheer amount of bounty hunters, pouring into the fortress base. These hunters were known to be heartless men, making their living by capturing and killing the underground freedom fighters who were seeking liberty for mankind. They came in all sizes, all shapes, some huge and muscular, some small and skinny yet devious.

Bammark, peer to the empire's leader, had summoned all the top brass, who, after seeing what happened in mid sea, no longer treated the mystery man offhandedly. Drakkar was fuming over the repetitive failure to capture the mystery man, and was determined to get him and break the resistance's spirit once and for all. Irma was surprised to see that she too was summoned to the great gathering in the outer coliseum of the empire's palace, a structure reminiscent of the Roman style from thousands of years ago. Drakkar stood like the Roman emperor, by his side his friends Bammark, Vaskov, and Bartholomew in bandages. A huge crowd of empire soldiers filled the large coliseum. Trumpets rang out, and all types of mercenaries and bounty hunters made their way through the arena, their faces turned to the honorary seats of the empire's leaders.

After a few minutes of chaotic movement, all the hunters settled in their places in the great arena, and the moment the trumpet calls died out a loud cheer rose from the crowd in the coliseum, "Long live the empire's leaders!" They all saluted toward the four leaders, and a silence befell them.

Drakkar took his stand on a small stage. He gazed around him at his tens of thousands of soldiers, feeling the might of his arms and the strength of his rule over the world. He waited a few seconds, confirming that the silence around continued. Not far from him sat old Irma, entirely wrapped in a black cloak that covered her face, but Drakkar could feel her gaze fastening on him from far away. He turns to the crowd and loudly calls, "Brave soldiers and glorious hunters! Today I am about to make an offer I have never made before." It was quiet all around; the hunters in the arena didn't make a sound. Some were caressing their weapons as if they were their beloved children.

Drakkar continued speaking, while behind him rose a huge screen, playing out the satellite footage of the marine battle between the *Black Octopus* and the *Oracle*. "As you can see, on the screen behind me are the images of the cursed freedom fighters, as they dishonor the empire. Look at this man!" Drakkar pointed directly to Adam Swandon's figure, frozen on screen, and everybody stared at the man riding a whale, a single grenade in his hand, on his way to blow up the submarine. "This is the man I want!" Drakkar looks down at the hunters in the arena. "This is the man I want captured and brought to me dead or alive, I will show all the miserable freedom fighters that they cannot match our great empire!"

The audience began whistling and cheering for the empire leader, a great din of cheers and cries of praise for Drakkar rose to the air. The leader spoke on and his voice echoed throughout the entire area, "The first to bring me this man, dead or alive, will be rewarded with enormous sums." The leader stood tall and silent for a few seconds, then suddenly slammed his fist into the podium in front of him and shouted, "Now go, my bloodthirsty hunters, and bring me this man, the faster the better. If you bring him to me dead, my only regret will be that I haven't killed him myself. Loud laughter came from the crowd, Drakkar participated with an evil, mocking grin, and continued, "And if you bring him to me alive, I'll have him executed in utter humiliation, supplying us with a form of entertainment that will break the resistance's spirit once and for all!"

At these words, the crowd rose to their feet, clapping and cheering the leader as he entered a cabin decked in red fabrics threaded with gold. Before he entered, though, the leader looked at Irma from afar and in his thoughts summoned her to his office, immediately. From afar, Irma nodded her head, signaling that she agreed. The hunters stood in long lines in front of narrow tables, where empire soldiers handed out pictures of Adam and a summation of the meager information they had to start off the hunt after the mystery man.

Two soldiers escorted the old witch through the fortress's hallways. They didn't dare look at her from fear that she would cast a spell on them. Irma easily read their mind and smiled to herself at their foolishness. She went on thinking, has Drakkar finally decided to make her a party in the occurrences? Will he put his faith in the prophecy now, respect it more than before? Her thoughts ceased as she reached the office doors of the empire's leader, and two soldiers moved aside, daring to steal one quick glimpse of the witch. They managed to see only her evil eyes, which unsettled them so that they immediately left the place. Irma opened the doors herself with her magic powers and entered.

Drakkar was alone, seated on his black couch, dressed in a sparkling uniform as if he was about to go to battle. He gestured for Irma to sit and so she did. She tried to penetrate the man's thoughts but he noticed and asked her to stop. He rose from his seat, turned to a collection of elongated wine bottles, poured himself a drink, and asked the witch if she wants any. With her eyes, she signaled no. The leader stood before his desk, near Irma, who was waiting for his word. He took two small sips from his drink. Irma noticed the beads of sweat gathering under the hairline near his temples and perceived that though he was trying hard to seem serene, he was actually very disturbed. She could feel the tension in the air.

The leader rested his goblet on the table and turned to the witch. "Well, I never imagined anyone would dare commit such an act of defiance against my empire's realm, I still can't believe those satellite images, but if you think I will start believing in nonsense tales and prophecies, you're wrong." Drakkar paused to sip some more from his wine. Irma's curiosity increased, but since she didn't want to awaken Drakkar's fury she made no attempt to penetrate his thoughts. She asked herself, if he doesn't want to draw on the prophecy, why did he summon her?

After she saw the man has finished his drink, she asked him what she was asking herself, "Why did you call me here, Drakkar?"

Drakkar stretched his uniform on his body, sidestepped the table from the right, sat again on his couch, and said, "After the failure of that miserable attempt of the freedom fighters to attack my officer's event, my soldiers killed all the invaders besides an old man and a young female. I know that you went to them, tried to interrogate them, but managed to discover nothing of the mystery man."

Irma began losing her patience now, but she said nothing, only waited for the bearded man to continue. "I also understand that you sent them to slave in the work camps of the Sardinian mines," said the leader, and leaning forward he added something he usually doesn't say, "You did well, Irma." The old witch was taken aback by the compliment, but she simply went on listening. "Today I launched hundreds of mercenaries on a hunt to annihilate the mystery man and bring me his body, which we will publicly display, putting the entire resistance, all over the world, to mockery, demolishing any possible hope for them. That's it for that. Now I want you to leave for Sardinia, with a group of special people that you select from among our spies. They will pose as newly arrived slaves, sent there to work, and they will get close to the old man and the woman and draw from them information regarding the mystery man."

Irma felt the thrill move through her ancient body, being very flattered that the leader of the realm of terror turned to her to command this mission. She rose from her seat, holding her black cloak close to her body, the lights of the great room illuminating her wrinkled face. She approached the great leader's desk and said, "I will select the people today, Drakkar, and will have briefed them on their mission before the day ends. You are showing a commendable initiative, my lord."

Drakkar seemed to ease more into his seat at her words. The old woman bowed curtly with a short smile, and as she was departing tried nevertheless to dig a little into the leader's mind. She managed to glimpse from the man's thoughts that he is afraid; the dark lord, controlling the planet with an iron fist, is afraid. She was not happy with this discovery. She steered herself to the path that would lead her to the double-agent units, where she would direct the agents to spy for the empire and maintain information from the captive freedom fighters. She commended herself for her decision to keep the old man and girl alive; they were more useful to the empire alive than dead. She smiled to herself thinking that with a wave of her hand she could have the captives killed. She wound her black robe tighter around herself as she made her way through the palace hallways, while soldiers from all direction scattered out of her path, making way out of fear from this strange figure with powers of sorcery.

Chapter Thirty-Four

A soft, pleasant scent of perfume hung in the air of the wooden cabin. The walls were decorated with fragrant roses and an array of colorful flowers, the cabin seemed to be filled with light, the vibrant mixing of colors created a feeling as if the walls were blazing with a sweet-scented fire. Adam felt how he was captivated by this heady aroma. Paola Katarina occupied herself in the kitchen making dried-fruit tea and soft, tasty cookies. When she returned they both sat down in the center of the cabin's living room. The vapors rising from the hot tea filled the air with a sweet aroma that mingled with the perfume of the red roses on the cabin walls. The two sat by a round oak table, illustrated with images of gypsies, traveling the world for centuries. The drawings told of their adventures wandering the world. Adam's eyes examined the details of the designs, and he was deeply impressed by the art in front of him.

Paola Katarina began suddenly to speak. "Adam, my dear, you said you are seeking the solution for all evil in this world. You told me your goal in this life is to help mend the world."

Adam nodded and said, "Yes, Paola Katarina, yes." He began telling her of that accursed day on the alpine mountain range, of the horrible massacre, of his own helplessness and terrible heartache, and above all about the odd decision to leave on a quest seeking an answer to the realm of horror and evil over the Earth. He told her of the lightning that split the skies on that bloody day, a day with no sign of a storm on the horizon.

Paola Katarina's eyes grew wide and she thought in her heart, "Is the person in front of me the man who will deliver humanity, is he the man?"

Adam noticed that the woman's hands were trembling and asked with concern. "Paola Katarina, are you all right?"

The woman did not reply; she rose from her seat and walked to a large wooden chest covered with heavy quilts. She removed the coverings from the chest and revealed a golden lock. She reached under her colorful dress and removed from her neck a long, golden key. After an effort of a few seconds, the wooden chest opened, and inside laid seven stone slates, slightly cracked, covered with odd engravings. Paola Katarina removed the slates carefully and laid them delicately on the oak table. Adam couldn't resist and felt he must ask the kind woman what these planks meant, she didn't reply. It seemed even as if she was ignoring him. As she concentrated on arranging the tablets in a certain order, an action that took a few minutes to carry out. Adam decided to leave the woman alone and not disturb her with further questions. He decided to trust her anyway. He sipped from the tea and savored its sweetness. He took a bite from the soft cookie that melted in his mouth, and when he finished, he noticed that the woman was still occupied with arranging the stone planks on the table. He couldn't understand the etchings on the tablets, but he managed to notice drawings of weird symbols. With all his curiosity, Adam decided to continue waiting patiently.

A pleasant breeze blew gently through the cabin window, which was especially low, and through it, one could see the ocean waves turning into white foam at the end of their journey from the blue depth to the soft, cool sands of the shores of Esperanza Island. The night air began to turn chilly, and outside not a sound was heard except for the hiss of the waves, softly whispering in nature's voice. Paola Katarina spoke up, her soft voice breaking the silence of the night, "Adam, look at these tablets, they were found about three hundred years ago by one of my forefathers, traveling through the ancient lands of Spain. They were found buried in a deep cave, in the heart of the Mount of Blessing—these slates are called the tablets of hope. They were passed on from hand-to-hand in my family until they were given into my hands. The gypsies had no knowledge of what the inscription meant, until they were found by one man, known for his kindness and intelligence. He went one day to herd his sheep, and one of his lambs fell into a water hole far from the rest of the herd. The man ran to rescue the little lamb. He himself didn't know how to swim, so he was risking his own life to save the little lamb. After a short struggle, the man managed to haul the lamb from the water before the little creature drowned to death. Suddenly he heard a voice behind him, and he noticed a blue light enfolding him in the middle of the field. When he turned, he saw, to his amazement, four beautiful blue figures, which he called 'the blue spirits.'

"They told him they came from the blue world, far from here. The four figures from the blue world taught him their alien language, a language never spoken on Earth, a tongue from a faraway place, from beyond the stars that surround us. The man's name was Eillidor. He was a kind man with a good heart. He asked the blue spirits why they chose him, and taught him their language. They replied that he was chosen for his kindness and honesty, that by their calculations, his positive side outweighs the negative, and that he holds the stone tablets that came from their world and were laid deep in a cave in the heart of mount blessing. They told him that a day will come when humans' evil acts before the creator will become worse than ever before, and they themselves will bring on the destruction of their world. They told him that men have a positive side and a negative one, but with the passing of the years, they will forget the truly important things. They will forget the creator that gave them an entirely good world. They will forget their task is to improve this world with every new generation, they will forget to respect each other, they will whore, giving themselves up to crime and materialism, forgetting what true love is, forgetting their spiritual side, judging others by their financial situation; they will go the easy and fast way to obtain their wants, by trampling their brothers and sisters. They will build powerful weapons that endanger all life on Earth. Still, the spirits told him, a spark of hope exists; there is some good in the world that could rise against the destruction coming from the negative forces in humanity; that is why in the Earth's depth, in the most secret hideaway, they concealed the answer. The solution. The special power that only one man could operate one day. A man with a pure heart that will sacrifice his own life to save the entire human race. This certain individual will have to go on a hard, dangerous voyage and overcome many obstacles before he discovers…

"Gim Nigma."

Adam was mesmerized by Paola Katarina's story. He felt the hair on his body rise and his hands were visibly shaking. It was an effort to speak, the words left his mouth almost in a stutter, "Gim Nigma? What is Gim Nigma?" Paola Katarina held Adam's hands, and they relaxed a bit until the tremor ceased, then she replied, "Gim Nigma, in translation from the alien language of the blue spirits from the blue world, means 'the solution,' the counter force to crime and malice. Gim Nigma is the special power buried here thousands of years ago by the alien spirits from the other world. They knew humans may destroy themselves, harming the innocent and breaking the balance of the universe, so they developed Gim Nigma so that one day, one unique person will be chosen to save the Earth from self-destruction. This person has yet to be found, and in the meantime, the Earth is dying, and so is the human race. With the language I learned from my mother, I can read the inscription on these seven stone tablets, and it conveys the story I just told you."

The woman paused for a moment and stared at the stone slates in front of her. She pointed at the seventh tablet, engraved with a symbol shaped like the sun. "This symbol conveys hope and the light, and here is the mention of the ancient libraries, concealed in the heart of the North African desert, where an old solitary priest, wiser than any other man in this world, is guarding the ancient libraries. The tablets tell that he is waiting for the chosen man to open the book of light and discover where on Earth Gim Nigma is."

Adam did not speak; he was still taken aback from the tale of the gypsy who found the tablets. Paola Katarina rose from her seat and went to the kitchen, returning in a moment with a glass jug filled with cold water. "Here, boy, drink and refresh yourself," said Paola Katarina. She poured some water into an earthen cup and Adam drank to his fill. He looked through the window at the sky darkened by the night as Paola Katarina carried on, "The tablets tell of this special soul, that will try with each reincarnation to complete its destiny, and it's destiny is to save the world, the humans and the animals, this special soul will set them free, this soul lives in a man that will go on carrying a beacon of hope for all living creatures who choose to live with honor, and as free as the wind blowing through the mountains."

Adam rose from his seat, glancing at Paola Katarina suspiciously. He retreated from her a little, as if trying to escape the place. The woman looked at him without speaking, understanding immediately that the man was expressing, without words, a heavy doubt in all she said. She accepted this with understanding, and without words smiled at him gently. Adam began to speak to her, "What are you trying to say? That this pretty legend is real? That these tablets have really been brought here by aliens from another planet? What are you trying to say with this, Paola Katarina?" Adam spoke heatedly, and it seemed for a moment he was not about to stop, but he noticed the kind woman was about to answer, so he curbed his tongue.

He still kept away from the tablets lying on the table. "I'm trying to tell you that it's not a legend. I believe such a thing indeed happened hundreds of years ago, and perhaps it did happen to one of my ancestors—a special man that came from a recluse gypsy tribe. The gypsies don't have greed. They live their lives as God intended it, with modesty and respect for nature. And perhaps for one of those reasons the strangers chose Eillidor, from the gipsy people." For a brief moment, the woman looked down at the tablets thoughtfully. Adam slowly approached the table and the slates, and finally sat back in his chair.

"What are you thinking of, Paola Katarina?" he asked. The woman looked at the young man and said, "I believe you carry that special soul." Adam nearly choked hearing Paola Katarina's words, but she went on, "You yourself said you decided to leave on a quest after the solution to the evil that swallowed our world, and here you have an opportunity. The tablets speak of the priest guarding the ancient libraries, where the book of light is kept, the book that can be opened only by the pure-hearted man, who's true and pure intentions are to save our world from devastation."

Paola Katarina sensed she now has Adam's full attention, so she carried on: "Look, Adam, I may not know everything, but I know this: the tablets indicate the location of the solution for the negativity in this world, and you are the right man for this quest."

These last words echoed in Adam's mind, and he felt suddenly as if he was going back in time to the rocky cliff on the horrible day of the massacre in the Battery-Nile village: he sees in front of him the kind and dear Peter and Dorina. He sees the orphanage home burning, he sees how through his courage, faith, and thirst for justice, he manages to blow up a fearsome empire hovercraft; he feels a strange sensation travel through his entire body. The blood runs hot through his veins as he remembers that evening when he considered his will to change the world, how the wind blew strongly that night, as if telling him to go on with the voyage, he remembers how he decided at that moment that he would carry on despite everything. Paola Katarina's words were so powerful they penetrated the depth of

Adam's thoughts, reawakening his faith and his will to carry through his wishes. He touched the stone tables, his fingers caressed the narrow cracks, and he felt that material was not from this Earth. He never saw a stone of this kind his entire life; this just reinforced his conviction. He looked at the woman and smiled at her. "I'd like to thank you for all you told me. Sometimes I doubt myself and the decision to leave on this journey to find a final answer for our world. Occasionally, I lose faith that there is a hope for a world without evil," said Adam. Paola Katarina took his hand gently and said, "I know if you wish with all your heart to succeed in this journey that you will indeed succeed, I know it won't be easy but your will shall declare victory, so I believe. It's late, Adam, we should go to sleep now. Tomorrow we can continue examining how to proceed with the journey to fulfill your resolve, a resolve uniquely connected to all our lives."

The woman rose from her seat and showed Adam a bed in the corner of the room. Adam felt he would like to continue talking to her of his journey, where it may lead. He wanted to tell her that he was thrilled to know he may be that special person to bring an end to the enslavement of humanity, but in some peculiar way, he could see in her face that she knew, as if she read his thoughts, and she understands, yet she said nothing until she led him to the bed. Then she smiled at him and said quietly, "Don't worry, tomorrow we will have time to discuss everything. Now sleep, gather your strength for the road ahead of you. Good night Adam." She left Adam and turned to another room.

He sat on the bed, testing the softness of the covers, and said, "Paola Katarina, good night… and thank you."

Chapter Thirty-Five

This is a strange dream, thought Adam to himself. *I feel as if I'm awake yet I know that I'm sleeping and dreaming. How do I feel this way?* Adam sensed himself standing on a high cliff, the sky around him dense with clouds. It seemed a storm was imminent. His heart whispered ill omens. He wanted to wake up but the dream held him captive; suddenly he heard strange voices, which from moment to moment sounded more and more like weeping. He looked up, into the eye of the looming storm, and to his surprise, he spotted two figures. He strains his eyes and recognizes the figures; it's Joshua and Heralda. Their faces are fallen and stamped with pain, Adam calls their names but they don't hear him; suddenly he feels how far he is from them, he yells and yells, but the more he yells the sense of detachment grows, he sees Heralda crying, her showing despair, while Joshua is speaking to her, Adam hears every word.

"Don't worry, sweet Heralda, Adam will save us, he won't forget us." The words from the old man's mouth echoed in Adam's mind; he felt a terrible helplessness and frustration at his own powerlessness. There he was, safe on the hidden island among friends, while Joshua and Heralda were suffering terribly in a work camp not far from there.

Adam began shouting to them, "I will save you! I'll save you!"

Paola Katarina came running quickly from her room, and before he spoke she said immediately, "Relax, Adam, it was just a bad dream, just a dream."

Adam caught his breath and said to her, "No, it wasn't just a bad dream. Joshua and Heralda, they need me, I must save them."

She gently laid him back in the bed and said, "This dream was created in your own sub-conscience, your soul is pure, it wants only to help, that's why it's restless when your dear friends suffer. Your eyes say everything, the eyes are windows to the soul, and you can see everything through them. Now you must rest. There's a long road ahead of you, and tomorrow when the sun shines we can see things clearer." Adam rose from the bed again, saying, "But they showed up in my dream, they're expecting me to come save them…"

"I know," replied Paola Katarina softly. "Their hopes and dreams reach the center of the universe, where they reach whom they should reach. They believe in you very much, Adam, and so do I, now you should believe in yourself and in your decision to find a solution. God helps those who help themselves, just as problems exist, solutions exist for everyone, one only needs to want to find them." The woman served him a glass of cold water. "Drink, Adam, and calm down. Lay back and rest without dreams this time, so you can really sleep and gather your strength for tomorrow."

Adam did not reply, but in his mind, an idea began forming to leave and save Joshua and Heralda from the work camp in Sardinia. He said nothing of it to the woman but she looked at him and sensed something, yet she sensed nothing.

She kissed his forehead gently, and he replied with a smile and then closed his eyes. The decision to leave and save his friends made him calmer and he fell asleep immediately. Paola Katarina stepped out of the cabin and gazed at the dark sea laying in front of her abode, then said, "Oh, God, creator of the world, higher force of nature. If Adam is the man carrying that special soul, please help him fulfill his destiny, that is linked to every living creature on Earth." She completed the sentence and went back inside.

Dawn broke, the sun lit up the new day, the people of the island of Esperanza left their cabins with a smile on their faces, being among the few free people on Earth, some of them went out fishing while some joined the crew of the *Oracle* to help them finish repairing the ship. Bright sunrays burst through Paola Katarina's cabin window. The wooden table was already laid out with a jug of fresh milk, goat cheese, and a freshly baked loaf of bread. This mixture of aromas woke Adam up; he washed his face and came to the table. On the rim of an old couch rested the seven tablets of hope. Adam stared at them for a few seconds and thought to himself, "I will continue my journey, this is a sign showing that a solution exists, hope exists, but first I must save Joshua and Heralda, I have to."

Paola Katarina returned from the kitchen carrying a warm omelet. The two sat and ate silently. When Adam finished he couldn't hold it back anymore, he wanted to tell Paola Katarina that he now goes to save Joshua and Heralda, but before he opened his mouth, Paola Katarina read his mind and said, "I know, Adam."

Adam's eyes grew wide and he asked himself, "What is she talking about?"

The woman carried on. "I know you want to go and save your friends, I read your thoughts. I'm sorry, I've been doing this since I was a child, I apologize for invading your mind. Please forgive me." Adam didn't reply so the woman continued, "You must understand, Adam, that it's very dangerous for you right now. This morning, rumors arrived from the underground that an army of mercenaries have left on a hunt, and you are the hunted, Adam."

Adam's heart began pounding fast and hard, he felt a hard pressure in his chest, nearly suffocating him. "What will I do?" he asked, the anxiety showing on his face. The woman drew an odd powder from her pocket, which she mixed into the glass of milk and handed to Adam. Adam cooperated, and to his surprise, he felt within moments that he was calming down; his heart's pace returned to normal and his breathing came easier.

When Paola Katarina saw that Adam was calmer, she resumed speaking, "Adam dear, don't worry. Everything its on time, you will save your friends yet, but now you must leave for the continent of Africa and find the ancient libraries and the old priest. You must find the book of light and open it, to know and learn of Gim Nigma. What is it? And where is it?" Adam insisted. "The dream was so real, I felt their pain—they need me! I must go to them! We must do something!"

Paola Katarina left the cabin, leaving Adam behind her so he could calm down. She understood that it's a dead end, trying to convince someone who already made up his mind. She turned to a group of sailors on the shore, who were pulling thick ropes, working to finish the repairs on the *Oracle*. She asked them for the location of the captain and they pointed her in the direction of the nearby forest. Her feet paced quickly over green patches of vegetation. She knew that time was short and Adam's quest after the solution was first priority. Her heart was full of apprehension since she understood the young man was determined to save Joshua and Heralda from the claws of the empire even with the terrible danger of the hunters chasing after him.

A few minutes later, she saw Captain Nelson and Simon standing in a clearing, examining weapons smuggled in by the men of the New Dawn Hawks. Simon noticed the woman and approached her. "Good morning, dear." The man kissed Paola Katarina's tanned hand. Captain Nelson came near them also. "So what did you discover? Do you think Adam is the man?"

The woman did not answer at once; she looked down for a few moments and when she lifted her head, she answered, "Yes, I believe he is the pure hearted man that will go on the journey to save life on Earth." The faces of the two men showed both excitement and astonishment. They smiled at each other, but the woman continued speaking and cut their joy short. "His heart is so sensitive, the man cares so much, that he wants to leave now to save his friends, who are in the work camp on the shores of Sardinia," she finished quickly.

"What!" the captain yelled, and Simon continued after him. "He has a pure heart, but also a crazy head! Didn't you tell him of the army of head hunters after him to kill him?"

Paola Katarina told them of all that passed in the special conversation between her and Adam, and she told them she warned him of the dangers and asked him to wait with the matter of saving his friends. The captain of the *Oracle* turned around suddenly, hearing a suspicious noise in the nearby bushes, his hand on the laser gun that was hanging from his belt. "Who's there?" shouted Captain Nelson in the direction of the bushes, and immediately a voice called back, "Don't shoot, Captain, it's me, Jeremiah," and he stepped out of the bushes, panting.

"What the hell is the matter with you, lad?" the captain asked his sailor.

Jeremiah tried to answer breathlessly, "Sir... Adam... He..."

The captain lost his patience and urged the young sailor on, "Adam? What of him? Something happened to him?" Jeremiah calmed down a tad and managed to answer, "He took one of our boats, and he was heading to Sardinia!" Simon's roar broke the forest's peace. "Damn. This boy is mad!"

"His heart gave him no peace, like I said before, he cares so much he would risk his life for others, that is his destiny," said Paola Katarina to everyone, and Nelson cut her short. "His destiny is not to die by the hands of the empire," said angrily and went on, "We must stop him, on to the *Oracle*!" As he finished speaking, the four were already running toward the shore. As they drew near, they already noticed people standing on the water line, calling Adam's name, yelling for him to come back because it's dangerous, but all for nothing.

Adam was locked on his goal to set his friends free; he would not abandon them in the hands of evil forces, his muscular arms pulled on the wooden oars and rowed vigorously toward the large island laying ahead... Sardinia, he doesn't even know exactly where they are, but he keeps on tirelessly rowing. He hears Captain Nelson's voice ring in the air, calling him back to Esperanza, and as he rows, he cried back to the people on the shore. "I must save them, Captain, I have to!"

Simon signaled everyone to stop trying to shout at the figure quickly disappearing into the blue horizon. He turned to his friend, captain of the *Oracle*. "Well, old friend, your man is certainly stubborn. He's just making the work of the hunters easier," Simon remarked.

Nelson rubbed his white beard and said, "We must go after him and help him. If he is willing to risk his life for us and for others, we should be brave enough to help him help us."

Paola Katarina drew near the captain and said, "Now we all understand, that this man is a beacon, trying—be that intentionally or unintentionally—to light the road for us and guide us to an enlightened life." All present felt, in that unique moment, a sensation of a concentrated heat in their chests. United by this common feeling, they all agreed unanimously to go after Adam, and together they called, "We will come to his aid!"

Chapter Thirty-Six

After an hour of rowing, Adam's little dinghy approached the shores of Sardinia. He could see from afar the watchtowers overlooking the work camp; he knew there was only one such camp on Sardinia. He looked around him, the sky was clear of clouds, the sun was shining brightly, and besides the murmur of the waves, not a sound was heard. Adam surveyed his surroundings and saw only the blue of sea and sky. A moment of silent peace, and as he was savoring the beauty of this untamed nature, a sudden deafening wail of a siren sounded, nearly knocking Adam unconscious with the terrible force of the sound, it came from two black ships, heavily loaded with deadly weapons. Those were empire coast guard ships, blocking Adam from all directions. Adam didn't know where to turn; he had no weapons, no manner of communication to ask for help, he found himself helpless, unable to do anything but pray. One of the ships shot a blast of bullets nearly shattering Adam's wooden boat; the shots were followed immediately by a screechy voice emanating from the ship's speakers. "Hey, you there, you are under arrest by empire forces, we warn you—one false move and we won't hesitate to shoot you down!"

In one moment, the peace and quiet were crushed by the realm of evil. Adam understood he was trapped. He felt fear choking him, for the first time in his life, the empire had him, and now that he was known and wanted by the empire, he knew that his life was in grave danger. He said nothing, but whispered a quiet prayer, "God, protect me from evil, please." He repeated again and again, "Please, God, protect me." One of the soldiers stepped out of his vessel and came close to Adam's boat: he gazed at the figure sitting motionlessly in a wooden boat, and was astounded to discover no other than the mystery man the entire empire was after.

The soldier immediately transmitted the information to his entire crew, who came out of their vessel gloating and booing at Adam. They were all happy for the capture of the mystery man; they mockingly thanked him for the millions they would receive in prize money thanks to him. Within seconds, the entire Sardinia base heard the news: the mystery man was captured by a marine patrol unit, very close to the base itself. The incredible tidings were immediately passed on to the top leaders: the moment Drakkar heard of it he ordered the administration's entourage to prepare for departure to Sardinia, where they would execute the mystery man to the eyes of the entire world.

The empire soldiers beat Adam, tied his hands, and led him to the work camp on the Sardinia shore. He could never imagine to himself that for choosing to save someone, for doing the right thing, he would be publicly executed. Sadness flooded his heart. His body ached from the thrashing of the empire soldiers, but he quietly whispered through clenched teeth. "Too many special things happened in my life for me to lose hope now. As hard as it is, I won't lose hope." Again, he repeated his silent prayer, "Please, God, help me get out of this." He was thrown into a narrow, dark cell, with no food or water.

One soldier came near the door of the cell and said contemptuously. "This is the mystery man? Only a miserable, stupid man, who practically handed himself over to the empire."

Adam gazed with his hawk eyes directly into the laughing soldier's eyes, and said, "As long there is life in my body, I know there is hope." The soldier's laughter awkwardly died in his throat, with a forced snicker he said, "Hope? What hope are you talking about?

Did you think you could confront such an enormous empire and save all its slaves? In a few days, you will be executed, and the slaves will slave on forever." The soldier left and Adam remained alone, his body scratched and bruised, the thirst and hunger torturing him, but he forced himself to concentrate on Joshua's words, who once told him never to lose hope, so he began focusing on positive thoughts.

Outside the base laid the empire's work camp, which they enslaved people in the mines, to mine and supply energy for the empire. The sun hung in the center of the sky, a remarkable heat weighed down the air; the slaves were sweating profusely and feeling very weary. Joshua and Heralda looked over each other from afar, when suddenly an announcer called out to all slaves, "Hark! Your Mystery man was captured, and tomorrow he will be executed for the entire world's eyes, for all to see how a man who goes against the rule of the empire is punished!" the announcer finished his proclamation. A great shock appeared on all the slave's faces, they stared at each other unbelievingly.

Heralda was stunned; she simply couldn't believe what her ears heard. As the turmoil among the slaves whispering to each other grew, Heralda moved closer to Joshua and before she could speak Joshua smiled at her. "He came to save us, Heralda, he came for us," said the old man, his eyes gleaming. Heralda didn't understand his words but she saw his old eyes fill with tears of hope. "He's here, Heralda." Continued the old man, "I knew he was special."

Heralda thought the old man must be hallucinating; she left Joshua and stopped one of the people who ran by them. "Is it true?" she asked. The man stopped in his tracks and answered, "Rumors are that the mystery man was captured nearby. Nobody understands what he was doing here." He finished the sentence and ran back to his work post, fearing to be punished with the whip. Heralda realized that Adam was truly captured. She felt all her hopes fade away; the announcer declared the execution would be tomorrow at high noon.

"Could it be?" the young woman asked herself. "Could it be that this is how it all ends? That all the hope Adam brought to all these people will disappear with his death?" She looked at the sky and with trembling lips and tears running down her soot covered face and said, "Dear God, all my life I believed there was hope for people to overcome this evil, as long as there is a spark of goodness that still exists in man. But now the only man who dared challenge the forces of evil is about to be sleighed by their hands, to the eyes of all. Please, God, spare his life, allow him to fulfill his destiny."

She lowered her head and her curls fell over her face. She sunk into bitter sobbing. The crack of a whip on her back brought her back to the harsh reality. She cried out in pain, and her cry carried far, echoing through Adam's narrow cell, who called, "Heralda, I'm here, I'm here!" Adam was filled with rage; he strained to break his bonds, uselessly. His cell darkened and he understood night was falling outside. The darker it got, the more he doubted his quest to save the world. He laughed at himself with pain, mocking himself as tears of pain filled his eyes. "Who am I anyway? I'm only another simple man, another victim to the happenings."

Suddenly his eyes fell on the wall to his left, on the only space in the cell that still held some light, where to his surprise he saw a tiny ant, holding in her chops a crumb of dry bread. He focused all his attention on the tiny creature's efforts, trying to climb the wall while hauling a crumb ten times its own size in its mouth. He saw her slip, fall, and climb up again, fall and climb up again, time after time. This tiny being and its amazing determination deeply moved Adam; even though she fell down time and time again, the ant kept gathering up her crumb and relentlessly attempted the wall again. For a moment, Adam considered assisting the ant, but then, oddly, he decided to just pray quietly for its success. Long moments passed, but indeed after a few more failed experiments the ant managed to make her way up the wall, the scrap clasped in her teeth. *She made it*, Adam thought to himself, she managed to climb and defeat that wall, even with all the hardships she didn't give up. The ant completed the steep climb along the wall and strolled through the narrow window out to freedom, carrying her reward with her. A shiver passed through Adam's entire body, and he thought to himself, "How is it that I, a human, much bigger and smarter then the ant, doubt my own abilities? How is it that I despair? If that little ant can make it, so can I." he began to repeat to himself out loud this forceful sentence, "As hard as it is, I will make it anyway! As hard as it is, I will make it anyway!" Outside his cell stood two guards, hearing Adam they laughed and mocked him, but within the cell, Adam no longer heard anything except his own voice, "As hard as it is, I will make it anyway!"

Suddenly on the windowsill appeared a butterfly, its wings glossy in the moonlight. Adam looked at the butterfly and remembered his mother once told him that a butterfly is a sign of good luck. He smiled at the being that kept him company and went on loudly repeating, "As hard as it is, I will make it anyway!" Within a minute, Adam noticed a shadow of a figure pass across his window, he was startled for a moment but was immediately soothed by a familiar, dearly loved voice, "Adam, my dear, how did you get here?" Heralda's pretty face emerged in the narrow, barred window of the cell Adam was sitting in. Thrilled, Adam's eyes shined in the moonlight.

"Heralda!" he called. "Be carful, don't let the guards discover you." Heralda wiggled her fingers through the bars and touched Adam's bruised face, as tears came tumbling down her face "What did you do to yourself Adam? Why did you come back here?" Savoring the touch of the beautiful girl's fingers, Adam said, "I came for you and for Joshua, I came to save you, I couldn't move on knowing that you were here, suffering."

Heralda's large eyes kept filling up with tears; she couldn't believe how special Adam was, how much he cared for her and old Joshua. She thanked him, kissed one finger, and then touched it to his face.

Adam felt warmth and hope from this simple human contact, he saw the helplessness in the young woman's expression, but he gazed at her with a determined look she did not expect at all, and told her, "Have no fear, Heralda, because I'm not despairing one bit." Heralda was a little amazed that with everything Adam wasn't giving up, she felt she had to ask him, "Adam, tomorrow they are going to execute you. How is it that you're not even scared?"

The man looked at her with his hawk eyes, glittering sharply in the moonlight and said, "As long as there's a breath of life in my body, I won't despair and I won't lose hope." He sealed his words with a wink, and felt a little encouraged just by the fact Heralda sneaked up to see him. They suddenly heard voices of approaching soldiers. Adam asked Heralda to leave so she won't get caught, she wished to stay a moment longer but he insisted, and before she went back to the slaves' quarters Adam told her, "Tell Joshua that Adam said to think positive, always."

She wiped the tears off her cheeks, parted with Adam, and promised him to pray for a miracle the entire night. After bidding her good-bye, the caged man went back to his intonation with even more determination, "As hard as it is, I will make it anyway!" Heralda reached the lodgings and discovered Joshua sitting in a special meditation pose. She told him what Adam asked her to tell; the old man burst into laughter and said, "Adam already learned something very important, and now he is giving this lesson back to me for my own good." The old man asked Heralda to sit with him and meditate for Adam's rescue. The other people glanced curiously at the two but did not interfere; some turned their eyes to the moon with a short plea, a mix of hope and despair. "Dear God, protect the mystery man."

The entourage of empire men landed, and the four leaders couldn't disguise their eagerness to get a close look at the man who slighted their fearsome empire. The four were impatient to see him killed in front of their eyes. The base commander of the work camp informed them that all the preparations for the execution tomorrow afternoon were already completed. The empire's leadership turned to drinking and celebrating their impeding victory over the freedom fighters, whose great hope was about to be executed.

The night brought silence with it, and from all the slaves' lodgings rose the prayers for the mystery man, who was willing to sacrifice his life to save his friends and all the slaves. The good wind carried the slaves' prayers high into the depths of the sky.

Chapter Thirty-Seven

Dawn broke over the Sardinia work camp. Red tinted clouds filled the sky, decorating the horizon of this fateful day for Adam Swandon, who was sitting in his cell, still praying. He hadn't received any food or water, exhaustion was taking over him, and he felt his strength ebb, but still he stubbornly repeated, "As hard as it is, I will make it anyway." The call of a rooster woke the slaves. They were in for a momentous and rare occasion. They would not work today, since at noon, the mystery man whom in which they found hope of salvation and freedom will be executed. He was to be executed before the eyes of the entire world, before the eyes of those who wished for a savior, for hope.

Today, the leader of the fearsome empire will prove to the world that he is the only ruler. Drakkar arranged for the satellite media to cover it all, broadcast to every corner of the world, as to break the hope of every underground member and freedom fighter, who believed Adam was the man that would save them from oblivion. Heralda woke up with her hands shaking. Joshua noticed this and he took her hands in his and calmed her. "Don't worry, child, you mustn't lose hope, no matter what's happening." Heralda couldn't understand how Joshua was remaining so positive even though in a few hours Adam would be brought to the gallows, but she said nothing of it, she listened to the announcer calling, "Today, by high noon, the mystery man who slighted the empire will be executed.

All slaves are invited to observe the death of their hope for freedom." The announcer concluded his words with a short, rolling laughter.

In the center of a hastily constructed arena on the beautiful shore of Sardinia, not far from the empire's work camp, stood a heavy-built empire soldier, the upper half of his face covered by a black mask, and a diabolical smile on his face. He will be the man to kill Adam Swandon with a swing of his huge ax, as customary in rebel executions around the world. He stood by a brown, wooden platform, covered with dry blood of former human sacrifices, killed long ago. He raised the huge ax with his massive arms, and with one arm slammed down the sharp tool and split another fissure in the thick wooden floor. He thought to himself that the mystery man hasn't the thinnest chance to escape him or his ax alive.

Free from work, in the hours remaining until the execution of Adam Swandon, Joshua and Heralda passed from shack to shack, asking the people to pray for the well-being of the mystery man. Many of them consented, and those tired, exhausted and emaciated people dropped to their knees and turned to the heavens in a prayer to the infinite force, to the God that created life, freedom, and goodness; they did the thing they hadn't done for themselves for years, they prayed for hope, and tears filled their eyes when they understood there was one special person who thought that they all deserved a good life, filled with freedom, honor, and values—one man that chose to risk his life to save them from the terror rule of the empire. The empire soldiers watched their actions and burst in peals of loud laughter, mocking the people on their knees during their last prayer for a shred of hope.

A group of armed soldiers secured the passage of the leader's entourage to their chairs. A crowd of soldiers and empire staff settled into their seats, arranged in a semi-circle. Two soldiers were dragging Adam, who could barely walk; his eyes, brimming with tears, were turned to the heavens as he asked the good Lord for his help. He was led to the wooden gallows, toward the fearsome soldier holding a large ax. He looked around him and saw laughing soldiers, and an area fenced with barbed wire, where the slaves were gathered, all looking painfully at the mystery man. Adam's arms were still tied. After a short, shrill siren call, Drakkar rose from his seat, looking down at Adam, who looked directly back at him with his hawk eyes. The empire leader raised his hands, commanding silence, and then silent it was. He turned toward Adam and called, "All of you, see what happens to this man who dared slight my empire. This is a warning to all puny freedom fighters around the world who dare try and release my slaves."

Drakkar's eyes swept over his peers, who replied with a smile of agreement. Heralda and Joshua followed the happenings from behind the barbed fence, as did the rest of the slaves. Suddenly, without a warning, Adam cried out to Drakkar, "And who do you think you are, holding free men as slaves? We are all sons of freedom. We all have the right of a free life, a life with honor." A loud silence fell over the entire crowd at the words Adam spoke. A fury rose in the empire's leader, his face turned crimson with anger, "How dare you open your mouth in front of me? I am the supreme ruler of the entire world, and you are about to die before the eyes of everyone, so they may see what their prayers and hopes deliver them." Drakkar shouted, the anger holding him turned into a loud, nervous laughter, "Who are you, lowly and paltry man, to dare challenge my glorious dominion?"

Adam took a step forward, looking at all the audience around him, and suddenly he felt a surge of power, a strange energy filling him, and he called out, "You are not the lord of the world, the creator is the Lord of the entire universe, he created every man and animal for freedom, and no human has a right to contaminate this great thing called freedom! God is the Lord of this world, not man. That is my belief, and it will always remain my belief!"

The crowd of both soldiers and slaves were mesmerized, following this charged exchange between the leader of the empire and the mystery man, Adam Swandon. Drakkar was furious again, but he tried to disguise this with a false smile when his friends looked at him. Bamark called out to his peer that the impudent man should be whipped; the slaves in the crowd began shouting in protest, Joshua remained silent, his eyes were shut. Heralda saw how the old man continued to pray silently and joined him herself, in the midst of the shouting and yelling of the slaves she and Joshua continued praying relentlessly. The soldier raised the whip in his heavy arm and brought it down on Adam's back. Every cry of pain was followed by a gloating burst of laughter from the empire soldiers and leaders, and in between came the calls of the slaves, begging again and again to stop the beating. Drakkar called out to the huge soldier, sweating from the task of whipping, "Enough! It's time to finish this, terminate him!" The huge soldier smiled a cruel smile under his black mask. He placed Adam, slashed and sore from the whip, with his head laid against the wooden platform. Heralda's large, pretty eyes grew wide with terror; she turned to Joshua, but he paid her no heed, his eyes were still shut and tears squeezed through the shut lids as his lips continued to mouth a prayer.

Adam felt terrible. He couldn't believe it would all end like this. The empire's crowd whistled and called out to the soldier to behead Adam. Suddenly Adam gazed with his hawk eyes directly into the eyes of the empire's leader, who froze in his tracks. Adam whispered wrathfully, "If I die now I die, but until then I will fight and I will win." He closed his eyes, waiting for the swing of the ax.

Drakkar shouted to the soldier to complete the job, the soldier raised his arms, about to bring the ax down, and at that moment Joshua opened his eyes wide and called to Heralda, "Now is the time, look Heralda!" As he spoke, the shriek of a laser shot sliced the arm of the soldier holding the ax. A great battle cry rose, "Go on friends!

Fight brave!" Adam lifted his head and saw the beautiful sails of the *Oracle* and all its armed crew, running toward the arena, shooting in all directions while pushing forward forcefully; at the same time the *Oracle* kept bombarding the stunned empire soldiers from the sea, practically demolishing the large arena. Around the *Oracle* zipped four jet-fueled engine boats under Simon's command, ceaselessly shooting laser blasts. Captain Damtry Nelson yelled the battle cry. Adam smiled with emotion, understanding they all came to save him and the slaves in the camp. Nelson ran to Adam as the maimed, one-armed soldier raised a weapon to kill him; Nelson drew his silver blade from its sheath and raised it high, and with one swing, he beheaded the soldier about to kill Adam, calling, "You will not harm the son of light!" The stunned empire soldiers retreated while shooting back at the bold men of the *Oracle*. The leader's entourage was flabbergasted; the royal guard swiftly led the four leaders into an armored hovercraft that took off immediately. Within a few moments, five black hovercrafts rose to the sky and began shooting at the sailors of the *Oracle*, who made special maneuvers to avoid being hit. Adam noticed the large ax lying on the ground, the same ax that moments ago was supposed to bring his life to an end, but that's not how it happened. That is not how God intended it. This ax will serve Adam in breaking the bonds of slavery holding down free men. In the midst of all the yelling and the shooting Adam rose slowly to his feet, the great ax in his hands, and began walking heavily toward the barbed wire enclosure holding the slaves. He lifted the ax high, and with a cry of pain from the whip and the hunger, brought the ax down on the heavy chains and shattered them. The gates of the fenced encampment flew open, and through them the slaves burst out, now free men and women. They ran out and the *Oracle* men led them toward the fast jet boats that would carry them to the large sail-boat. Tears rose in Adam's eyes. He felt immense happiness but his body was weak, exhausted from the hunger and the beatings, he felt dizzy; he looked around him and saw men and women running with all their might toward the blue sailed ship, everything became blurry, and in one moment Adam Swandon collapsed to the ground.

Seeing this, Captain Nelson was startled; he ran quickly to Adam, lying unconscious on the ground, Jeremiah joined his commander and they both examined Adam quickly. Captain Nelson sighed with relief: "He is alive, thank God—he just fainted." Jeremiah exhaled with relief and happiness, and sheltered the unconscious Adam so he wouldn't be hit by a stray shot.

Two figures carefully drew near Adam, the captain of the *Oracle* and the young sailor. It was Old Joshua and Heralda. They called out Adam's name and were increasingly worried when he didn't answer them. Jeremiah calmed the two, telling them Adam merely fainted from exhaustion. Nelson took hold of one of Adam's arms, Jeremiah took the other; they rose and took Adam with them. The captain spoke to all in a commanding voice, "We have to move out of here quickly, the element of surprise has lost its affect and the deadly empire hovercrafts are an immediate threat. Make haste."

Joshua nodded in agreement to the words of his old friend, but before moving on, he drew near Adam's limp face, rubbed his palms together for a few seconds, and laid them immediately on Adam's cheeks; to everyone's surprise, Adam awoke at once and gazed at Joshua, who stood in front of him, smiling. "Joshua, are you all right?" whispered Adam, his face lit with joy, and the old man replied, "Yes, my son, I'm fine, we are all fine, thanks to God almighty and thanks to you, thanks to that special fighting spirit of yours." Is made all of this happen, the strength of your spirit, your will to help and save others has influenced all these people to do just so. Because of your deep caring they care for you also, and they followed you here to save us all." Everyone was overcome by emotion, Heralda's little chin quivered and tears formed in the corners of her beautiful eyes; only Nelson remained attentive to the hostile surroundings. Adam tried to answer, but his strength left him and he fainted again, falling back into Captain Nelson's and young Jeremiah's faithful arms. The voice of the captain echoed sternly in the air, "We must leave, now!" He noticed the small figure of his friend Simon waving his arms in the air, pointing Nelson's gaze toward the black hovercraft closing in on the captain's group.

The black vessel began shooting orange laser blasts at them. The veteran captain signaled Simon with a nod that he grasped what was happening, and at once ordered Jeremiah to assist him in carrying Adam to Simon, who was waiting on the last jet boat. All the other slaves were already swiftly boarding the *Oracle*, which continued to blast the black, threatening empire hovercrafts with grenades and laser beams. Heralda pulled a pair of pistols off the belt of a dead empire soldier, passed one of them to old Joshua, and the two began advancing as they shot at the threatening hovercraft, thus covering the captain and Jeremiah as they quickly carried Adam toward the shore. The hovercraft commander cursed his soldiers for failing to hit Heralda and Joshua or maneuver through their shots. He himself took hold of the manual machine gun, armed with old style bullets from the past century. A malicious smile grew on his face when he gets pretty Heralda in his sight, and with a wicked pleasure, he squeezes the trigger.

From the barrel of the machine gun that extrudes out of the bulk of the hovercraft, a stream of deadly bullets pours out and quickly hits the ground, reaching the figure of Heralda, and one bullet pierces young Heralda's abdomen. She lets out a short cry of pain, then her delicate form falls and hits the ground. Joshua sees this, his old eyes fly wide open and a cry breaks from his mouth, "Heralda!"

Jeremiah and the captain hadn't noticed yet what happened; they were busy carrying Adam to the jet boat. Joshua focused all his strength in one hand that rose with abnormal speed up in the air, then came down and hovered over the bullet wound; he began mumbling, "The bleeding will stop right now!" Again and again, he repeated, "The bleeding will stop right now!"

Tears filled Heralda's eyes; she sobbed without a sound, the bullet penetrated her body, and as she cried in pain the beautiful Heralda looked into Joshua's worried eyes and spoke, "Joshua, I feel the life leaving my body, I can no longer see the open sky."

Joshua's heart clenched with deep pain, his hand pressed down on the bleeding wound and again he repeated, "Right now, the bleeding will stop!" He whispered in Heralda's ear, "Close your eyes, dear, let the positive force of the universe pull you back into life, you remember what I once told you, you must never give up." Even through the bitter pain, Heralda heard Joshua's words and shut her eyes. The flow of blood ebbed, the wound stopped bleeding. Joshua felt encouraged by this, but knew her life was still in danger.

Once Adam was laid in the boat, Simon jumped off it, holding in his hands a deadly grenade launcher. He stared directly at the approaching hovercraft, drawing dangerously near Heralda and Joshua, who were lying helpless on the ground. Simon aimed the barrel of the launcher at the front of the rapidly approaching hovercraft. The eyes of the hovercraft commander picked up the figure of Simon; he nervously squeezed the trigger of his machine gun. Trails of bullets hit the ground but before they reached Simon, he himself squeezed the trigger of the launcher, releasing one deadly accurate grenade. It trailed along tail of fire in the sky and left only a cloud of debris where just a moment ago was the hovercraft about to end Heralda and Joshua's life. Simon made his way to Joshua and helped him carry the wounded woman to the boat, where she was laid by Adam's side, both of them unconscious.

Simon took hold of the boat's steering wheel and with jet speed turned it to the large sailboat that was already drifting far from the smoky shores of what was not long ago a slave encampment. The remaining empire hovercrafts decided to withdraw, having reached the conclusion that the freedom fighters already won this battle. Not one of them expected such fierceness and bravery from the underground. The deck of the blue sailed ship was crowded now with three hundred and forty seven men and women who could not believe they were now free. The crew of the *Oracle* handed them food and medicine, but everyone was anxious for the well-being of Adam and Heralda.

Joshua promised them all he would do his best for them and went to small room in the hull of the ship where Heralda laid, still unconscious. The old man sat by the silent form of the young woman, only two hours passed since their escape from the slave camp and now Heralda's life was in danger. Joshua shut his eyes and began praying for her. The captain of the *Oracle* asked all the people on the ship to join in a true, strong prayer for the two, and they all said yes, with great emotion and passion. Some began crying tears of gratitude to the creator and the few that sacrificed their life to save them. One of the sailors approached the captain with a casualty list of the *Oracle*'s crew, the captain poured over the list for a long moment; eleven men lost their life to protect their faith, which is true freedom for all. The sailor noticed the gleam of tears in the captain's right eye as he requested to prepare the bodies of his friends for a respectable and noble burial when they reach Esperanza.

Chapter Thirty-Eight

The ocean waves were slices in two opposing directions as the *Oracle* sailed on through hostile waters. She was now the main target on the empire's sights. Every headhunter knows that the name of the mystery man is Adam Swandon, and that he's on board this large sailboat. The ship's doctor made frequent visits to the wounded. The crewmen were recuperating quickly, to Nelson and Simon's great joy, who were thanking the Lord for their friends' quick recovery. The bodies of the other sailors, killed in the great battle to free Adam and the slaves, were wrapped in soft white fabrics, and over it was placed a peach colored cloth on which words were embroidered: "With hope, with faith and with courage the maker has blessed thy."

Adam was lying alone in a dark room, on a damp wooden bed. The ship was swaying from side to side; Adam's eyes were tightly shut, his face sweating, his eyebrows frowning, his face hardened. He is dreaming something that makes his blood boil, he sees Heralda's figure falling into an abyss as he stands and watches her from the edge of the cliff; in a heartbeat, he decides to jump after her, even though he knows he himself will smash at the bottom of the abyss, but as he comes closer to the falling figure of Heralda, a strong, blue light envelopes them, his hand grasps hers and they are halted in midair, as if gravity does not exist. She smiles at him and he replies with a smile, her lips do not move but he hears her voice in his mind, thanking him for trying to save her, but she is dying. She is about to return her soul to its maker. Adam opens his mouth and answers that it is not so, but Heralda lets go of him and continues to fall. At that moment, Adam wakes, he rises quickly from his bed and calls out loudly, "Heralda! Heralda!" two stunned sailors watch him as he runs through the wooden hallway, crying the girl's name, "Heralda! Heralda!" His senses direct him to a small room deep in hull of the ship, the young girl's figure was lying silently on the bed, a few sailors stood by with grim expressions while old Joshua stood in the corner of the room and tears of sorrow were flowing from his elderly eyes. He did the best he could. It was useless; he was failing. Heralda's vital signs were fading fast.

Adam said nothing when he saw Joshua, but the old man's face showed joy at seeing the young man back on his feet, fully restored to life. Adam's expression was questioning, inquiring to the state of the young woman, and the old man nodded grimly, signaling all hope was lost; despite that Adam drew near Heralda, laying still on the gray sheets, he lifted her delicate palm, suddenly his eyes grew wide, the hair on his body rose, and he began breathing the air of the room heavily; to the astonishment of all around, Adam opened his mouth and his voice thundered through the room, "Heralda, hear me, you will not die for you will live!" His voice echoed through the entire hull of the ship, causing a crowd of sailors to come running to the room to watch what was happening. Over his hawk eyes Adam's eyebrows were lifted high, his muscles tensed, and his voice kept on echoing, "Heal yourself, Heralda, heal yourself. There is hope, there is a grain of battle spirit, you are stubborn. The maker brought you to life so that you may fulfill yourself, you have yet to complete your mission in this world. Rise and live, win with the help of the good maker, rise and live again!" A mysterious wind began to blow from through the open window in the room, tossing objects around, the people around stood unbelieving, dazed. At first they thought perhaps a storm was coming, but then, they noticed the ship wasn't moving. The old man stood perfectly still, silent. He just closed his eyes through all the excitement and mumbled a silent prayer. The wind blew harder and harder, the whistle of the gale sounded just like a shout. The sailors had to cover their eyes to protect them from the gale blowing harshly from the small window, then suddenly Heralda's eyes flew open and she cried out, "Where am I?"

Joshua and the sailors were overwhelmed with joy and wonder; everyone eyes were filled with tears and they called out their thanks to the good maker. All understood that this was a miracle from the almighty. They leaped with joy at the sight of the young woman back amongst them, alive.

Chapter Thirty-Nine

Ten empire soldiers in shiny black uniforms were standing in tense attention, weapons loaded and charged in their hands. They were guarding the entrance to the empire's meeting hall, and they could not disguise their dread of the terrible screams coming from inside the hall.

"It's a total disgrace!" yelled Bammark at everyone around him. His entire body moved restlessly, shook by anger. "How could this possibly happen?" continued the man with the long golden mane. Kraus, top commander of the Hovercraft fleet, answered coolly, "Calm down, sir. We must be practical and act now for this man's annihilation." Bammark stared with furious eyes at the tall and skinny Kraus, who froze on the spot. "Calm down you say, commander Kraus? How can we calm down when a daring rescue of this man takes place right under the empire's leaders' noses, and our mighty empire can do nothing to prevent it?"

Kraus gulped and remained silent, not answering his leader. Suddenly Drakkar opened his mouth and cried, "Silence!" In an instant, everyone around fell silent, and the man with the black curly beard carried on in a thunderous voice, "We will persist with our plan to capture this man, we will kill him, no one can stand in the empire's way, not the underground and not this miserable man the underground managed to rescue. Hundreds of bounty hunters have embarked on a chase after this man, and in the mean time, we will proceed to suffocate the populace even more. I plan to execute a wide scope idea, to build a unique army that will find and destroy the underground wherever it is. Until this plan is carried through, one of the many hunters will probably have brought us the head of this scoundrel who humiliated our great empire." He completed his sentence and Bammark jumped up with an expectant smile, "A plan, Drakkar? What plan? What army are you going to raise?"

Drakkar smiled malevolently and wrapped one arm around his partner in power. "I will tell you everything, but first come have a drink with me in my headquarters, and bring the others with you." They all fell silent at once, wordlessly exchanging curious glances, then they all followed Drakkar to his headquarters to hear of this mysterious plan.

Chapter Forty

Far out on the horizon the green trees of Esperanza, a shelter island for the underground freedom fighters, became visible. The *Oracle* was merely an hour away from shore, and the crew were looking forward to step on safe ground, to rest, relax, and also bury their dear friends, fallen in great battle on the Sardinian shore. Simon stood with his old friend, Captain Damtry Nelson, watching the two wooden boats slowly making their way to them, to escort the *Oracle* to a safe hidden docking place. The island men cheered with joy at seeing their friends return safely from the daring operation, that no one really believed will pass with such success. Simon, leader of the men of Esperanza, stepped on the safe ground of the Island and was filled with a warm joy. He thanked his maker for allowing him to go on a just crusade and return safe to the free people, living secretly on this little island. After him came some of the island men, who joined the *Oracle*'s crew in the struggle against the empire soldiers. The crewmen were also thrilled to touch solid ground. Only Captain Nelson stayed behind, watching all dismount his precious ship, caressing the wooden banister and smiling to the blue sails, slowly being lowered by two strong sailors. He thought in his heart how deeply he loved the *Oracle*, and how faithful she always was to him, and through all the adventures and all the storms and dangers, they were still together, one with each other. He admitted in his heart that the *Oracle* was his one true love, that he would feel lost without her, like a husband without his beloved wife. The hand caressing the banister now grasped it tightly, like a loving embrace; the captain wished he could receive some sign from the *Oracle* that she knows how much he loves her, and as he was thinking these things in his heart suddenly one of the ropes the sailors were tying came loose, and a part of the blue sail carried in the wind and was stopped by Nelson's body; the blue fabric wrapped itself around the thrilled captain, who took this as a divine signal that this ship is alive, and it's embracing him with love. The sailor handling the ropes was startled when the knot he tied somehow came loose, he ran to his Captain to apologize, but the captain replied with a warm smile, reassuring the sailor that all was well.

Many people gathered in a secluded strip of land, lined with large stones with names of man no longer alive carved in them. This was the Esperanza's cemetery, where the underground fighters, living in hiding, gave their final respects to their brothers in arms against the empire's rule of horror. The wounded were absent from the burial ceremony about to start. Adam stood by Captain Nelson, his eyes roaming over the people gathered there. He was thinking that if given the chance, he would prevent such things in the future. Groups of diggers opened wide holes in the ground. Here and there, muffled whimpers could be heard, of young women who lost their loved ones in the great battle to free Adam and the slaves. Bodies wrapped in peach colored cloth were lowered gently into the ground, and within a few short moments, the Earth that was just dug out from the ground was returned to it, with the addition of a body of a man who lived free and died for freedom. Simon read out loud to the people attending a few words written by Captain Nelson: "These great people died a worthy and triumphant death. They lived and fought for the spirit of freedom, and for it they died. There are many people living in the world, but only a few die fulfilling their destiny in this world. That is why the people whose bodies we bury today live on in a better place, because they were privileged enough to fight and to die for something they truly believe in. and to them, gentlemen, we salute."

The entire assembly, including Adam, lifted their heads and saluted with their right hand toward the fresh graves. Adam was filled with a fierce inspiration when he saw then a solemn, grave event such as this could become uplifting and inspiring. Within an hour, the assembly dispersed; everyone went back to their business, tending to the wounded and mainly preparing for a possible attack of the empire forces.

Within a few hours, the sun hung in the center of the sky, noon arrived. Inside Paola Katarina's fragrant cabin wounded Heralda laid on pleasantly soft sheets. The texture of her bedding was so different from the hard damp bunk she was confined to only a short time ago. She looked up from her bed and her large, pretty eyes saw flowers all around, and the perfume of Jasmines filled the wide room. In the corner stood Paola Katarina, who was toiling over a potion for Heralda. She sensed the young woman's gaze and turned to her, smiling. Despite the pain from her wound, the girl smiled back at her. The older woman approached her, holding an earthen bowl filled with something like foul smelling porridge.

"You were very lucky, dear," said Paola Katarina as she lifted the yellow sheets from Heralda's stomach, exposing the wound, and gently swathed it with a cloth soaked with the concoction she just made. Heralda squinted at the hot; stinging sensation the medicine left on her wound, but made no sound.

"I am Paola Katarina," said the smiling woman.

Heralda opened her mouth, meaning to introduce herself, but the woman continued, "You're Heralda, I know. It's all right, dear, I know enough about you." Heralda lightly lifted her head off the pillow. "I thank you for treating me. I heard you could tell the future, is that true?" asked Heralda. The woman smiled again. "Well, I do have a talent noticing things deep in people's souls," said Paola Katarina.

Heralda remained quiet for a long moment then decided to speak. "then you must know I…"

Before she completed her sentence Paola Katarina did, "That you love him?" The young woman blushed and answered with a smile, "Yes."

"Well, dear," said the woman, sitting on a wooden chair and moving closer to Heralda, "I'm sorry to have to tell you this darling, but Adam may not fall in love. His mind must be focused on his destiny." Paola Katarina noticed the questioning wrinkles form on Heralda's forehead and she hastened on. "Adam is not like most people we know. His soul is very ancient. I believe he is in the last cycle of his reincarnation, and his soul will not rest until it fulfills its destiny… And its destiny is quite different from the usual course human lives take. He feels he must save humanity from destroying itself. There is an ancient legend, telling of a special force buried in the Earth thousands of years ago by someone not from this world. This force is called Gim Nigma, which in the foreign language means 'the answer,' the solution for humanity's ancient condition."

Heralda looked at the woman with excited curiosity and asked, "What is humanity's ancient condition?" Paola Katarina looked into the youngster's large eyes. "Humanity's ancient condition is its destructive tendency. Humans don't understand or appreciate the kindness of their maker or the bounty the world has to offer every living creature, and the wonderful freedom of all living beings. They make negative choices when they could have been making positive ones, enriching their lives with prosperity and success. Until today human beings did not learn how to appreciate the good in their lives, and it's a fact that man created the nuclear weapon, thus bringing a disastrous threat on themselves—people have lost their freedom over their own stupidity," concluded Paola Katarina. Heralda bowed her head lightly and said, "You are so right. These are the things I learned from Joshua. I lost my family during the mayhem that followed the empire's rise to power, and Joshua adopted me then. Together, us and many more, try to eradicate the empire, but with no success."

Heralda lifted her head when she remembered Adam. "You are right when you say Adam is not like other people. It's incredible how much he cares for others. That is why I love him, and even though the idea that I can't love him and be with him greatly pains me, I understand the importance of his mission," finished Heralda, as her pretty eyes filled with tears. Paola Katarina spoke softer and quieter then usual now. She understood how the young girl felt, and with soft hands, she gently wiped Heralda's tears. "I'm very proud of your mature capacity to understand this. I believe in the lad and his determination to carry on. Even though all odds are against him his fighting spirit is strong. We must all stand behind him and encourage him to carry on, for his own destiny, the purpose of his life, and for the entire human race."

The woman went into the kitchen, and returned after some time with a dish of cooked vegetables, smelling quite appetizing. She carefully served the youngster, saying, "Eat, darling, grow stronger, and remember, we live on faith and hope, and those will lead our way."

In a few hours, the sun will set, thought Adam to himself, as he was standing barefoot on the seashore of Esperanza, his hands in his pockets and his face to the sky. The wind blew gently through his dark hair; he relished the wind's gentle caress and took a deep breath to his lungs. The ocean waves crashed into the soft sand time and time again. Above his head white seagulls glided, their screeches wounding the calm. The blue view in front of him made Adam grateful to be alive to see the beauty of God's creation. In his heart, he felt great gratitude to the supreme force he believed in, and in whom faith was just growing from day to day. He was thankful to the maker of this world for saving him from sure death only one day ago. His eyes filled with tears from the intensity of the joy filling him. He was astonished how his own fierce faith doing good and helping others brought a large group of people to dare and face the empire, to fight for his sake and for the liberation of the slaves on the Island of Sardinia. In his heart, he felt a grave appreciation of what was happening, and again he thanked his maker for his friend's good will, for their faith in freedom and the little good left in the world.

Adam closed his eyes and the tiny tears trailed down his cheeks, the wind blew and gathered his tears to heaven. Adam spoke to God from his heart, "Supreme force, maker of man and Earth, give me the strength to continue my journey, for the sake of the ones suffering, the ones in need. Give me the strength to follow through, to overcome the obstacles, not to fall, and if I do fall, I will rise again, and I promise you, Lord, as long as there is a breath in me, I will not leave my journey until my destiny is fulfilled!"

The sudden touch of a hand on his shoulder cut Adam short, he turned around and called with a smile. "Joshua!" The old man opened his arms slowly and the two embraced. "I'm so happy to see you Joshua, alive and well," said Adam with a wide grin. "Me too, dear friend, you brought me great joy, that even in my age I can still witness miracles that would wake an old heart, making it believe in more then it did in the good maker," said the old man. Adam turned back to the sea and Joshua slowly sat down on the soft sand, inviting the young man to sit beside him.

"You see these waves, Adam?"

The young man replied at once, "Yes, they're beautiful, aren't they?"

"True," answered the old man curtly. A long silence fell between the two as they watched, transfixed, how the blue waves made their way from the center of the ocean to their feet. Then the old man began speaking again. "You know, Adam, a lot can be learned from anything in nature, if you give it a little attention. For example, the waves." The old man pointed the young man's gaze to a large wave advancing from deep in to the shore. "You see how big and scary it is, making everyone who sees it fear? But as it comes closer to you and draws near, it finds its end as a small white curl of foam when it meets the sand," said the old man. Adam watched the big wave make its way to them from the sea until it turned into white foam caressing the yellow sand, and still Adam asked for an explanation for the sight. The old man clarified, "Every time a problem arises in the journey of life it seems large and threatening, we fear it and lose our faith in good, but nature teaches us that just like the problem so the wave seems big and scary in the beginning, still the shore does not move or draw back in fear, it remains steadily in its spot, and in a short time, just like the wave shrinks until it turns into delicate white foam, so the big and scary problems come to their end in peace. All that is needed is for us to keep the faith and have no fear, none at all." Joshua's words made Adam feel good. "Those are wonderful things you say, Joshua. I remember when I was on the ship, you and Heralda were locked away in the empire dungeons. I heard you speak in my mind, warning me from the danger coming to us in the shape of an empire submarine. I learned to see that there is an immense and special power in thought," said the young man, and the elder stopped him for a moment. "That is very true, Adam, and you are beginning to understand this special force, but you are still only in the beginning of this road. I believe that if you continue on your journey to Africa you will discover more of the power of thought, you will learn the might of a positive will and what you can achieve through it, with the faith in the almighty. I remember how all your wounds healed through that meditation I did with you, and I believe that there is even more hidden in you, and that is why you must carry on."

Adam stood up and looked at Joshua. "I am ready to continue the voyage, Joshua, with full power." The old man took Adam's hand in rising and said, "Then we must prepare you for the rest of the journey."

Chapter Forty-One

The row of empire leaders made its way to the headquarters of the empire's ruler, Drakkar. The three other rulers took their seats on coal black couches. In the center of the office stood an oval table made of black marble. Drakkar stood behind that table, his friends sat in front, then the lights were dimmed and suddenly from the wall behind Drakkar a large screen emerged. The three remaining leaders were full of curiosity: what kind of plan was this? What was it that Drakkar thought could bring them a crushing victory over the underground? The empire's leader approached the screen and pressed on the bottom right corner.

A special film started immediately, a series of graphic images flashed one after the other quickly. One could recognize huge robotic forms, each equipped with a variety of deadly weapons that emerged from every possible angle. Then a simulation a huge army of huge combat robots advance toward a populated area, full of helpless people trying uselessly to shoot down the robot army closing in on them. A smile appeared through Drakkar's black beard. He glanced at his friends, who stared at the screen with awe, occasionally throwing a quick glance at Drakkar. On the screen, the huge robots were shooting their destructive weapons, demolishing every populated area. In a few seconds, the film was over and the lights came on. Bammark was the first to speak, "So that's your plan, ha?"

The man with the golden hair quietly snickered. Vaskov decided to react also, "A new army of huge combat robots to destroy the freedom fighters?" Bartholomew remained silent, afraid to express his opinion in case the great empire leader might choose to use the opportunity to take out his rage on him again. Drakkar stood in front of his people, not answering their curious questions, waiting for better ones to come. It came soon from the mouth of Bammark, "But, Drakkar, my friend, the freedom fighters are no fools, they are like moles, they will find a way to hide from your huge robots," said Bammark, some disdain in his voice, then continued, "so why should we invest so much in building an army of huge combat robots when we have millions of soldiers, deadly hovercrafts, canons and many other destructive war vehicles?"

A wide, wicked smile spread on the empire leader's evil face. He decided to answer now because he found Bammark's question most to the point. "Well, my dark companions, we won't build this army of deadly robots to fight the freedom fighters." Drakkar paused for a long moment to make the suspense to rise, the curiosity nibbled at Bammark who asked irritably, "So why the goddamn robot army?"

Then Drakkar replied, "My plan isn't to search for the underground people all over the world. My plan is to use this robot army to destroy entire settlements of men and slaves. We will present the freedom fighters with an ultimatum: if they do not surrender, give in their weapons, and cease any subversive activity to our empire, we will continue destroying more and more settlements and cities around the world." The three other leaders remained dumbfounded; they did not imagine to what extent the head of the empire was heartless and evil. "So you mean to threaten the freedom fighters by hurting people all over the world?" asked Vaskov.

"Yes, my Vaskov, we will finish the resistance once and for all. For this I need your agreement and cooperation, to get this project going as soon as possible." Bartholomew stood up, carefully approached his leader, and said, "I'm with you, Drakkar. With this army of deadly robots we could break the resistance." Drakkar was slightly taken aback by Bartholomew's willingness and with a rare gesture he embraced the stout leader with one arm then asked his friends, laughing, "Well, are you with me?" They all broke into an evil laughter, accepting the dark leader's plan, who summed, "Well, we will commence immediately with building this army. The last day of these worthless freedom fighters and their mystery man draw near."

Chapter Forty-Two

The sun made way for the colors of the night, slowly taking over the entire island of Esperanza. The hiss of ocean waves mingled with the cries of the aquatic birds, the sound of their screeches diminishing as the hour grew late. Simon, leader of the Island of Esperanza, gathered a special meeting in his house, including his old friend Captain Nelson, accompanied by the loyal one-eyed wolf Arak, Paola Katarina, old Joshua, and Adam Swandon. They all sat by a round, wooden table, set with jugs of natural fruit juice and gold ornate china plates laid with crispy cookies, the handiwork of Simon's wife.

There was a slight tension in the air, and everyone felt it. Simon was a practical man, with both feet firmly planted on the ground. He believed in practical and strategic fighting against rule of the empire. Joshua, on the other hand, was a more spiritual person; he believed they must build their victory not only on fighting the empire with weapons, but also with their faith in a higher force, a force stronger than any other human weapon. The tense silence was broken by Joshua's words. "My honored lady, my dear gentlemen, the recent events strengthen the idea that we should put our faith in a unique salvation, that will finally release humanity from its suffering, and I believe with all my heart that Adam is the special man who will do this."

Adam was slightly embarrassed, but the old man carried on. "For years now, freedom fighters all over the world have been trying to bring the empire's reign of terror down to no avail. For all our efforts, we are like bees trying to sting an elephant. I believe in our strength and in the justice of our ways, but above all I believe in the higher force, instructing us that our victory depends not on the sword, but also on our faith in the path of goodness, in finding a true solution for the entire human race."

Simon's expression darkened hearing the old man's words, but Joshua continued anyway, and all listened, "Our lady Paola Katarina told us all of the prophecy, passed through the gipsy tribes for generations." As Joshua spoke Paola Katarina laid out the seven tablets on the table for all to see. "These tablets came from another world, to one day assist humanity in saving itself from self destruction." Joshua paused for a moment to look at the people around him, and then Simon said, "Dear sir, I understand what you say well, but we don't have a clue if these tablets are real, if they truly came from another world, or if they are here to help us. I, too, have believed in the creator, but what you're talking about sounds too fictional, and now, after the success of our latest operation against the empire, we have a better chance in confronting it."

Suddenly, Captain Nelson interrupted, "That's true, my friend, you are right, but after what happened the empire will probably retaliate hard and strong against the underground, and unfortunately, our forces are weak compared to the empire's. We probably can't withstand the next battle with the empire." Simon looked with surprise at his old friend and said, "The underground is scattered all over the world, and we have a chance now to overthrow the empire."

Joshua interrupted Simon. "The underground is strong, but the empire army is massive and well armed. I think that we all must give Adam a chance to fulfill his destiny."

Paola Katarina sat quietly. She watched Adam and sensed what he was about to say.

Adam rose abruptly from his seat and began pacing restlessly through the room. Then he began speaking to the people around, "Dear friends, I don't know much of the prophecy, and I don't think you should…" suddenly Paola Katarina got up quickly and completed Adam's sentence. "And you don't think we should put our trust in you? Is that what you wanted to say, Adam?" The young man stared at the woman, surprised of her knowledge of what he wanted to say, and the woman continued, turning to all the other people in the room. "Gentlemen, we all saw the events unfold in the last few days, we all saw how this man standing here chose to risk his own life for the sake of others. He himself chose the destiny that the creator intended for him. That is why I believe he must continue his journey to find the solution to humanity's suffering. I believe the prophecy to be true, but that is merely my own opinion. Simon dear, you are a brave and clever leader, and I know that deep within you too want to believe in the deliverance of mankind by a higher force. We all want to see men live free, only this time they will appreciate the idea of freedom in a positive way and won't take for granted the beauty of the world that God gave as a gift to us all. I know everyone has a different opinion, and I respect you all, but in my heart I feel for his readiness, will and pure heart. This man here will fill a crucial part in humanity's salvation, and I will do my best to help him go and fulfill his destiny."

The woman completed her sentence and looked into Adam's hawk eyes, and a wide, warm smile spread on her lips. Adam was in awe of her words and the faith she expressed in him. He took her hand and said, "Thank you, Paola Katarina, for having faith in me and for encouraging me to carry on with the journey. I feel inside that I must do this. I must save the next generation of children from suffering and slavery. I don't know how I will do this, but I remember a story that my dear father told me years ago, when I was a child. A man falls into a swamp and tries to grab anything to stop him from sinking to his doom. He sees a tiny weed, so he reaches out and grabs it. Then nature surprises the man doing everything in his last moments to hold on to that last spark of hope. The little weed has a strong root, growing deep in the ground, and that saved this man. He also said that if a man just simply wants something, he won't get it, but if a man realy, truly wants something with a deep passion, he will."

Captain Nelson rose from his chair in great excitement and called, "Those are strong words, lad, and I'm sure that Simon agrees with me." Nelson patted his friend's shoulder, and the other smiled, stood up also and said, "I have no doubt that you are one hell of a guy, Adam, and though this journey is dangerous and possibly fictional, I appreciate your courage and determination in going on anyway. So I will give you my blessing, and I will do my best to help you, in any way possible." The captain was happy to hear Simon's words and said with a cheer, "Hooray Adam, I will see it as a great honor for my grand *Oracle* and its faithful crew to take you to your next destination." Joshua smiled, stood, and he, too, embraced the young man. "Well, Adam, it seems we agree to believe in the idea of your journey, and we all want to help you do it. So let's go Adam, let's get you ready for the rest of the voyage."

Arak, Nelson's faithful wolf, affirmed the merriment with cheerful barks. Adam patted the one-eyed wolf, embraced him, and said, "If all of you believe in me, then I'm sure I'll succeed."

Paola Katarina looked at Adam from the side and winked a "victory wink" at him.

Adam understood he must do it anyway. He felt great faith in himself even though the doubts tried to suffocate him, and in his heart, he asked the creator to help him to succeed.

Chapter Forty-Three

Morning overcame the night, the sun painted the sky with a brilliant glow. Seagulls glided over the yellowish shoreline of Esperanza. The island men were tirelessly loading the large sail ship with food, water, and weapons. Captain Nelson stood on the shore, overseeing the work, and at his side the loyal wolf, Arak.

Simon was commanding a group of few people who were installing weapons in hidden places on the *Oracle*. They all worked swiftly and diligently, for the *Oracle* was meant to take sail today, and on its board was the man who chose to continue the journey to find a solution to all evil that exists in the world. He lit a beacon of hope in the heart of the people, and they were willing to do their best to contribute to the liberation of their brothers around the world, enslaved by the empire's reign of terror.

Adam sat on his bed, in a cabin near the seashore. He took his little laser switchblade from his pocket and a great excitement overtook him; he tried to calm himself but the excitement still had hold of him, he asked himself if he wasn't deceiving himself with this whole idea that he, one man, will go on a journey to resolve all the evil in the world. Then he realized that this is the destiny he chose for himself, he realized he is walking the path he chose to walk. He always felt himself to be different than other people, always shying away from the company of his peers at school, always daydreaming; no one understood him as a child, they always treated him like a dreamer living in a fantasy. He felt now that all these things he passed in his life have led him to these days. Today's reality would seem like a bad dream those days, but today, when humanity was in its era of social destruction and freedom was a fictional concept for most people, he decided to leave and not give up until he will find that thing called Gim Nigma, that special force that legend tells was buried here many years ago by someone from another world. In his head, many questions circled, demanding more details: what is it, actually, this thing called Gim Nigma? Where was it? And is there even a small chance that this story of Gim Nigma is real? But even more than that. He wanted to know, does this lonely priest guarding the ancient libraries deep in the deserts of North Africa really exist?

Just as the questions running through his head began to give way to a gnawing doubt, he heard a familiar and pleasant voice behind him. "Adam, everything is ready"

Paola Katarina stood in the threshold of the cabin; the sun glowing behind her made her look like a celestial figure. The sun was shining today brighter then any other day since Adam's arrival on the island. The kind woman came close to him. "I know what you are going through, Adam. Your mind is full of many questions, but I know you understand that only by continuing in your journey and believing in it you can get the answers. Remember, all is possible in life, bad as well as good, and you should always choose to do good. The creator made the human heart so it could pump blood through the man's entire body, so man can live, and function, and carry on the creator's work by doing good in the world. Everything has a reason, all that you have to do is believe in that, and under no condition to allow negative thoughts to penetrate your mind."

Adam listened to the woman, who was holding his empty hand, while in his other hand he was holding his faithful laser pocket-blade. He chose to see it as symbolism, that in one hand he held a weapon while in the other he held the faith this woman was giving him. He answered her with a voice resonating with confidence. "I'm ready to go on, and I hold on to wings of faith so they may carry me to my destination."

The two left the cabin and walked toward the *Oracle*, where everyone was gathered. The ship's crew was already on it, preparing it for a mysterious adventure in the depths of the sea. The island men were waiting to part and wish good luck to the man who chose to do all he could to save humanity from the bondages of suffering it was trapped in. Among these people stood Heralda, who was feeling better now thanks to Paola Katarina's devoted care. She came to the shoreline to say good-bye to the man who caused her heart to beat faster than ever before. Adam came near her, his eyes showed happiness for seeing her on her feet and out of danger, but he felt sadness in his heart, and noticed she was crying.

"Don't cry, Heralda my dear, we parted before and managed to meet again. I'm so proud of you, and I want you to pray for me, that I will succeed against all odds to fulfill my destiny the best I can." He gently wiped her tears and now his eyes were also brimming. Nelson, standing close to the pair, made an effort to hide his own emotions and tears. Paola Katarina hugged Heralda warmly and said, "We will all pray for you, Adam. You are our hope." The young man kissed the kind gipsy woman on her cheeks, then looked into Heralda's beautiful large eyes, held her face gently with both hands, and softly kissed her lips. The young woman felt her heart bursting within her, but she rose above the pain within and said in a broken voice, "Adam, I never knew a man like you, who cares so much for others and he is willing to sacrifice himself for a legend that may save mankind. Of course I will pray for you, I believe in you and your destiny. Go and succeed."

Joshua slowly drew near, embraced Adam, and said, "I pray to God that when we meet again, we will all be free. Go and do well, my boy." The old man couldn't hold back his tears, and turned to the two women holding each other. The tears ran down from Adam's hawk eyes, his heart ached terribly in his chest. He shook Simon's hand

and thanked all the people who came to bid him farewell and good luck. Accompanied by Captain Nelson, Adam made his way to the deck of the *Oracle*, and then the entire crowd on the shore cheered as one for Adam and the *Oracle* crew, trumpeting farewell wishes. The wind filled the blue sails of the *Oracle*, pushing the great ship deep into the blue sea.

Chapter Forty-Four

Within the vast empire fortress, the home of the four fearsome and evil leaders who held the world in a cruel grip, sits an old woman, deep in the cellars. Irma the witch is draped in her black cape, her narrow eyes busy with the book her grandmother Trudy left her when she was young. She is reading of the son of light, she is reading of the man who will choose himself to face the evil that will take over the world. The man has a special soul, created by God to bring hope to mankind. She reads that the carrier of this soul will be of a pure heart, caring for others more than for himself. She discovers, diligently reading, the words of Trudy, who tells that what ties the pure heart to its fierce will to save humanity is the faith in the path of good, in the goodness of the creator, and in himself.

Her eyes suddenly widen and her heart beats rapidly when she realized that what could break this pure heart is doubt; doubt could gnaw at him, causing him to lose faith in his journey to save the world. When he figures for himself that man is evil by nature his will shall fade, his faith will die out, and he would forsake the idea and the way to save humanity, thus the prophecy threatening the empire's reign will disappear, and the evil rule will go on forever, generation after generation. A wide grin cracked the aged features of the evil witch. She realized she stumbled upon the true solution that would truly destroy the mystery man and his will to carry on his journey to demolish the empire. Then she began asking herself, how can one break a man's faith? She continued wondering, when the pure heart's faith breaks, will the prophecy also break? And how can she reach the heart of the man and make him doubt what he believes in?

Despite these disturbing questions, Irma felt proud of finding the way to impede the prophecy's realization. She realized, though, that she needed help. She could count on the cooperation of only one of all the empire's men: her mouth opened and she called out, "Bartholomew!"

Chapter Forty-Five

Captain Damtry Nelson stood by the *Oracle*'s steering wheel, his face worried. He could feel the wind blowing fiercely across his short white beard, and he thought to himself that this wind doesn't bid well of the weather. The *Oracle*'s sailors knew the frown on the captain's face, and they became tense. Adam woke up for his midday work shift on the ship, like the rest of his friends the sailors. He has already learned much of the life of a sailor in mid-sea. He learned much but he couldn't recognize the meaning of this mysterious wind, blowing so strangely. Adam's body grew stronger since he first stepped on the *Oracle*, his muscles developed through the hard work on the ship, he decided to jump to the main hull and ask the captain why everybody was running around, looking worried. The captain noticed Adam and asked him to strengthen a few ties connecting the mast to the floor of the ship. Adam approached the task briskly, but he was feeling the tension in the air growing stronger, he sensed something was about to happen. When he was done, he came to the captain and asked him about all the commotion. The captain held his hat to his head, with his second hand he supported the wheel, then he answered, "A big storm is about to break, Adam." The words echoed through Adam's mind. "A storm?" he repeated.

Now Nelson was holding the ship's wheel in both strong hands, "Yes, a colossal storm—look at the sky." Adam lifted his head to the horizon, which began filling quickly with black clouds. A smell of moisture rose in the air, as if the sky threatened to fall into the sea, and the wind began blowing harder. Nelson shouted to his sailors, "Men, lower the sails, fast!" the loyal crew rushed to carry out their captain's order immediately. "What do I do?" asked Adam when he realized he was about to experience the first great storm at sea in his life. As a kid he heard the tales of courageous adventurers who in their journeys at sea fought through fierce and deadly storms that only a few survived. His heart pounded hard and a great anxiousness flooded him. He tried to tell himself to think positive and gather his courage but the captain's shouts at his men sliced through his thoughts. "Tighten those ropes there!"

In one instant, the wind tripled its force, and some of the men were tossed as if they were mere toys, Adam also fell but he rose immediately and helped the sailor that fell near him to get up. Rain began pouring down and the captain looked at his men as he alone held the ship's wheel. "Friends, the storm is upon us! Be ready for everything!" the captain called to his people. The rain beat hard, nearly blinding them, and shouts rebounded from one end of the ship to the other. The waves began rising to incredible heights, Adam couldn't believe how fast this storm formed, he was washed entirely by a sheet of water that crashed into him from the sea, the rain threatened to drown the *Oracle* but the ship seemingly had a mind of its own, it fought relentlessly, not giving up. Adam ran through the jets of water that hit him time and time again, reached the captain and helped him balance the ship's wheel. He noticed the captain smiling at him through the sheets of rain, he heard him cry out loudly: "You see Adam, God must be testing your determination to carry on!" Adam heard every word, and he called back loudly to Nelson, "We won't surrender, Captain, we won't surrender, we will fight and win!"

A loud creaking noise was heard, a huge wave broke the top of the mast, Nelson was alarmed when he saw the huge wooden mast was about to fall on a few of his sailors, together with Adam they called out to them from the wheel, "Look out, move away!" But it was too late; the half-mast fell on two sailors and injured them. Adam immediately tore himself from his position, calling Jeremiah to help the captain hold the wheel.

Jeremiah did that immediately. He realized something astounding was about to happen, and Adam ran through the sheets of water, calling the sailors around him to come help him lift the half mast to save the wounded sailors. The ship rose and sunk incessantly, threatening to sink into the depth in any moment. They all reached the place where the half-mast crashed and tried with all their might to move it, uselessly. The sailors cried out in pain, their blood painted the wet wood red, and the sailors trying with Adam to lift the heavy wood off their friends began losing hope. For a moment, Adam was with himself, and he spoke to the creator, "Please, Higher Force, help me to help them. Don't fail me, I will not give up, I won't let this storm stop me from fulfilling my destiny, I must go on, and I'm asking you, dear God, help me overcome this obstacle."

Suddenly, through the din of the storm and the waves ceaselessly breaking against the ship, lightning tore through the sky and split the mast in half. The sailors didn't wait, Jeremiah and Nelson together saw what happened and they saw it as a sign of a miracle—because of the lightning strike the sailors managed to move the heavy wood with more ease, and they managed to rescue the wounded men and lead them to shelter. Adam called loudly to the sky, "Thank you, Lord, thank you, I will continue believing in you and in the path of good, I won't cave in, no matter what I will continue my journey through my faith in you. Thank you, my maker!" He was greatly moved and he called out to all his friends, crazed, "Look, the good Lord is with us, don't give up, we will emerge strong, let us fight and win!" All the sailors felt their spirits soar and their physical strength rise; they shouted in agreement with Adam's words, and the captain again realized that the good Lord wishes for Adam's journey to succeed. The storm didn't stop, but it seemed that with their spirits high they had a better chance to survive. They all worked together tirelessly, telling themselves that the storm will not break them.

A new dawn rose over the *Oracle*. The great sailboat was only slightly injured by the terrible storm that occurred last night. The skies were calm and quiet, except a few thin feather clouds. The sky's deep azure ruled everything.

The men woke slowly, one after the other. The few wounded sailors were supported by their friends. Some turned to the bow, kneeled on the bottom of the ship, and called out an elated prayer of thanks to their maker that no one died during the fierce storm of last night. Adam and the ship's doctor helped bandage the wounded. The experienced Captain Nelson, who has seen storms as bad before, had never witnessed such wonders and miracles like those that occurred the night of the storm. He was deeply excited by the thought that he indeed must be transporting the man meant to save humanity from the bonds of slavery.

He looked at Adam, working tirelessly and without pause, tending seriously to his wounded friends. In his heart the captain thanked the Lord for giving him the chance to be a partner in this young man's journey, bravely off to find a solution to all the evil that accumulated in the world. Then again, Nelson reminded himself, they may be on a totally fictional journey, the story of the lone priest living alone in the heart of the African desert may be no more than a simple children's tale. But then Nelson remembered the ancient saying: "he who seeks shall find." The seasoned captain was an experienced sea traveler, and he was not quite excited by the idea of a spiritual journey that will lead to the defeat of the forces of evil through a mysterious special force buried in the Earth hundreds of years ago, like the legend described. Still, he was a man of logic, a realist, and he summed the inner argument going on in his mind with the thought that the ancient saying makes sense—that it doesn't matter if that old monk exists or if he knows anything of this mysterious force. Adam was a determined man, seeking with his entire heart a solution to empire's evil rule over the world. A strong sentence, he thought to himself, he who seeks shall find.

That actually means that anyone seeking something, longing for it with all his heart, will find it. Adam looked from afar at the captain holding the wheel, and Nelson, noticing the young man looking at him, raised his thumb in the air and smiled, signaling, "All is well."

Adam was diligently dressing the wounds of a sailor, whose leg was slightly injured. He still couldn't stomach the astounding experience he just went through; he was never a seaman and he never experienced such a storm, especially so deep out in the sea. He read about it in books, he remembered the pirate movies he loved watching as a kid, of hidden treasures on desolate islands. He was amused by the similarity between his journey to the journeys of the pirates and the treasure seekers; he, too, of course, was looking for a treasure, a treasure he believed to be priceless, something whose value can't be measured in gold or diamonds, which are actually only rocks and metals. The treasure he was seeking had to do with the entire human race. He remembered that he had a difficult childhood, and as a child he used to escape into an imaginary world, where he was a special hero, saving the world. He dreamt of this when he was a kid but he would never believe that one day he would embark on a quest after the treasure that would save this hurting bleeding planet.

Adam's thoughts disappeared at once when Allator cried loudly, "Africa, friends, Africa!" Arak the one-eyed wolf stood at the bow of the ship, barking at Captain Nelson, who left the wheel in the hands of one of the sailors and ran to his loyal friend. "What's with you, my friend Arak, why do you bark like this?"

The large wolf continued to bark, as if trying to speak, to tell the captain to look. The captain strains his eyes then pulls from his pocket an old telescope, he focuses his gaze on the strip of land laying on the horizon, and a curse escapes his mouth, "Damn it!"

Adam also raced to the bow, but before he could speak a word the captain turned to Allator and cried out loud, "Lower the sails, right now, stop the ship!" For the moment, he ignored Adam, who was standing behind him, then he called to the rest of his sailors, "Drop the anchor! Drop the anchor!" The sailors carried out their commander's orders immediately, the *Oracle*'s blue sails were swiftly lowered and folded, the chains scraped against the hull of the ship as the great anchor plunged into the blue ocean. The captain went on watching the distant shores of Africa through the telescope. Adam asked, "Captain, what happened, why are we stopping here? Africa is right there."

The captain turned to face the young man. "Look through the telescope, Adam," he said, passing the old telescope to Adam. Arak has only one eye, true, but it's sharper than a human eye. He noticed the danger even from this distance. Adam put his eye to the telescope and aimed his gaze to the thin, distant strip of land. "Captain, beside the land, I don't see anything special," the young man replied. "Focus your gaze, focus a little more and you'll see," Nelson answered at once. Adam followed the captain's bid, and his eyes could now pick up the little black dots scattered along the strip of land. "What are those dots?" asked Adam naively.

"That's the empire's army, Adam. The entire shore is swarming with empire soldiers. Those dots you see, those are hovercrafts and war vessels of the empire," said the captain, his voice grim.

Adam looked through the telescope again; now he could indeed recognize the black hovercrafts, scattered along the entire length of Africa's shore.

"What shall we do?" asked Adam. The captain signaled to his sailors to come to him, then answered, "There isn't much we can do, Adam, we must stop here. The *Oracle* is wanted by the empire, and if we come closer they could recognize us and easily shoot us down. You saw it for yourself. The shores are crowded with empire forces, we have to keep our distance. but I have to get there," said Adam determinedly.

"And you will get there, my friend, don't worry. But I'm afraid you'll have to go on without us," Nelson said.

"So this is where we part?" asked Adam

"For now," the captain answered, with a touch of sadness in his voice. Adam's heart filled with a mixture of sorrow and fear, for parting with his good friends; Captain Nelson and the *Oracle* crew and carrying on by himself. "But don't worry, Adam, a good friend will join you and keep you company further on," Nelson called with a smile, trying to disguise his sadness for parting with Adam, and Arak's barks immediately filled the air, as if he knew he was the one who was going to join Adam. Adam himself was surprised, "Arak? But he is your loyal wolf. I wouldn't want to separate you two, Captain." The captain knelt on one knee and patted Arak warmly, who liked the bearded face of his friend. "Don't worry, Adam, when you have Arak with you it will be as if we are all there. He is loyal, brave, smart, and strong, and besides, under that patch covering his eye is a secret that will be of help further on."

"A secret?" Adam exclaimed. The captain laughed lightly. "Yes, Adam, but you will discover it later, and as long as Arak is with you, he will connect us. And I know one more important thing." Adam looked curiously at Nelson, who swiftly carried on. "That we are not parting for long, Adam, we will meet again, I feel it in my heart. Leave for Africa now, with the payers of all the *Oracle*'s men, and don't worry, we will stay in this area for some time. You have to go on without us now, together with the loyal Arak, and with God's help you will succeed." The faces of the sailors crowding around Adam and the captain were sad; they all liked the brave fellow, they were sorry that they couldn't join him, but they trusted Arak and their captain, knowing he is not a regular wolf, and only the captain knew his real capabilities, there were many things hidden from the eye about this wolf.

A blue jetty was lowered to the surface of the water. The captain ordered his men diligently so that everything will function properly. Adam came to shake the captain's hand with an excitement mixed with the sadness of parting. The captain looked at him, his eyes brimming a little, then he threw his arms wide open and held Adam in a warm embrace. Each of the sailors shook Adam's hand by turn, blessing him and saying farewell. The captain hugged Arak warmly one last time, and then the large wolf leapt into the jetty awaiting the two passengers. Adam went down into the jetty using a rope ladder then looked up at his friends, calling out their good-lucks, and the captain added, "Don't worry friend, we will meet soon, remember Arak isn't a regular wolf, he will surprise you yet!" At Nelson's words, Arak barked loudly, in a voice that carried over the roar of the waves slapping against the great ship.

Adam started up the engine of the jetty. He hid from his friends the tears, running slowly down his cheeks. He looked up to the sky and asked his maker, "Please, take care of them."

The little jetty sliced through the ocean swiftly, and the *Oracle* behind it became smaller from moment to moment, until it disappeared entirely into the horizon, while the shores of Africa became larger and closer Adam thought to himself, "What awaits me there? Who will guide me to the whereabouts of the lonely priest?" He made an effort to think positively, to focus on his objective to discover more about this recluse; he dismissed the possibility that the story about this mysterious priest was false. Adam noticed a certain area where the empire's hovercrafts weren't patrolling at the moment, a small cove, a good place to stop—as if he was reading his thoughts. Arak barked in agreement. The two jumped out of the jetty and within minutes had the small vehicle entirely covered by the green vegetation growing around.

Arak barked and began walking toward an area that seemed crowded with many people; from afar it seemed like a large pier market. For a moment, Adam wondered why would Arak lead him into a place filled with soldiers and people, but he remembered at once that to get information or anything else to further his goal, he must make contact with people. So he began walking behind the large one-eyed wolf and said, "All right. Arak, I trust you."

Adam covered his head with a hooded cape, made of a brown material. He was now looking now like a Bedouin, a man of the desert, he was covered with heavy fabrics from head to toe. When Nelson gave him these clothes; he explained that the locals, Arab descendants, dress this way and he should do the same. Adam hoped very much that it would work so he may blend in seamlessly.

Chapter Forty-Six

The market was filled with all kinds of produce, and besides the soldiers in black uniforms surrounding the entire area, the place looked like a colorful heaven, with men and women colorfully clad from head to toe in garments similar to Adam's. Adam began to feel more at ease, and Arak clung to his heels, as if trying to tell him, have no fear, I'm here and I'm guarding you. The two made their way through the vendors, who cried out to the by-passers to buy their products, which were better than their neighbors'. Adam's eyes wandered over stalls crowded with mouth-watering food. He could feel his hunger mounting at the sight of the piles of food lying on the damp wooden booths. The hunger was also bothering the large wolf, and he began barking toward one of the vendors; a man draped in blue and red garments, his head shaded by a blue cloth. The man noticed the hungry expression on Adam's face, and through his curly beard, his tanned, skinny features broke into a wide smile. "Sir, here you will find the best smoked fish in Morocco, also the best cheese—for you, sir, at a special price!" Adam looked warily at the man, he seemed to be about fifty years old, the merchant saw Adam eyeing the food longingly, but his smile receded as he noticed the large wolf.

Adam noticed that and said, "Oh, don't worry, sir, this is a special wolf, he doesn't harm people." The merchant's smile reappeared. He seemed reassured by Adam's words, he called Arak and served him a smoked fish, which Arak grabbed with his teeth at once and proceeded to eat it. Adam began searching his pockets for some money.

The merchant saw the young man struggling with his garment's pockets to find some money and called out, "It's all right, sir, I like the big wolf, the fish is a gift."

Adam thanked the man, "Many thanks, sir, do you have anything for a hungry person like me? Unfortunately I can't pay you, but I would gladly help you with your work as payment." The merchant looked at Adam for a moment, a little shocked, then burst out in a laughter swallowed by the din of the people around. "Oh, you are very funny, young man. If I gave food to a wolf, wouldn't I give a human? After all hospitality is a very important tradition, going back to the days of our father Abraham. Take whatever your heart desires to eat." Adam's face lit up. He was happy for the merchant's kindness and his wariness of the man disappeared. He thanked the man politely and chose for himself one smoked fish and a long loaf of bread. In his heart, he thanked the creator for introducing him to good-hearted people, even while the world is oppressed by an evil empire. The merchant noticed Adam's restlessness when once in a while a black clad soldier passed by, holding a long barreled laser guns, patrolling the area and supervising the normal activities of a market in a pier town. The merchant continued peddling his products to the people passing by. He let Adam and Arak eat in peace, and when they finished, he asked them both to stay by his side. From Adam, he asked to help him occasionally load new fish to his stalls, which became empty from time to time.

Arak, lying on the ground, felt someone watching them. He noticed that nearby, by a stand of red and green peppers, stood two figures, also clad from head to toe in a purplish garment, constantly staring at him and Adam. The one-eyed wolf rose and replied with an ill-tempered gaze in his one eye toward the two mysterious figures. He took one step forward a growl rose in his throat. The two withdrew and disappeared behind the vegetable stalls. Arak lost them and after a minute returned to his friend who was helping the merchant with his work. At the eve of day, the market began dwindling of people, the place that was so crowded and loud during the day began falling quiet. The shouts of people and peddlers diminished, as did the presence of the empire soldiers in the area. The merchant offered Adam and Arak a place to stay for the night, and Adam gladly accepted. He wished to ask the kind man with the curly beard if he knows anything of the legend, of the mysterious priest or the ancient libraries, but he held himself back, thinking that he will allow this night to pass quietly; tomorrow was a new day, in which he could examine the facts clearly and decide if he should ask the merchant about these things.

Night fell as the merchant led Adam and the wolf to his house, located on the top of a steep rise, in the center of the pier city. Arak walked behind them, stopping every now and then to verify they weren't being followed. They advanced to the merchant's house, and all the while, the two characters in purple robes silently followed the small group. Finally, Arak's sensitive nose caught the scent of the strangers, and he began barking. The two figures quickly drew pistols from their robes and hid behind an old building wall. Adam asked Arak to stop barking, afraid he will wake the merchant's household, but the merchant told Adam that if the wolf is barking like that, there may be a reason for it. The merchant drew near to Arak and asked, "What do you see, friend?"

Arak stopped barking and merely fixed his gaze on the two dark silhouettes on the street corner. The merchant began advancing cautiously, Adam looked from afar and his heart began racing, the merchant came very near the two dark figures and then called out, "Who's there?"

The two laid their fingers on the trigger, preparing to shoot the merchant, when suddenly the rumble of a black empire hovercraft sliced through the tension in the air; the odd figures used the opportunity to quickly run away. The merchant didn't have the opportunity to see them before he turned back to his house. The patrolling hovercraft flew away; curfew fell on the city. The laws here were the same as anywhere else in the world, at this hour all people except those in the work-camps, who were defined as slaves, are supposed to be in their houses, and may not leave under any condition. If they broke the empire's law, they would be immediately killed by one of the hovercrafts wandering over the cities.

The merchant's family was sleeping peacefully, not at all disturbed by all that happened outside. The night was so quiet it seemed as If the entire world was sleeping. The large wolf Arak immediately sprawled on a colorful rug by the entrance door. The merchant smiled at Adam and said, "I see our friend took care of himself, he already found his spot."

Adam replied, "Yes, Arak is very intelligent, he's not a simple wolf." As the merchant arranged the covers on a low bed in the corner of the large room, Adam came near him and said, "I'd like to thank you, sir, for your great kindness. I'm overwhelmed every time that I meet good people like you, especially in these difficult times, when people lose faith in each other."

The merchant continued arranging the sheets, and when he finished, he said, "Look my friend, in this world we live in, every day might be our last, and if a man has the chance to do a deed, it might as well be a good deed. This is how my grandfather lived his entire life, and my father after him, and now I carry on their ways. I believe that in this way they live on through me." Adam remembered he hasn't introduced himself to the merchant yet, so he reached his hand out to him and said, "It's an honor to meet you, sir. I'm Adam Swandon." The merchant shook Adam's hand and replied, "And I am Abdul Asam."

In the shelter of the quiet night the two mysterious figures stood beneath a broken lamp light and conversed, "I'm sure it's the mystery man, I saw his face," said the first. "We'll slit his throat and bring his head to the leader of the empire. We'd get a big reward for it."

"We must hurry before the others discover where he is, the loot will be all ours," said the first man. "You're right," said the second, and drew a sword that seemed like a local artifact, a gleaming sword with a curved, very sharp blade. These two were mercenaries, sent by the empire's ruler on the mission to trap or kill the mystery man, Adam Swandon. They agreed to do it at the break of dawn.

Chapter Forty-Seven

Adam couldn't sleep. Many thoughts raced through his head: he thought of Heralda and Joshua, who remained on the island of Esperanza together with Simon and the freedom fighters of the New Dawn Hawks, he was glad they were safe; Abdul's kindness and hospitality reminded him of Peter and Dorina's kindness, somewhere out there in the forests of the Alps; his thoughts collided with everybody's expectations of him, that he be the one to free humanity from the empire's reign of terror. He remembered the words of the veteran Captain, he missed his friends the sailors, Arak's presence made him feel safe, as if his friends, the *Oracle* crew, were right there with him; but overall he was preoccupied with the question of how he may discover more information about the lonely priest, the ancient libraries, and the illusive Gim Nigma.

He remembered the kind face of Paola Katarina and how much she believed in him. Abdul observed Adam sitting on his bed, not sleeping. He sat down next to him and said, "This is something that normally shouldn't be done, but come with me." Adam looked at him questioningly, but the man rose and signaled for Adam to follow him. The merchant led Adam to a small terrace, hidden by bushes, at the back of the merchant's house. On the terrace were chairs and a little wooden table, and on the table were two red cups, decorated with golden ornaments. Next to them sat a pitcher of the same color and ornaments. Vapors of steam rose from the pitcher into the night air.

"Sit, my friend, let us drink some tea, that will bring some order to all your thoughts," said the merchant, smiling. Adam sat down and looked up at the half moon pinned to the dark horizon. "What did you mean when you said this isn't allowed?" asked Adam.

The merchant Abdul poured the hot tea into the two ornamented cups and said, "Thirty years ago, when I was twenty five, freedom was a natural thing. We could be anywhere we wanted at anytime. Nowadays, under the empire rule, we are restricted, and empire law forbids us from being outdoors at this hour. It's curfew time now, until dawn." The merchant laid an old fabric bag on the table and took out a pipe from it. He swiftly filled the pipe, lit it, and within seconds the air was filled with the thick scent of tobacco. The pillars of smoked curved up and dissolved unto the night air. The merchant offered some to the young man, who politely declined. Adam could feel the man's curiosity and he knew that the questions will soon come, and indeed, after a long moment of silence, Abdul began to ask what was Adam's business in a foreign land, accompanied by a large wolf with a weird patch over his one eye. Despite the man's generous hospitality, Adam was still wary of him, he didn't want to take a bigger risk then necessary knowing that he was wanted by the empire and there was a large bounty on his head, so he was careful with the details he told the merchant: "a long time ago, I heard an interesting story from a fortune teller, on an island far from here. It's a story of a lonely priest, guarding the ancient libraries in the heart of the desert of North Africa. They say that this tale is nothing more then a fairytale, but my heart tells me there is more to it than that. This story fascinated me so much that I came here." Abdul looked at Adam strangely, as if he didn't understand a word of what was said. He inhaled deeply from his pipe and said, "Interesting…"

The merchant laid his pipe by his teacup and carried on, "I never heard of such a priest, or of these ancient libraries." His words caused Adam some disappointment. He was hoping for a breakthrough. Abdul asked, "A fortune-teller you say, ha?"

Adam nodded, waiting for Abdul to complete his sentence. "And why are you looking for this man?" asked the merchant, lifting his pipe again. Adam didn't reply to the man's question. He sipped the hot tea carefully, and complemented the man for the tasty tea. The merchant did not repeat his question. He considered leaving the young man alone, and then said, "Tomorrow morning, we go together to my old uncle. He's a hundred and seven years old. He's old, but his mind is still sharp, and perhaps he heard something about that story of yours. After that maybe you could come and help me around the market, what do you say?" Adam was encouraged by these words, and answered gladly, "That's great, Abdul! Does your uncle live far?"

"Not far," answered the merchant, yawning a big yawn that showed just how tired he was. Adam noticed this and said, "I think we both need a good measure of sleep, Abdul. And I'd like to take this chance to thank you for your great kindness." The good merchant rose from his seat and walked to his and his wife's bedroom. On his way he said, "It's nothing, Adam. In our family, it's customary to be kind and good to each other, regardless of who rules the world," and before he entered the room he added, "The empire allows us to sell in the markets only because it serves its interests. But we choose to see the market as a reminder to the fact that we are free in some way, do you understand...? Oh, by the way, tomorrow is my daughter's birthday. I would be more than happy if you could join the celebration. Of course we will have to celebrate in secret, unless they ban the occasion and arrest us for being happy." Abdul concluded his words with a tone of anger in his voice. Adam thought in his heart. "If Abdul only knew why he was searching for the ancient libraries, if he only knew that he was searching for the solution to end the suffering of humanity in the entire world... but still he decided to keep the complete picture to himself, at least for now. "Don't worry, my friend Abdul. The sun of freedom will shine upon our world once again, don't despair," said Adam, summing the night with these words. He remained sitting on the small wooden chair, looking at the half moon. It seemed as if, with that moon, the sky was smiling a white, hopeful smile at him.

The two hunters crept closer to the merchant's house, their swords drawn in their hands, on their feet special shoes that made no noise. Pacing swiftly, like two cats, they flatten themselves against one of the merchant's walls. The entire household is fast asleep; Adam, too, is lying on the bed in the guest room, his eyes peacefully shut. He doesn't know that a few feet from him are two men that are about to kill him and bring his head to Drakkar for a fair prize. The hunters whispered among themselves, discussing their plan, Arak was sleeping by the entrance door, he hears nothing, the hunters' special shoes muffled their footsteps. They discovered Adam's bearing. One of the hunters, holding a curved sword, its blade gleaming in the rising dawn, leapt through the window close to the bed Adam was sleeping in. his veiled face revealed only a pair of evil eyes. He reached out with one hand, intending to grab Adam's head; in the other, he lifted the deadly sword high.

In a few fatal seconds, he will have the head of the mystery man who offended the empire, the man who threatens the empire's reign, so thought the mercenary, the hand holding the sword came down over the sleeping man's throat, but suddenly sharp teeth pierce the mercenary's raised arm, he cries out with pain, Arak the one-eyed wolf jumped on the assassin. The entire family was woken by the hunter's cries of pain, as he struggled to free himself from Arak's fearful teeth. Adam awoke with a start and leapt out of his bed, grabbing a wooden chair and smashing it over the withering form of the assassin. The second assassin jumped through the window and saw his friend laying on the floor and Arak standing over him threateningly, he drew a pistol from his purple robe and aimed the barrel at the large wolf, but before he could squeeze the trigger, Adam forcefully kicked the hand holding the sinister gun, a shot escaped, but it missed the large wolf, the gun fell from the hands of the second hunter, who now stood in front of Adam with a drawn sword and in his eyes nothing but death.

Adam was anxious, he never confronted a situation like this, he was sure that the sharp sword will do him harm. At the same time the first hunter, blood flowing from the wound Arak inflicted on him, rose, and stood by his friend. Now the two assassins loomed over Adam with sharp swords that promised death. Arak backed away, barking loudly; Abdul, rushing to defend his family, ran into the guestroom holding an old hunting rifle and shouted at the hunters, "Who are you, what are you doing in my house?"

The second hunter gestured to his friend to kill Adam while he takes care of the merchant. And evil laughter escaped though the veils covering his face. The merchant held up the old rifle in order to shoot the hunter but he couldn't work it on time, the hunter raised his sword and slashed a wound in Abdul's stomach, who fell to the floor, crying with pain.

"Abdul!" Adam cried out with horror. Something had to be done, yet in front of him stood the bleeding hunter, his sword slicing through the air in all directions, apparently about to end his life, Adam called Arak but the wolf did something that seemed very weird to Adam and everybody else in the room; he laid on the floor, whimpering, trying to remove the patch from his eye with both his front paws. For a moment, everyone's attention was solely on Arak as the wolf suddenly leapt back to his feet, the patch fell, and they all saw an incredible vision: Arak's unseeing eye, hidden behind that patch, was actually a round metal mechanism, which rotated on its axis, stopped on a certain location, and clicked. After the click came a drawn out, shrill tone, getting louder and louder, Arak made a brief roaring sound, looking directly at the two threatening hunters. An immensely powerful laser beam was released from the bionic eye of the large wolf, slicing through the two hunters and leaving them on the floor, without a breath of life in them.

Adam was shocked. He checked the hunters and saw they were indeed dead. Abdul's wife and three children were huddled around him, crying bitterly over the wounded merchant whose stomach was bleeding profusely. The woman cried out to Adam, begging him to do something for her suffering husband, the young man was still trying to digest whatever happened here in the last few moments, but he focused on his wounded friend immediately removing his shirt and tightening it over Abdul's bleeding wound. "We have to close the wound, or he will lose a lot of blood," said Adam, his voice concerned. Suddenly Arak came to Adam and nudged him with his head, as if asking him to move aside. Adam made way for the special wolf, Arak stood near Abdul, looking directly at the gaping wound, and again the odd eye rotated on its axis and clicked into a different location, and within a second thin thread of red light came from the wolf's eye and began miraculously welding the wound closed. Abdul was stunned by the occurrence, and the woman relaxed once she saw her husband was no longer moaning in pain. The wound was entirely closed, only an etched line showed across the merchant's stomach.

The woman rushed to the kitchen and returned with a pack of white bandages and a jar with some aloe vera. She began spreading the ointment carefully over the closed wound, and after a minute, she gently applied the bandages. Adam sat down on the floor, his bare back leaning against the bed. He looked with wonder at Arak, who looked back at him. "You are indeed full of surprises Arak, Captain Nelson said you were a special wolf for a reason." The young man smiled at the wolf. "You saved us, Arak, I thank you. You are indeed special, my friend." The wolf came to Adam, holding the eye patch between his teeth; Adam patted the head of his loyal friend, who astonished them all with what he did. The wolf gestured for Adam to put the patch back over his special eye, Adam understood, and with a warm smile he covered the eye, then hugged his friend, thanking him again for his actions. As he was holding Arak, Adam noticed Abdul's family watching him questioningly. The woman shielded her little children and the wounded Abdul rose slowly from the floor, throwing another glance at the two dead bodies sprawled across the floor, who a short while ago were about to kill Adam, himself and his family. He sat on a large wooden chair, padded with the fabrics typical to this exotic land. The merchant signaled for his wife to take the children back to their room and pacify them then politely asked her to make breakfast. Only then did he turn his full attention to Adam, who was sitting on the floor, shirtless, with Arak by his side.

"Would you like to tell me the truth now, Adam? Why did these men break into my house, why did they want to kill you?" asked Abdul angrily. Adam felt he must now explain to the merchant who he was and why the two hunters were trying to kill him. He told Abdul of all his adventures, beginning with the slopes of the Alps, where he witnessed the terrible massacre, and of the night he saved the children from the orphanage, which was also the night when for the first time, a man managed to destroy an empire hovercraft unarmed. Abdul remained speechless, now the merchant recalled the rumors he heard from far away ends, of the man who saved dozens of children from a burning building, the rumors that were passed from mouth to ear reached all the way to his country, rumors of the mystery man that the empire declared a hunt after him, to bring him in dead or alive.

He remembered the empire announcer, calling out in the market to turn in this man wanted by the empire. Abdul cared for his family, he took no interest in these far away rumors that the mystery man will be humanity's savior, but then again, he never considered these rumors might be true. Now the mystery man was sitting here in front of him, in his own humble house. "So you are the mystery man the empire is trying to capture and kill, you are the one who dared confront the regime that made us all slaves, you are the savior of humanity?" asked Abdul, his excitement mounting.

Adam lifted his hands as if in defense, "Please, Abdul, I'm just a simple man. I don't know what rumors are there of me, I do know that I embarked on a journey to find a solution to all this pain in our world. I'm fed up with seeing people suffer everywhere; I'm fed up with seeing pure children born into a world of suffering and pain. I don't know exactly how to stop the empire and the death she reaps in this world, but I heard of a legend telling of a mysterious force, buried somewhere in the Earth, that may be the answer, the response to all evil. I know it's just a legend, but in these days, what do we have left but to try whatever we can?"

Adam paused for a moment and concluded, "I just feel inside me that I must do my best to find this force that may save our dying world." Adam stopped speaking and felt embarrassment flood over him. He spoke with passion and now that he finished his words, he felt as if he was speaking nonsense. Abdul noticed that and said, "I'm a simple merchant, Adam, but I was always a man of faith, I believe in the kind creator. There are many people who lost their faith and their hope for a good life of freedom, honor, and morality. I raise my children humbly, under the empire's reign of horror. We go on living carefully. I teach my children to preserve hope and faith, without which we have no life, and because of that, I tell you I'm proud of you for trying to find the solution. I know nothing of it, but like I said, my old uncle has plenty of knowledge up his sleeve of the mysteries of this world. Your coming to my house is in fact the fruit of my faith and hope. I see it as a sign that the good creator is showing me that it pays to go on believing." Abdul stood up, apparently feeling much better, reached out to help Adam up and said, "If those bounty hunters found you it means the place must be crawling with them, and they won't rest until they get you. Please understand, I don't want to risk my family's life."

"I understand..." said Adam, his face embarrassed and continued, "Arak and I shall leave immediately for your uncle, if you could just please show us the way..." Abdul looked directly into Adam's eyes and said, "Adam, you must understand that I thank God for the right granted to me to help someone who aims for the greater good, that's why I will lead you to my old uncle." The merchant concluded and a warm smile showed through his coiled beard. And he knew that Adam agreed with him when he replied with an understanding smile. Then the merchant called his entire family and explained to them that everything is all right. He asked his daughter, celebrating her seventh birthday, to come near Adam because he wanted to give her a gift, that this year it is something extra-ordinary. The little girl awkwardly edged close to Adam, who looked at her with a smile. Then Abdul spoke to her softly, in front of them all, "Look, Dahab, my dear, this is your gift." Adam didn't understand what he meant, neither did anyone around, then the merchant continued his words in a soft, warm tone, "Look, Dahab, the present I give you this year is hope. Here it is, standing in front of you. Take a good look, because Adam is the mystery man everyone is whispering of in the market place, he is the man they say is humanity's hope of salvation, he was chosen by the good creator to set us all free."

Even though Adam could not agree completely with the words of the man, being himself choked by doubts again, he said nothing, respecting Dahab's birthday gift. The little girl drew near Adam, spread her little arms and warmly embraced him, and with her angelic voice she said, "Thank you, Adam, thanks for the best present in the world." Adam felt his throat tighten with tears at the little girl's words and actions; he knelt to her, hugged her back and said, "I will try not to disappoint you, with God's help." A single tear fell from his hawk eyes, and as he wiped it with one hand, he noticed little Dahab's tearful eyes. Then he uttered the words: "I won't give up as long as there is life in my body, I won't give up until everybody's dream for freedom is fulfilled."

The child looked at him with a sweet smile on her lips. Adam smiled back at her and said, "Happy birthday, Dahab."

Chapter Forty-Eight

The harbor market began its bustle again, of merchant's persuading the people passing to buy merchandise from their stalls. Black uniformed soldiers make their way through the intimidated crowd, black rifles in their hands, scaring the people of the market into submissiveness, so they carry on their daily activities without daring to object to the presence of the soldiers.

Suddenly everybody turned and looked toward the sea, at a dot coming closer to the harbor, growing larger from moment to moment, turning into a vortex that sprayed water in all directions, making a deafening noise; the empire soldiers stood tense, weapons ready in hand, the merchants hid behind their stalls, waiting to see what was happening: then, to everyone's eyes, the Parakees burst out of the water, the large, armored vehicle of the four Parakees men. The massive vehicle kept advancing toward the pier and stopped when it reached the edge of the dock. The door of the Parakees opened and out came the four sturdy men. The soldiers recognized the famous Parakees crew at once, and they dispersed the gathering of curious bystanders. Kardo and his men shoved the people and merchants aside as they plowed their way into the market courtyard.

Chickon pushed a merchant standing by a stall of vegetables, grabbed a few grape bunches, and began devouring them, juices spattering all over his face. Baltimore looked at him mockingly, came to a stall of grilled chicken, and grabbed one for himself. The four men began pillaging the merchant's stalls, who stood by, not daring to speak out, merely watching furiously as the four men devoured their fares. The empire soldiers looked from the sidelines, enjoying the sight, some even laughing. When they finished eating, Kardo turned to one of the merchants and grabbed him by the collar of his white shirt. The terrified man begged Kardo to leave him at peace, but Kardo ignored his words entirely, and drew a small picture from his pocket, showing the image of Adam Swandon.

Kardo asked the man if he saw the man in the picture, the frightened merchant replied that he didn't, and Kardo threw him to the ground at once and proceeded toward the other merchant, as did the rest of the Parakees crew. They moved from merchant to merchant, questioning them if they saw the man in the picture, no one had any idea who the man was, then suddenly from among all the people around a short and skinny man, with a thick moustache covering his upper lip, approached the Parakees men with a mean smile on his face. "Good morning, dear sirs," said the man, rubbing his palms together.

"And who the hell are you?" asked Asan, resting his hand on the handle of the large gun on his belt.

"I am Zartan, at your service," groveled the mustached man. "You said you are looking for a certain person. Well, I think I've seen him."

Once they heard this, the Parakees men immediately closed on Zartan, raining questions on him, "Where? When?" the man asked to be paid for the information, then Asan drew his pistol, put the barrel to the astonished Zartan's temple, and said, "Perhaps we will let you live after you tell us where he is." Zartan stammered and withdrew his request, begging not to be hurt. Kardo asked Asan to put down his weapon, and after a few seconds, Asan sheathed his gun. "Now talk, Zartan. Where is this man?" asked Kardo threateningly.

Zartan calmed down a little and said, "I saw him helping Abdul, the fish vendor, yesterday."

Kardo raised his voice ominously. "And where is he now?"

The man signaled for them to follow him and led them to Abdul's house, but when they arrived, they saw the place was empty. Kardo grabbed Zartan and began yelling, "Tell me, are you trying to make a fool of us?"

Zartan was shaking with fear, cursing himself for turning to them, but he quickly pulled himself together. "Sir, this is the merchant's house, look, his name is on the door."

Suddenly Chickon called from inside the house. "Hey, come here quick!" They all entered and were surprised to see the two bodies covered with blankets. "these must be two of the mercenaries on Drakkar's hunt," said Kardo, spitting at the covered carcasses. Baltimore examined the bodies quickly and said, "Kardo, this man is armed with some special weapon, look at these shot wounds."

Kardo looked at the bodies and their wounds for a long moment then began pestering Zartan again. "Tell me, fool, is there another place he could go? The terrified man thought for a moment and said, "he has no relatives here, except for…"

"Except who? Talk if you want to live?" Kardo yelled at Zartan.

"Except his old uncle, who lives up the hill," the scared man answered hurriedly. Asan looked at the other Parakees men and called, "So that's where we go." They all agreed, drew their weapons to make sure they're fully loaded, and went toward the hill, following Adam and the merchant.

Chapter Forty-Nine

Adam and Arak paced behind the merchant, who was walking slowly, due to his fresh wound. The sun blazed in the center of the sky, the streets became narrower as the group climbed up the hill. Very few people wandered outside in this hour of day, because of the heavy heat, they preferred to sit in coffee shops and cool themselves with cold drinks. In each coffee shop, the empire soldiers with their black uniforms were sitting, sipping bitter black coffee, and looking threateningly at the people passing. Their gazes also passed over the two men followed by a large wolf with an eye patch. The soldiers suspected the odd group, but were too lazy to stop them. The weather made them too heavy and tired to do anything, so Adam and the merchant continued walking uninterrupted. They came to the old uncle's house, looking quite strange standing apart from any other house on the hill and entirely enclosed by ivy. Abdul stopped a few steps from his uncle's house and said, "It's been a long time since I've last been here. There were times when my uncle would tend the garden surrounding the house, but nowadays he's simply too old, he stays inside the house the whole day. He gestured for them to continue and they entered the house. The air smelled of mold. Arak seemed troubled by the smell, he began wandering through the house, sniffing.

"Who's there?" came the hoarse voice of the old uncle from another room. The entire group rushed to that direction, and they all saw the old uncle, sitting by a wooden table, bent over an old clock from the last century.

"Dear Uncle, it is I, Abdul, your brother's son," said the merchant in a voice louder then usual. After a few moments of staring at him suspiciously, the old man managed to recognize his nephew. "Ho, my Abdul! You finally came to visit me." The old man abandoned the old clock and turned to greet his nephew. The merchant hugged the old uncle gently.

"Uncle, meet Adam," called Abdul in introduction. The old uncle raised his frail arm slowly toward the young man and said, "come close, my boy." Adam bent a little toward the old man, who laid his shaking hands on Adam's face. The old man of a hundred and seven years old shut his eyes and mumbled ancient phrases, and in a minute, he opened them and said in a hoarse voice, "You came from far away, young man…"

Adam raised his head and looked directly into the old man's eyes, and he felt as if the old man was reading the tale of his life so far, a sensation that ran chills down his back. He bent closer and continued to listen to the uncle's words, who spoke in a slow, rasping voice, "And your road leads you far further…" The old man rested his shaking hands on his knees and sighed, "Oh, dear Lord, today is the day."

Adam and the merchant stood by each other, mystified by the old uncle's words. "What day are you speaking of, dear uncle?" asked Abdul, glancing at Adam, who was also intrigued by the old man's words. "I am a hundred and seven years old. Through my long life, I saw men destroy with their own hands what the good Lord gave them, desecrating the gifts of creation. I saw how they robbed each other, how they raped, how they killed. I saw them choose the evil side of their mind, do evil deeds that hurt others around them, and all this was grounds for the rise of this evil rule of the last thirty years…" The man cleared his throat and coughed in length. Adam was slightly taken aback, impressed by such an old man having such a sharp mind, the old man bowed forward in his chair slowly and carried on, "but all through my long life I never presumed I will live to see the son of light, the pure hearted one, on his way to fulfill the ancient prophecy."

With these words, Adam froze in his spot. How did the old man know about the prophecy, about the son of light?, Adam asked in his heart. He swallowed hard, his entire body trembling as he drew closer to the old man, who was draped in a red cloak tied by a black leather belt, to his head a blue kerchief with black stripes, partially covering his wrinkled face. Adam knelt on his knees and looked at the old man. "Dear uncle, tell me, how do you know these things about the ancient prophecy and the son of light? What else do you know?" asked Adam with great excitement, the old man raised his right hand slowly and said: "I know that you are the son of light." These last words caused the merchant to stumble back and nearly fall over; he stared at Adam unbelievingly. "Could this be, Uncle?" he cried with excitement. "Could Adam be the man that carries within him the soul of the pure hearted?"

Adam stood up quickly, trying to defend himself, "Now hold on for a minute, Abdul." The merchant drew near to Adam, smiling, and grabbed him excitedly with both hands "Could you, Adam, be the man to bring salvation to us all, could you be God's messenger?" Adam stepped back and cried, "I'm not the man, Abdul! I'm merely seeking a solution to the evil in this world, I learned there may be a special force, buried somewhere in our world, and I'm trying to find it."

The uncle's grave voice broke into Adam's words: "Gim Nigma."

Adam's hawk eyes grew wide. "You know of Gim Nigma?" he asked, stunned. The merchant didn't understand what the two were talking about but he waited patiently.

"Many years ago, as the empire's reign of horrors rose and cast a long-lasting darkness over our lives, the rumor spread of an ancient prophecy, that one day a certain individual would choose to go on a quest to find Gim Nigma, but I don't know what the word means. I only know that there is a very ancient book, hidden in the heart of the Sahara desert, disclosing the location of this mysterious force," the old man summed. Adam could hardly feel his legs, his head began spinning and he had to sit down. He could feel his body heat rising and his heart beat twice as fast. "I can't believe this is happening," Adam said out loud.

All the signs pointed to this. Could the tale of the lonely priest guarding the ancient libraries be true? Adam asked himself. Deep inside he always thought the story might be fiction, just a legend, but it seems that even in far away lands the story of Gim Nigma was well known. *Is there really a prophecy about a mysterious force buried in the Earth decades ago? Am I really on my way to find it? Am I truly that man?*, Adam asked the people around him.

The old man cleared his throat and said, "For a few years now, I have been dreaming the same dream almost every night, and in my dream I see fire burning all over the world, and then from the sky bursts a bright ray of light, and a figure steps out of it—the figure's faces is your face, Adam." The merchant Abdul was mesmerized, he couldn't believe his ears, never before in his life was he so wildly excited, the son of light had come into his life. Strong chills gripped him. Adam sat quietly on his chair, trying to digest the old uncle's words. Abdul no longer felt any pain from his injury; he came quickly to his uncle and began eagerly questioning him, "Oh, dear uncle, would you know where is that priest guarding the ancient libraries?"

The old uncle mumbled unclear words, Abdul's attempts to understand him were useless, then with a hoarse whisper the old man asked his nephew to hand him a pen and a parchment to write on, which the merchant did with no further questions. Adam watched them silently. "I have dreamed that dream so many times because of the countless times I prayed the good Lord for salvation, but my age made it impossible for me to leave on the journey myself. So I waited, like my heart told me to, for someone special to knock on my door one day. In my dreams I saw where the ancient libraries lay, I remember every stone and every dune as if I walked that route hundreds of times". Abdul's face glowed with joy, "and you think you could draw a map to show us its location, a map from the memory of your dreams?" the merchant asked excitedly. The old man bent slowly over the parchment his nephew handed him, and to everyone's surprise, with his eyes shut and his hands trembling, he began drawing the map that would lead Adam to the ancient libraries deep in the Sahara desert.

Chapter Fifty

The four Parakees men pressed Zartan to hurry and show them where the merchant's old uncle lived. The people passing by had to move out of the way of the Parakees men, unless they will be harmed by their cruelty. The empire soldiers watched how the Parakees men treats the people in their way with mocking, leering gazes. The local population's hearts filled with frustration; the empire holds the guns, and they must obey if they wish to live. After some time, Zartan stopped and pointed to a hill decorated with small houses. "There," he called, attempting to rush away, but Kardo held his robe and didn't allow him to leave. "You have to show us exactly where, and you're in big trouble if we don't find him."

A grim laugh fleeted across his face. His other friends smiled at each other, enjoying their feeling of supremacy. In his heart, the mustached man cursed himself for the moment he offered them his help, seeing that this is his penalty for trying to join with the forces of evil, it never pays, thought the man to himself, but perhaps, he could still escape, he tried to cheer himself as he climbed up the hill, the Parakees men marching behind him.

Arak the wolf was restless, he could smell danger approaching, his edginess caused Adam to turn and ask him, "What is it Arak, do you sense danger?" Arak began barking wildly and his barks reached the ears of the Parakees men as they ascended the hill; they looked at each other and Kardo signaled to draw their weapons, they hastened their pace, with Zartan still leading in front. Abdul looked through the window and called out, "We have guests with wicked faces and weapons in hand. They must be after you, Adam." The merchant came near Adam and said, "We must leave now, Adam, we have the map that my old uncle drew, now you have to move on and not stop. If they get here and find you they will kill you, we have to leave and fast." Adam drew near the old man and held one of his shaking his hands. "Oh, dear Uncle, I will walk down the paths drawn on your map, and will try with all my might to find Gim Nigma." The old man looked with eyes weary with age at Adam and said, "I know that, Adam. The good Lord will be with you always. Fear nothing, and more importantly, don't let your doubts fail you."

Adam tried to lift the old man from his seat, "Come with us," he called. Even though the old uncle was a hundred and seven years old, he resisted, then said, "No, Adam. This is your journey, I've had mine, today I can close my eyes, content and peaceful, for what I wished for many years came true in front of my own eyes. Thank you, Adam."

The old man remained seated in his chair and asked the two men to leave quickly, before the Parakees would reached the house. Arak leaped out of the back window, Abdul parted from his uncle with tears filling his eyes, and the three managed to depart through the back exit.

The old uncle remained alone, looking at the walls of his house through aged eyes, his heart brimming with joy. He got to see the son of light with his own two eyes, now God could take his soul back to the heavens above. The old man laid one shaking hand on top of the other and they both rested upon his ancient knees. The old man smiled blissfully and drew his last breath. He left this world in peace; no one could take that away from him. His soul returned happy to its maker.

The door of the house was kicked open with Asan's wild entry. With drawn weapons, the Parakees rummaged through the rooms searching for Adam and the merchant, but their swift, feverous search was fruitless. Kardo began spewing curses; after a few moments, he turned to look furiously at Zartan, and with no remark, he shot him down. The small, mustached man paid with his life for his attempt to turn in Adam; blood spouted from his chest and his soul left his little body.

The four identified the figure of the old man sprawled in his chair, and after a brief examination figured, he was dead. The smile on the dead man's face raised Kardo's fury, who began kicking the furniture; Chickon tried to calm him down, "Kardo, we have to stay practical. They couldn't have gotten too far away, let's follow their tracks." Kardo saw the sense in his peer's words he commanded his men to check for signs of them, then Baltimore called out loud, "Here is some fur from the wolf he has with him." He showed his friends the bits of gray fur Arak left behind when he leaped out of the back window, Kardo was encouraged by this, he said, "The bastard isn't far. We will capture him, and when we do, I will kill the scum with my own hands."

The two men and the wolf ran with all their might far from the hill and the impending threat of the Parakees, luckily the fact they were running down hill made their escape easier. Abdul had to slow down because of the pain from his wound; Adam delayed in order to support his friend the merchant, who asked to stop, no longer able to take the pain. Arak suddenly barked at an old structure, apparently an old well shaft, signaling that it is a safe hiding place. Adam helped Abdul to reach the well and the three sighed with relief. "We shouldn't delay Adam, these people are still behind us," gasped the merchant, panting heavily. Adam replied at once, "Recover, Abdul, then we go on." After a minute, the merchant caught his breath and said, "You have the map now, Adam, all you need to do is get there." Adam looked at the map but he couldn't recognize anything, he knew nothing of this place, knew nothing of the roads of this land, filled with sand and deserts. He felt helpless, knowing that he couldn't ask his friend the merchant for any more help, since he had his family to care for. For a moment he felt despair flood him, but then he remembered old Joshua's words. "Think positive, Adam, think positive." He began repeating these words over and over in his head, then suddenly Abdul called out with a smile. "I remember, I have a friend who lives out of town, he's a mechanic of hovercrafts and land vehicles. He services the empire but that is from a lack of choice. He hides parts from them and smuggles them to the underground, right under the empire's nose. He is the man you should reach." It seemed as if Arak understood Abdul words, for he started to bark happily, signaling the two men that the time has come to move on. He could sense the Parakees approaching them.

    The trio moved on quickly, occasionally checking to see if the Parakees were anywhere on the horizon. After an hour of running, they made it to a wide tent on the outskirts of the city. The tent reminded of ancient times, as if time didn't touch this place. Camels and horses wandered around, tended, and fed by Bedouins in black and white robes. Abdul approached one of the Bedouins and conversed with him. Adam looked around himself and was astonished that there was not even one empire soldier in the place; the place was remote, forgotten, and the locals did not carry weapons, or do anything else that might call upon the empire's military presence. Adam saw veiled women, moving in groups, carrying their children on their shoulders. He felt as if he moved back in time. The large tent, far from the pier city, cast a sense of safety on him. The Parakees where nowhere to be seen but his heart was trembling within him; a long, mysterious road still lay ahead of him. He clutched the map tightly; this bit of parchment was the key for the rest of his journey, and according to the old man's words, the tale of the ancient libraries must be true. He felt eased a little. He remembered all the people that put their faith and hopes in him and was encouraged by this. He saw Abdul return, smiling, leading a camel behind him.

"The *Camel* is the ship of the desert. He's not noisy, he needs no fuel, but he's fast and strong, and he will bring you to my friend," said Abdul, handing Adam the reigns to the Camel "But how will I find my way to the ancient libraries? The Sahara desert is immense…" asked Adam.

"God will guide your way, Adam," Abdul answered, opening a small metal parcel, containing pills against the pain. He put one in his mouth and sipped some water. Within a few seconds, the man was smiling, apparently feeling better. "I suggest you move on Adam, in case the bounty hunters track you here," Abdul said. Adam felt that the time had come to part from his friend, a friend that was so kind to him. He hugged Abdul gently and thanked him warmly for all his effort. The merchant answered, "Look, Adam, my dear friend. In my life, I learned that when a man helps someone he is really helping himself; as if he lit another man's torch so that man may find his way in the dark, and by doing this he throws more light on his own path. I learned we must help each other, because that makes the whole of humanity work better."

Wise words, thought Adam to himself as he saddled the large desert beast. The merchant pointed to a sparkling dot in the sky and called: "you see that dot over there…? Well, that is the North Star. Walk in its direction and by night you will reach my friend." For a moment, the two looked at each other and they both felt the pain of parting in their hearts, but a fierce bark from Arak reminded them both that it was time to leave, Abdul prepared food and water for Adam and Arak; and he said that usually there weren't any empire forces on the route that leads to his friend, there're usually no empire forces, but Adam should still keep his eyes open. The camel began moving away from the large tent; Adam mounted the large animal's back, and Arak paced by his side. Adam looked back and saw the merchant waving good-bye, and he waved back. So many good people helped me throughout this journey, thought Adam to himself. There is still a spark of hope for this grim world, for these people it was worthwhile to go on this journey, for these people it's worth while to save the world. Far away now stood the merchant Abdul who raised his hands to heaven, calling out a prayer to his maker, "Ho, God almighty, please, I pray for this special man's well being, I pray to you to make him strong and bless his path, so he may fulfill his destiny and save this world which you created."

Chapter Fifty-One

Irma stood in her dark room, Bartholomew by her side. Both were staring silently at her crystal ball, in the center of which wisps of yellow smoke swirled. Irma is strains to locate the mystery man; she needs to know where he is, where he's hiding, what he's doing, for that she uses her powers of sorcery, which mightily drain her strength. Her eyes are tightly shut, her body trembling a little. Bartholomew sees this, but has already learned not to interrupt the old witch as she works her spells. He merely waited in silence. The witch told him that by the words of Grandma Trudy, the way to break the prophecy is to destroy the pure hearted son of light, who carries within him the soul, which is destined to bring light to the world and force the reign of evil out, forever. The way to do that, she said, the key is to break the man's spirit, make him understand that his quest to save the human race is useless, that man is evil from his youth and is not worth saving. They must find a way to make Adam believe his efforts are futile and he should forsake the idea of saving this world. But how is that done? Bartholomew asked himself. Now Drakkar is again embarking on some grandiose plans to remove the problem of the mystery man by sending out hundreds of bounty hunters to find the man threatening the empire. He's trying to solve this problem by brute force; he's not really concentrating on it thought Bartholomew to himself as he quietly watched the witch concentrate on her crystal ball.

The chubby leader was thinking that he and Irma here were truly getting to the bottom of the problem of the ancient prophecy, and they understood that by the words of the former witch Trudy, who served the dark dominions a century ago, that they should break the wings of faith that carry this man, who will launch a great war against the four kings. Bartholomew laughed quietly to himself: how does one man embark on a war against four rulers who have control over the world for decades now? How could one simple man possibly challenge an army of millions? But still, there is an ancient prophecy warning him against Adam. Could this be the man?

His chain of thoughts was broken with Irma's sudden cry, "Here, I got it! I got it!" Bartholomew glanced at the crystal ball and indeed, he could discern an indistinct figure, becoming clearer from moment to moment, and then they saw Adam, mounted on a camel and the large wolf, Arak, pacing at his side. "How did you manage to do that Irma? Even our satellite system couldn't track him down," The chubby leader cried gleefully. The old witch swayed from side to side, seeming to lose her strength, her life energy drained by her mystical feat.

"He is in Africa," she whispered, and after a few moments she added, "He's in the African desert, he apparently learned more about the prophecy, and continues his voyage." Bartholomew slammed his fist into the table and shouted angrily, "Damn! Our hunters couldn't capture or kill him!" The figure of the man and his companion disappeared from the crystal ball and Irma collapsed heavily into her red couch, "There is a way to break him, and I believe it's the spiritual way," whispered the witch.

Bartholomew came closer to the sofa Irma was laying on, "What are you talking about, Irma? What spiritual way?" the stout leader asked. The witch recovered a little and sat up on the corner of the sofa. "Well, Drakkar tried to sink the rebels' ship, with the mystery man on it, and he failed. The forces of nature rushed to the man's aid and overcame the deadly submarine. Drakkar unleashed on the mystery man great forces of hundreds of hunters who scattered all over the world to find him and kill him. Drakkar is flaunting the strength of his empire with vanity and arrogance that have not proven themselves right," Irma said. Bartholomew considered the witch's words, though he didn't like hearing what the old evil crone had to say, he found a measure of logic in what she said. He inhaled briefly and asked, "Well… what is this way you were talking about?"

The witch turned to face the stout leader and said, "Always, a man's best friend and a man's worst enemy are him himself."

Bartholomew seemed baffled by Irma's words, she noticed this and explained, "We all have our demons, Bartholomew, we all have our fears and doubts, because we all a mixture of good and evil. The mystery man too has his doubts, and we can nourish them until they overwhelm him and banish his will to carry on his foolish attempt to bring down your empire." The witch paused; she could feel her exhaustion overpower her, her eyes closed and her head lolled back.

The stout leader could see her efforts had finally got the best of her, and he said, "Rest, dear witch, gather your dark powers, and when you wake tell me how we can destroy this man and his path."

The witch remained with her eyes shut, accepting the leader's words. He got up quietly and stepped out of the dark room of the sleeping witch. He knew that the empire dearly needed this witch, and that he must wait until she wakes with renewed dark powers. He was eager to know what her way was to destroy the mystery man but he knew he must wait patiently. As he made his way back up the corridors of the Argma fortress he thought that he should keep this information to himself; he didn't want the other leaders to ridicule him for joining with the witch and her mystic ways, for they acted and believed only in practical solutions, in the military and physical strength. The single thought racing through Bartholomew's mind was to return to the witch's quarters the moment she awakes, he wanted all the glory to be his, that he would be the man who brought down the mystery man and his will to overthrow the empire. He thought that would finally earn him the respect of his friends, who always mocked him. When he reached his own room, he called one of the guards and asked to be notified immediately when the witch Irma woke up.

Chapter Fifty-Two

Night fell over the desert, and Adam didn't remove his eyes from the star twinkling on the darkening horizon. Follow that sparkling dot, told him Abdul, the kind merchant; he had been riding for hours and still no sign of the mechanic's house. "I never rode a camel before," mused Adam. He looked at Arak, slowly and faithfully walking beside him, and he thought how unique this wolf was, he thought of the way Arak saved him from the clutch of the hunters that almost killed him, and how he dealt with Abdul's injury, and suddenly Arak stopped, perked his ears and listened motionlessly, apparently hearing something the human ear couldn't pick up. Adam stopped the camel and quickly slipped off him, he came near Arak whose one eye was fixed on the darkness.

"What do you hear, my friend?" asked Adam with a whisper. Arak began moving forward, and Adam walked after him, gently leading the camel. Trusting in the special wolf Adam walked on confidently. Suddenly his ears picked up a faint and astonishingly beautiful tune. The melody became stronger as they advanced. Such a lovely melody, in the middle of the desert... it reminded him of the sound of Joshua's violin, playing in the blue house where they first met. Adam paced on after Arak as if captivated by the magical melody. Suddenly his eyes were blinded by a bright spot of light. "Hello, anybody here," Adam called out questioningly. In front of him stood a small, lit tent, and right by it stood a small cabin with its doors locked. Adam repeated the question, ready for anything, "Is there anyone here?" The pretty tune coming from inside the tent diminished, and in the entrance of the tent stood a tall, muscular man, with a big white towel tied around his waist. His hair was smooth and golden. His face was partially covered by shaving lather. He did not look like any of the localities. In one hand, he held a shaving blade, and in the other he held his face. "Who are you? And how did you get here?" the man asked threateningly. Adam glanced at Arak and saw he wasn't reacting defensively; he derived from this that he had nothing to fear, remembering his mother telling him as a kid of the special gift for recognition wolves had. They could tell if the person in front of them had a kind or evil nature. This thought boosted his confidence and he answered the man with a smile.

"Good evening, sir, I have been sent here by your friend, Abdul the fish merchant." The man glanced at Adam and returned to shaving his bright beard. "Abdul, ha?" said the man, and from beneath the shaving foam a tiny smile showed. "I haven't heard from him for months. How do you know him?" asked the man, in a softer tone of voice. Adam began to tell the tall man of his adventures with Abdul, how Abdul hosted them in his house and how he helped them escape the bounty hunters following them. The man with the golden hair was about to finish his shaving, but before he did, with the last section of foam still on his face, he called to them with a cheer. "What are you waiting for, come in, every friend of Abdul is also a friend of Vanderbraken the Dutchman." Arak began barking and wagging his tail, and Vanderbraken added, "Tie that camel up and come in lad, I was just about to sit down and eat this stew I prepared."

Adam was glad for the invitation, being tired and hungry from the way. He entered Vanderbraken's tent, and in the center of it, he saw a large stove, ancient, at least two hundred years old. A strong fire burned in the stove, lighting the entire tent. An enticing aroma rose from a large pot hanging over the flickering flames. Within a few minutes the sturdy Dutchman returned to the tent and handed

Adam, who already took his seat on one of the many cushions scattered in the tent, a spoon, and a plate. The two ate wordlessly, Arak was busy chewing a large bone with remnants of beef still clinging to it. Vanderbraken finished eating first, and he laid back quietly on a large cushion, decorated with silver ornaments and beaded with tiny, colorful stones. "So how is the good Arab doing?" asked Vanderbraken. Adam stopped eating, his stomach full with savory stew. "Truth is that during our struggle with the bounty hunters he was injured by the blade of one of the hunters." Vanderbraken almost jumped from his seat, alarm apparent on his face. "Abdul is hurt?" He was indeed injured, but Arak managed to take care of it immediately. Adam calmed the man. Somewhat appeased Vanderbraken asked curiously: "How did this wolf take care of Abdul?" Adam stood up, came close to Arak, and patted him, while Arak was enjoying his friend's caresses Adam gently removed the eye patch covering the special eye.

"Wow!" The Dutchman leaped from his seat and came over to the two. "Amazing!" he called while closely inspecting Arak's unique eye, with no resistance from Arak. "It's a bionic eye with a self adjusting laser mechanism. I never saw anything like it before!" Vanderbraken patted Arak, who gestured to both of them he would like to resume his meal now. The Dutchman turned off the stereo playing the beautiful tune that filled the air of the tent, and took his seat by Adam. "So you want to move on and find these ancient libraries and the lonely priest guarding a special book that will reveal the secret of Gim Nigma…? I must admit, this whole thing sounds like a child's fable to me," said the blonde man.

"I've been living here for years, ever since my family was killed by the empire years ago. I know nothing of what's happening beyond this place. Every now and then, empire soldiers pass through with faulty hovercrafts, and I have to fix them. If I don't they would burn down this place and kill me. But within me, I carry the desire for revenge over the murder of my wife and two kids…" For a moment, the sturdy man paused, his face growing sad. Adam wanted to say something but sensed the man was not finished, and the Dutchman carried on, "Years ago, I was a junior robot mechanic in Holland. I was eighteen years old when the empire rose to power, terrifying the world into submission by wiping Australia and all that lived there off the face of the Earth. Together with a group of other people, I sought shelter in the great continent of Africa. I met my late wife here. We lived in a relatively desolate area, not far from the port city Abdul lives in. We lived quietly, hidden from the threat of the empire, but to my sorrow—not for long. One day I came home, carrying engine parts from a neighboring city, I saw from afar pillars of smoke rising, and my heart sank. I realized something was wrong, when I got to the house it was burned down to the ground, the bodies of my friends, my wife and kids were scattered on the ground, pierced by shots from the cursed empire soldiers' laser guns. I swore that day that one day I would avenge them."

With these words, the Dutchman's eyes glazed over, his face turning red with anger. Then Adam spoke, his eyes suddenly brimming, "I understand your pain, Vanderbraken, and I hurt for your wife, your friends and your children, but you, you are alive, and you must do something meaningful with your life. Help me reach the place I'm looking for, help me so I can confirm if these ancient libraries exist or not, and if Gim Nigma is truly the solution that will save our world." The Dutchman pulled himself together at once, and with his large hand he clamped Adam's shoulder and called, "So how can I help you, Adam?"

Adam rose to his feet. "Dear Abdul told me you have a vehicle you occasionally hand over to the underground. Could you arrange some transport for me to reach my destination?"

Suddenly Arak leapt to his feet, his ears perked up: strange rumbles came from outside. Adam and Vanderbraken exchange suspicious glances, feeling the presence outside. The Dutchman peeked through the flap of the tent, and his eyes grew wide when he saw ten armed empire soldiers, mounted on black motorcycles whose glaring headlights nearly blinded him momentarily. "Damn it," whispered Vanderbraken.

Adam came closer and curiously asked, "What is it, Vanderbraken?" The mechanic turned and whispered, "Empire soldiers, ten at least, all armed. Hide now, damn, if they see you they will kill you and me alike." Adam looked around, where could he and Arak hide? There was no furniture or objects in the tent to give them cover. The footsteps of the soldiers came closer and they began to call out Vanderbraken's name. The Dutchman looked at Adam and Arak tensely then ran quickly to the center of the room: by the foot of the stove lay a dusty, thick rug, he swiftly whisked it away, exposing a wooden door covered by a layer of yellowish sand. The mechanic lifted the wooden door and whispered, "Quickly, get into here. I will try to get rid of them as fast as possible." Arak and Adam hastily slid in, the wood door closing over them, but not entirely. They were left with a thin crack, enough to let in some air. The Dutchman quickly went out into the night to receive the empire soldiers.

"Gentlemen, it's late at night, I was just about to sleep..." But before he could complete his sentence one of the soldiers shouted, "Shut up, Vanderbraken! We are empire soldiers, and you have to service us—now." Vanderbraken was filled with rage, but he dared not show it, he merely smiled apologetically at the soldiers and asked how he may help them. They pointed at their black motorcycles, and one of them complained that the last job Vanderbraken did on the motorcycles was lousy, the jet fuel engines had broken down again. The soldier ordered the Dutchman to fix it immediately, and began walking toward the tent, his heart violently pounding, Vanderbraken ran to the entrance of the tent and blocked the soldiers' way. The soldier that yelled at him earlier yelled again, "Get out of the way, lousy mechanic!" The soldier laid his hand on the grip of the gun hanging from his belt; through the narrow opening, Adam could see what was happening and his heart beat fast, fearing for Vanderbraken's life.

Having no choice, the mechanic moved aside and said, "Rest, gentlemen, and I will go and fix your motorcycles." Adam caught his breath as he saw the black boots pace across the tent floor, coming so close to his hiding place; the Dutchman forced himself to come up with something quickly, and suddenly called, "But I'll need your help, I'm having problems opening the door to my garage." The soldier in command sat down on a pillow pointed to four of his men, "Go out there fast and help him, I want to get out of this rat hole as fast as possible." Vanderbraken was hoping that they would all come out to help him, but following him to his garage were only four soldiers. The night was pitch dark; he asked them to light the way with their flashlights.

Inside the tent, the remaining six toyed with objects scattered on the floor of the tent. The commanding officer lay back on a heap of pillows and turned his gaze to the large stove in the center of the tent, the stove that at its feet Adam and Arak were hiding. Adam's eyes met those of the soldier; his heart skipped a beat. The soldier suddenly stood up and walked toward the stove; Adam's heart nearly burst out of his chest. He braced himself for anything. The soldier advanced slowly and stopped exactly in front of the hiding place; Adam was about to jump out and fight, but the soldier drew a thick cigar from his pocket and lit it with the flames flickering in the stove. Then he turned back, a wisp of smoke trailing behind him. Adam breathed a silent sigh of relief. The place they were hiding in was a tiny secret chamber, hardly large enough for Arak and him to crouch. Despite the discomfort they were silently coordinated, both not moving an inch.

Within a few minutes, Vanderbraken and the soldiers accompanying him returned to the tent. Suddenly the commanding officer asked Vanderbraken a question that caught him off guard, "Tell me, Vanderbraken—did you see an unfamiliar character wandering around with a large wolf?" The Dutchman laid down his toolbox and answered quickly, "No, I didn't see anybody. You can see that I'm in the middle of nowhere here, only soldiers like you stop here, and like you, they just fix their vehicles and move on." His answer apparently satisfied the officer; because he laid back on the pillows, shut his eyes and said, "Tell me, Vanderbraken, when will you finish the repairs?" The Dutchman didn't like the idea of having the soldiers in his house with Adam under their feet, that was an extremely dangerous situation, an idea came to his mind, and he answered cautiously, "The work will be done faster if you come and help me." To his surprise, one of the soldiers said, "Come on, let's help him so he can finish the job fast. I don't feel like staying too long in this miserable place". The officer thought for a moment, then gestured for his men to step out and help Vanderbraken fix the motorbikes quickly.

The soldiers left the tent at once, to Vanderbraken's joy, but the commander remained sprawled over the cushions, his eyes shut. Adam remained tense in the soldier's presence; he tried not to move even though they were nearly running out of air. Outside, the Dutch mechanic was fixing the motorbikes, with the help of the soldiers, who complained for having to dirty their hands and for not having enough light outside to see the work. Inside him, Vanderbraken loathed the empire soldiers. He kept looking at the lighted tent, where he left the officer with Adam and Arak under the carpet. He forced himself to work faster.

Indeed, after half an hour he got to his feet and called out, "That's it guys, you can get on your bikes and ride on, I'm done fixing them," and in his heart he continued, "and may you crash into each other, bastards."

The bunch of soldiers looked at the Dutch mechanic with disdain; they didn't even thank him. They told their officer the work was done, and he asked them to wait for him on their bikes. Then he turned to Vanderbraken, who was busy cleaning himself, "I hope you did a good job on these bikes this time, Vanderbraken, because if I have to come back here I'll burn this place down to the ground, got it?" said the soldier indifferently as he straightened his black uniform and dusted it off. Vanderbraken was a proud, rugged man, and he barely restrained himself from smashing the officers rude face with his fist, but thinking of his revenge on the empire he swallowed his pride, smiled to the soldier and said, "Of course, sir, I got it."

The soldier was about to leave, then suddenly stopped and turned back around, "Vanderbraken, is there something that you're hiding from me?" hearing that Adam's fists tightened, ready for anything now. Vanderbraken answered, "I'm here, a day's walk from the city, I live alone, I like living alone, and besides buying food from the nearby town now and then I don't see people at all. All I do is service the empire, I've been serving it for years now, and I hide nothing from the empire." The soldier looked at Vanderbraken and smiled contently. "All right Vanderbraken, all right, I just heard you've been helping the local underground lately." Vanderbraken opened his eyes wide and said at once, "No way, sir, I have nothing to do with the miserable little underground." The soldier laid his hand on the tent flap, laughed, and then said with a serious face. "For your own good, Vanderbraken, I hope you're saying the truth. Oh, one more thing…" The Dutchman couldn't stand the soldier's annoying presence a second longer, but he asked anyway, "What is it, sir?" The soldier stared at him threateningly and said, "If you see a stranger wandering about, accompanied by a large wolf, you should notify the empire immediately, is that clear?"

"Of course, sir, of course!" Vanderbraken answered without hesitation. Finally, the officer joined the others waiting on their bikes, he gave the order, and they disappeared quickly into the dark night. Vanderbraken sighed with relief then ran quickly into the tent,

"Adam! Adam, are you all right?" called the Dutchman. Arak and Adam burst out from the tiny underground room, breathing heavily. "Almost… we almost ran out of air," Adam said, catching his breath again. Arak stepped out to breathe the night air and recuperate.

"I'm sorry, boy, it was the only way to keep you hidden. You heard them, they're looking for you," said Vanderbraken as he helped Adam to his feet.

"I heard it all Vanderbraken. That's why you must help me, I have to move on—and I need a vehicle that fits the desert conditions," said Adam, his breathing steady again.

"I know Adam, maybe this way I can have my revenge on the cursed empire. I'll help you, my friend, I admire your courage, going out into an unfamiliar wasteland to follow a legend that may be the hope for all of us," said the Dutchman enthusiastically, then added, "We should rest now, we must gather strength. Tomorrow with dawn, my friend, I'll introduce you to my "Dragon Rider." It will be a great help to you, it's as if I made it especially for you," said Vanderbraken proudly.

"What's the Dragon Rider?" asked Adam curiously. But he could feel exhaustion already taking over him. Vanderbraken answered with a smile, "Oh, the Dragon Rider is something special that took me months to build, you'll see it in the morning. We should sleep now, tomorrow a special day awaits you."

Adam laid down on a carpet, covering himself with a thick blanket; the nights in the desert were very cold. His weariness took over and he fell asleep at once. Vanderbraken lowered the heat in the large stove, looked at Arak who laid across the tent's opening and thanked him for guarding his Abode. Within a short time, they all were sleeping.

Chapter Fifty-Three

Bartholomew was eagerly running through the fortress corridors. He was told the witch Irma was awake, and ready to tell him her plan to stop the mystery man. The stout leader was so excited he almost tripped with his awkward running, for Irma's doors opened for him just as he reached the entrance.

"Dear Irma, I'm happy to see you," said the fat man with a wheezing gasp.

"Calm down, Bartholomew, and follow me," said Irma mysteriously. She led the leader to a dark room, without a gleam of light.

"What are we doing here, Irma? I don't like the dark," he complained. Irma shut the door behind them, leaving them both in utter darkness. Suddenly there was a spark, Irma lit a long match, and the dark room was now dimly lit; she lit a number of black candles, arranged in a formation of a pentagram with five points. A shiver ran through the fat man's body, despite his curiosity he kept quiet and waited patiently for the situation to become clear. The pentagram was spread out on a low dais standing on the floor of the room, which in the candlelight turned out to be round, the walls empty; besides two cushions on the floor beside the podium the room was entirely empty. Irma gestured for Bartholomew to sit on one of those cushions, and he did her bidding. She sat across from him and began speaking: "One of the ancient methods to communicate is through telepathy—with the power of the mind one can reach another's thoughts directly and influence them." Bartholomew's eyebrows rose with astonishment and he continued listening to the witch quietly. "Through the strong force of my mind, I can reach the mystery man's thoughts and penetrate them, weakening his will, weakening the force of his thoughts and wishes," said the witch, each word echoing through the round room. "Is that possible, Irma? Can it truly be done?" asked Bartholomew with excitement. "I'll have to strain my dark powers to their limit, and I'll need to use your mind as well, Bartholomew. The matter can be compared to an electric light: the further we wish to cast that light, the more battery it takes," said Irma.

"What? You want to use my mind," asked the leader with a voice full of fear. "Don't worry, fool, nothing will happen to you. I simply need support, you must help me so we can remove the threat of the mystery man together, preventing the prophecy of the son of light from coming true," the witch concluded. She asked the man to take her hands and close a circle around the podium. "We must focus our thoughts on the mystery man, infecting his mind with negative thoughts that will overcome his own positive ones, this will destroy him," said Irma. Bartholomew did as the old witch said. They both united their thoughts, with Irma steering the entire process. Suddenly the candle flames rose high and flowed over the walls in a spiral of fire; Bartholomew was startled, but Irma asked him to remain calm, with his eyes shut and to continue sending negative, destructive thoughts to the mystery man's mind; carried by her magic powers, these thoughts will reach the man and affect him so that he will abandon his quest to bring down the empire. As the flames ascended in a spiral around them, flowing in a circle along the circular walls, Irma mumbled ancient words filled with evil, and her words flowed through space, moving toward the mystery man's mind.

Chapter Fifty-Four

Far beyond the sea, an old man sits on a yellow beach, his long white beard blowing in the wind. Beside him sits a young woman, they are both looking at the blue sea. The wind carries an exotic scent from the far land of Africa. They are both thinking about that special man who chose a special destiny for himself, a quest to find the solution for the evil that rules the world, both are praying that the good Lord will bless this man's journey, the man who wasn't thinking of himself but of the entire world. The old man feels something strange in the blowing wind; he feels as if the wind was suddenly tainted with a dark, noxious color, which caused him a deep distress, that grew deeper from moment to moment. The young woman peers into the old man's face with worry, seeing him pale more and more, and she feels increasingly troubled. She expresses her worry, asking the old man about his health.

He looks at her grimly and tells her that an evil wind is blowing, a wind, which moves toward Adam, to poison the spirit of the man trying to save humanity. She asks the old man what he was talking about; he answers that he can feel the evil energies coming from the empire, energies which are toxic to the heart, sent to hurt Adam and stop him from his vocation. If that happens Adam will die, and the hope for salvation will die with him. He explained he could feel an evil source, making efforts to send negative energies directly into Adam's mind through the power of thought. The young woman is shocked by his words, and asks him what they could do to help

Adam. He answers that they must gather their friends and together they shall pray in meditation, thus sending out a positive force to resist the destructive, negative energy. The young woman rises to her feet, helps the old man up, and they both march toward their friends. They have to do their best to help Adam.

Chapter Fifty-Five

The dawn was rising. Vanderbraken was on his feet already, looking through the tent flap at the rays of the rising sun, spreading the precious light of a new morning filled with hope. He wakes Adam and the two men step out to the fresh desert air, with a light wind blowing and caressing the golden dunes. Arak and Adam stand by the tent and notice now, in the light of day, that there is nothing around them but sands, beside them is the little makeshift home of the mechanic, near it a small hut where probably he keeps his tools—but where does he keep the vehicles he hides from the empire?

The place was empty, no other structure to be seen. Vanderbraken asked Adam to be patient. Holding a contraption with antennas, the Dutchman comes near the two friends patiently waiting. The three stood across from the tent quietly, only the wind whistling around them. Adam looked curiously to see what the Dutch mechanic was doing, and the man smiled at Adam and Arak.

"Now you shall see how I deceive the empire soldiers." As he finished speaking, he pressed one button on the electronic device in his hands, and the ground suddenly split open and a silver dome rose up slowly from the Earth to the open air.

Adam couldn't believe his eyes; the crafty Dutchman hid his entire treasure underground, tucked away from any human eye! Vanderbraken pressed another sequence of buttons and the dome split open, and as it unfurled sideways it exposed a flat platform, staked with many unique vehicles, all of them polished and shiny as if they just now left the factory. Vanderbraken's treasure was now exposed to Adam and Arak's eye, who were stunned by the sight.

"Amazing, Vanderbraken, simply amazing," said Adam reverently at the sight of the gleaming vehicles.

Vanderbraken stood proud by his creations. They were all unique, looking like large motorcycles, yet with some features different then any other vehicles. Adam's hawk eyes settled on a certain bike whose color matched the desert sands, and was patterned with earth-toned stripes, like the hide of a tiger. The design was so exceptional Adam couldn't take his eyes off it. Vanderbraken came close, chuckling with pleasure, "I see you have a good taste, Adam," said Vanderbraken, laying one arm around Adam's shoulder. "This is the Dragon Rider, my friend, and it's yours." Adam's face lit up, the mechanic's words caused him to forget his morning grogginess, "You're giving me the Dragon Rider to complete my journey?" asked Adam, understanding at once that the question is rhetorical. Excited, he came near the collection of vehicles and stopped by the Dragon Rider.

"The Dragon Rider is no regular transport, Adam. I put the best existing technology in it regarding its operation, controls, and weapon systems," said Vanderbraken, pointing out all its different accessories and parts.

Suddenly Adam remarked, "Now that I think of it, I never rode a motorcycle before, how will I know how to operate the Dragon Rider?" The Dutchman comes close and taps his shoulder, "Nonsense, you'll know by the end of the day," said Vanderbraken confidently. He leaped on the motorbike, pressed some buttons, and the Dragon Rider made a sound like the battlecry of a wounded wolf, a tongue of flame burst from the jet engine's pipes, and the extraordinary motorbike suddenly leapt ahead, the spiked wheels spraying the desert sands aside. Adam and Arak looked on, astonished at all the maneuvers the practiced Vanderbraken showed them.

After a few minutes of wild driving, the Dutchman stopped short.

"Well, Adam, what do you say of my Dragon Rider?" asked Vanderbraken, a bit smugly. Adam came near, clapping enthusiastically. "Vanderbraken, you may know how to build amazing motorcycles, you may know how to fix hovercrafts, but you are definitely an insane driver," laughed Adam. The Dutchman dismounted the bike, laughing as well "you're totally right—put me on one of these and I lose my head."

Arak came close to the two and his one eye said it all; if the Dragon Rider was Adam's new transportation to the ancient libraries, then where will be his place? Vanderbraken understood the special wolf's wisdom and said, still laughing heartily, "Ho, my friend Arak, don't worry, I will arrange a place for you. My Dragon Rider could contain even a special wolf like you." With these words, Arak leapt for joy and barked loudly at the two, who couldn't stop laughing.

Many hours passed with Vanderbraken teaching Adam how to ride the Dragon Rider, and ride it well. Every time Adam fell off the vehicle, Vanderbraken would shout from afar: "So you fell! Now get up and try again!" These words echoed in Adam's mind, and every time he repeated to himself: Go on, Adam, you can do this, you're improving yourself with every fall. And truly, after many hours of excruciating practice he could control the Dragon Rider as if he'd been riding it for days. Then he remembered something his wise father used to tell him when he was a kid:

A great will bears great achievements. He was very happy with himself for succeeding. He had the map from the old uncle, he had a loyal companion, and now he even had a unique vehicle to carry him through the rest of his journey to find the lonely priest guarding the ancient libraries, but above all, behind him were many people who believed in him. Adam drove close by to the Dutchman, who stood waiting with a leather contraption in his hands—a seating arrangement for Arak.

"Well, I think you're ready to move on, Adam," said Vanderbraken. Even with all the positive developments Adam felt, deep inside, a fierce fear of the rest of the journey. Difficult questions assailed him: what if he loses his way in the desert, what if the old man's map turned out to be false? What if the tale of the lonely priest guarding some secret libraries in the heart of the Sahara is really nothing but a legend?"

The doubts washed over Adam, and the Dutchman noticed that immediately. "What happened, lad? Why do you seem sad? You should be proud for advancing so well."

Then Adam spoke, "I'm scared, Vanderbraken. Scared I will fail, that all this is for nothing, no one has ever met this priest before, no one has ever been to the ancient libraries. It's all rumors. What if those are just some made-up stories, meant to give people hope?"

The Dutchman was surprised by the sudden drop in the young man's motivation. He was considering how to answer this, then he saw something that enlightened him. Even though he was a pragmatic man, a realist, and spirituality wasn't his thing, he saw in it something of a sign. He gestured for Adam to come near a segment of the platform, paved with heavy slabs. "Look Adam, do you see that?" The Dutchman pointed at a paved walking path, leading from the vehicle's platform to the little tool shack behind it, but Adam didn't understand what the Dutchman was showing him. When they reached the paved path, Vanderbraken directed Adam's gaze to a tiny green bud, growing between two heavy pavement slabs. Adam didn't see what Vanderbraken was trying to show him, and he asked listlessly. "So? What are you trying to tell me?"

Vanderbraken was shocked by the sudden low spirits of the lad, who only minutes ago was eager to continue his adventure in search of a solution to the evils of the empire, yet he insisted on speaking his mind; it was an odd feeling, as if he was somehow directed from above to speak and act this way. "Look at this tiny plant, Adam. Even though it's surrounded by heavy, hard stone, it has the audacity to push its way through the pavement and hard Earth toward the open air and the good sun."

Adam gazed for a long time at the little sprout and came to life as if he overcame some evil spell. "You are right, Vanderbraken. If that tiny delicate thing can force its way through these big hard stones, so can I go out to the desert and succeed in my way." Vanderbraken was astonished by the sharp changes in Adam, he felt like he must ask about it: "Tell me Adam, what's going on with you? It seems you're changing your mind every moment." Adam walked on the yellow desert sand, away from Arak and Vanderbraken, turned his back to them, grabbed his head in both hands, and said, "I feel as if some power is taking over me, penetrating my brain and making me weak on one hand, and some other power is fighting this power to prevent it from weakening me in the other hand, as if two powers are fighting inside my head, and this affects me."

The Dutchman didn't know what to say, he was just asked about Adam's well-being. "And now Adam, how do you feel?" The young man answered with an uncertain tone: "I feel fine Vanderbraken, I'm fine." A little smile returned to Adam's face, he drew near to his Dutch friend and said, "Thank you Vanderbraken, thanks for everything, Abdul has good taste in friends." The Dutchman wasn't at ease with the situation; he was concerned for Adam, who seemed influenced by some evil force, something that was holding him back from his former excitement. He decided to lighten the spirits anyway, and he slapped Adam's back affectionately and called, "All right, Adam, move on, I will mark my place on your map in case you lose your way, or need to fix something on your bike."

Adam saw he was now all set to go. After a few last arrangements, the Dragon Rider was fully loaded with food, water, a mysterious map, a large wolf and one special man heading out to a destination that may not even exist.

After a short time, the jet engines of Dragon Rider screeched through the desert emptiness; Adam lifted his hand and parted with the Dutchman who gave him this unique vehicle to continue his voyage on. Adam and Arak were speeding through the desert when they suddenly heard a loud explosion from afar, causing Adam to nearly lose his control over the Dragon Rider. "What was that, Arak?" Adam asked and realized that the explosion came from Vanderbraken's direction.

His heart pounded loudly, something inside him told him the Dutchman was in grave danger. He looked in the one eye of his faithful Arak and the wolf said it all in one loud bark, Adam turned the Dragon Rider around swiftly, pulled the turbo-levers and the vehicle began racing with incredible speed through desert sands toward the sound of the explosion. Within seconds, Adam could see a fire blazing where just minutes ago Vanderbraken's house stood. Empire bikes circled around the flames, mercilessly shooting and destroying the house of the Dutchman, who so far was nowhere to be seen. Adam came closer to the spot, until the empire soldiers noticed him and began to shoot. With incredible speed, Adam maneuvered in between the shots, making the soldiers miss time after time; all the time calling out the missing Dutchman's name: "Vanderbraken! Vanderbraken!" Arak laid his paw on Adam's back, signaling for him to stop, Adam stopped the vehicle and Arak leapt to the sandy ground and immediately began to search for Vanderbraken through the flames. The empire soldiers on their black bikes drew near, shooting at Adam, who began moving away at once, drawing their fire away from Arak, who was still searching after Vanderbraken. Suddenly a loud howl sliced the air; Arak had found Vanderbraken. Adam grasped this from afar and began heading in Arak's direction, as the Dragon Rider leapt ahead it occurred to Adam the Dutchman taught him nothing of the weapon system. He will have to rely solely on his maneuvering skills. Luckily, the Dragon Rider was much faster than the empire bikes, with incredible speed Adam made it to Arak and Vanderbraken, who was trapped under a pile of wood and metal that was once his home.

Adam jumped off the large motorbike to help the Dutchman and tried with all his might to pull his friend free, but the wood and metal rubble was too heavy. While Adam was struggling to free his friend the empire soldiers came near and stopped not far from Adam and the trapped Vanderbraken. With evil smiles on their faces, the heartless soldiers aimed their weapons toward the two. Arak didn't stand by idly, with one paw he removed the patch from his special eye and once again the special mechanism adjusted itself by rotating on its axis and within seconds the locking sound was heard again, Arak was ready, and just as the evil soldiers were about to shoot the two men down Arak dashed in the direction of the black motorcycles, his special eye releasing deadly, powerful laser blasts, which hit some of the riders and their bikes.

The rest of the riders simply could not believe what they saw: that a one-eyed wolf was shooting laser blasts at them from its mechanical eye. As a result three soldiers and their bikes turned to specks of ash on the desert sand. The rest began maneuvering to avoid the wolf and his deadly eye; Adam called out ecstatically, "Go, Arak! Show them who you are!" Arak continued moving around, covering for Adam while he strained to free the trapped Vanderbraken. "You have to help me, Vanderbraken!" Adam shouted. "You have to join your strength with mine and push this heap of rubbish with me!" Adam urged the Dutchman.

"Okay, I'll make an effort," replied Vanderbraken and laid his hands on one of the metal scraps sitting on top of him and waited for Adam's signal, who gathered his strength for one last effort to remove the heap from the Dutchman's body. Then Adam called out, "Push, Vanderbraken, push!"

Both men strained together as one, and indeed, the pile shifted and Adam managed to pull the mechanic free, unharmed except for some scrapes and scratches; they both jumped on the Dragon Rider and began moving out. Adam shouted to his loyal friend Arak. "Let's go, Arak, come on!" The wolf saw they were both safe and ready to leave and began to run toward the Dragon Rider, which was already in motion. Vanderbraken reached his arms out toward Arak as he approached, and at once, the wolf gave a mighty leap toward the moving vehicle. Arak almost fell short, but Vanderbraken managed to grab his front legs and haul him up. The three were safely on their unique vehicle, but still the empire soldiers were hot on their trail, never ceasing fire, but due to Adam's evasive maneuvers, they just kept on missing. In the midst of all this mad driving Adam turned and called out to Vanderbraken: "we have to do something to lose them!"

The Dutchman nodded in agreement, and turned himself around, so that he was now facing the black motorcycle riders. He asked Adam to press a certain button on the control panel up front, Adam did, and two little doors opened in the back of the vehicle. Two barrels of laser guns unfolded from them. Vanderbraken took control of the guns, aimed, and began blasting the black motorcycles pursuing them. "Way to go, Vanderbraken, way to go!" Arak kept on shooting potent laser blasts, which blew the empire agents to bits. Only two riders remained now, and their fear caused them to turn their vehicles back and run. Vanderbraken shouted with exultation, "We did it, hurray, we did it, we destroyed them all, only those two cowards got away!"

Adam slowed down a bit. The sun began sinking, tainting the desert horizon red. Night was falling. The group drove on silently. Then Vanderbraken spoke, "We have to leave this area. The two that escaped will pass the information on, and more armed forces and soldiers will come to kill you." Adam said nothing; he just went on steering and listening to his friend. "Don't worry about me, Adam. Nearby there's a small Bedouin village, I have friends there. They will help me. You, on the other hand, must continue your journey and never stop. Those worms killed my family, now they burned down my house, I have nothing left." When Adam heard those last words, he stopped the vehicle at once and turned back to his friend, saying, "Vanderbraken, my friend, the empire forces may have killed your family, they may have destroyed your house, but they can never kill the eternal hope in your heart, don't say you have nothing, the hope for a good free life no one can take from you. Hope, Vanderbraken, hope." The Dutchman's eyes filled with tears but he didn't let them roll down his cheeks. He said, "You are right Adam, one must never give up hope. Let's continue, I'll direct you to my friend's village." The group began moving forward once more, with a wind of hope on their back, pushing them forward.

Chapter Fifty-Six

Far away on the island of Esperanza, a small group of people gathered around a bonfire on the shore. The group included the kind Paola Katarina, Simon, the leader of the island's men, and Heralda, who was now entirely healed. They all united in a special meditation for Adam, to keep his spirits high. Joshua warned them against the evil influences carried on the wind, and that they must send Adam a force to counter this evil power aimed at Adam's mind, to poison his heart and fail him. He sensed that this power came from the empire, he was almost sure this was the work of the old witch.

They all focused their thoughts, Paola Katarina and old Joshua used their own unique powers of the mind they gathered and steered the positive energies of the rest of the group. Everybody's eyes were shut; everyone was concentrated on Joshua's words, who kept repeating, "Adam, believe in yourself, believe in the good creator, fight the evil thoughts and banish them from your mind. Continue the journey you believe in, fortify your will to succeed. Don't fear any obstacle on the way. Let your faith in your destiny grow, remember Adam, a man with no faith is a man with no path, and a man with no path is a man lost." The positive power of the group on the island of Esperanza began sailing through space, toward Adam Swandon's mind.

Chapter Fifty-Seven

In the port city, the Parakees bunch were sitting, angry and frustrated for losing the tracks of Adam and the merchant. They were flinging accusations at each other and sipping from the alcoholic beverages, served by the shaking hands of the terrified saloon owner.

Kardo slammed his glass on the table, splashing a bit of his drink in the air. "I swear that when I get my hands around this man's throat, I will pull his head off without so much as blinking," raged Kardo. Asan continued, "We have some really bad luck with this man. A few times already we came after him, and every time we lose him."

"Don't bring luck into this," raged Kardo at his friend "we will carry on until we find him and kill him." The gang lit one cigar after the other, drinking and smoking.

Suddenly two empire soldiers entered the saloon; their black uniform's covered with desert dust, their faces full of fear. They approached the bar and yelled at the bartender to pour them something, and quick. The four Parakees men looked at the pair quietly. They could hear their loud conversation with no effort at all.

"I can't believe the entire unit went down. This is a disaster, the commanders will punish us!" said the first soldier.

"Shut up, I don't want everybody hearing us," said the second one. "Don't tell me to shut up. That wretched wolf alone killed three men with that freaky eye of his!" With these words, the four Parakees men rose as one and approached the soldiers. Kardo turned to the saloon owner: "two mugs of mead for these two empire troopers, on me." The owner urged the bartender to do what he was told; the two soldiers thanked Kardo warily and dusted the sand off their uniforms.

Asan raised his arm and embraced one of the troopers as he was sipping from the mug he was served. "Dear soldier, we couldn't help but overhear what happened to you. We are the Parakees. Did you hear of us?" Asan asked. The embraced soldier raised his eyebrows "The Parakees? Of course, we heard of you. You're the deadly warriors working in service of the empire, famous for your cruelty."

At this, Baltimore laughed out loud "Famous for our cruelty? We aren't cruel. We just do what we are told," he snickered. Kardo decided to move the conversation to more useful tracks. "Tell me, troopers, was the person you fought with accompanied by a large wolf?" The two soldiers exchanged glances and answered as one, "Yes!" Chickon looked at Kardo and said, "it must be him." The first soldier interfered, "you should know that he's equipped with a really fast vehicle, with deadly weapon systems we never saw before." Kardo laughed quietly and answered, "Don't worry about it, soldier, just tell me which way he went."

"He went into the desert—he'll probably pass through the nearest Bedouin village, a little to the east from here." Kardo gestured for his men to get going, the four headed to their armored vehicle, and Kardo summed, "Okay, boys, let's go on a desert hunt." They all mounted the Parakees, and the monstrous wheels of the great automobile rolled out of the dock city and into the desert, pursuing Adam.

Chapter Fifty-Eight

The Dragon Rider crossed the expanse of desert sands with immense speed. Vanderbraken drowsed off in the back, while Arak the wolf kept looking forward in the direction they were heading, his gray fur billowing in the wind. His eye was covered with the patch again, protecting the special mechanism.

Adam's hawk eyes were fixed on the horizon he was driving to. He had to bring his Dutch friend to the Bedouin village, where he would drop him off. Then he and Arak must continue on their own, guided by the map Abdul's old uncle drew for them. He felt the excitement build up in his body from moment to moment—he could hardly believe it, but apparently, he will soon meet the lonely and mysterious priest Paola Katarina told him of. He was excited by the fact he was living and breathing his destiny, and for a moment he was perfectly content, aware that he was now walking the path he only dreamt of his entire life. His muscular hands were holding the Dragon Rider's handle bars steady and with force. The fatigue did show on his face. After a few miles of riding through the golden dunes Adam's hawk eyes distinguish a cluster of tents, and the three friends reached the Bedouin village at the break of dawn.

Three men in black robes and white mantles came to greet them with outstretched arms.

"This is the nature of the locals. Hospitality is crucial," said Vanderbraken, after dismounting the big motorcycle, he walked toward the welcoming Bedouins. Their hosts ushered Arak and the two men into a red colored tent, and served them a bounty of food. "How is it that this place escaped the claws of the empire?" asked Adam as he chewed down the goat's cheese.

"Well, my friend, the empire has no use for remote little places like this, they would rather stay away from the smells of camels and men. I myself find the Bedouins to be unique, fascinating people—they don't get caught up in worldly nonsense, they exist apart from the rest of humanity, just like the gypsies in Europe," answered Vanderbraken as he enjoyed a glass of cold camel's milk.

A few hours later, with the sun hanging low in the sky, the Bedouins parted with Arak and Adam, who began pacing away from the cluster of tents. Vanderbraken escorted them. "Thank you, Adam and Arak, for coming back for me and saving me from a certain death," said the Dutchman "thank you, for your help, for giving me the Dragon Rider so I may continue my quest for ending all evil—but what will become of you?" asked Adam. "Don't worry about old Vanderbraken, I'll stay here, the locals are good people, they'll take good care of me here." The two men shook hands and promised each other they would meet again one day, when they were all free men. Arak barked loudly, reminding them it was time to move on. Adam mounted the Dragon Rider, pulled the handle bars of the large motorcycle back, and the exceptional vehicle began racing with jet speed across the desert sand—though now Arak and Adam were truly on their own, their only guidance was the map that Abdul's old uncle drew. With Arak by my side, and the Dragon Rider carrying me to my destiny, I'm determined I will make it, thought Adam to himself. The Bedouin village was far behind by now, and according to the map, he had to continue southwest, toward the Sahara desert.

Chapter Fifty-Nine

The Parakees parked by the sputtering heap of what used to be the home of Vanderbraken, the Dutch mechanic. Kardo and his men prowled through the wreckage quietly, searching for Adam Swandon's tracks. "I hate the desert," Chickon mumbled. "It's bad luck to go into the desert," the man continued.

"Quiet!" shouted Kardo irritably at his companion. "We will go into the desert, and we will come out of it with this bastard's severed head," said Kardo conclusively. Baltimore paced slowly toward him, "We must remember the man is riding an extremely fast vehicle, one designed especially to move fast on the desert sands," he said and continued, "our Parakees can't match that speed." Kardo looked around him angrily, his eyes wandering over the empire trooper's corpses lying by their bikes. Then he called to his colleagues, "Listen, men! We'll take these motorcycles back to the Parakees with us, fix them up, attach additional jet fuel engines to them, and make them much faster." So the Parakees gang gathered the motorcycles, all still in working condition, and a few minutes later the large armored vehicle began moving into the vast ocean of a desert, its destination: Adam Swandon.

Adam stopped the Dragon Rider facing the setting sun. Arak leapt off his special seat and went to stretch his limbs; Adam remained alone, his back leaning on the Dragon Rider, his face painted in the golden hues of the sun setting on a gilded horizon. An overwhelming wave of sadness filled his heart, and thoughts began troubling his mind, "What am I doing?" he asked himself "I went alone on a quest which seems impossible to fulfill. I'm heading for a destination I don't even know exists. My heart wants love." He remembered Heralda's beautiful face, her magical eyes "I haven't experience true love yet," he thought to himself "I decided to go on a long, strange journey—why don't I find love, raise a family, and live my life quietly with a loving woman by my side and kids whom I can play with and hold." These strange thoughts took Adam by surprise, and tears rose in the man's hawk eyes.

The wind blew lightly over the golden dunes, and only the sun witnessed the man's painful thoughts: "I'd like to find a real love, and love the woman with me with all my heart, a fierce and wonderful love. Why am I clinging to this escapade, with a goal that may not even exists."

Adam felt a heavy loneliness and a deep depression began rising in him. The tears rolled from the corners of his eyes down his cheeks, through the dark stubble of his beard. The sight of the sinking sun made his heart ache; he hurt for the fact he was alone in the world, that the only reason for him to live on is the fulfillment of his destiny, that he was alone in the midst of a sandy desert, and the light was fading now. The night was falling.

Adam's thoughts came to a halt when Arak came back from his spin. The special wolf sensed Adam's sadness, and sat down at the feet of the man, who quietly wiped his tears.

Adam felt very tired; his eyelids grew very heavy. He laid down by Arak's side, covering them both with a heavy blanket, and a heavy sleep fell upon them both.

Adam dove deep into the ocean of a peculiar dream. He finds himself standing on a blue tainted mountaintop, surrounded by a blue mountain range; above him, he sees two suns, shining blue, painting the entire scenery in a soft blue hue. He hears a sweet voice call out his name from afar; his heart twists with a sweet pain, like a deep longing for someone dearly loved. The wind blows gently, carrying with it blue and green leaves which dance around Adam's feet as he stands and wonders over the enchanted view in front of him. The sweet voice is coming closer and closer, then he can see a figure sailing in the wind—it is a beautiful woman, draped in many robes, green and blue. The breeze carried her long flowing hair softly, and her blue eyes were the prettiest eyes Adam had ever seen. Adam stood on the summit silently; hypnotized by her beauty, awaiting whatever came next. Her green blue robes billowed in the wind and her gentle face smiled at him, making him feel wonderfully safe. "Adam," she called to him and her voice sounded like the most beautiful thing ever to exist. Adam grasped that he was falling in love, stronger than any love he knew before.

"Yes," he answered. He remembered movies, books he read about love at first sight, but he never imagined that such a thing truly existed, that one could truly feel this way. He felt as if he was in love with this woman before he was ever born, and a boundless joy flooded his heart. He smiled at her, abashed, and she called out his name again, "Adam." Her voice sounded like the clearest water flowing through an enchanted river. She came to stand on the summit near him, and they looked at each other silently. Sweet tears of love began rolling down Adam's cheek, he felt as if he was reborn into a world filled with light and love, he was grateful for his existence, for the first time in his life he felt whole—but he asked himself, who is this magical lady? And where was he?

And as if she was reading his mind, the beautiful woman answered in her soft, tender voice, "We will meet again, my love, we will meet again." Her words pierced Adam's heart, and she said more, "But in order for us to meet, you must continue your journey, Adam, and not give up even with all the troubles that will assail you, even though it will all look so grim and painful—don't ever give up. I'll wait for you, my love, I'll wait." Her soft voice started fading away, like a magical tune vanishing into endless space. Adam's heart hurt like it never had before, he desperately wanted her back, but the wind carried her away till she vanished behind the Blue Mountains. He began crying out to the distant figure to wait, to come back, but she was gone already. He knelt on the blue mountain and began to weep for the fierce pain in his heart—he had found the true love only for her to disappear. The wind began whispering in Adam's ears, "No need to weep Adam, remember, she said you will meet again."

Adam rose to his feet and gazed at the two suns, which looked like a pair of torches lighting the blue ranges. "Yes," he said, "she said we will meet again." He wiped his tears and smiled once again. "I have to go on with my journey, I have to go on, I won't fear the obstacles. I'll overcome every obstacle and make my way to you." A wave of excitement welled within him, and he shouted at the Blue Mountains, "I will do everything to reach you, my true love, I will fight hard and I will win, we will meet again—we will meet again!" he woke up shouting these words into the star-filled desert night. "We will meet again!"

Arak woke up with a start and looked at his human companion with concern. Adam looked around him and felt a sweet pain in his chest; he raises his eyes to the sky and saw that among all the other stars one shone especially bright, its light tainted blue. Adam breathes heavily, understanding this was no common dream. Slowly he calms down and says to the one-eyed wolf. "I'm all right, Arak, everything's all right, let's go back to sleep now."

The wolf laid his head on Adam's legs as if saying, "I'm here, friend, and I'm looking after you."

Adam felt the same way toward Arak. The two quietly fell back to sleep.

Chapter Sixty

Chickon and Baltimore were busy repairing the black empire motorcycles. They installed them with extra jet engines to make these vehicles faster than any normal vehicle. The Parakees moved heavily through the desert night. Every few seconds Asan would check the radar on the control panel to see if there is any trace of Adam.

Within a few hours, as the first rays of sun began pushing back the night, Chickon called Kardo and reported that the bikes were now ready for action. Satisfied, Kardo ordered his men to also install the black motorcycles with a deadly missile launcher, cruelly emphasizing, "I want him blown to bits and pieces." The men were laughing as the Parakees continued to make their way toward Adam.

Adam and Arak finished breakfast quickly, and Adam took out the old uncle's map and studied it carefully. There were a lot of curves and scribbles he couldn't make out, but he was determined to make some sense of it. He followed the lines curving into something that looked like a grouping of trees—suddenly Adam cried out with joy, seeing that it must be a desert oasis, because right in front of him he could see a patch of bright green. Cheerfully he called Arak to hop back on the Dragon Rider, for the oasis was proof that they were on the right track. The two jumped on the large bike and zoomed toward the oasis, which unfolded before their eyes in the morning light.

Within minutes, they reached the spot. To their surprise, they discovered the oasis wasn't only a small patch of greenery mid-desert;

it was actually quite large. Beneath hundreds of trees, small, blue lakes could be seen. Adam, stunned by the sight, remained frozen with awe on the back of the Dragon Rider, while the one-eyed wolf leapt out of his seat straight into the cool lake water. Seeing Arak splashing around gleefully, enjoying the water's coolness, Adam laughed and called out to him, "Actually, why not?" He took off his cloak and leapt into the blue pool as well. The two friends played around in the water like little kids. After some time, they laid on the lake's shore and relaxed, the green palm leaves sheltering them from the warm sun.

A few miles away, the bulky Parakees halted behind a desert rock. Their radar picked up two large figures within the oasis. "It's them," called Asan.

Kardo ordered his men to leave the Parakees and go demolish the mystery man and the wolf. The Parakees door opened, and from it, Kardo, Chickon, and Baltimore shot out, mounted on black motorcycles with fast jet engines attached to them. Asan stayed behind to maneuver the monstrous Parakees, which also advanced toward the oasis.

Arak suddenly perked his ears, then immediately lifted his head and began sniffing. Adam saw this and grasped Arak was sensing danger; he looked through the tree trunks toward the sand dunes and his head and his sharp eyes registered the riders on their fast motorcycles, rushing toward the oasis, with a fearsome looking vehicle rolling behind them. Startled, Adam cried out, "Quick, Arak, jump on the bike!" Within seconds, Arak and Adam were mounted on the Dragon Rider and the mystery man swiftly started the engine of his special bike. The Parakees men daftly maneuvered their fast bikes through the trees. Suddenly, Kardo cried out, "There he is, kill him, kill him!" All three men opened fire, bombarding Adam with laser blasts. Adam dodged them with evasive maneuvers, and the stray shots tore through trees and bushes, which flew in all directions in fiery explosions. Adam's heart beat fiercely in his chest; only a few moments ago, they were idly enjoying this small haven, and now the gang of murderers at their heels may butcher them. Adam began to pray silently. "Dear Lord, please help me, please help." Arak barked, signaling Adam to remove the eye patch from his special eye—Adam understood and did exactly that, all while driving on at an immense speed. With his special eye exposed, Arak stared directly at Baltimore's bike and released one laser blast at the highest strength. The beam penetrated through the shocked Baltimore's black motorcycle and split it; within seconds, Baltimore and his bike exploded to smithereens. The sight drove Kardo mad. He drove his motorcycle straight toward Adam at the highest speed. The wolf kept shooting laser blasts from his special eye, but he missed the other two riders. Adam took fright, hardly imagining what he might do next; he just kept dodging the shots of the other riders as he weaved through the trees—trees and bushes that stood in this peaceful place for years were now exploding into shards all around him. Kardo suddenly appeared at his right, taking Adam by surprise. The man looked into Adam's hawk eyes with a murderous, evil stare. Then Kardo powerfully slammed his bike against the Dragon Rider. Adam nearly lost control but quickly regained his balance and straightened the large bike. Arak barked toward his enemy, and again, Kardo slammed his bike against the Dragon Rider with even more zest; this time, the impact threw Arak off the Dragon Rider's back and flung him powerfully against a tree trunk. Adam was horrified to see his loyal friend Arak lying beneath the tree, motionless.

He immediately swerved the Dragon Rider toward the wolf, while Kardo aimed a pair of deadly torpedoes at him. Adam started circling the tree in order to protect Arak from the riders. The wolf lifted his head weakly and looked at Kardo as he approached, his gaze following the course of the two missiles that were supposed to end his and Adam's life. Despite his injury, the special wolf managed to lock on to the missiles in their flight, and with two accurate laser shots he wiped out both missiles. Adam saw this and was merely relieved that Arak was still alive. He stopped his bike short, as did the furious Kardo. They stood facing each other from afar. Chickon wanted to come close but Kardo signaled him to stop; he wanted Adam for himself. He wanted to kill this mystery man with his own two hands. Then Kardo began moving toward Adam with great speed, and Adam did the same. The two motorcycles rushed toward each other; Kardo was sure the mystery man would take fright and swerve at the last moment, crashing into one of the trees.

Adam remembered Vanderbraken's words, that the Dragon Rider was a very special bike, and swiftly, while driving, he pressed a few buttons on the control panel—at once the two spiked wheels withdrew into the frame of the bike, and three jet blasts suddenly lifted it up like a missile; at the same moment, Kardo should have crashed into Adam. The Dragon Rider took off and glided right over Kardo's head, who continued staring at it, astonished, as he drove on. Chickon called out to him to beware, but it was too late; Kardo smashed into a tree, his bike immediately bursting in flames. Chickon was horrified to see his commander, who lead them all for years and years, suddenly devoured by flames. He called Asan on the radio to come to his aid; having lost two companions, both were severely shaken.

Adam jumped off the bike and quickly ran to Arak, examining his wound. He was grieved to see that Arak's ribs were apparently broken. Adam took off his shirt, soaked it in cold water from the nearby spring, and gently laid it over Arak's damaged chest. Chickon yelled, "I knew it was bad luck to go into the desert!"

Asan moved the Parakees heavily toward the two, simply trampling over the dense greenery in his way. He flips a single black switch, and a missile is released, exploding right next to Adam and Arak. The blast throws Adam far in the air. He is badly hurt. Even through the haze of his injury, he notices the Dragon Rider standing nearby and starts crawling toward it. Chickon came near, a wicked smile on his face; he will be the one to kill the mystery man! He dismounted his bike, drew his gun, and advanced slowly. Adam strained to reach the Dragon Rider's control panel. He felt Chickon standing very near now. He whispered a prayer, "I don't know what I'm pressing, but be what it may—it's all in your hands, God." He pressed a blue button. Two narrow, silvery barrels immediately protruded from the front of the Dragon Rider, releasing a short laser blast, killing Chickon in an instant. He dropped dead on the sandy ground.

Asan remained alone now inside the Parakees, facing the mortally wounded Adam and Arak. He was horrified to discover that he was totally alone, his friends all dead; only a few minutes ago, they were all with him, Kardo, Chickon, and Baltimore, they're all dead now, the mystery man did this, him and his big wolf. Rage flooded the last Parakees man. He turned the engines on full power. Adam crawled toward Arak, intent on defending him. The Parakees advanced toward Adam—wounded, bleeding on the green foliage and desert sand. As he was crawling toward his friend the wolf, he thought to himself, "I made it so very far, with such tremendous efforts, only to die here in the heart of the desert."

With great efforts, he made it to Arak, who was in agony over his broken ribs. Adam's mind kept lamenting, "I let them all down, Joshua, Heralda, Simon, Paola Katarina, Captain Nelson and his men—even Peter and Dorina. I failed. I will die here, in the first and last oasis I shall ever see." A great sadness fell upon Adam, who knew the severity of his wound, and knew the doom facing him in the form of Asan and the Parakees he drove. He felt his end coming, yet something prevented him from closing his eyes and dying. He remembered the magical dream of that night, the beautiful woman, and those unusual eyes, he remembered he fell in love in the dream;

he remembered she said they would meet again, but first he must fearlessly complete his journey. Once again, his heart retuned to beating powerfully and steadily. With his last ounce of strength, he held on to that sliver of hope he dreamt of. Suddenly he was filled with peace. It didn't matter anymore if he died; he had to keep on, like the woman in the dream told him to, with that sweet voice. The Parakees was very near when it drew to a halt. From within the monstrous vehicle Asan called toward Adam on the microphone, "You, mystery man, you killed my friends and disgraced the empire. I will kill you now, and your death will be horrible." Asan began laughing an evil, mad laughter.

"And you thought you were humanity's hope! Ho, that's funny, because now there's no hope left for you. You're going to die like a dog—you and your furry friend!" Laughing and mocking the two injured beings lying beneath the palm tree, he aims one last deadly missile at the two and prepares to launch it.

Adam whispers in Arak's ear, "Arak, my dear, we may very well die here, in the midst of the desert. But before we do, let's strike them one last time." The special wolf looked at Adam with his one good eye and made an effort to lift his head off the ground. Adam—he, too nearly paralyzed by the pain—held up Arak's head with his two bleeding hands and directed it to face the Parakees.

"What are you trying to do?"

"Now, Arak, now!" As the words left Adam's mouth, Arak shot a single laser blast, with Adam helping him aim with his two shaking hands supporting the wolf's head. Asan, the great warrior, couldn't believe his eyes, but before he could do anything, the Parakees was blown apart in a great explosion that thundered through the entire desert the Parakees remains scattered all over the ruined oasis. Arak passed out; Adam's vision began to blur, and he laid back. He couldn't feel his body anymore. He could sense death gathering near. He stared up into the blue skies and tears flowed from his eyes. "Dear

God, I did what I could, I tried to help, to save, to find the solution to all evil in the world. I must have been fooling myself, though. I'm just a man about to die, without his true love, without seeing his dream come true."

Suddenly Adam's ears heard a distant shriek of a hawk. He thought that he and Arak might be food for vultures while they were still alive. He didn't want to believe that this could be God's retribution for one who tried to follow his destiny, he didn't want to believe that this could be the end for someone who tried to do good in the world. "Could it be?" asked Adam. Just as his eyes rolled shut, he could feel a strong wind blow over his face; the shriek of a hawk was heard again, closer this time. A huge shadow passed over him, and then Adam Swandon, left alone in the desert with his loyal friend Arak, finally shut his eyes.

Chapter Sixty-One

The flames burning along the walls of the room where Irma and Bartholomew were sitting went out at once, the flaming pentagon extinguished, and darkness settled over the room. Irma was pushed back by a mysterious wind, as was Bartholomew. He couldn't understand the meaning of these events. His curiosity expressed itself with the question. "What's happening, Irma?" The old witch groped in darkness until she found some kindling to relight the candles. Once again, the room was faintly lit. "Well, my dear Bartholomew, there is a strong resistance from the forces of light, they outnumber us, and somewhere in the world there is a group of people doing a meditation similar to our own transmitting of dark energy. There's a struggle between our telepathically transmitted forces, and this time they managed to drive us back."

For a moment, Irma fell silent, as if listening to far away voices, then she carried on, "I feel something terrible in the air." Her voice trembled, and her eyes began darting in all directions.

Bartholomew, intrigued, asked at once, "What is it you're feeling, Irma?"

The woman gulped and said quietly, "The Parakees, Bartholomew—the Parakees crew, they are all dead. Aided by the positive energies sent by his friends directly into his brain, the mystery man managed to overcome the force of the four men who served the empire for so long. They are dead." Irma shut her eyes, seemingly concentrating deeply on a distant place.

Bartholomew was beside himself; he couldn't believe that the Parakees men—known for their fierceness and cruelty—were killed by the mystery man. His fear of Adam was now greater than ever before. He began trembling.

"Irma, what will we do?"

The skinny old woman's narrow eyes grew wide as she stared at the chubby leader facing her, and she said, "I feel the man is mortally wounded, and I feel some other presence with him. It is not human."

Bartholomew leapt out of his seat. "Is he dead, Irma? Is that man dead?"

Irma asked the leader to calm down. He did as he was asked but still waited impatiently for her answer. The gloomy room was silent for a few, long seconds, and then Irma called out, "I can't catch anything!" Bartholomew was disappointed, but Irma carried on, "We need more people, Bartholomew, more minds to enhance our dark energy, so we could break into the mystery man's mind and neutralize his will to bring forth the prophecy." The old hag seemed exhausted. She asked Bartholomew to keep their actions secret and asked him to arrange for more people. He nodded in agreement and went on his way.

Far away on the island of Esperanza, the group that gathered in a special meditation, whose purpose was to help Adam overcome the negative energies and continue his special voyage bravely and with confidence, rose to their feet suddenly with great joy. Joshua's face filled with light; he knew that they succeeded in pushing back the dark forces. He knew that for now, the dark forces failed in their attempt to conquer Adam's will to fulfill his destiny; he also knew they would try again and return stronger than before. He turned to his friends, "Dear friends, this is an important day. Adam has managed to overcome the dark forces. But don't think it's over. They will come back, and they will be much stronger, bent upon breaking into Adam's mind and conquering his will."

Simon stepped forward and said, "Well, we must prepare ourselves and be ready for anything."

Only Paola Katarina was sitting alone, far from all the rest, and Heralda noticed that tears were running down her face. She signaled the other members of the group to check what was wrong. Joshua approached her and asked gently, "Why do you cry, Paola Katarina? After all we have succeeded. With our common prayer, we stopped the forces of evil from poisoning Adam's mind," the old man spoke softly.

Paola Katarina lifted her head and met her friends' gazes. "I feel Adam is in great pain. He is badly hurt, somewhere deep in the desert, and his loyal wolf Arak is also badly injured, I see it in my mind."

Concern took its place upon all the faces, and Heralda broke into tears. Only Joshua spoke, "What else can you see, Paola Katarina, with your powers?"

The good woman shut her eyes and concentrated, using her spirit's eyes too gaze far, far away. Then she said, "I see a pair of enormous wings and hear the shriek of a hawk." The woman opened her eyes and looked around.

Heralda sobbed, "Oh no, hawks are coming to hurt Adam now. He's lying deep in the desert, all alone, badly wounded. It's so sad."

Then Joshua asked an intriguing question, which took all of them by surprise, "But how do you feel about these sights and voices, Paola Katarina?"

The woman understood the old man's intention and answered unexpectedly, "It's funny, but I have a good feeling about Adam, a very good feeling." Paola concluded with a smile. The old man answered with an understanding smile of his own.

Chapter Sixty-Two

The desert looked like a plateau of gold, the dunes so beautiful, and the air warm and pleasant. The wind caressed Adam's face; he felt himself floating through air, sunlight filling his eyes, so far from the ground—*am I dead?* he asked himself. *Where am I?* He was gliding high above the desert ground, silence all around him, only the beat of great wings echoing through the desert air. Adam no longer suffered from pain; he felt as if he was dreaming a dream that was all peaceful and graceful. He asked himself where his loyal friend Arak was, and tilting his head a bit, he saw that he was clasped by the claw of an enormous hawk, and Arak was held in the other claw. He was sure he was dreaming a strange, magical dream, yet the shriek of the hawk was so real it made him see this could be no dream.

How did he and Arak come to be in the claws of a great hawk, gliding over the desert? Where was it heading, and why hasn't it hurt them? But from moment to moment, the assurance grew that the hawk was actually their savior and guardian. The loud shriek resounded again, as if the great hawk was trying to tell Adam something. Adam looked ahead in the direction of their flight and couldn't believe his eyes. In the middle of the desert stood a huge boulder, standing apart and somehow different than all the other rocks. As the hawk drew near, he could see the boulder was enormous, looking like a great fortress in the heart of the desert.

What is this place? Adam asked in his heart. Suddenly he remembered the old uncle's map; he drew something like a large stone in the middle of the empty wilderness. A thrill of excitement rushed through Adam's body. He couldn't believe he made it to the place! He couldn't believe this giant hawk carried him to the place he wanted to reach. But how? Adam wondered as the hawk spread out its giant wings and began to glide lower. It softly laid Adam and Arak on the desert ground. The wind caressed them softly, and the weather was pleasant. The hawk gathered his great wings to his body and shrieked again, standing by the odd-looking stone formation. Adam looked around, and his eyes saw nothing but golden dunes and a few rocks, scattered far from the gigantic boulder.

Suddenly, all the pains returned at once to his body. He collapsed on the sand; Arak's sudden howl echoed through the empty wilderness around them, yet despite this pain, Adam felt oddly confident that all was well, and there was no need for fear.

A voice suddenly echoed through the empty space. "Ayakon!"

Adam, drained by pain, strained to see where the voice was coming from. "Ayakon!" Again came that thundering voice, which ran shivers down Adam's wounded body. The huge hawk let out a long shriek, which sounded especially happy, and once again came the thundering voice, louder this time, "Ayakon, my friend, welcome back!"

Adam could now see a figure coming from the direction of the huge rock; the figure was of an old man dressed in silver and blue robes. A gray mane tumbled down his head; his long hair flowing seamlessly into a long gray beard, which covered his upper body entirely. To Adam's amazement, the great hawk rose in the air and started shrinking to the size of a normal hawk. What was only seconds ago an enormous predatory bird was now perched comfortably on the old man's arm. Adam, feeling that he was about to faint, made an effort to speak, "Who... who... are you?" asked Adam in a weak voice.

The old man smiled at him and said, "A great will brings to great accomplishments."

Adam didn't understand the meaning of this answer; he looked toward Arak, who was lying beside him motionlessly on the ground. He called out to his loyal friend, "Arak?"

The old man turned to the one-eyed wolf and patted him, "Don't worry for your friend, he'll be just fine."

To Adam's astonishment, as soon as the odd old man with the long beard touched Arak, the wolf rose to his feet and shook himself off, as if he was just waking from a long, refreshing sleep. He barked in Adam's direction, as if asking the gray-bearded man, "What about Adam?"

"Don't worry for your friend either. He, too, shall be taken care of." Arak approached Adam in perfect health and began licking his face.

Adam's vision began to blur. "Am I dreaming?" he asked weakly.

The man with the gray beard answered, "Don't worry, son, you arrived where you wanted to be." The wind softly scattered the old man's beard as he knelt by Adam, who was moaning in pain. Adam's gaze met the gray eyes of the bearded man, eyes that had something odd about them, and just before he passed out, Adam heard the man with the gray beard say, "Welcome to the ancient libraries."

Adam awoke on a large stone slab. He looked around and saw he was in a large room, cluttered with many objects, many books of different sizes, all stacked on shelves and tables; in the corner of the room stood a giant globe with what seemed to be planets spiraling around it. There were old chairs in the room, an old wooden desk stacked with paper, writing utensils, and many other contraptions that Adam couldn't even identify. Adam looked down at his own body and saw his wounds have been dressed. He looked around him, wondering where Arak was, and where was the odd man in the silver and blue robes, as he heard footsteps approach. He raised his head to see who was coming and saw Arak; the one-eyed wolf look at him happily from his side. "Arak, my friend, you're all right!" called Adam gladly, and the wolf replied with a cheerful bark.

"You too will be all right soon, son," came the voice of the gray-bearded man.

Adam looked at the unusual man who approached him. He could see him clearer now. His face was full of light. Adam never met a man like him, with such an impressive demeanor and fierce gray eyes. The man had an overwhelmingly powerful presence.

The man laid his hand gently on Adam's forehead and said, "You came a long way, my boy." The touch of his hand was warm and soothing, and it wiped all of Adam's pains away. "What is your name, son?" asked the gray-bearded man.

"I'm Adam Swandon," Adam replied, filled with awe by the gravity of this moment. He took courage and asked with a shaking voice, "And who are you, sir?"

The man looked into Adam's eyes seriously and replied, "I am Karan, the lone priest, guarding these ancient libraries for the past

350 years." Adam almost choked as the man finished his sentence. His entire body trembled. He made it to the ancient libraries! It wasn't a legend, it was real. The old tale of a priest living in the heart of the desert and guarding an ancient library is as real as the sun burning in the sky above, as real as water flowing in rivers, as real as the eternal existence of God! Adam began to weep with exhilaration. He wanted so badly to be able to share this with Captain Nelson and the men of the *Oracle*; he wanted to call out to Paola Katarina and tell her she was right. He wanted to shout out to Joshua and Heralda and to all his friends out there in the distance that yes, there is hope.

He is facing the solitary priest in the heart of the desert. People have risked their lives to help him get this far and face Karan. God himself helped him; God helps whoever helps himself. God helps whoever truly wants something with all his might. Now he understood the words of Karan when they first met: great will brings great achievements. Karan waited for Adam to calm down then gently covered the young man with a blanket.

He asked him again to quiet down. Adam did the man's request. Karan spoke to him in a fatherly tone. "Close your eyes, Adam Swandon, close them and allow yourself to relax." Adam closed his eyes and let himself be carried by Karan's guiding voice. He felt entirely secure in what was happening. His injuries still pained him, so he went along with Karan. Arak backed away and allowed Karan to do his work uninterrupted. Adam slowly sunk into a hypnotic like state, guided through stages by Karan's voice.

"Adam, allow your muscles to relax. Allow your spirit to relax. Your mind is now tuning to my voice. You sink deeper, deeper into a pleasant state of relaxation."

Adam's breath became peaceful; a deep ease flowed over him. Karan continued, "Now focus on your body, Adam, and begin sealing your wounds. Focus on your body's own healing powers. Concentrate your life energy in speeding the natural process of healing in your own body, decide that now your body is healing itself with great speed. God has given you life and special abilities to use for the good. See in your mind's eyes how your wounds are completely healed, how your skin is healed and becomes whole again, healthy and smooth with no scars on it. Everything returns to full health, you grow stronger and heal completely."

As the priest spoke, Adam focused on this process of self-healing, and indeed, his wounds began to cure and seal. From moment to moment, the tissues and bones were mended, the skin became whole, his wounds closed until there was no sign left of them, not even a scar. The process took about an hour, and Karan, satisfied with the results, called Adam to wake up.

Adam, thrilled by these recent happenings, slowly walked behind Karan, thoughts frantically running through his mind. He wanted to ask, how was it that his wounds healed so quickly that not even scar remained? How was it this man has been guarding the libraries for 350 years, and he seems to be only about sixty years old? How did the giant hawk Karan called Ayakon suddenly shrink to the size of a regular desert hawk? And why did Arak jump to his feet after being merely touched by Karan?

Many questions troubled him, but to his surprise, Karan read his mind and answered, "Don't fret, Adam, all in good time. These questions have answers, but now, you must eat. Follow me."

Adam remained silent, simply walking quietly after the priest, Arak pacing behind him. Karan leads them to a huge room, in its center a table laden with food: a bounty of fruit, vegetables, bread, and cheese. Adam couldn't believe his eyes. He looked at Karan as if questioning—where did all this food come from?

Karan, reading his mind, replied, "Eat, Adam, later we will speak of everything." Adam's appetite grew as he gazed at all the delicacies spread out on the large table. Arak immediately came close to the food and began feasting to his heart's desire, and Adam followed his lead. Karan let the two eat in peace. They didn't even notice when he left the room. Adam was filled with a wave of gratitude toward the creator as he relished the tasty food filling him and the feeling of peace, after such a long time.

After a short rest, Karan returned to the room where Arak and Adam were eating and spoke to Adam, "Now that you're healthy, full, and refreshed, you can ask whatever you want. Follow me please." The priest gestured for the one-eyed wolf to remain where he was for now. Since Karan spoke directly into the wolf's mind, Arak understood him perfectly and did as the gray-bearded man asked him.

Adam could see that Karan was capable of reading and transmitting thoughts. He remembered the good Paola Katarina who knew how to read his mind and understood him with no words. He followed the priest silently.

As they walked, he began slowly digesting that fact that he was truly here, in the abode of the lonesome priest, led here by the tales, by mysterious signals and dreams.

Adam could suddenly smell a scent of pine; before he could question where the scent of fresh pine could come from in the midst of a barren desert, an amazing sight was revealed to him: an expanse of lush, green vegetation. A small waterfall trickled through green and brown moth-covered rocks, bubbling springs of crystal clear water all around; different types of plants grew everywhere abundantly.

Adam was enchanted by this little paradise; he looked around him with his mouth wide open and then looked at Karan. The place was uncannily vast; in one corner, there was a plot of fruit and vegetables, with a few cows wandering through a green field right by them. Adam understood now where the fruit, the vegetables, the cheese, and the rest of the delicacies he consumed came from. *Amazing, simply amazing*, he thought to himself. The priest Karan can survive here, only thanks to the magic of this place. He must make all his food by himself. Karan walked to a stone bench, sat down, and gestured for Adam to sit by his side. Adam reclined and gazed up to the ceiling of this vast space; above him he saw a patch of blue sky peeking over the high stone walls that protected the place from sand storms and unwanted visitors. Then Karan turned to Adam.

"Tell me, Adam, why are you here?" Adam was taken aback by Karan's question. *Why would he ask me such a thing?* he thought. *When he can read minds? He knows I came here for him and for the ancient libraries.* Karan looked at Adam with his peculiar, gray eyes, still awaiting an answer.

Adam saw what he must answer. "I'm here, Karan, seeking a solution to the reign of evil over our world, to the suffering mankind has endured for many years. I always felt something burning in me, that I must do something about this. One cursed day on the face of the Alps, I was a far-away witness to a great injustice. The empire army massacred an entire village, mercilessly killing women, babies, kids, old and young men alike."

As he spoke, Adam's eyes filled with tears; his chin began to quiver, the terrible sights played out before his eyes again, affecting him so that he had to pause for a few moments. When he gained his composure, he carried on, "I came here following the faith inside me, the hope inside me. I refuse to accept the rule of evil over the world. Good people told me the legend of you and of the ancient libraries, which hold a book disclosing the whereabouts of this mysterious force called Gim Nigma, which is the solution to all evil, wickedness, and pain in this world. I made a decision to embark on a voyage to find an answer to the evil reign of the empire, which enslaves all humanity. Many good people who resist those dark forces have helped me. They believe with all their heart in my idea and my will to find an answer. That is why I am here, Karan. The empire soldiers are on my trail, trying time and time again to kill me, but I believe that God rescues me time and time again so I may fulfill my destiny. I choose to continue fighting, not to give up. I choose to make the ultimate effort to change the state of the world, to banish evil and bring hope to the next generations of humans and animals living on this Earth."

Karan said nothing; he merely watched Adam talk excitedly. When the young man finished speaking, Karan turned Adam's gaze to the ground. "Look, Adam, this ground endured many wars, bloodshed, fires, floods, and storms; yet it keeps on living and allowing life to grow from within it. See all the plants around us, all reaching out from the Earth into the air of the world. The purpose of life is this growth, this reaching out. See how in nature every part is aiding the others to grow, blossom, and exist. God made it all one harmonious whole. The clouds carry rain, which waters the Earth, which grows life, which nourishes other life forms. God created it all as a wondrous perfection. See the beauty around us, the foliage, the flowing water, the rocks, the birds flying above, no one breaks the balance of forces in the universe—only one species does that. Only one of God's creatures destroys the world he lives in, pollutes it, builds things, and does things that bring disaster upon itself and upon the world he is living in, disturbing the peace of the universe itself. That species is mankind, the mankind you are trying to rescue. Since the dawn of their existence, mankind brought destruction to the perfect balance of creation."

Adam didn't know what to say. He knew Karan's words to be the truth. He was ashamed to be part of the human race that, even though it advanced with technology, was moving backward regarding its understanding of the purpose of life. Clean lungs, made purely for breathing, were polluted by cigarette and industrial smoke. Men brought evil and destruction upon themselves. *Karan is right*, thought Adam, and remembered at once that the gray-bearded priest can read his mind, yet he insisted and said out loud, "But among all men, there is a good, positive kind, that believes in God almighty and in the freedom given to him and any other living being," Adam tried to defend his stand.

"Is that so?" Karan replied with a question. Then he rose from the bench and said, "You are a special man, Adam Swandon, and you don't even know quite how special you are. We are going to embark together on a unique journey." Karan began walking down a path enclosed from both its sides by two flowing rivers.

Adam rose and called out to the man with gray eyes, "A journey? But I just came from a long journey! And what of the evil rule of the empire over men, violating their birthright to live honorably and freely?"

Karan turned on his heels, looked directly at Adam, and said, "Everything in life has its own time. You will come with me now, if you wish to fulfill your destiny."

Adam sensed he was acting impatiently, and he must put his trust in this special man if he wants to find a solution. He began walking down the narrow, winding path and felt as if the water following him was smiling at him. He cheered himself on, telling himself he should be happy; he has already come far, to a place most people considered to be a mere legend. Every step he took after Karan, he felt more confident; everything in life has its own time, so Karan told him, and his words were of deep wisdom. *Everything in life and in nature is a process, requiring patience and ease*, Adam told himself, *so keep on believing and don't give up*. He remembered the many people who helped him in his journey because of their faith in him, and even with all the suffering and darkness suffocating the world, some of these people remain positive, still believing and hoping for the victory of light over darkness. *Yes*, Adam answered himself, *I will go on, Karan. I will go on.*

Karan lead Adam down the narrow path, which grew wider as they advanced. To his astonishment, Adam saw that the space seemed boundless; from the outside, the stone walls seemed as big as a fortress, but he couldn't have imagined how immense it was from the inside. Adam was already acquainted with some of the place; he saw the room where they ate and the room where he was nursed by the priest, and of course that huge, astonishingly beautiful garden.

Karan stopped by a round stone table, with small stone stools on both its sides. The two sat opposed each other. Colorful birds were flying above them; Karan gazed at their flight and his gray eyes shone in the sunlight. Then he lowered his eyes to Adam again and said, "Well, Adam, go ahead and ask your questions."

Adam looked around him, took in the carpets of green grass and colorful meadow flowers, the trees with their wide trunks, the blossoms, which scents were carried gently by the breeze, as if there were no stonewalls surrounding them. He took the air into his lungs and calmed down. He was fascinated by the idea that the man sitting in front of him was at least four hundred years old, yet seemingly young. Before Adam could voice his question, Karan, reading the young man's thought, replied, "Many years ago, I came here from a faraway world. I was chosen to be the messenger who would guard this special location, created especially to protect the hope for humanity's salvation, one day. The species that I belong to is quite progressive and wise. For a long time now, concepts like war, pestilence, and other forms of negativity do not exist for us. We lovingly accept what the Lord chose to put in the universe, and we accept our responsibility to maintain the balance and the sanctity of life in this universe created by the infinite force. These ancient libraries are dedicated to preserving the good hope—a hope that exists in the most important books. The books kept in these libraries go back to the dawn of humanity. They are books of the victory of good over evil. All the wisdom, good will, and kindness of the greatest writers are preserved in this place."

The man with the gray eyes halted for a moment, and at that moment, Ayakon the hawk swooped down and landed on Karan's shoulder. Karan continued, "This is Ayakon, the desert hawk. You must be thinking how this bird managed to change its size. Well, it was especially trained in the world I came from. He is my companion, and since we both came from a different world, Earth's atmosphere maintained our bodies well, so we may do a good job here—and our job is to wait for the son of light with the pure heart, whose intentions to save this planet are pure. Our job is to keep this place safe till the moment you showed up. You are the only one who ever made it here. You carry the special soul chosen by the maker to embark on a journey to save mankind, to fight the forces of evil and defeat them once and for all."

Adam still couldn't digest that he was actually standing in this magical place. Now that he heard these strange words coming out of the mouth of the man with the odd gray eyes, who claimed he comes from another planet, Adam was simply at a loss for words. Karan carried on, "Give yourself some time, Adam. Time will do its thing, and you will be able to accept all these occurrences. In the meantime, tell me of yourself. Where were you born? Where did you grow up? What did you want more than anything when you were a little child?"

So many questions, Adam said to himself, *why can't Karan just lead me to the ancient libraries so I can find Gim Nigma?* He looked at Karan imploringly, hoping that the man with gray eyes and hair flowing down to his shoulders would read his thoughts and answer his questions, but nothing of the sort happened. *Apparently, I must be patient—like Karan said earlier, everything in life has its own time, so I'll be patient then.* A faint smile played across Karan's face, as if he agreed with Adam's conclusion.

Adam thought of how to start unfolding the story of his life before the priest. His eyes wandered around the magical garden then paused on the silhouette of Ayakon the hawk, resting peacefully on Karan's shoulder. In his mind's eye, he skipped through visions of his childhood, which wasn't an easy one. He recalled his grandmother who died when he was six, of who he heard wonderful things, things that inspired him later throughout his entire life. His family told him she was a wise woman with wise sayings.

"It's a bit hard for me to recall everything, Karan," said Adam. The man with the long, gray beard rose from his seat, and Ayakon took to the air. Karan approached Adam, asking him to trust in him and close his eyes and relax. Adam did as the man requested.

"I will help you remember," whispered Karan, laying his hands on Adam's temples. Adam felt as if he is falling through a time vortex, everything blurred for a while, then visions began flowing in front of his eyes; he saw himself being born, in an obscure city in the Middle East. He saw himself as small child, crying, running from the kids at school, who taunted him and excluded him from their company because he came from a poor family, because of his weirdness and the place he came from. Karan sees everything Adam's memory calls up, and Adam keeps moving on through time; he sees himself growing up, going through high school surrounded by impenetrable walls. No one could reach him; he would open to no one. His thoughts were of God and of true love. He lived in his own world of imagination—that was his refuge. That's where he felt alive. That's where he was the hero, saving the world and winning the love of the beautiful girl. Adam sees himself drawing, watching sad movies, and crying over them alone. He dreamt of a true love, of the one and only, the dream, which till this very day existed in his heart.

Adam sees himself as a teenager now, in love with the most popular girl in class, but she is beyond his reach; he comes from a poor, uneducated home while she is from a rich family. She keeps company only with the most popular kids. From here, his feelings of inferiority developed. He saw films and pictures of people massacred, killed, burned for the color of their skin or for their race, films which made him furious with God and furious with his own helplessness. He developed a fierce passion to save this world and help the suffering people with which he felt he had so much in common. He grew up as a very lonely and very sensitive child. He dreamt of helping his family escape the harsh place they lived in. Karan continued viewing these sights, and his own heart was moved. With his eyes closed, he continued to move through Adam's history, his childhood, and his adulthood.

Many times Adam's life nearly came to an end, yet he always somehow managed to survive, almost as if he was being watched over from above. The rise of the fearsome empire changed the face of Earth; men created the nuclear threat to protect themselves from other countries in the world, but ironically, it was used against them all, turning them within a few years from a race of free men to a race of slaves.

During the war, on his way back from a small food smuggling operation to the area his family and a few others lived, Adam discovered to his horror that all his people were gone, his family among them. There were rumors everyone was taken to work camps. He went searching for them for some time, until his friends—men who harbored and assisted the underground rebels to escape the empire soldiers—told him the situation was too dangerous, that the empire army was capturing all free men and the young ones are taken to toil away as slaves in the work camps. Adam, who always believed in the right of every living being to be free, was forced to escape to the mountains where he hid away from the claws of empire soldiers and grim work camps. He hid, but in his heart, the wish to save the world from this evil burned mightily. Decades ago, he knew a similar empire existed, which nearly succeeded in taking over the world; the

Nazis in Germany, who murdered millions of free people for their race and for the color of their skin. Innocent people who harmed no one, children, babies, mercilessly killed for no fault at all. Seeing this horror repeat itself made Adam's blood boil in his veins in rage. Karan then sees in his mind's eye that miserable day on the mountain face, the massacre that occurred at the feet of that mountain; he sees Adam cry to the sky, cry out to God above, "Why?" He sees the signal, a shaft of lightning splitting the cloudless sky, and he removes his hands from Adam's temples. Both men open their eyes.

Adam felt a little lightheaded. Karan returned to his seat. "You went through a lot in your life, Adam Swandon," said the man with gray eyes and continued speaking while Adam regained his bearings. "Why do you want to save the world?" Karan asked.

His question caused Adam's eyebrows to rise high with bewilderment. "What do you mean, why?" Adam replied with a question.

"What would it give you?" Karan asked.

Adam thought Karan's questions were becoming quite troublesome. He made this long, arduous journey, narrowly escaped death countless times, and now he must endure these troublesome questions. "What will it give me, you ask? Let me explain," said Adam, with a tone that reviled his impatience. "There are people in the world suffering pain, hunger, poverty. There are lives out there being tortured to death by hard toil, children are being born who never knew the taste of freedom, or of having a mother or father, so much pain and suffering is going on, women being raped, the honor of elders trampled upon, everywhere around the world men live in fear, what the Nazis did years ago returns now tenfolds, and you ask me what will it give me? I can't go on living and accept that this is how things are. I believe something can be done, something should be done. We must struggle against all this evil. I tell you that I'm here, I came all this way, because I always believed that there has to be some force that could destroy all this evil once and for all. Call me crazy, but what I've seen so far makes me believe that it's my destiny to go on this quest, and that somehow, I will save the world. I can honestly tell you I don't know how I will do this, but if I got so far, and the God above helped me on my way, I see that as a sign that I should go even further. And another thing"—Adam halted for a moment.

"Another thing?" Karan repeated.

"Yes, one more thing—since my early childhood, I felt something within me, that this injustice should be changed from its roots, that no one should hurt anyone else for being poor, or disfigured or an invalid, or different in color or race. We are all equal. We are all God's children. I feel as though I can't die before I do my utmost to save this world." Adam finished his words, and a long silence fell upon them. He waited for a response from Karan, who merely listened quietly.

After a few minutes of silence, Karan stood up and beckoned Adam to him. "Follow me, Adam. I'd like to show you something."

Adam stood up at once, confident now that he expressed what was in his heart, now Karan would finally show him the way to the ancient libraries, so he may find the path that would take him to the mysterious Gim Nigma.

The two walked down the path they came from. Approaching them now was Arak the one-eyed wolf, clinging happily to Adam's feet, who reached down at once and patted him warmly. The path ended abruptly at the threshold of a tall door, made of a light, bluish metal. Karan stood in front of the door and waited for Adam to come near. When he and Arak came to the door, it flew open suddenly, so abruptly it caused Arak to back away, startled.

Karan walked into what turned out to be a huge hall, its tall ceiling curving into a pale blue dome, its walls rounded and of the same metallic blue color. The floor was a shade of yellow, glowing and shiny as if the place had just been scrubbed. Karan doesn't cease to surprise, thought Adam, remembering that all this time they were actually surrounded by the desert in all directions. Karan walked toward a pedestal, positioned in the center of the hall. He pressed a few green-lit buttons on a flat metal plate, which looked a little like a tall, narrow table. Within seconds, the wall facing the entrance door split open, and an elliptical screen rose before them, making a horrendous noise. Adam gazed at the screen with wonder, surprised to see Arak hiding behind his legs. Adam patted him and told him to relax. Karan called Adam to come stand beside him—the two stood facing the huge screen, with Karan's hands resting on the metal plate, lit by the green buttons.

"What's this thing?" Adam asked curiously. The gray-eyed man looked at him gravely and replied, "Well, my dear Adam Swandon, you came to a unique decision—you decided you want to save the world." The man paused, and Adam waited impatiently till he spoke again, "You want to redeem humankind of its suffering because you pity them, you want to help them. Let me show you a few things." Karan pushed one of the green buttons, and the screen before them flickered to life. Karan took a few steps back and allowed Adam and Arak to focus uninterruptedly on the visions in front of them. It seemed to be some kind of film, beginning with the view of planet Earth from a distance, a planet drawn in green, blue, and brown, teeming with life.

The picture came closer and one could see the ocean waves move in the ocean and break upon the rocks. Animals were abundant on the shores. Penguins and seals played in the water, wild birds hung like jewels in the blue sky. Tall graceful trees lined the shores; the picture turned into one of a lush forest, green and wide. Animals were crowding the tree branches; a multitude of monkeys leapt from tree to tree, a burst of colorful birds suddenly took off in all directions, chirping marvelously.

How beautiful, thought Adam, when suddenly he noticed Karan draw near, his voice thundering through the great hall. "Look, Adam, see creation's beauty. Nature is a perfectly balanced and beautiful harmony. Animals live freely, trees grow peacefully, the birds sing of liberty and joy. These sights lighten your heart, do they not?"

Adam nodded, focusing on the immense screen. "Now look," Karan's voice rang out angrily. As he spoke, a terrible sight flashed before Adam's eyes—large machines trampled their way through the forest, crushing the fragile vegetation, mercilessly chopping down the tall trees. "Do you see how men thoughtlessly kill the trees God created? Do you see, Adam, how a multitude of living beings die as they lose what was once their home, the forest?"

Adam felt ashamed, and with suddenly tearful eyes, he continued watching the painful sights; pictures of fishing boats filled the screen now, boats mercilessly hunting whales, shooting them down, their blood clouding the ocean water. Karan's furious voice echoed again, "Do you see, Adam, men massacring the great sea mammals, just for their teeth and fat?"

Adam's eyes filled with tears. He wasn't expecting such sights. Pictures continued to flicker on the screen; hundreds of dolphins were stacked upon the shore, where men systematically pierced them with daggers. The wondrous animals lie in pools of their own blood.

"Do you see how without an ounce of mercy, man drives his pike through God's creatures?" The tears are streaming freely down Adam's cheeks now. Arak drew back and hid his face between his two front paws. The sights rolled on… whole forests consumed by fire, the ocean face covered with black oil spills, sea animals coated with black tar, which brought them an unjust death. Huge chimneys spewing a dense smoke, which blackened the blue skies above, slaughterhouses, large animals systematically murdered so that a certain number of men could reap profits from their death.

Again Karan's voice thundered through the air, "Do you see, Adam Swandon, how men abuse their power over the other creatures of God, how they massacre them to wear their skin as a gaudy adornment, using their bones as jewelry, how they spread death for these wonderful creatures as a sport, as an amusement?" The scenes kept coming, showing men strike, shoot, slaughter, and abuse helpless animals.

Adam slumps to the floor, his hands covering his face, a strangled cry of pain emitting from him, for these sight made his heart explode in his chest. Again Karan's thundering voice rings out, "But this is not all, Adam Swandon, not at all… men don't only kill animals, trample forests, pollute the air, not only do they invade the sea with their black oil, killing the sea life, they don't merely destroy the nature God created with love. They turn on their own brothers and sisters, their fellow humans!" Terrible visions flickered in front of Adam's tearful eyes. Tanks trampling through villages, bombing people's homes, naked little children fleeing while soldiers shoot them down from afar, their little bodies dropping to the ground like puppets suddenly cut off their strings. He sees an infant trying to reach his mother, who is herded, along with many other women, into the gas chambers. He sees a Nazi soldier shove the infant out of the way, but the baby rises and tries again. He doesn't understand why he is being kept from his mother. He keeps trying to reach her, but once again, the soldier pushes him to the floor. Adam sobs, choking on his tears, but the images on the huge screen keep screaming out to him; he sees the soldiers drive naked women and children into the gas chambers, stealing their freedom, he sees how the gas is pumped into the sealed chambers, how the bodies twist and distort, then drop lifeless to the moist ground. The screen shows a crowd of people line-up along the edge of a huge pit, and an execution team shoots them accurately and mercilessly—the bodies drop into the huge pit—with no life in them, no freedom, not a shred of dignity—

"Enough!" Adam screams through his sobs, but Karan will not stop, he keeps projecting the images, the bodies are now heaped on carts, the bodies that were once living human beings, who had their own dreams, who wished for love, for success, who had ideas. "Do you see, Adam, how men plunder the freedom of their brothers and sisters?" Karan's voice rumbled again. The pictures flashed across the huge screen, a black man, his hands tied, is lead by a group of uniformed men, while they beat him with bats; he cries for help and no help comes. They bind him and lie him down in a field of wheat, where they shoot him from range zero. There is no mercy.

Karan cries, "Look at the screen, Adam Swandon, look now!" In front of Adam's crying eyes, a huge mushroom of smoke, fire, and dust raises in the air. Humans have used the most terrible weapon existence on their brothers and sisters. Slowly the screen washed itself clean from the horrible sights, remaining black and silent.

Adam lay curled on the floor, his head clasped between his hands. He wept in pain. He was about to drown in the deepest sadness he had ever experienced. He feared for a moment that he would drown in it and die, but Karan's gentle touch on his shoulder returned him to himself.

"Oh, Adam, I'm sorry that I had to do that, but these are the creatures you wish to save, these are the humans you pity so much." The good Lord always gives them an opportunity to do good, to choose the positive way, but time after time, they do the opposite. They chose the easy way, which is actually the disastrous one, the one that leads to self-destruction. It brings devastation not only to the human race but to nature itself, to all that grows and lives. It violates the inborn liberty of all other species living on this planet," Karan said, his voice softer this time. He reached out and helped Adam up from the floor, which was wet from his tears. Arak came to the two standing figures and rubbed his head against Adam's legs. Adam wiped away his tears and slowly calmed down. "I had to show you this, so you will know exactly what these humans are."

His breathing once again steady, Adam directed his hawk like gaze into Karan's gray eyes and said quietly, "I understand your intentions, Karan. I understand that humans come through as a cruel, horrible species, one that doesn't mind abusing its own brothers and sisters for its own ends. I understand that humans butcher animals, even when not needed for their own survival. I see all that," Adam's voice grew steadily louder. "But there's something else, Karan, something you didn't show, something you didn't speak of. It is that among these people there are also good people, men who help people weaker than them out of the kindness of their heart. There are people that struggle to save animals from extinction, people that do their best to keep the planet clean. There are some that still have the glimmer of hope in their hearts for a full life, one lived with honor, dignity, morality, and freedom. I choose to focus upon these individuals, because it's for them. They make this whole journey to save the human race worthwhile."

Silence fell upon the great hall. Even Arak didn't make a sound. Then Karan said, "Well, done, well done. You believe in the human race. You think it is worthy to be saved from oblivion. You care that much. I respect that," the gray-eyed man concluded and began walking toward the exit of the great hall, signaling the two to follow him.

Where to now? Adam wondered. He called the one-eyed wolf to follow him, and the two paced behind the man who led them on without a word, silently walking down the path. From afar, Adam noticed the mouth of a cave and turned to Karan. "Are we about to enter the cave?" he asked.

"Yes," Karan answered, his gaze fixed straight ahead. "In this cave, you and I will go through a very special, very important journey." He turned to the one-eyed wolf. "My friend, you will have to remain here for the moment. Only Adam and I must go in now."

The wolf obeyed without a sound, backing out. Adam continued walking behind the priest, who paced confidently through the pitch-dark cave. "Come after me," Karan called softly to him.

"But it's so dark here, Karan," Adam answered, his steps faltering for a moment.

Karan marched into the darkness and said, "Faith, Adam, it takes faith."

Adam walked on despite the darkness, and from moment to moment, the cave indeed became brighter, so much brighter it seemed to be bathing in full daylight. Adam was relieved when the place lit up. He was curious as to the origin of this light; the road in front of him was blocked by Karan's figure, but a few steps more and the tunnel ended in a large, rocky cavern, in its center a pillar of fire, spinning around itself with great speed. Adam understood this must be the source of light brightening the entire cave. He was awed by the vision.

Karan turned to him and said, "Come close, Adam, and fear not. This cavern is a place of blessing. It has been blessed with a spark of the fire the Lord has used to light the eternal hope in every living being's heart. Here you will go through the journey of your reincarnations."

Though Adam stood close to the fire, he was surprised to see he wasn't scorched by it. "The journey of my reincarnations?" Adam repeated, looking questioningly at Karan.

Karan lifted his hands above his head and called out, "Oh, higher force, in front of you stands the man who carries the special soul within him. I must do my duty. I must test his reincarnations to see that he is truly the one, the son of light, the pure-hearted, the soul destined to save an entire world."

Adam watched Karan silently but within him his spirit stormed, his heart pounded fiercely; he was taken over by exhilaration. Suddenly, with no warning, the Earth began to shake—small stones tumbled down from the cave's ceiling. Karan stood with his eyes closed and his arms outstretched. A fierce wind rose from the spinning column of fire, knocking Adam off his feet and slamming him to the cave's floor. Karan remained standing. The ground by his feet split open, and with a great clamor, a large stone chair rose from the depth of the fissure.

The wind calmed. Karan opened his eyes and allowed his hands to fall at the sides of his body. "Adam Swandon, take your seat on this stone throne," Karan commanded in a rumbling voice. Adam silently rose off the ground and sat on the large stone chair. A fierce chill ran through his body as it contacted the large throne; he had no idea what to expect, but felt he should put his trust in the gray-eyed priest. Although the chair was made of hard, cold stone, it was comfortable to sit in. Adam laid his arms on the two armrests at the sides of the chair.

"What month where you born?" Karan asked, standing across from Adam, with the burning column at his back.

"I was born in the month of March," replied Adam, growing accustomed to the feel of the stone chair.

"The month of spring. You are a Pisces, the sign that contains in it the qualities of all other signs. It's a sign of leaders," said Karan.

"I am no leader," Adam said quietly as if abashed.

"A true leader knows not that he is one, until others see him as one," replied Karan and swiftly carried on. "Lean your head back, sit comfortably and securely," Karan requested, folding his arms behind his back. Adam did as the gray bearded man asked him. Bluish flames rose from the center of the fiery column and began spiraling around the walls of the cave. Adam noticed that the flames emitted no heat. As his eyes followed the spin of the flames, Karan's voice echoed through the entire cave, "Adam Swandon, close your eyes. Allow your body to relax. Allow all your systems to sink into a deep, pleasant peace."

Adam shut his eyes and began to feel a pleasant drowsiness. Karan continued to guide him into a deep hypnosis. "At this moment, you are feeling relaxed, loose, free. All your negative thoughts disappear. Your mind is clean of any negative thought. You are entirely focused on my words, which will lead you into a deep silent relaxation, into a deep ocean of peace."

Adam could feel himself truly slipping into a sleep-like state. Following Karan's instructions, he felt himself flowing into a pleasant peace, which grew deeper and quieter from moment to moment. Karan's voice echoed through the space as the blue flames danced around Adam, sitting on the great, stone throne.

"I want us to check the rebirths of your soul together. I shall walk back through history with you, and together, we will see the reincarnations of your unique soul. Together we will examine the will of your soul's destiny."

Adam saw himself now, in his mind's eye, floating through the dark space, surrounded by countless stars. He looked down at himself and saw he was dressed in a black shirt and black pants. He heard Karan speak to him in his mind, "You have nothing to fear, Adam. You are completely safe. You are in space right now—do you see planet Earth?"

Adam turns in his spot and sees in his mind's eyes the breathtaking vision of planet Earth from afar. "What should I do now?" Adam asked in his mind, while his body sat motionlessly on the stone throne in the chamber.

Karan shut his eyes and stepped into Adam's hypnotic trance; suddenly, Adam saw him suspended beside him in the endless space. Together, they floated slowly, gazing at the Earth. Then Karan spoke, "Give me your hand. Let's move toward the planet." Adam reached out and took Karan's hand, and together they glided swiftly toward Earth; they moved with such immense speed that all the twinkling stars flowed into long, white stripes. Suddenly they were standing on the ground. Adam took a step forward, examining the terrain, while Karan stood back, watching him. "Karan, where are we?" Adam asked.

"We are standing on the land of Europe," Karan replied.

Adam's mental body moved forward, while Karan remained standing, his arms folded behind his back. "What are we looking for here?" Adam asked him.

"For one of your former reincarnations," replied Karan.

"And what period are we in?" asked Adam.

"Nineteen hundred thirty seven, Earth count." replied Karan. Suddenly, the rumble of machines tore through the silence—large army trucks loaded with men made their way up the chalky path. Clouds of dust rose from under their wheels. The drivers were in uniform, metal helmets on their heads. They were yelling incomprehensible words in a language that spoke clearly of threat and degradation. Adam came near the moving trucks; now he could notice tens of scared faces, women, elders, children. The sound of a baby's cry made Adam cry out at once to stop this, but his voice went unheard; he remains unseen. Evil continues, all trucks stop at once; a Nazi officer jumps off one of the trucks and instructs his men to get all the passengers off the truck. Adam runs back to Karan and says urgently, "You must stop this, Karan, I feel something terrible is about to happen!"

"All you see has already happened a long time ago," said Karan quietly, his voice laden with sorrow. Adam looked upon the happenings with a deep frustration for not being able to do a thing. Their expression blank, the soldiers lined the terrified passengers one beside another in a long procession, with their backs to the dark fir forest. Occasional bursts of weeping came from the women. They all understood their end was near.

"Where's the justice?" one old lady cried out bitterly. The metallic click of guns was heard; their weapons now loaded, the Nazis were about to murder what God had given life to. Could that be? Adam understood this was the Second World War, and those were Jews standing on one side and Nazis on the other, and the bitter end was now near. Suddenly, out of the crowd of people, a young boy jumps out and dares to come close to the soldiers, calling out to them to spare these people's lives, risking his own by defending the others. The sight made Adam's heart weep. The Nazis laughed wickedly, mocking the young man, yet he repeated his plea.

"Please," he begged, "spare these people." Again and again, he begged, until the soldiers' evil laughter turned into a nervous one. The guns were aimed at the line of weeping people. There was no justice, no logic, the horror of it; humans killing other humans for a difference in nationality, a difference in race. Suddenly the boy jumped on one of the soldiers, taking him completely by surprise, he yanked the gun out of the soldier's hands and began shooting at the other soldiers, yelling at the others to run, run as fast as they can. The people picked up and ran without thought in the direction of the forest, but the bullets of the other soldiers quickly pierced the young man's body. Through the gaping bullet wounds and the boy's cries of pain, the young man's soul escaped, and his bleeding form fell lifeless to the ground. The soldiers range reaches the escapees; with short bursts of fire, they shot them down one after the other, an old man, an infant… only a handful found their way to the shelter of the forest. The small body of the youth lay on the floor in a puddle of his own blood, which seeped slowly into the soil. It was over. A few dead soldiers also laid on the Earth, which did not discriminate between one death and another; it enfolded them all. A multitude of people whose only crime was being Jewish now littered the ground with their lifeless bodies. It was finally quiet—no trucks, no soldiers, no life, just the body of a courageous boy lying on the ground. Adam drew near the youth who laid on the red-stained floor.

"It's such a shame about this kid," said Adam, his eyes flowing with pity.

Karan came near him and said gravely. "A brave boy who tried to change the face of things. A special boy."

Adam gently caressed the face of the kid, removing the blood-soaked clumps of hair from the kid's beautiful eyes. "Who was this boy?" Adam asked in a broken voice.

Karan laid his hand on Adam's shoulder and said, "This boy is you."

Adam's heart nearly skipped a beat. "Me?" asked Adam, his voice trembling.

"This boy carried your soul. He is one of your former reincarnations. It is the same soul that is always bent on helping, fixing, healing, and saving others. It is that special soul, trying to fulfill its destiny."

"Could that be?" asked Adam, looking with pain at the beautiful face of the dead boy. Karan extended his hand to Adam and said, "Come with me, Adam, we must go on now." Adam began walking after Karan, turning his gaze toward the bodies who were only a few minutes ago living creatures. He shut his eyes silently, and once again, he and Karan were floating in the endless star-filled space.

When he opened his eyes again, he saw Karan standing by his side, arms folded behind his back. They were surrounded by white houses with green lawns. "Where are we?" Adam asked.

"We're in the United States," replied Karan as he walked toward one of the white houses with red roofs.

"And what are we doing here?" Adam asked.

"Waiting," answered Karan. Just as the words left his mouth, a red car took a sharp turn at the street corner, its brakes screeching so loud that a few tenants stepped out of their houses to see what was the noise, but when they saw what was happening, they quickly stepped back into their houses. Adam saw a group of men, all holding clubs, leave the car and walk toward the house Karan was standing by. The man of the house stepped out to protect his family from the gang, who yelled at him to take his family and leave this neighborhood, since they didn't want black residents in their neighborhood. Adam disliked what he was seeing and hearing, but he knew no one there could tell he exists. No one came to the defense of the black family; only one man stepped out of his house, a white man, just like all the other residents of the neighborhood.

"Let these people be, please!" the man called out to them.

The group turned their gaze to him at once. "It's none of your business, sir. You better just step inside so you don't get hurt," said one of the group.

"I can't do that, friend. I can't watch one man hurt another."

The black man looked at his neighbor and smiled at him with gratitude, still ready for anything. Rage became apparent on the face of one of the men as he tightened his grip on the wooden club.

"You don't get it—we don't want no black people in our neighborhood!" The young man came closer to the gang. Adam began fearing for him. "I don't understand you people. This is happening everywhere. Everywhere men are cruel to the different and to his different color. They are not different from us. Their skin is darker, but their blood is red like yours. In all of us, a heart beats just the same. We are all the children of one God," said the man, his voice thunderous. Many faces peered out of the windows of houses nearby; everyone sensed something was about to happen. The black man was sheltering his family; his wife stood behind him, a weeping baby in her arms. The man asked her to go inside, but she refused, fearing for his life. One man, his head shaved, drew near the young white man who came to defend the family, the club in his hand raised threateningly. "I'm warning you, man, go inside. If you're a black people lover, we'll kick you out with them," said the skinhead, his face angry and threatening.

"Like I said before, friend, I can't let you hurt another man. We're all the same, we're all humans. You have no right to come and try to drive out someone just because you don't agree with his skin tone." The young man concluded his sentence and stepped toward the black man. He stood beside him silently in the entrance of the house. The raging gang fell upon them, beating them with their bats. The neighbors hurried to withdraw into their houses and shut the windows. From afar, a police siren was heard; the wicked group of men leaped into their car and quickly escaped. The police arrived and examined the two bleeding men lying on the porch. One of the policemen was trying to calm the crying woman. The baby's wails mixed with the voices of the policemen talking among themselves, "Those two won't be able to walk again," said one of the cops. "The ambulance is on its way, ma'am. I suggest you calm down," said another cop to the weeping woman.

Karan drew near to the raging Adam and said, "You probably know who that young man was that came to his neighbor's aid and was beaten by that bunch of racists until he became paralyzed, right?"

Adam shut his hawk eyes tightly, and one tear rolled down the corner of one eye. "I know. That man was me, right?"

"One of your earlier reincarnations, in an earlier life," agreed Karan and reached out his hand to Adam once again. "Come, Adam, we're moving on," Karan summed, and once again, the two were suspended in the endless space. They went through different times and different happenings; in all there were men trying to defend the weak and helpless against an evil force, and time after time, they were pushed back by evil. The special soul never managed to truly fulfill its destiny.

"You see, Adam, each time this special soul tried to fulfill its destiny in this world and couldn't see it through—except for this time. You are the seventh and last reincarnation of this soul. You are the son of light. You are the pure heart that wants only to save, to heal, to fix, and now is your time to do so. So now that I am sure that you are truly the son of light, I will take you to the ancient libraries, so you may venture out to fulfill your destiny, your dream of saving the world. The prophecy exists to bring hope and courage to the positive forces in the world, but the fulfillment of the prophecy in which light overcomes dark depends on you and on God," said Karan as he lead Adam down a path of sparkling stars.

Adam was filled with a joyful sensation when Karan said he was about to take him to the ancient libraries. He thought of the long way he came, hoping and believing he would make it, and now after all the obstacles, his strong will brought him to his destination; he was happy, yet he knew that the road ahead was long. Karan asked him to shut his eyes and concentrate on his voice. Adam closed his eyes and listened to Karan's voice guide him, "Adam Swandon, you are about to return to the present. You are returning to your own body, here on this stone throne. You are filled with a forceful confidence, with a determination to come back and fulfill your destiny in the best way possible."

From moment to moment, Adam felt himself returning to himself, to his body sitting on the stone chair inside the cave; he began feeling the texture of the stone once again, and then Karan called loudly, "Open your eyes, Adam, and return to life!"

Adam opened his eyes and saw Karan standing in front of him, arms folded behind his back and a warm smile upon his bearded face. "Welcome back, young man," said the man with gray eyes.

The flames encircling the room withdrew into the column of fire. Adam rose from his seat and the ground opened once again slowly to swallow back the chair with great noise, and again it closed; the column of fire was now the only witness to all that happened.

"All my life, I sensed something within was driving me, and I didn't know what. It was you, Karan, you helped me see that my soul has a distinct mission that has to do with all human race. That is what I was feeling all this time, I didn't know how to define it, but now, after I saw my different reincarnations, I understand why I went on this voyage, I feel it burning inside me. I must do it, Karan. Please help me so I may do this," said Adam passionately.

"That's my job, Adam. I was meant to wait here for the special human that will make this unique choice to come here and seek a clear solution to the problem of evil in this world. And the solution exists, Adam, you must head out and find it. I can take you only to the ancient libraries, I can show you the books, but I can't show you the thing you must ultimately find," said Karan.

Adam came close, breathed in deeply, and said, "I understand, Karan, and I want to thank you from the bottom of my heart for your help and guidance. I'm ready to continue, Karan, I'm ready for the ancient libraries."

Karan smiled in agreement, and they stepped out of the cave.

Chapter Sixty-Three

Karan lead Adam down strange passages, winding in down sloping curves, which gave the impression they were descending deep under the Earth. The walls of the passages were made of odd, unearthly crystals, colored in blue, purple, and pink. Adam saw that as they walked down the winding passages the colors constantly changed, as if the walls were moving with them. After a long hour of walking, the two stopped before a huge stone door.

"This is the place," Karan declared. Adam tried to find some handle in order to open the giant rock door, but after a quick inspection, he saw there was no such thing. He looked at Karan questioningly, and as if he read his mind, the priest walked to the giant slab of rock door, he sat in front of it, crossed his legs, and clasped his hands together and called out loudly,

"Oh, great, positive maker of this world, the door will open by the force of the eternal faith in the positive way." As he spoke these words, the huge stone began to rise heavily, and the entrance to the ancient libraries was wide open to Adam Swandon, who escaped from Europe and was nearly killed on the way, who crossed the Mediterranean ocean and nearly drowned on the way with the rest of the *Oracle* crew, who crossed the desert and was nearly killed in battle with the Parakees men—all this only to reach this hidden place, which was mentioned only in fairy tales. Here it was in front of him. The smell of old books stood in the air. Rectangular tables of aged wood were organized in rows through the library hall. Adam was overjoyed; he reached the place where he would discover where Gim Nigma was hidden. He was so overcome with happiness he had to calm himself down and tell himself to be serious.

He looked around; it seemed the library was endless, filled with millions of books. *How will I find the one disclosing the location of Gim Nigma?* he thought to himself.

The deeper Adam delved into the library, the bigger he found it to be. *It will take me years to find that book*, Adam said to himself. Karan read his mind and said, "Just like you started your voyage, a long time ago, by leaving your mountain and coming here, so will you continue from here on." The gray-eyed man came close to a pile of old books lying on the table, one on top of the other, and said, "You know, Adam, books are a very unique thing. You can open one little book and find a whole huge world you knew nothing about." The priest opened one of the books. "Every one of these is a treasure. If men only knew how many treasures are hidden in books, they would rediscover life afresh with each one," said Karan. Adam paced slowly to the pile of books at Karan's side. "I never thought that way about books, Karan. I read a little as a child, but I found no treasures," said Adam, gently wiping the dust off an ancient cover.

"Is that so?" asked the priest. "Is that really so, Adam? Well, did you read the right books? That's the real question."

"The right books?" Adam asked.

"Yes, the right ones," replied Karan. "Follow me," the priest requested. The two walked silently by the many shelves, where dust and thin cobwebs coated the books. Suddenly Karan stopped and turned to Adam. "Look at this shelf, Adam. Here are the books of victory, of good men who did their best to improve the human race and the world they live in."

Adam looked at a long line of books of all sizes and managed to recognize the names of the books and the names of the authors:

The Power of the Subconscious Mind by Joseph Murphy
Think and Grow Rich by Napoleon Hill
How to Win Friends and Influence People by Dale Carnegie
The Monk Who Sold His Ferrari and *Leadership Wisdom* by Robin S. Sharma
The Alchemist by Paulo Coelho
Self Hypnosis by Valerie Austin
The Aladdin Factor and *Dare to Win* by Jack Canfield and Victor Hanson
Tuesdays with Morrie and *The Five People You Meet in Heaven* by Mitch Albom
The Seven Habits of Highly Effective People by Stephen Covey

"These are self-help books, or so men used to call them," Karan said. "Based on this concept, self-help, the idea these books manifest is that we can help ourselves to find solutions to the problems we encounter in life, by developing a correct positive approach, the problems are turned into challenges and the way to their solving becomes an adventurous experience."

Adam listened to Karan eagerly, thinking how true his words were and what a shame it was that people are too lazy to open a book and read about their possibilities in life.

Karan carried on: "Our maker made this entire universe, leaving one meaningful aspect under our control." Karan paused for a moment and turned to the large shelf, seemingly searching for something among the dusty covers.

"What's the one meaningful thing under our control?" Adam asked curiously. The gray-bearded man pulled out one of the many books on the shelf, blew the dust off it, looked at Adam and said, "The most meaningful power in our possession is the ability to choose. We can choose how to think and how to act regarding the events in our life. In front of your eyes are the books that hold the inspiring stories of many special men who overcame crisis and hardship, and declared victory in their own way." Adam was fascinated by the words of the gray-eyed man. He suddenly remembered the days he shared with his father, before losing touch with his family; he remembered his childhood and his father's words of wisdom. He was a simple man, yet he was full of life's wisdom. "How can I learn more of these things you speak of?" Adam asked.

"Well, young man, just go to the books, just go to the books."

Karan concluded, turned on his heels, and walked toward the exit. On the way out, his hands folded behind his back, he said, "You will find that books are good friends to man. I will leave you here, and when you finish reading these books, you will better understand the forces within you, and so, I believe, you will discover where the prophecy book is—thus finally locating Gim Nigma." As Karan's tall figure disappeared down the winding corridors, the huge stone door descended slowly and met the ground with a thud. Adam remained alone in the great ancient libraries, softly lit by torches extruding from the walls. He understood he must remain here now and dig through these wise books, learning more on the principles of wisdom and insight, so he may know more about himself and his abilities. He was wondering how he would survive here during the time he was reading and seeking answers then his eyes met, in a dark corner, a table laden with food and water. Karan thought of everything; he smiled to himself. He picked one small book off the shelf, *The Power of the Subconscious Mind* by Dr. Josef Murphy. He took a seat by one of the rectangular tables and cleaned the dust off the cover. Next to him, he placed an ancient contraption, a container holding an old wax candle, which gave enough light to read by, and he started reading.

The book spoke of the secrets of the mind and the spirit and of man's ability to get all he asks for by turning the request to his subconscious and repeating it over and over again, until the request sinks deep into the subconscious mind. Within time, it makes itself manifest. The way to do this, the author said, is to quiet the mind, clear away all the thoughts, and repeat the defined request out loud, over and over again, for about ten minutes. Something then occurs in the brain; within time, new neural connections are constructed, supporting a new behavior. By this action, a man slowly creates new neural passages that lead him to achieving his wants and goals. *Wonderful*, Adam thought. *That seems so simple. How is it that no one has done this before?* And then he remembered Joshua's advice to him, to recite certain sentences when he encounters certain situations. He remembered sitting in the prison cell in Sardinia, fending off despair by reciting over and over again, "As hard as this is, I will make it anyway."

The author mentioned that the idea is to be like a gardener, planting the seed of a wish, then watering it day after day until it blossoms into results. *This is what actually happened*, Adam told himself. *I repeated over and over to myself that I want to reach the ancient libraries. I repeated over and over that I'm seeking a solution, and these things did happen. All I have to do is to stick to an idea until it becomes real.*

He finished *The Power of the Subconscious* and continued with *Think and Grow Rich* by Napoleon Hill, which fascinated him. He read of man's ability to use his mind in order to obtain money, ideas, wisdom, and any achievement he may desire, merely by creating a positive state of mind in thinking of finding prosperity and abundance in life.

He studied about mankind's greatest achievers, how they managed to obtain great riches by pursuing their own ideas and goals. Despite being doubted by all, despite many obstacles, they relentlessly pushed on and managed to maintain their desires. He learned he couldn't let negative thoughts seep into his mind, that man must keep himself tightly shut from negative influences that may weaken his ability to achieve his desired goal.

Many days passed, and Adam continued reading the special books. He read Steven Covey's book about how real a man's concept of himself truly is and his concepts of the world, demonstrating that a man must be true to himself and take responsibility of the way he thinks, and if he suffers in life, he must take responsibility for himself and realize that his life is an expression of how he grasps himself and the world. There are people who may appear like successful men on the outside, but in their own eyes, they see themselves as losers, not truly worthy of success.

After finishing *The Seven Habits of Highly Effective People*, Adam began reading *The Aladdin Factor*. From this book, he learned of the art of expressing a wish, that life gives man exactly what he asks for, and he may choose what he requests, that with a strong will and confidence he will get what he seeks. Adam thought to himself that all the books he read so far spoke of clear and easily applicable ideas; he was amazed how simple things really are. *I supposed people were so busy with nonsense and focused on the mundane*, he thought to himself, *that they lost this simple and natural path, the true way.*

Adam didn't feel the days passing in the ancient libraries. He was driven by an insatiable appetite to keep on reading these books. He moved on to a book called *Self-Hypnosis* by Valerie Austin, from which he learned of man's ability to bring himself into a state of such deep relaxation that the subconscious remains wide awake, a state in which one could program his own mind to achieve any goal, whether it is recovering from a physical or mental illness, or strengthening the body. From book to book, Adam understood that the true power lay in the mind, in how one thinks, and how one channels this special force to succeed in anything.

The books of Dale Carnegie taught Adam that it's in his power to choose his reaction to certain situations in life, that he could affect people positively by exciting them about things that are important to them, and how one can release himself from the habit of worrying, leaving the mind peaceful and clear of all kind of silly worries, focusing its power on constructive things instead, using a forward and positive mind frame.

He zoomed through the book *Tuesdays with Morrie* and learned the importance of appreciating the simple things in life, treasuring them, for they are temporary. In order to enjoy them, one must be concentrated on the present. He learned how to forgive men, for ego, pride, and vanity lead to great suffering; and only love, loyalty, and compassion could lead man through a lighted path into a better, illuminated life. He learned one must learn how to give love unconditionally and learn also how to accept it—that by accepting something from someone, you are actually giving meaning to his life, by allowing him to give. *By accepting you are actually giving, that's wonderful*, thought Adam to himself as he continued with the book, which touched him deeply. It told of a wonderful old man dying of a terminal disease, a man who chose to see his last days as life lessons to his loyal student, thus giving these last days a grave importance. Adam was so touched that tears fell from his eyes, and the life lessons from the ancient book penetrated his heart and mind deeply. It must be understood once and for all that love is the answer to all the pain and suffering; it is the meaning of existence, it is the force that can overcome anything, it is always with us and always remains with us. All we must do is believe in it and accept it. Hate brings war, war brings death, while love is the closeness between man and woman, a closeness that brings children to the world, brings new life. Adam repeated to himself, "Hate brings death, love brings life."

The next series of books Adam delved into were Robin S. Sharma's books: *The Monk Who Sold His Ferrari*. It taught Adam to appreciate nature and the present, removing worry and negative thoughts from the mind, that man must focus only on positive thinking. *I must not think negative thoughts*, thought Adam to himself. He thought to himself that the brain is like a glass of clear, transparent water, which one drop of black liquid would turn cloudy—so one negative thought is enough to cloud the clarity of the mind. Adam concluded from that, that man must maintain a constant state of positive thinking, denying the negative force. He remembered the words of his father to him when he was a child; when a man rose in the morning and saw the day was cloudy and gray and let this fact influence him, declaring in his ignorance that today will be a bad day, by this, he is actually inviting the negative forces into his day and into his life, and this way, the day manifests itself, such as by man bumping into the corner of a table or being late to work. Man stupidly chooses to be a victim to negative thinking. The creator supplied a bounty of everything, and man must see and choose the good in the world and do even better.

Leadership Wisdom taught him that he must be systematic with his dreams and goals that he must focus on the things worth doing. He learned he must simplify life, not complicate ourselves with all kinds of unneeded things; it is as if a man has a messy desk, with many unnecessary things crowding it, and these things must be cleaned away, so one can focus on the truly important ones, the ones worth attention. A man must focus on the things that will advance him toward the goals he truly wants to achieve.

One tiny book remained on the shelf, which was by now wiped clean from the dust covering it for many years now. It was

The Alchemist by Paulo Coelho, a Brazilian author from the former century. Adam began leafing through the book and the hair on his body rose; he was astonished by how much this story was similar to his own voyage of self-recognition. By going on a journey to fulfill his destiny and what was burning in his heart for years, ever since he recognized himself; only that now he decided to take action. He read about the young hero, his dream, and his decision to go on a journey after his dream, after the treasure. An interesting metaphor came to Adam's mind; he imagined man as a large sailboat coursing through the ocean of life, and he saw the storms, the high waves, and the dangerous rocks threatening to drown the ship as the problems that assail man's life, threatening to drown him or to smash him against the rocky shore. Time and time again, still, man mustn't lose hope; he must continue despite all storms, whirlwinds, pirates… *But what could push the sailboat to continue?* Adam asked himself. Then an insight crossed his mind—that every ship needs a destination, and its purpose is to find, amidst the vast ocean, its own specific little treasure island, which holds a hidden treasure. Thus, a man navigates his life to find his own treasure; a man must dedicate his life to a goal, and like Robin Sharma said in his books, the purpose of life is for life to have a purpose. A purpose so high, so special, that it will enrich the life of man himself and the life of others, people, animals, and nature. A man mustn't allow fortune to guide his ship. He must take responsibility over himself and have faith in the good God that he was put on this Earth in order to do something with his life, something great and so meaningful it would influence the rest of the world in a positive way; it will light up the entire world with precious light. It will leave a positive mark on the lives of others who need love, heat, an embrace, food, medicine. A man must take hold of the steering wheel of his ship and maneuver it through all the obstacles toward its treasure island, and when it reaches the treasure island, and the man finds the treasure he was striving for, then he can continue toward other treasures; *because there will always remain someone who needs help in the world,* Adam thought to himself.

At the time, when humanity was free, all the rich people in the world could have joined efforts and abolished hunger from the world, they could have brought sight to the blind, found cures for the sick, and even if their efforts were not entirely successful, the life of the person in need would have been improved merely by the fact that they were trying. *Love cures,* thought Adam to himself, *that's why man must take hold of the steering wheel of his ship and guide it through all the obstacles and challenges in the way. Actually,* Adam thought to himself, *why treat all these challenges as something bad and depressing? Why not treat it as an adventure? Turn life into an adventure, instead of a journey of suffering and frustration?*

Adam closed the book called *The Alchemist*, overwhelmed with excitement. All these books spoke of one thing. Of a special force, of uniting with the way of the creator—he realized from all this that God put everything in this world, and man himself must choose the good. History teaches that every man or influential leader that acted in a negative way brought destruction upon himself and the world. Everything that begins with a negative tone will end negative. God created an endless bounty in the universe. *Man was given the choice of how to use this special force,* Adam thought to himself.

Man must create healthy, positive ways, leading him to a wonderful life, enriching his own existence and the existence of the world; he must focus on the positive force, and he must focus on the things that are worthy to be focused upon. Every now and then, a man must improve his ways, there is no problem when one decides that there's no problem, if a man focuses on the positive force he leaves no room for the negative one. When he does that, man would walk the king's road for the rest of his life. *A positive approach is the key,* Adam thought to himself and rose from the ancient chair he's been sitting on for many days now. He rubbed his cheeks and was surprised to feel the fuzz of a beard. "How long have I been here?" Adam asked himself. He walked toward the table in the corner and held up a green apple. "It must have been a few weeks that I'm here now," said Adam to himself as he bit into the apple. "In reading all these books, I realized that we humans can do anything within our own human limitations. We can overcome diseases, we can venture out in space and reach other stars in order to keep growing and developing and lighting the universe, but all this can be done only if humanity realizes that it must stick to the positive way, and believe in the positive way of our maker—that only on the path of love, forgiveness, tolerance, and good-will this can be done."

He finished eating his apple and looked again at the special shelf filled with victory books. He gazed at them with admiration. "These books truly are good friends to man. The weeks I'm here, I've learned so much from them. I'm beginning to grasp the special might in this path of power of the mind," said Adam to himself. "All I really need to do is to meditate, understanding that God is only good, that he wants what's good for man. I must concentrate on my belief that I'll find the special book of Gim Nigma, thus finding the special force that will help me rescue the world from the evil rule of the empire," Adam concluded.

He stepped to the center of the library hall, sat down cross-legged on the ground, and began speaking to himself, "I'm relaxing my body and my mind. I now empty my mind completely from any negative thought. I let nothing distract me. I'm focused on my wish to find the book of Gim Nigma, and indeed, I'll find it." Adam's Hawk eyes closed; he clasped his hands together with his legs crossed and began repeating over and over. "I'll find the book of Gim Nigma. I'll find the book of Gim Nigma. I'll find the book of Gim Nigma."

Adam was in a state of self-induced hypnosis; he heard nothing, saw nothing, but his goal, he was entirely focused upon his request to find this special book of Gim Nigma. Minutes passed, and Adam continued repeating the sentence, hours passed and still Adam repeated the sentence decisively and without pause. "I'll find the book of Gim Nigma." Suddenly, he felt a pleasant heat flood his body; he felt the muscles of his body charge with immense power, felt the blood gush through his veins as if it was about to burst through, as if he received a great jolt of energy. He realized he should now open his eyes. His skin was covered with sweat. With his eyes still shut he saw a bright flash of light; immediately, he opened his eyes and stared at the spot where his gaze happened to fall then smiled with great excitement; his eyes fell upon a high shelf, covered with dust and dimly lit, but nonetheless his eyes beheld one book among all the rest, and he managed to read its title out loud: *The Book of Light, Gim Nigma*. He quickly leapt to his feet, lifted his hands up, and stared at the high ceiling of the libraries, calling out loudly, "Thank you, my creator, thank you."

He came to the shelf, overwhelmed with excitement, tears of joy weaving their way through his young beard. He reached high up and gently took the book off the shelf, a book whose binding was made of a metal not from this Earth. On the front cover of the book was a golden emblem of the sun. He caressed the cover gently and the small tears fell upon the golden cover. A huge smile spread slowly over Adam's bearded face; he found the book. He did it.

The great stone door rose slowly, revealing Karan, the lonesome priest, standing in the doorway, with Arak the one-eyed wolf beside him. They entered the ancient libraries; Karan noticed that the place was lit more than ever before. He knew something special must have happened. A few steps later, the priest and the wolf stopped by Adam's sprawled figure, peacefully sleeping on the ground with a smile on his lips, his arms wound tightly around the book of light. Karan gazed warmly at the sleeping figure of Adam, turned to Arak, and said, "He made it, Arak. He managed to find the book. I'm here for so many years and no one managed to make it all the way here, to arrive and find the book that would change the course of human history." Karan pat Arak's head, who enjoyed Karan's caressing touch. "I guess no one wanted it as fiercely as Adam did. Apparently, there was no one special enough, pure of intention enough. The heart beating in Adam's chest is pure, and the pure truth always wins," Karan said loudly in order to wake up the sleeping Adam, and indeed, his voice woke Adam. The young man rose swiftly to his feet when he saw the gray-eyed priest and his one-eyed friend standing there. Arak was jubilant as Adam stood up; the special animal and Adam embraced. Arak warmly licked Adam's face while Adam excitedly showed him the book he found, the book of light. "Do you see, Arak? We did it, we did it!"

Karan let out a rumbling laugh, "Indeed, you did it, my dear Adam," Karan said, but then his laughter faded and he spoke in a grave tone. "You indeed found the book, written by a mysterious hand not of this world, but now you must learn to understand what is written in it and discover the location of Gim Nigma."

Adam looked at the priest with an astonished expression, realizing that finding the book of light was merely one more stage. Karan's gray eyes saw Adam's crestfallen face, and he laid his hand over Adam's shoulder and said, "Don't worry, Adam, I'm here by your side. I will help you. Together we'll find in the book where Gim Nigma is. Don't forget, I came from that other world hundreds of years ago. I know the language in which it's written." Adam's expression turned back into a smile that quickly changed into a laugh of joy.

"Karan, before we carry on, I have one small request," said Adam, rubbing his hand over his bearded face.

The priest looked at him questioningly. "Yes, Adam, what is your request?"

Adam replied, smiling hugely, "I've been in this place many days. I don't even know how many, and there is one thing I simply have to do."

Karan looked at the young man curiously.

"I need a decent shower," said Adam, laughing lightly.

The priest burst into a loud laughter that shook the ancient libraries and replied, "Of course Adam, of course."

Chapter Sixty-Four

At the bottom of the Argma fortress, hundreds of men gathered, all clad in black cloaks. Their faces were hidden but their eyes glowed red and evil. They were following Irma the witch, who led them into a vast underground hall, which looked exactly like the special room where she and Bartholomew did the special meditation, radiating negative energies in order to neutralize Adam's will to carry out his quest. The men were assembled together by the witch in order to concentrate a source of mental energy strong enough to overcome and trample the defensive walls of positive thinking that Joshua and his friends created in the effort to help Adam far off the island of Esperanza. Irma recruited men from the land whose hearts were governed by evil and destruction. Her goal was to bind all the evil thoughts from all these evil minds and transmit them as a concentrated blow into Adam's mind, utterly destroying him. Bartholomew watched it all from the side. He hid all this from his fellow leaders, especially Drakkar; he wanted to be the leader that saved the empire from the threat of the prophecy coming true. He rubbed his hands together and smiled wickedly, thinking that through Irma's work they could take the rule over the empire into their own hands. The stout leader's eyes saw how hundreds of people gather around the witch and the circular podium in an enormous circle. On the podium, black candles were arranged in the shape of a five-pointed star. Darkness fell upon the hall. The silence made the hair on his body stand on edge; he waited anxiously to see what would happen next. Irma opened her mouth and released a stream of incomprehensible words into the space of the room with a hoarse voice. The hundreds of black clad men repeated her words with a thunderous echo. The walls of the room were swallowed in raging flames, the black clad figures held hands and repeated the words of the old witch loudly, the candle flames rose higher than ever before, reaching to the hall ceiling. Irma read out loud, in a language Bartholomew could understand, "Our energies combined will reach this man's mind, trampling his will to continue his quest. They will cast a heavy weight of negativity that will crush his spirit and his will. Our dark powers will overcome the pure heart of the son of light, trying to fulfill itself through the prophecy. The negative force will be strong enough to break him. Let it be done!" With an ear-piercing screech, Irma lifted her hands above her head, gesturing oddly.

Bartholomew was spell bound by this vision; he felt the full force of the negative energy, filling up the great hall from wall to wall. He felt the energy flow as if it was a live creature making its way toward its prey. Bartholomew said with a smile, "This is your end, mystery man."

Ten floors up, there was a commotion in the fortress. The other three empire leaders sat by a black marble table, their arms crossed, silently listening to a bunch of scientists in silvery robes conducts a loud argument. Drakkar rose to his feet, pulled his laser gun from its sheath, and shot a short blast into the air. Everyone fell silent at once. The leader then returned the weapon to its case and took his seat by his colleagues. "Now what's all this noise about? Does anybody want to tell me?" asked Drakkar angrily.

One of scientists stepped near the table and said, "Your highness, some of us don't think the army of robots is ready for action. Some of us think we should wait a while longer before engaging the robots in actual battle."

One of the scientists from the opposing group burst into his words, "Your highness, that's nonsense. The giant robot army is ready to fight, but our colleagues don't have the guts to see that."

The leader gazed at the two scientists wickedly, stroking his thick beard. "Is that so?" said Drakkar and continued, "And why would you think my giant robot army isn't ready to go to battle, defeating the resistance all over the world and grinding it to dust?"

The first scientist stepped back and answered in a scared voice, "We checked all systems—everything seems to be in working order, but the robot army hasn't been tested in real field conditions."

The scientists all tightened back into one group, facing the three leaders, awaiting the decision of the top ranks. The leader of the empire then rose from his seat and called out, "I say that the robot army is ready to fight. I want to execute my plan now. My robot army will trample city after city, forcing the resistance all over the world to surrender, unless they want innocent blood on their hands." The leader finished his sentence with a rasping, evil laughter. The scientists looked at each other nervously, forcing themselves to join in his laughter.

Bammark and Vaskov rose from their seats, patting Drakkar's shoulder as a sign of agreement. They all agreed with Drakkar's diabolical plan. This was how they would bring down the underground worldwide. The giant robot army will overrun the cities and wipe out entire communities; the resistance will have no choice. They will give up their arms and submit to slavery like most of humanity over most of the world, handing the empire its crushing victory. The scientists then said that the new army will be ready soon, and Drakkar demanded they speed matters up. As Drakkar was speaking with the scientists, Bammark turned to Vaskov. "Where did the fat guy disappear?" asked the man with the greased back golden mane. His colleague answered indifferently, "I don't know where he's been roaming, but rumors say he's been seen in the cellars a lot lately, in the quarters of the old witch." The two men walked toward the group of scientists, who were discussing last details with the empire leader before activating the giant robots. Drakkar turned to the two and called, "Excellent, the scientists informed me we can commence our plan next week."

He noticed the questioning expression on Bammark and Vaskov's faces. "What is it?" he asked, and Vaskov replied with a whisper, "Do you know where Bartholomew is? And why he wasn't in the meeting?" Bammark continued,

"Are you aware that our friend has been spending a lot of time with Irma in Argma's cellars?"

Drakkar's forehead creased, his eyebrows rising with wonder. "Is that so?" he asked, and continued with a whisper, "Well, Bartholomew is of no interest to us now. We need to prepare for the launching of our new robot army. I want to finish off the underground once and for all."

The two leaders looked at each other, agreeing that their leader was right. Bartholomew was of no importance now; let him play his silly games with the old witch, while they manage the upcoming battle.

Chapter Sixty-Five

Dawn broke over the island of Esperanza. The sky was clear of clouds, the weather pleasant. The palm trees swayed softly in the breeze. Paola Katarina was sitting outside her house, watching the waves roll in from a distance and slowly merge with the white sands on the island shore. She shut her eyes and rested her wrists on her knees, which were folded in a cross legged sitting position. She breathed the perfect air deep into her lungs, her hair billowing in the light wind, and suddenly scary images flashed through her mind. She felt a great concentration of negative forces inside her. She opened her eyes at once and looked around; besides the blue waves washing onto the magical shores and green trees, there was nothing different to behold. She looked out at the sea and the flashes appeared again, one after the other, casting terror upon Paola Katarina; she saw in front of her hundreds of dark figures in black cloaks, all gathered around one main figure, also in a black cloak. She felt an extremely high concentration of negative energy and sensed from within that all this negative force was being aimed at Adam Swandon. She rose at once, heart pounding, and paced quickly toward the large cabin where the representatives of the New Dawn Hawks resided—Simon, the leader of the island's men, old Joshua, and young Heralda. She remembered a time when she was young and her parents told her that she holds unique powers to see things far beyond the reach of the human eye, and that one day her powers will serve all humanity in an important way. These words touched her; she remembered her family, the gipsy tribe, wise and special people that usually didn't receive the respect they deserved from society. She arrived at the large cabin panting, swung the door open, and looked anxiously at the people gathered in the room.

Simon rose at once and ran to her. "What's happened, dear? Are you all right?"

As the good woman gradually caught her breath, Joshua came to her and held her hand. "Calm down, dear, calm down," he said, patting Paola Katarina's sweaty palms with his old hands. Heralda served the good woman a glass of cold water. The woman sipped it slowly, and since her hands were shaking a little, the water spilled a bit from the corners of her mouth.

"Friends, Adam is in grave danger," she called loudly to all those around her.

Simon knelt by the woman. "What are you talking about, Paola Katarina?" he asked.

The woman handed the glass back to Heralda and said, "In my mind's eye, I saw visions from a distant place, a great force of negative mental energy gathering, about to be transmitted into Adam's mind—to kill him."

Everyone, besides old Joshua, turned pale. Heralda cried anxiously, "Oh dear, what shall we do?"

Joshua stood up and gazed out of the window facing the sea. "I assumed this is what would happen. The dark forces want to prevent Adam from bringing light, hope, and freedom to humans and the world in general. They tried to stop him before and failed, because Adam's will is pure and fierce, yet a high concentration of negative energy may indeed have an effect, unfortunately. That's why we must do what we did before. We must unite our forces and resist the dark power's negative energies. We must gather as large a number as possible of good-hearted people and focus all their positive thoughts in a giant communal meditation. That is what must be done," summed Joshua.

Simon stood up in front of his friends and said, "Well, Joshua must know what he is talking about, so what are we waiting for? Let's start rounding up the island men."

Paola Katarina stood and looked at Simon. "The island men aren't enough, dear. In my visions, I saw hundreds, perhaps thousands, of dark figures with dark hearts. We will need more people."

Joshua came to the two and said, "She's right, Simon. A greater force is needed."

Simon understood the two and said, "All right, friends. We will leave immediately for a round in the neighboring islands and gather as many people as we can find, free people, with a positive spirit, and we will bring them here, and with them, we will build the largest meditation possible."

Old Joshua coughed lightly and said with a smile, "Wonderful, Simon, that's a brave and kind decision on your behalf, but we must be very cautious so that the empire forces don't spot us."

Simon laid his hand gently on Joshua's shoulder and said, "Thank you for your words, Joshua." He looked around at his men and called, "Well, what are we waiting for? Adam needs our help, and we will help him big time!"

Chapter Sixty-Six

In the heart of the Sahara desert, in a great secluded structure made of massive stone, sits a man who holds in his hand the book that discloses the secret of Gim Nigma's location, the mysterious force, which is the answer to all evil in the world. Adam Swandon is now clean and shaved, waiting for Karan, the lone priest, who guarded the ancient libraries alone for many years, until the right man came along, the man with the pure heart, bent upon saving the world. Arak the one-eyed wolf paced around Adam's legs, impatient for the gray-eyed priest to come. After a few more minutes of waiting, Karan appeared, smiling, and spread his arms wide, "Oh, Adam dear, you look much better without that beard!"

Adam answered, lightly laughing, "Well, I'm ready, Karan, ready for you to help me decipher what's written in the Book of Light, so I can see my quest through."

The man with the flowing gray hair sat down on one of the chairs. "What did you learn from all the books you read while you were in the ancient libraries?" asked Karan, taking Adam by surprise.

"Well..." said Adam, thinking how to reply the priest's wise question. "Well, Karan, I learned that there is one huge, infinite force, the force of the creator, and the creator is nothing but good. He made a world with an infinite bounty of both good and evil and gave man the choice between them. How is a man to make his choices? The decision is in man's hands. There is always the mistaken approach to think that the creator is sometimes evil and wishes his subjects to suffer. I learned that the creator is a mother and father to everything. Can parents who bring a child into this world to grow, and prosper, and bloom, could they ever wish him bad? I believe the creator wants only what's good for us, and all we must do is be wise enough to see his way. It is a way of harmony, of unity, of respect—respect toward man, or animal, or plant. I learned this great force is always attainable, for good or for bad. I will give an example from human history. Two leaders that changed and fashioned the world by their own vision, using this special force. The first is Adolf Hitler, a German that became the leader of Nazi Germany. He used this great force to conquer the world, and he almost succeeded. He was responsible for the death of millions of innocents. He believed his race to be superior to others. He attempted to slaughter the Jewish people, killing six million of them—men, women, children, babies, elders—but the creator wanted it differently. The free world rose against him, almost too late, fought the Nazi regime back, and after many years and many casualties, the Nazi regime was defeated. Hitler's end was wretched and pathetic. History tells us he killed himself with a shot to the head, hiding in his bunker, toward the end of World War II. That's how it ended for the one who tried to influence the world in a negative way. He wanted to conquer the world and enslave other people, all children of the creator, he started his way with evil intentions, and so it ended for him and for the people he represented. Nature will not allow one nation to rule over all others. They are all equal, all born for freedom, all deserving respect. There is not one better than the other. They are all different, and the differences must be respected, for hate brings war, and war brings death and destruction.

"There was another special person, though, an Indian—Mahatma Gandhi. He led a nation of hundreds of millions, freeing them from the rule of another nation, without using arms. He caused an army of millions, armed with deadly weapons, to retreat and leave the land they conquered. He did this with persistence, love, and tolerance. The English hurt him more than once, and yet he didn't give up. He was adamant that the struggle for freedom be carried out with tolerance, not war. He fasted many days, torturing himself so that peace could come to his people so they might unite against the conquering army, only through love and tolerance could they achieve their goal, and indeed, this road brought this humble, skinny man to free his people. History praises this person, which left a positive and inspiring imprint of tolerance, brotherhood, and love, for love brings children, and children are life.

"History praises the many special people that brought inspiration and honor to the creation of man throughout the world: Martin Luther King, Mahatma Gandhi, Yitzhak Rabin, King Hussein, Helen Keller, Mori Schwartz, Abe Nathan, and many more that sought justice, equality, and peace for all humans. But there is another special man that touched my heart, a man who walked the path the creator led him through and believed in the mission cast upon him—Moses. He was the prince of Egypt, which was a great empire at the time, yet his heart was pure and special. He gave up the kingship, the gold, and all the riches, and went into the desert following the quest God gave him. He went to free the people of Israel from the hands of the pharaoh of Egypt, who made another nation into slaves. This special man did all this with only a simple staff of wood in his hands and eternal faith in God in his heart. Against all odds, the faith in the positive way of the all-powerful creator, who made us all equal and free to choose between good and evil had won. It was faith that split the ocean and drowned the forces of evil within it.

"The creator helps whoever wants to help himself and others. One must be wise enough to choose the road that would lead to his goal. Life's purpose is to fulfill yourself and your destiny, keeping in your heart hope, faith, and the courage to succeed. Any vocation will bring a man pure happiness as long as it enriches the life of others, be they humans, animals, or any other thing in nature. Man must use the treasures the creator planted in him in order to enrich the world and light it with a precious light. Rather than wasting their life's energy in hating, killing, and destroying, it is possible to build, to plant, to love, and give yourself to others with unconditional love, to do just for the sake of doing, without expecting anything in return, for the return will come from your own acts. Everything is possible in life, good and bad. I realized that man should choose the good. It's so simple, if you do bad, the result will be bad. If you do good, it can only come out good."

Adam ceased talking and looked at Karan, waiting for his response. The man with the gray eyes looked at him with pride. The lonely priest knew that in front of him stood the special man with the special soul, the one bound to save the world from its misery. In his heart, he felt a circle close, a unique sense of calm over the fact that someone finally chose to do the right thing, to be selfless, to stand up for the rights of others. Adam was the pure-hearted one, and Karan believed that God would always be with him, now and later on. The priest stood up, smiling widely, and called out, "I'm proud of you, Adam. You spent days and nights in the great libraries. You learned much from the wonderful books written by the best and most positive men in the world, and you are now ready to continue toward the fulfillment of your destiny, which is tied with the destiny of all humanity. Together, you and I shall study the book of light and discover where the mysterious force of Gim Nigma is hidden."

Adam rose from his seat and shook Karan's hand warmly. "Karan, when I was a boy, I dreamt I would change the world. Everyone told me to forget about that idea, but in my heart, I never gave up despite all the difficulties, the obstacles, the wars, and the horrific tyranny of the empire, and as long as I'm alive, I won't cease believing that I can bring a real change to the world. I thank you for all your help," Adam said with emotion.

The priest laid both his hands on Adam's shoulders and said, "I will give you all the help I can, for because of you my destiny also is fulfilled, and that fills my heart with joy. That's why tomorrow, with first light, you and I shall open the book of light and discover where in this world Gim Nigma lay."

Arak the one-eyed wolf leapt with joy; apparently, he understood what was happening and he began barking jovially at Adam and Karan.

A new dawn rose over the desert. The wind gently caressed the golden dunes, the sun shone brightly. Karan lead Adam outside the huge stone structure that stood in the midst of the desert, and together they marched a mile from the large structure. Arak stayed behind with Ayakon, the great desert hawk, at the entrance to the large stone cove.

Karan bent down to the sandy ground and brushed some of the sand aside, exposing to Adam's eyes a round, colorful stone. The priest then pressed the center of the round stone and a rounded pedestal rose up from the ground. Karan asked Adam to step toward it and place Gim Nigma's book of light in a rectangular hollow that seemed like a template for a book. Adam placed the book as Karan asked.

The book merged with the stone at once, opening before them, and as it opened, a bright shaft of light burst from the book up toward the sun in the sky and then back upon the open book. Adam and Karan stood facing the stone podium in which the book of Gim Nigma was now embedded, wide open, and before both their eyes, colorful lights began shimmering, lifting from the book toward the desert. The patterns of light slowly came together and began creating an image of breath-taking landscapes, blue seas, tropical forests, tall mountains, and green valleys. The picture settled on a beautiful mountain view, and suddenly by the colorful, lit landscape appeared something that seemed to be an enlargement of one of the pages in the book. The page was covered with a strange writing, composed of geometric shapes and triangles in many sizes.

"What does it say?" Adam asked.

Karan looked at the writing on the large page projected from the book and began translating for Adam, "Well, it says here, congratulations to the son of light, the pure-hearted one who found the book of Gim Nigma. The fact he found this special book means that he carries the special soul destined to follow the quest to locate Gim Nigma and save the human race and all of planet Earth."

Adam patted Karan's shoulder, smiled, and said, "That means we are on the right road, right?"

Karan replied, a smile in his eyes. "We are on the right road, but you are the one who will leave here alone to find Gim Nigma."

Adam nodded curtly, showing he understood, and said, "If so, Karan, tell me where Gim Nigma lays. What does the rest of the book's pages say?"

Karan approached the book, which was enveloped in a rounded sphere of light, passed his hand over the pages of the book, and another page turned over and was projected out large to the eyes of Adam and Karan. "The pure-hearted one must continue the journey he took upon himself and arrive at Victory Mountain, located in the continent of South America on Earth. There he will be tested—should he pass these tests successfully, Gim Nigma will reveal itself in all its glory to the man carrying the unique soul. The pure-hearted one must hold fast to the Book of Light and never lose it. The book will guide him on how to act later on the journey." Karan finished reading the writing on the page and took one step back.

Adam remained standing by the tall podium to which the book of light was attached, still projecting the image of a beautiful mountain terrain. Adam turned to Karan and asked, "I look at the picture of these beautiful mountains and I don't understand. Is one of them the Mountain of Victory? And if so, where is it? And how will I reach it?"

Karan cleared his throat and answered Adam. "The book tells of the place where Gim Nigma is buried, and that place is Mt. Victory, where Gim Nigma was buried thousands of years ago in case the day would come when the human race are under threat of destroying themselves, thus shattering the balance of the entire universe. The people of my world took upon themselves the responsibility to do the deed and protect the balance in a universe that God created for all, so they hid Gim Nigma here. Gim Nigma is the solution to all evil in the world. It is the answer to all crime and suffering that is going on in the world for thousands of years now. The fact that there exists one man with a special soul who cares enough to embark on such a difficult journey shows us that there's still a spark of hope for the human race, making this world a place worth saving. Indeed, one of the mountains you see here is Mt. Victory, but I don't know exactly which one. From here, you must continue to South America, following the book's instructions."

Karan came close to the book once more, waved one hand in the air, and said, "Let's see if the book tells us how to get there." The priest passed his hand over the lit book once more, and again, another page turned, its contents displayed before the two men. The page that was projected contained a colorful map, displaying the continent of South America, focusing on Peru. In that area, many marks were concentrated, looking like little circles and triangles.

"This is the map that will show you the way. Mt. Victory is near a city called Inca Drakna. Inca pyramids will surround the mountain. Beyond this the book tells no more, the rest of the pages will be displayed only later in the journey," said Karan, summing what was written on the projected page.

Adam sat down on the sandy ground, laid both his hands on his knees, and asked with his head bowed low. "Later on in the journey?

You said I will go alone, how am I to understand what the rest of the book says?"

The priest came close, facing him, while behind him the book of light still glowed, projecting the giant map beside the picture of the mountain range. "Listen to me, Adam, you are not alone. God will always walk with you, and I will be with you as well as you continue your journey. You can communicate with me when you need me. Remove fear from your heart and persist with your goal."

Despite Karan's encouraging words, Adam felt a strange force weakening him, and he was frightened by it. Karan noticed this and said, "Adam, the forces of evil are straining to weaken you from afar. They are concentrating all their negative force and projecting it into your mind to weaken you. Get up, Adam, you mustn't give into it."

Karan's voice rose higher, yet Adam felt more and more miserable, until he simply lay down on the sand without moving. Karan was worried for the young man's well being; he realized that the telepathic forces of an immense negative meditation were making their way into Adam's mind, poisoning his thoughts. The priest wasted no time; he lifted Adam in his arms and hurried back into the great stone structure. Ayakon and Arak showed their concern as they accompanied the gray-eyed man back in. The book of light remained outside, glowing brightly. Karan continued to speak to Adam, who fell into a restless daze. "Adam, don't give into the negative forces. You have the power in you to resist the negativity, you are special, believe in yourself."

Karan's words went into Adam's ears and found their way into his befuddled mind. Karan managed to hear Adam mumble, "I'm not giving in, Karan, I won't give in, but I need help." Adam then sunk into a slumber. Karan laid him on a bed with soft white sheets, sat beside him on the floor, crossed his legs, pressed the palms of his hands together, and began praying, "Oh, great higher force, our Lord and creator, before us lay a special man. Please, don't allow him to surrender to the forces of evil. Don't let his soul sputter out. I pray for him that you may give him the strength to overcome this obstacle, so he may carry on his quest, fulfill his destiny, declare victory." So the gray-eyed man continued to pray without cease for the special man's salvation.

Hundreds of miles away, on the island of Esperanza, hundreds of men gathered from all the islands around. They all held hands around a great campfire burning under the open sky. All this was to help one special man, who took it upon himself to go out and save them and the rest of the human race, to take them from slavery to freedom, from darkness to light, from suffering to happiness. They believed in his fierce will to succeed. Not one of them knew if he could carry out his mission, not one knew if he found the place he was looking for yet, but still they believed in him. Those were people with hope in their hearts, with hope for salvation, so they did it anyway.

Chapter Sixty-Seven

Old Joshua stood by Simon, who was diligently looking over the positioning of the people, and said, "I'm very proud of you. Look what you accomplished. You managed to arrange thousands of men with goodwill, with faith in salvation, and through your efforts, we will unite our powers and help Adam repel the oppression from his heart and mind, so he may go forth and fulfill his mission." Simon looked at him, his eyes shining with the reflected light of the huge fire.

"Thank you, Joshua. I have to admit at first I had my doubts about all this, but as the days pass, my heart grows surer in its faith. That's why I believe there is hope now, with all my heart, I hope for this young man's success. That's why I'm doing all I can to help him, so he may help us all," said Simon. He looked around at the crowds of people gathered around the campfire. They were all here because they wanted a better life, because they were told that one special man exists, which refuses to give in to suffering, and he intends to bring salvation to them all. They heard of the man that took a daring quest upon himself for the good of the entire human race, and they were touched by this. When they heard that this special man had a problem they immediately rushed to do all they could to help.

Suddenly, a sharp scream cut through the commotion of all these people. They all turned to look at the source of the shout and discovered Heralda, terrified, standing by the slumped figure of Paola

Katarina, lying on the ground. Simon dashed toward Paola Katarina. While a few men and women calmed the crowd, asking them to remain calm and await instructions. Simon knelt by the unconscious woman and cried out loudly, "Paola Katarina, can you hear me? Please, answer me!"

The woman opened her eyes with difficulty and whispered, "He is in terrible danger, the dark forces have begun poisoning Adam's mind and spirit." The woman's eyes closed again, her head lolled back on her shoulders. Simon didn't give up, he held both her shoulder's and gently shook her.

"Wake up, Paola Katarina, we need you. I understand your mind is linked to Adam's, but you must stay with us and not let go, do you hear?" Again, the good woman's eyes slowly opened.

"We must hurry, Simon. We must hurry with our work before it's too late," said Paola Katarina weakly, her eyes shutting again. In a broken voice, Simon called out to the crowd of thousands of worried people. "Did you hear that? We have to hurry! Let's go, people, go!" The crowd rushed to fulfill his request; they all fell into place, took each other's hands, and awaited further instructions.

Joshua stood on a small wooden stage, tightly shut his old eyes and called out to the cool air of Esperanza, "Dear public, people of all races, colors and nations—all respected, all equal, and all united under one God. United in order to roar a prayer of light that will defeat the darkness threatening to swallow our dear friend, Adam Swandon. I ask you all to focus the power of your thoughts, make them positive, make them utterly victorious—as all our positive thoughts combine, they will flow through space directly to the mind and heart of our Adam. This will give him the strength to resist the dark force's negative energies. They want slavery to go on forever. We won't give that evil a hand! We will reinforce Adam's strength, for his intentions are pure and good, and we must help him so he may help us all." The old man paused, saw that he had the full attention of the entire immense crowd, and carried on, "Let us unite our positive forces, let us send this positive power to Adam, let us pray for him together, let's do it!"

As he finished speaking, the entire crowd of thousands roared, "Let's do it!"

Tears formed in the corners of the old man's eyes, deeply touched by the occasion.

In a moment, they came together, thousands of people of different races and groups, united in their fierce, unshakable will to help Adam overcome the negative forces. They all shut their eyes and a colossal prayer rose to the sky, a prayer of hope, a prayer of goodwill, of light over dark.

Hundreds of men in black cloaks gathered round the old witch Irma, who assembled them all in order to unite their evil minds in a destructive meditation that would destroy Adam's spirit. The witch was sitting in the center of the podium, in the center of a pentagon of burning black candles. Her craggy mouth opened, and she cried out to the great hall. "Unite your minds, gather all your negative energy. We shall transmit the full might of our evil into the mystery man's mind, far away. It will trample his spirit. It will kill his will to carry out the prophecy of the son of light!" Irma's usually croaky voice rang loud and thunderous, echoing in every corner of the huge underground hall.

The hundreds of black clad figures with their glowing red eyes replied with a long growl that grew louder and louder until it turned into a deafening shout. Even the soldiers patrolling outside heard the shout and took fright. The shout moved through space and reached the mind of Adam Swandon, who lay unconscious on a bed in the heart of the desert. The priest Karan was sitting by his side, constantly praying for him.

Adam opened his spirit's eyes. He saw his own body lying on a crisp white bed. He saw the gray-eyed man by his side, feverishly repeating a prayer. He felt himself float above the room; he looked around and realized this was a certain spiritual state. He realized he was now outside his body. For a moment, he was frightened, but then something drew his attention—the sound of a long, mysterious growl. He moved through the rooms of the great stone structure and found himself outside the huge cove. He had reached the open desert. By the entrance, he noticed Ayakon the hawk with Arak, both quietly sleeping. He continued to float toward the mysterious growling sound; the closer he came, the louder the growl became. Suddenly, a dark figure in a black cloak appeared before his spirit's eyes. As he advanced, he could see behind this figure hundreds, perhaps thousands more figures, all clad in black, all with evil eyes. Adam was startled; he looked around but all his spirit's eyes saw was sand and more sand, and the ancient stone structure, home to the priest and the ancient libraries, far in the distance.

"Who are you?" Adam asked. Silence surrounded them. Not one of the thousands of figures replied, only the drawn out, disturbing growl rang in the desert air.

"Who are you?" asked Adam again, louder. Suddenly he saw one figure, standing in front of the others, slowly float toward him. He considered moving away but was too eager to get an answer for all that was happening. He could see the face of the figure now; it was the wrinkled face of a very old woman. The woman stopped before him and answered him in a rasping voice. "I'm Irma the witch. I serve his highness Drakkar, the leader of the empire, ruler of Earth. I'm here to stop you from fulfilling the prophecy."

Adam felt as if he was suffocating. The witch's narrow eyes penetrate into his own hawk eyes. She continued speaking, "What happened, young man, that you took into your head to go on a journey to save this world? You knew right from the start that's an impossible mission."

Adam listened, and the witch continued, "Walk with me," she told him. The both began pacing over the desert sands; while in the background, the thousands of figures continued growling that incessant, droning growl. Adam felt disoriented; a part of him wanted to hear the witch speak. As they walked across the desert, the witch continued, "Don't you think you are wasting your precious time? Instead of living your life, enjoying all that life has to offer, you go and try to sacrifice yourself for this miserable race of humans, that doesn't even deserve to be saved. Through history men did only evil, destroying themselves in their pursuit after money and power. They learned only to hate each other, covet, and slaughter. The human race doesn't deserve to be saved." Adam's ears picked up every word. He felt confused. The old woman's words started to make sense to him. She continued, "Why carry on this useless voyage, do you think you can change them? Do you think once they're free, they'll change? They deserve a rough hand like Drakkar's."

Adam's spirits began to fall. He processed all she said in his mind and saw logic in her words. The witch carried on, "You can live an enjoyable life. The empire will allow you a comfortable and pleasurable life. Desert this silly notion of saving the world and join us." The witch held out her hand to Adam. Snakes were twisting round her skinny arm. Adam was swayed by Irma's words.

Why should he put in such an effort, really? For who? For what? Humans will stay like they are, evil, treacherous, greedy, and corrupt, war mongrels, yes, the witch is probably right, thought Adam. He looked down at the witch's outreached hand. She noticed this, and an evil smile stretched her withered lips. Adam lifted his arm and reached his hand out to take the witch's hand. "Forget your mission and join us," the witch said, knowing that once Adam willingly took her hand the prophecy will crumble and darkness would rule forever.

Adam's hand inched closer; he could feel his spirit leaving him… but suddenly, a thunderous sound rolled over the desert, instantly breaking the disturbing growl of the thousands cloaked figures.

"No, Adam, don't you give up!" Adam halted before his hand reached the witch's hand, and turned back. Before him, he saw old Joshua, Simon, Paola Katarina, and Heralda—and behind them stood a great multitude of people, their faces all alight. "We won't let you succumb to darkness, Adam. We love you, we believe in you and in your pure, honest will to save this world. Come back to the light, come back to the path of the creator, don't give up, fight the negative and destructive thoughts, don't let them destroy you and your dream, stand up and fight, fight and win. You can't give up. Hope is eternal. God is always with you, the choice is always yours to walk the path of victory. So do that, Adam. We believe in you—now believe in yourself." The voices of all the good people rang out as one. A new, immense might flowed through Adam. He turned to the witch and called out, "Why should I carry on, you say? For these people—and for anyone else in this world with a kind heart beating in their chest. That's why, damn witch, I will not give up! I'll carry on my journey despite you. I will fight fiercely and won't surrender, because I believe in my maker who made everything for the best. I won't surrender. I will make my dream come true, I will fulfill my mission and my destiny, I will fight you, and I will win."

In an instant, the witch was powerfully thrown back. Adam has made up his mind; he will carry on despite the difficulties, despite the dangers he will make it, and no negative factor will stand between him and his goal. Irma and all the cloaked figures faded from the desert landscape and disappeared completely. Adam remained standing before his friends, deeply touched. "Thank you for not losing hope in me."

He looked at the sky and whispered, "Thank you, God, for giving me the strength and hope to continue." Adam felt himself float back in the great stone structure, back into the room where his physical body was laying on the bed. He felt himself filling his own body once again, once again he is filled with the energy of life, reviving him. His eyes opened. He sat up and looked at Karan, who rose from the floor at once.

"You returned to us, Adam! Welcome back, my son," said the priest with a satisfied smile. Adam stood on his feet, examined his body, and said, "It's good to be back, Karan. I'm ready to go on now, despite the danger, despite the pain, despite everything I will go on. Far from here I have friends, and they still believe in me and in my will, so I have to move on now."

The priest listened quietly then took Adam's hand and called out, "Well then, dear Adam, let us continue from where we stopped. Step out to the desert air, Gim Nigma's book of light is still there. You have to take it with you for the rest of your journey to South America."

Adam walked behind the priest and suddenly halted. Karan stopped too and turned back, "Why do you stop, Adam?" asked the priest.

Adam looked down at the ground for a moment then lifted his gaze and asked, "How will I continue my journey to find Gim Nigma? I can't move through the desert again. I got here on the Dragon Rider, and that special vehicle was badly damaged in the battle with the four assassins that were trying to kill Arak and I, and besides, it's also far from here. How will I go on from here, Karan?"

The priest resumed walking toward the entrance of the great stone structure. The moment he opened the door, the entrance was flooded with a bright light, so bright it almost blinded Adam for a moment, and then a flap of great wings sliced the desert air. Karan's voice echoed through the desert space, "Don't worry, Adam, Ayakon the desert hawk will take you forward!"

The huge hawk spread his enormous wings and sounded a loud shriek, piercing the silence around. Arak stepped forward, nudging Adam's knees with his head. Adam was happy to meet his faithful friend again; he patted his friend and saw Karan approach him with the closed book of light in his hands. "Here, Adam, take this unique book with you. I, too, will be with you as your journey proceeds, and when you need my help, all you have to do is meditate, and then I can communicate with you telepathically. I will do all that's in my power to help you. Now go on your way, my son, go with God's blessing, go assured that you will obtain what you wish for and fulfill yourself. Believe in what you want, believe in your dream, and let nothing stop you on your journey to your goal."

Adam took the book and placed it in a green side bag. Ayakon was patiently waiting for his riders to mount. Arak scrambled swiftly up his back. Adam faced the priest and said, "Dear Karan, you taught me so much. I thank you for all your help. You made me realize just how much I want to fulfill my fate and my dream. Because of all I experienced here, I realize I must carry on fearlessly, driven by a burning faith and with relentless force—for there is one infinite force and it is God. For we are all equal—animals, humans, and the rest of the world. For there is a solution for evil, there is a solution for suffering, and I'm going to find it."

Adam finished his sentence and the priest embraced him warmly. In a moment, Adam too was seated on the back of the giant Hawk, who once again shrieked loudly. Ayakon spread out his wings, and the giant hawk began rising from the golden ground into the blue sky. Together with Arak and Adam he flew high, high above the pristine white clouds. Below them, the giant rock construct looked like a little dot. Arak and Adam were crossing the desert on the back of the huge hawk, toward their next destination. Deep inside, Adam knew who he was about to meet soon. He sensed Ayakon knew the way with no need for words or instructions. The hawk flew on, and

Adam's gut feelings were turning out to be true; before them was the place he missed dearly while he was in the desert for so long. He missed the scent of water, he missed the company and comradeship of the *Oracle* men, and here was the place in front of him in all its glory—the great ocean.

Upon the big sailboat, the *Oracle*, the veteran captain Damtri Nelson was standing on deck, gazing toward the faraway shoreline of the African continent. He was reflecting on the special man who left on a quest against all odds. He was missing his newfound friend. He prayed for Adam's well being every day, asking God in his prayers to keep the young man safe from all evil, that he may succeed in his way and find what his heart was seeking for. He knew in his heart that the entire crew missed Adam; he stole their hearts from the first day he set foot on the ship. It's been a long time since he last saw him… as long as Arak's by his side, he thought, Adam was safe, but still apprehension was rising in his heart for the safety of his friend. As his thoughts were colliding with each other, Alator's cry sliced the air.

"Look over there!"

The entire crew hurried to the deck, surrounding their captain. All heads turned to a dark dot on the blue horizon, a dark dot rapidly growing from moment to moment. The sailors looked at each other anxiously, then the captain called out, "Relax, friends, it's only a hawk flying in the sky."

Jeremiah the sailor stepped forward and said, "I've never seen such a giant hawk, Captain." They all saw the truth in Jeremiah's words. From moment to moment, the shape of the hawk grew larger, they all realized that the carrion bird was approaching them rapidly. The crew was startled, and the captain called out at once.

"Don't panic! Man the canon at once!" Within seconds, two sturdy sailors, awaiting the captain's orders, manned the ship's canons. As the seconds passed the tension mounted in the crewmen, they all were preparing for any development. The hawk's shrieks came louder and louder as it approached the *Oracle*; Captain Nelson ordered the two soldiers to aim the barrel at the huge bird and prepare to shoot it down.

"Get ready," Captain Nelson called out to his men. The gun was aimed directly to the center of the body of the huge hawk, but before the sailor squeezed the trigger of the canon, a familiar and well-loved voice rang out, "Hello, friends, it's me, Adam. I'm back!"

The captain and the *Oracle* men thought they were dreaming, but then they noticed Adam and Arak straddled on the huge hawk's back. Adam, all smiles, waved his arm to his friends on the blue-sailed ship. The crew couldn't hold back their overflowing joy and they all shouted as one: "Hurray, hurray, he came back to us!"

A huge smile spread on the captain's lips. He felt joy flood through him. He winked at the sky and thanked the good Lord for keeping Adam safe and returning him to them in one piece on the wings of a huge hawk. The captain immediately ordered his crew to prepare for Adam's landing on board the *Oracle*.

The joy was great—though Ayakon tried to land gently, the large ship rocked like a shard of wood on the water when his feet touched the deck. The *Oracle* crew were brave men, but wary of the bird's size, they kept a safe distance. Only Captain Nelson dared come close and stand only a few feet away from Ayakon; Arak leapt directly into Captain Nelson's arms. The wolf was ecstatic to be back with his old friend. Captain Damtri hugged Arak powerfully.

"God bless, you came back to us, safe and sound. This is wonderful!" Nelson called out happily. Adam dismounted Ayakon and ran to the captain, who awaited him with open arms. The two embraced for a long moment.

"I missed you all so much," said Adam. The *Oracle* crew all hugged Adam with great love; they lifted him on their hands and raised him with a victorious cheer. Arak accompanied everyone's joy with loud, happy barks.

"Come down here and tell us all your adventures!" called Captain Nelson. The sailors helped Adam down.

He stepped to Ayakon, who was waiting quietly, "Thank you, Ayakon, thanks for your help. You're a dear, loyal friend. Return to our dear Karan, return to him safe, and I will go on to my next destination. Remember, you are my dear friend, and I'm grateful for your help." The captain and crew were amazed at the way Adam spoke to the giant hawk, and at the way the hawk appeared to listen. Adam patted Ayakon's beak warmly; their eyes locked on each other, and the hawk apparently understood every word.

A few seconds passed, then the hawk lifted his head and let out a shattering screech, deafening the ears of the *Oracle* men. Then Ayakon spread his mighty wings and took toward the sky. The *Oracle* men sheltered their faces from the gusts of wind created by the mighty bird's wings beating. Adam raised his arm and shouted, "Good-bye, Ayakon, we will see each other soon. Good-bye!"

The bird replied with a powerful shriek, and flew far away, back toward the continent of Africa, to the golden deserts, to Karan and the ancient libraries.

Adam looked at his friends, a huge smile still hanging on all their faces.

"Come, friends, we move on, to where goodwill, determination, faith and hope lead us," Adam said excitedly.

"Where do we go, Adam?" Captain Nelson asked curiously, and the entire crew joined in the query with questioning faces.

"I discovered that the tale of the lonesome priest is true. With the help of God almighty, I found the ancient libraries, and I found the Book of Light that tells us where Gim Nigma lays," Adam replied. Trembling with excitement, he opened the green side bag and took the Book of Light out. Exhilaration took hold of all the ship's men.

Captain Nelson was overwhelmed. "Can it be? Can it be all that exists?" Captain Nelson asked, almost stammering, "Can there really be a solution to all this evil in the world, and you are holding the book that will show us where it lays?"

"Yes, Nelson," Adam answered, trying to control his excitement. "The book tells us where's Gim Nigma, where's the solution, our direction is South America, to a place where there is a special mountain called Mt. Victory," Adam summed.

The captain and crew stared at Adam, somewhat stunned. They listened to him attentively, then a long silence fell upon them all, until Captain Damtri Nelson cried out, "So what are we waiting for? Take the wheel, stretch the sails, our next stop is South America!" The entire crew leapt with joy; they were all swept up by excitement. They all shouted in agreement, "Forward, to South America!"

Adam joined Captain Nelson, who asked his friend to tell him all his adventures, and Adam began telling him.

Chapter Sixty-Eight

Bartholomew ran with all the speed his body could muster. His heart was beating furiously in his chest. His men gave him the bad news. They told him the witch has failed once again to destroy Adam Swandon and the prophecy threatening his and his friends dark rule. The corridors seem longer then usual; Bartholomew thought to himself, as his lungs strained to deliver oxygen to the entire bulk of his fat body. He paused for a moment and stared at one of the corridor walls, trying to catch his breath. "I hope Drakkar's plan will be executed soon. I hope the robot army will be ready for action," said Bartholomew to himself. He resumed the quick pacing toward the underground hall where old Irma and her hundreds of dark men lingered. He noticed a few cloaked figures standing outside the hall, guarding it. Their red eyes stared directly into the stout leader's frightened eyes.

"Let him pass, he's a friend of the witch," one of the cloaked figures hissed. The way was opened and Bartholomew entered a hall silent and still, with no candlelight, no raging flames, only an exhausted old woman lying on a podium stacked with extinguished black candles. She sensed Bartholomew enter and asked her men to leave them alone. They did as she asked.

Irma looked tired and weak. Bartholomew sat by her side and asked to her health. She looked at him with those narrow eyes surrounded by a web of many wrinkles, lifted herself up a bit, and turned to him. "I'm spent, Bartholomew. I tried to use the magic powers of my men and myself. We tried to penetrate his mind and poison it, make him forget about his idea to challenge the empire. I almost succeeded in dissuading him, until the freedom fighters showed up, countering our negative energy with their own positive energy. They managed to convince him to fight our dark forces and push us back."

For the first time, the old woman seemed touched by despair, but Bartholomew helped her lift her head and look into his eyes. "You could try to poison his mind and spirit again, Irma dear," Bartholomew said.

And the old tired woman replied, "It's useless to even try as long as he has such strong support from the resistance, who believe in him and aid him."

Bartholomew rose to his feet and spoke to the witch, his voice louder than usual, "Drakkar will execute his diabolical plan to wipe out the resistance. He will threaten them with a new deadly army, forcing the underground to crawl out of their burrows and surrender, for if they don't, hundreds and hundreds of people all over the world will be hurt. This is Drakkar's methodical plan, and when he carries it out, you and your men can destroy this man and his quest to bring light to the world and threaten our realm."

Irma opened her eyes wide and stood up. "And when will this genius plan be fulfilled?" An evil smile spread across Bartholomew's rounded face, and he said, "Very soon, Irma dear. Very soon."

Chapter Sixty-Nine

Around the huge campfire on the island of Esperanza, hundreds of people danced and jumped with joy. They learned that their prayer meditation for Adam's well-being was a success, that it indeed overcame the negative energies trying to break his spirit and discourage him from continuing on his quest to fulfill the ancient prophecy. They were all embracing each other, joy swept over the entire island, everyone except Paola Katarina. She stood apart from them all, barefoot on the wet sand where it met the soft foam of the breaking waves. She was staring at the moon, which wasn't full, yet it shone in a bright white light, which lit the night on the entire island. Among all the people celebrating, only Joshua noticed the worry on her face. He walked toward her, stepping away from the thousands rejoicing over the fact that hope has been resumed for Adam and his brave quest. The good woman sensed the presence of the old man, who stood beside her wordlessly.

"You must feel it in the air, don't you, Joshua?" Paola Katarina asked.

"Yes, Paola Katarina. I feel it," old Joshua replied.

His old eyes met the woman's gaze. The wind softly scattered his white beard and hair. "It's not over, Joshua. Something terrible is about to happen, something bigger than ever before," Paola Katarina said.

"What is this terrible thing about to happen, Paola Katarina?" the old man inquired.

"I don't know, but I feel it in my heart." The old man drew near her and hugged her with one arm, saying, "We must never lose hope. Adam is a unique man. He chose to direct his life to fulfill his destiny, and he goes on with his quest. We have to trust in him, we have to trust in God. I myself believe that Adam can do all this and succeed. He can overcome all the fears. He can beat all obstacles. He can rise above them all and complete his quest victorious, helping us all by this. God has chosen a path for him, and he is indeed walking it."

The woman patted Joshua's old hand embracing her. "I believe in him too, Joshua, I believe in Adam with all my heart, but the weight of the threat makes me fear for him, and for us all." The old man left the woman's side and walked toward the ocean, stopping only when the cold water touched his feet. "The best way to make the negative disappear is to dismiss it. If a hand is holding something good, it doesn't have the room or the time to hold something bad as well," said Joshua.

Paola Katarina smiled at him from where she was standing and said, "I understand what you mean, Joshua. We must hold on to the idea of victory of good over evil, and so it will be."

The moon shining upon his face and white beard, the old man replied with a smile, "We must go on believing, Paola Katarina, we must continue believing in the positive way, and leave no room for negative energy in our lives." The two stood quietly and looked toward the horizon, where the sky met the sea, and asked their maker to protect Adam and bless his way.

The *Oracle*'s blue sails were tightly stretched by the strong arms of the ship's crewmen. Through them all, a revived hope flowed; there was yet a chance to defeat the forces of darkness. Adam and the faithful Arak have returned to them, safe and healthy, delivered by a giant hawk. If there was ever any doubt as to the authenticity of the prophecy, that the son of light shall come and save humanity, that doubt was now gone. Now they were all united in their goal to bring Adam to the shores of South America, so he may continue his quest to save the human race from the evil empire.

Adam told them all of his adventures in the desert, up to the point where Ayakon the hawk brought him to the priest Karan and the ancient libraries. The entire crew, captain included, were amazed by his adventures. They all could see how God protected Adam and guided him to his heart's desire. It seemed like the wind; the blue sea and the waves were also cooperating with the great ship, so it may swiftly reach the continent of South America. Captain Nelson showed great interest in the Book of Light in Adam's satchel and began questioning him, "Tell me, Adam, does this book tell you how to find Gim Nigma?" Nelson prodded.

"Karan told me that the book will tell me more as the journey continues, and also that I will be tested," Adam replied.

"Tested?" Captain Nelson asked.

"Yes… the book tells that the son of light will have to reach the mysterious city of Inca Drakna, where he will have to pass a series of tests," Adam replied.

"What tests?" Nelson inquired. "I haven't the faintest idea, but whatever it is, I will get through it, whatever it takes. We came so far, we went through so much together, and we will remain determined to continue, whatever we are faced with," Adam said decisively.

The captain smiled and patted Adam's shoulder. "Those are true and solid words, Adam. I'm very proud of you for your determination. I'm happy you came back to us safe and sound, I believe that in a few days we'll reach South America, and you will finally find the thing you've been searching for so long," Captain Nelson said.

The entire crew worked diligently and energetically to get the ship to its destination, where they were told they will find Gim Nigma, the solution to all the evil in the world, the answer to all the injustice and crime, and this information drove them to function better than ever before. The crewmen felt they've been given a chance to partake in saving the world from the dark empire; they refused to rest, they refused to pause in their work. They were tremendously inspired by Adam and his determination to carry on. Adam in turn was impressed by the crew, and he joined them morning and night in the trappings of the ship; they were all as one man, marching fearlessly ahead, no doubts in their minds, only the fierce wish to attain their goal.

As they were working diligently, a familiar and threatening sound captured everyone's attention. The crew turned its eyes to the blue horizon and saw the dark dots coming closer and closer to the ship. Alator's eyes grew wide with fear, and he cried out loudly, "Empire hovercrafts! Dozens of them!"

They all dropped what they were doing and ran to the deck. Alator was right; thirty armed empire hovercrafts, making their way through the air toward the *Oracle*. "Damn! They must have spotted us on their radars!"

He turned to his men and called out to them, "I know we never faced such a challenge, with dozens of armed hovercrafts pitted against us, while we are alone in the midst of the ocean, unbacked, but remember, God is with us! The shores of South America aren't far now, and that's where hope lay, that's where our solution is. That's where Adam needs to go, and we will help him!"

The men all looked at their captain. Though they knew the *Oracle* to be uniquely fitted and heavily armed, they also knew that she simply couldn't take on so many hovercrafts. It seemed a lost battle.

The veteran captain saw the fear in his men's eyes and called out loudly, "We went through hardships before and we made it through, and we'll pass this one as well! We'll jump this great hurdle together!

Together we will fight fiercely! Uproot the fear from your hearts and take up your battle stations!"

The crew looked at each other then looked at Adam standing quietly by their side, and at once, they were all shouting madly, "We'll fight! We'll win! For life or for death, go!" Every crewman grabbed a laser gun and took his place for the coming battle. A few men proceeded in opening the ship's sides, exposing the many gun barrels, and immediately aiming them at the approaching hovercrafts. The captain handed one laser gun to Adam and took one himself. They all waited anxiously as the hovercrafts rapidly closed in. "Ready…" called Captain Nelson. "Aim…" he cried again, his outstretched arm aiming the gun at one of the hovercrafts overhead. He saw another hovercraft already shooting laser blasts at their direction, and let out a mighty cry to all his men: "Now! Fire! Fire!" as soon as the captain gave the order, all posts began firing frantically.

Adam joined in at once, but there were just too many hovercrafts. It was going to be a short and bitter fight, it seemed. Yet Adam refused despair, even as he saw it reflected in his mates' faces. He found shelter behind a laser pierced wooden mast, shut his eyes, and concentrated on the prayer he let out into the air: "God, my maker, please help us in our struggle, please send us help."

As the words were spoken, a shiver ran through him and the spirit form of Karan appeared before his eyes. "Don't worry, my dear Adam, help is on its way," said the figure and faded. Some of the crewmembers were injured, some were covering for the injured; they were fighting fiercely yet they hadn't managed to take out even one hovercraft. Damtri Nelson grinded his teeth nervously. He didn't want to think that this was how it all ends, that they would die here, in mid-sea, while close by the shores of South America loomed, Gim Nigma was so near and yet so far. He looked at Adam and his eyes said despair, but to his surprise, Adam smiled and his hawk eyes sparkled as he gazed up to the blue horizon. The captain didn't understand the meaning of this. He saw one of the hovercrafts draw in close, so close he could see the wicked smile on the face of the pilot as he aimed his guns at them. Nelson saw his death closer than ever before.

But suddenly, the skies echoed with a loud screech, which changed everything.

The giant hawk Ayakon suddenly appeared, and at once, he pushed the looming hovercraft away with his feet. Adam shouted victoriously, "Way to go, Ayakon! Show them what you got!" The empire soldiers were stunned; an enormous hawk hovered before their eyes, defending the ship. Ayakon screeched again and flew low over the ship. Adam realized he is to mount the hawk. Just when he felt someone else was missing, Arak appeared behind him, barking. The man and the wolf understood each other perfectly, without a word. The *Oracle* men looked on in wonder. "Don't worry, friends!" Adam called out to his shipmates, as he and Arak leapt on the giant hawk's back. Ayakon's wings beat fiercely as he rose toward the cluster of hovercrafts.

"What does he think he's doing?" Captain Damtri asked his men nervously. The brave sailors remained silent, watching the scene in the sky with a shade of a smile on their faces and their eyes wide with wonder. The giant hawk, the one-eyed wolf, and the mysterious man were now operating as one single being. Ayakon maneuvered between the hovercrafts as they ceaselessly fired at him. Adam held Arak tightly and signaled that he's about to remove the eye patch and expose the secret weapon. Arak cooperated immediately. The hawk flew directly into the cluster of hovercrafts and Adam screamed, "Now, Arak, now!" the moment the cry left Adam's lips Arak's special eye released a chain of powerful laser blasts. One by one, the hovercrafts dropped into the ocean. The *Oracle* men fought along with them, hope renewed on their faces, and within a few minutes, the blue ocean surface was covered with the burning wreckage of what a moment ago were fearsome, armed hovercrafts. Captain Nelson and his men cheered for Ayakon, Adam, and Arak, who were also exhilarated in their common achievement.

The hawk hovered over the deck carefully, and Adam and Arak jumped off his back. With one last piercing cry, the hawk took off and swiftly disappeared, his distant image swallowed in the high clouds.

"You did it again, Adam," said Captain Damtri as he embraced Adam warmly. "No, Captain Nelson, we all did it. You saw today how man and animal cooperate in their striving to repel the forces of evil. Karan told me that when I call for help he'll answer," Adam started explaining to the entire crew, but his words were interrupted by Alator's cry, "Land ahoy! Land ahoy!" Alator shouted from his nest on the top of the mast.

The greenish mass of the South American continent was revealed to the eyes of all. The joy on deck knew no limits. Captain Nelson ordered the wounded to be taken to the infirmary to be tended. "Adam, you are closer than ever to what you have been searching for all this time," said Captain Nelson, gazing at the looming land as if hypnotized.

"Faith, hope, and courage are what got me this far, and I couldn't have done it without your help and the help of many other good people who risked their lives for justice, for freedom, and for the well-being of all living creatures. Only together this could be done, only through faith in the eternal good God, for when faced with peril we didn't despair, we believed in the infinite positive force and overcame every obstacle, time after time," said Adam, his voice choked with tears. The captain wrapped his arm around Adam's shoulder, and they both watched how slowly they moved closer to the place they wanted so much to reach. "A great will brings great achievements," so said Karan to Adam in the desert.

Chapter Seventy

Captain Nelson poured over his navigation maps, looking for the best docking spot for the *Oracle*, somewhere they won't be discovered by the empire forces. He instructed the ship's navigator to sale the *Oracle* into a small hidden bay, surrounded by thick tropical bush. Then Captain Nelson called Adam to his quarters to discuss how to proceed.

"Look, Adam, I checked all the maps I posses, and I simply can't find that mysterious city of yours… how'd you call it?" Nelson asked. Adam came near his desk and peered at the maps scattered one on top of the other.

"Inca Drakna, that's the name of the city," Adam said, his eyes roaming over maps seeking the name, but Captain Nelson was right. Inca Drakna wasn't on the map.

"We're pretty safe in this spot," Captain Nelson said, looking out through the command room's window. "Are you sure the empire soldiers don't wander about here?" Adam asked.

"This area is crawling with deadly reptiles, like alligators and anaconda snakes, which the empire soldiers prefer to keep their distance from, which makes it a safe, a good place for us," said Captain Nelson, taking his seat on a wooden chair beside the desk. "What do we do about Inca Drakna?" the captain asked.

"The Book of Light mentions Inca Drakna to be by this mountain chain, one of the mountains being Mt. Victory, where Gim Nigma is," Adam said, following the marks on the map pointing out the mountain chain. The captain said, "We have to go ashore and ask the locals about Inca Drakna," and Adam nodded in agreement.

Half an hour later, a small group of sailors dismounted the *Oracle* and accompanied Captain Nelson, Arak, and Adam to shore. The ship was well hidden in a natural bay, dense with lush, tangled vegetation. Even if a hovercraft did happen to pass by, it would be difficult for it to spot the *Oracle* hidden in its tiny bay.

Arak the one-eyed wolf led the way, sniffing the path as he waked. Behind him marched Adam, Captain Nelson, and a group of sailors armed with laser guns, for safety's sake. The pack slung across Adam's shoulder held the Book of Light. As they marched deeper into the jungle thicket, the captain paused every few minutes to consult his map. Suddenly he stopped and called out loudly, "Wait, friends! The map shows a track going through the jungle, which leads to a small village, called Kallag'aro Chicko, and we can reach it through here." Captain Nelson pointed into the jungle and all eyes followed his finger; through the dense vegetation they saw a small path winding into the thicket. They all decided to follow the captain's lead. Various colorful insects and weird sounding birds surrounded them. The weather here was different from what it was in the open sea, the heat heavy and the air humid. Through the lush green the sun could glimpse, rolling high in the sky. The sailors frequently complained of the mosquito bites and the tiring heat, but they pushed on, prepared for anything.

Suddenly Adam cried out, "Hey, where did Arak disappear to?" They all suddenly realized that the large wolf leading the way had disappeared.

Captain Nelson became anxious for the fate of his loyal friend. He advanced while calling out, "Arak, where are you?" But besides the chirping of birds a silence hung in the air. Everyone could feel the tension mount. Adam began searching after Arak, but it was useless, all he could see was green plants.

"I don't like this quiet," called one of the sailors, cocking his gun.

"Relax, friends, I trust Arak, he must be somewhere around, but still, be ready for anything," Captain Nelson said, and suddenly they heard barks, bringing everyone a sigh of relief.

"It's coming from over there!" One of the sailors signaled. "Arak must have found something, let's go," said Captain Nelson, and they all began to run in the direction of the barks. A few seconds later, they found Arak across from a short man of Indian ancestry, who seemed quite frightened. Arak was barking at the man, who stood frozen on the spot. "Quiet, Arak, let the man be!" Captain Nelson scolded his old friend, and Arak immediately backed away and returned to the captain's side, who patted his head.

Adam approached the Indian. "Who are you, please?" Adam asked politely.

The man seemed more at ease now, and he smiled shyly at the group. "My name is Anado, and I come from the village of Kallag'aro Chicko, behind this jungle."

Captain Nelson charged forward. "Kallag'aro Chicko!?" he repeated.

"Yes," Anado replied, retrieving his colorful pack that lay discarded on the greenish ground. "I'm here gathering healing plants for my sick aunt," he continued, "but who are you? What are you doing here?" Anado asked, gathering a bunch of thin green reeds into his colorful pack.

Adam came close to the short, colorfully clad man. "I am Adam Swandon, and these are my good friends, Captain Nelson, Arak, and the brave crew of the *Oracle* ship," said Adam.

"Nice to meet you, gentlemen," Anado replied, "but what do sailors seek in this remote area of the world?" Anado asked curiously.

Adam looked at his friends, waiting for someone to reply. No one spoke.

"We're looking for the city of Inca Drakna," Adam said, wondering in his heart if telling Anado their destination was the right thing to do.

"Inca Drakna?" asked Anado, his slanted eyes opening wide.

"Exactly," Captain Nelson replied.

Anado turned swiftly on his heels. "Come with me," he said. The men looked at each other questioningly, but the captain signaled them to follow the colorfully dressed man. After half an hour of silent marching, the path surrounded by tangled vegetation came to end at the diameter of a large clearing.

"Gentlemen, welcome to my village, Kallag'aro Chicko," Anado said. Before their eyes lay a full and lively village, far from the fearsome empire's reach. Children ran everywhere, busy playing with each other. Several woman carrying baskets and urns on their heads turned to examine the strange group of men invading the village, that were standing at Anado's side. Anado signaled that it was fine; they weren't dangerous.

Captain Nelson ordered his sailors to lay down their weapons, and they were lead to the head of the village, who was sitting in a large straw cabin, decorated with colorful flowers.

"Welcome to my home," called the heavily built man, his head decorated with colorful feathers and his torso exposed. His undergarments were made of many colorful fabrics, layered on top of each other. "I am the head of the Kallag'aro Chicko village, and my name is Indiago. I can sense you are good people, not emissaries of the evil empire, so come my friends, sit," said the village head to the *Oracle* men. The captain shook Indiago's hand and introduced himself, as did Adam and the rest of the crew.

"We thank you for your hospitality, sir," said Captain Nelson to his host.

"Oh, please, call me Indiago!" immediately tropical fruits were served to the guests, who devoured them quickly, enjoying the refreshing juicy morsels. The head of the village enjoyed seeing his guests enjoy the fruit, and when they finished, he asked them, "Tell me, why do you seek the secluded city of Inca Drakna?"

Looking at the village head, Adam felt he had to be direct and say what was in his heart.

"We're searching for a certain mountain close to Inca Drakna," Adam replied.

"Mountain, what mountain?" the village head inquired.

Adam hesitated for a few moments, doubting if he should continue, but when he looked into Indiago's eyes, he felt an odd calm, encouraging him to speak on with confidence. "The name of the mountain is Mt. Victory," Adam said.

The head of the village seemed to pale momentarily. He looked at Adam suspiciously. "And why are you looking for Mt. Victory?" Indiago asked in a trembling voice.

Adam and Captain Nelson exchanged glances. "Well, since you made it all the way to this point, you might as well tell him why you're looking for Mt. Victory," the captain said sardonically.

Adam realized that it was the time to do this; there was no point in waiting any longer, so he turned to the village head and said, "I'm looking for Mt. Victory because I went on a long quest to find a solution to evil in our world, a solution to the evil reign of the empire that denies men a life of freedom and honor. I came all the way here looking for Gim Nigma."

The eyes of the Indian village head grew wide. He drew back in his chair. "You're looking for Gim Nigma?" Indiago asked in a trembling voice

"Yes," Adam replied. Indiago rose from his chair and walked out of the straw cabin, and the *Oracle* men followed him at once. Indiago stood gazing at a distant mountain range. "Even when I was just a child, my ancestors told that thousands of years ago people came from another planet, and they buried something in one of those mountains, which would one day help humans find the way back to their hearts to the things that truly matter. Gim Nigma can only be revealed to the one worthy of it. The man who would free Gim Nigma from the mountain must be one of a pure heart, with pure intentions to change the world and expel evil from the face of the Earth, once and for all," said the village chief, his face solemn.

Captain Nelson suddenly leapt forward. "Adam is that man, Indiago. Adam came a long way here, for he's the one of the pure heart," said the *Oracle*'s captain with emotion.

Indiago came close to Adam, laid both his hands on Adam's shoulders, and gazed directly into his hawk eyes. "So Adam is the one, before me stands the man who will fulfill the ancient prophecy. We all must come to his aid then, so it may be fulfilled, for the sake of mankind and all living beings."

The *Oracle* crew and Captain Nelson were happy to hear Indiago was willing to help. "You know of the prophecy?" Adam asked.

"Yes, Adam. The prophecy has been passed through generations in our tribe, it foretells that one day, things would be so bad for mankind, the world will come to the brink of oblivion, and it's only spark of hope will come in the form of one man, one man with a will to change things. He would sacrifice himself to save the world. His heart will be pure and dedicated to this purpose only. And one day, this man would pass through our village. After he overcomes the tests awaiting him on the way, he will release Gim Nigma from its grave of thousands of years, where it was waiting for the right man, the pure-hearted one, the one with the will to destroy evil on Earth—and Gim Nigma will bring eternal peace and true harmony to all human's in the world," said Indiago to all around him.

"Indiago, please, show us where we can find Gim Nigma. Where is it buried?" Adam pleaded.

"It is a great honor, for my village and myself, to live through the time of prophecy," said the village head, and continued, "I will help you, Adam. My loyal Anado will lead you to the right place. He, too, knows of the prophecy, and he will be of great assistance to you. But remember, Adam, the voyage will not be easy, and you will have to complete it alone."

Indiago's last words echoed through Adam's mind. "Alone," he said. Adam will have to continue alone, but Adam's answer was swift and unwavering: "I'm ready," Adam said in a determined voice.

The village head smiled and called Anado, "Anado, you must lead Adam and his friends to where they need to go. I assume Adam already knows that he must continue toward the fulfillment of the prophecy and his destiny in life by himself," Indiago told them all. The sailors didn't know what to say. The captain felt a pang of sadness; the moment of their parting would come soon, he sensed. But he stepped forward and said, "Don't worry, Adam, we're all counting on you. We're all with you in spirit and in prayers, that you may succeed in fulfilling your destiny, fulfilling the prophecy that will bring an end to the forces of evil, letting light rule over this world."

Adam looked at them all. "My life was never easy. There were times when I suffered much, like when I was a child. Yet all that time I never lost hope that I, little Adam, could change the world, and do something for all the little boys and girls, so they wouldn't have to suffer anymore. I dreamt the same dream ever since, and I finally became this dream. Here I am, standing with you in South America, close to finding that thing I searched for all my life. The rumors became reality, the tale of the prophecy gave hope back to a multitude of people all over the world resisting the rule of evil, and from day to day I realized that I chose a destiny that gave meaning to my existence on Earth. I realized a man can't live only for himself. He exists in order to serve the world, in order to offer himself up in good will—that's what makes his life full, special. Each of us has his part in life to fill, and we choose how to manifest ourselves—in a positive way that would enrich the world, or in a negative way, that would destroy it," Adam said, and the people around him listened, spell-bound.

"My father once told me a beautiful saying, which I remember till today. God gave man a match and told him he has two choices: he may use it to light the world, or he may use it to burn it down," Adam concluded.

The village head, touched, said, "That is truly a beautiful saying. Your father is a wise man for saying those words." The men gathered around all nodded in agreement. "Anado is an excellent guide. I suggest you leave while there's still light in the sky," said the village head to the general agreement.

The *Oracle* group stocked itself with food and water, and after briefly parting with the villagers, they embarked on their journey once again, their next destination being the mysterious city of Inca Drakna. Adam reflected over what Karan told him, of the tests the Book of Light will assign him before he may find Gim Nigma, but in his mind he was resolute that no matter what he will carry on, he won't give up, and he won't let dark thoughts and doubts poison his mind and spirit. The group advanced quickly, but suddenly, Anado stopped and said, "Halt, friends!" Everyone immediately froze in their spot. A total silence stood in the air. They felt a sudden gust of wind hit their faces, and suddenly, they noticed they were standing close to the edge of a cliff, a giant, gaping abyss beyond it. The jungle ended with this deep chasm, a gushing river flowing below.

A long hanging bridge, made of rope and slim wooden beams, was the only thing connecting the two pieces of land. Adam suddenly noticed that his satchel was quivering, and a bright light was coming from it. He quickly opened the bag, and the men all witnessed the book of light shimmering brightly. Adam laid it gently on a nearby rock, and to everyone's surprise, the book opened on it's own accord, and a glowing beam of light was projected off the pages onto another rock, depicting the image of the bridge that lay before them and at it's side a written page. Adam saw he must ask for Karan's help again. He sat down across from the book, crossed his legs, and shut his eyes. The men stood back and didn't interrupt, merely observing him quietly. Adam cried out loud, "Dear Karan, I seek your help. Please, I came this far, but now I need you to read this page for me." Moments after the words were spoken, Karan's glowing spiritual figure appeared and smiled at them all. "Hello, Adam, and hello to all the good and brave people accompanying you on this great quest that will determine the fate of all humanity." Some of the sailors were rubbing their eyes in disbelief. "Karan, we reached the edge of huge precipices, and the book began glowing. It's trying to tell us something, but I can't read what's written," Adam said to the bright figure. Karan turned his gray eyes to the book and said, "Adam, you have come to the first test. The test of the bridge." Adam looked at the long rope bridge, swaying from side to side with the breeze.

"The test of the bridge?" he asked.

"Yes," Karan replied and swiftly continued, "in this test, you are meant to carry on alone, burning the bridge behind you, leaving no way back. From here on you must go only forward, and this is the spot where you solemnly declare that you fear not to go on alone, you don't intend to turn back, and by burning the bridge behind you, you will know that there truly is no way back. You can only go forward." Karan's mental image faded into thin air, but his words stirred the sailors.

"What does he mean? Did he mean we must part with Adam here, on the edge of a cliff?" one of the sailors asked his friends. The captain and Adam exchanged glances.

"I guess that's what Indiago meant when he said you will have to continue alone," Nelson said, the sadness ringing in his voice.

Adam looked to the far away land beyond the abyss then back at his friends. "There's no choice, this is what I have to do. This is my destiny. I can feel it, deep inside my soul. I'll cross this bridge with courage and then I'll burn it behind me so I can't go back, only forward, to our great victory," Adam declared, his voice choked.

"This is a hard moment for me," said the captain of the *Oracle*, his eyes glazing with tears. "I'm parting with a beloved and dear friend," he said, and one tear rolled down his wrinkled cheek and disappeared between the hairs of his short white beard. The group of sailors were also beginning to tear up; they were parting from a man they came to appreciate, respect, and love through all the journeys they had together. One of the sailors embraced Adam Swandon warmly, bidding him farewell. Adam's tears flowed freely now, and Arak the one-eyed wolf came and licked his face lovingly. Adam hugged the beloved wolf tightly and then let him go. Arak retreated and rejoined the *Oracle* men. Only Captain Damtri Nelson slowly approached. The two men who became fast friends hugged each other and wept for long minutes.

"Take care, Adam," the captain said with a broken voice.

"Thanks for everything, Nelson," Adam said, choking on his tears. "I feel this parting isn't forever," said Adam, wiping the tears off his cheeks. "The good Lord will have us meet again, and when he does, we will all be free." Adam continued, "So I believe." The captain looked into his friend's hawk eyes and said, "You are a special man, it is a great honor to be your friend, and we will continue praying for you and for your success until the moment of the great victory itself, with God's help. Farewell, Adam, go walk the path of victory, and know that we will always love you and believe in you."

Adam hugged the captain fiercely. "I'll do my best, Nelson. I'll give it all I got, I won't give up, and I will carry on no matter what, as long as I'm breathing. Good-bye, friends. May God be with us all."

Anado the Indian guide approached him with a smile. "You are a brave and special man. I'm happy I've met you and I'm sure you'll succeed." Anado handed Adam a burning torch and said, "Go forward, be entirely without fear, leave room for courage and strength alone to exist within you."

Adam slung his satchel across his shoulder with the Book of Light, which was once again locked until the next time, across his shoulder. He took the burning torch in his right hand, looked back at his dear friends, the men of the *Oracle*, and called out with a smile of hope upon his face, "I will return with Gim Nigma, and light will overcome darkness, once and for all!" He turned toward the long rope bridge and began crossing it slowly, the Book of Light in the satchel on his shoulder and a burning torch in his right hand. Adam felt the bridge sway from side to side beneath him, but he insisted on pushing on. Looking only forward, not right, not left, not down, not up, only straight ahead, and after half an hour of slow pacing, he made it to the other side of the bridge. Then he looked far away to where Anado and his friends were waving to him and answered by waving his free arm, then he looked at the burning torch, raised it to the sky, and brought it down on the rope bridge. The ropes were immediately engulfed in flames.

Adam was burning the bridge behind him, and in his heart, he asked God to be with him as the road continued. Slowly the long bridge was consumed by fire, it began crumbling into burning refuse, piece after piece dropping into the gushing river at the depth of the abyss below. He looked at the faraway figures of his friends on the other side of the abyss and said, "God, help me to help them, and all the other good people in need. Help me succeed." He finished the sentence and turned toward the jungle, walking confidently into the green thicket.

The *Oracle* men saw their friend disappear inside the green jungle. They remained standing in their places, looking at each other silently. Only Anado turned and began walking back toward the village. The captain signaled his men to follow the Indian guide, and as they were all marching back, the captain stopped to take one last look at the jungle on the other side of the abyss, at the spot where Adam disappeared a moment ago. "May you succeed in your mission, Adam. Oh please, Lord, help him to succeed," said the captain and rejoined his friends on their way back to village, and from there on back to the sailboat, the *Oracle*.

Chapter Seventy-One

Many empire soldiers were called to man tanks and hovercrafts that would accompany the first attack of the giant robots upon one of the big cities. The empire sent out a notice to the freedom fighters hiding under the surface that if they don't leave their shelters and surrender to the empire forces, the giant robots will destroy the city; they would wipe it out, leaving no one alive.

The local resistances were dumbfounded. They didn't know what to do, so in the meantime, they did nothing. Drakkar then issued the order to activate the army of deadly robots to demolish the city and all its inhabitants. Now, shortly after the order was given, dozens of giant robots marched out of their hangers with a deafening roar of engines. Thousands of empire soldiers clapped their hands and cheered for the large convoy of robots, whose heavy steps shook the Earth. Old Irma watched the proceedings from afar. "I hope your robot army can defeat the resistance, so I can fulfill my own duty, of killing the son of light," said Irma to herself out loud, and her voice was swallowed in the din of the robots, which were advancing into the city designated for demolition. The crowds of empire soldiers were shooting in the air gleefully, calling out for death and destruction. Drakkar, the head of the empire, stood watching from his palace balcony, seeing his demonic plan come to life.

"In just a few hours, the resistance all over the world will see what I'm capable of. For years, the resistance around the world irked me, but today, my new army will wipe out an entire city, killing thousands of men, women, and children, breaking the resistance once and for all. They will all fear me, they'll be forced to surrender, I will trample anyone resisting me, and each time the freedom fighters refuse to lay down their weapons and surrender, I'll destroy another city, and another, and another!" said the leader of the empire to himself, and a surge of mad laughter burst from his lips.

Bartholomew stood behind him, watching Drakkar and listening silently, pleased that the empire leader was finally doing something against the freedom fighters. He knew that once the freedom fighters surrendered Irma could carry out her own plan, obliterating the prophecy of the coming of the son of light.

The robot army reached the city, and dozens of robots commenced in systematically turning buildings into rubble, buildings that inhabited countless living humans. The desperate screams of women didn't prevent the robots from shooting powerful laser beams all around them, killing thousands of people. Crying children scattered everywhere, looking for their parents and never finding them, for they were no longer among the living. Drakkar kept his word; he executed an entire city of innocents.

Who would come to the aid of the murdered ones, who might rush to stop this injustice? Those questions echoed through the mind of an injured woman, as she helplessly watched the giant robots trample the lives of the people she knew all her life. She whispered a silent prayer amidst all the deafening racket of the fearsome war machines, that from moment to moment slowed their activity, as the lively city had fell silent already. In her prayer, the woman asked that a day might come that those behind the killing would crumble to dust, be wiped off the face of the Earth. She asked that the next generation of men would be a free one, that humans may know mutual respect once more, and that they honor and protect their values so such a holocaust would never repeat itself. Then the woman shut her eyes and her soul left her body.

Only a few hours passed since the robot army entered the city holding a population of twenty-five thousand living human beings. Now the city was perfectly silent. Blood flowed through the still streets, piled with corpses of all sizes and genders. They say that hope is eternal, yet hope was not to be found for the men of this city, whose blood now became one with Mother Earth.

In Argma, the empire's fortress, the sight of the city being demolished by the new army of robots was broadcasted on giant screens. Thousands of soldiers laughed and enjoyed the heartbreaking scenes. Men killing men, evil reigned, and there was no one to stop it. The fate of the free people was doomed. Drakkar sat around the black marble table together with his colleagues, the leaders of the empire, all looked at the large screen before them with diabolical smiles on their faces. They enjoyed seeing Drakkar's plan succeed, for numerous notifications from around the world were already pouring in, announcing that many freedom fighters were lifting their hands and surrendering, yet there also came word from heads of militias that declared they would not surrender.

They would continue to oppose his regime, they would continue to fight the empire with the little they have, for life without honor, morals, and freedom is not a life, so they have no choice but to continue fighting. Drakkar was furious and decided to send his robot army to every place in the world where the resistance still remained, they will bring their cities down; they will slaughter the innocent, until any resistance left is brought down. So with his command, the army of deadly robots proceeded to the cities where the opposition still held, to destroy city after city until any resistance breaks and his hold on the world is complete.

Chapter Seventy-Two

Far from there, on the shelter island of Esperanza, turmoil was raising among the residents of the island as the dreadful rumors spread of the giant robot army and their mass murders and of the evil plan of the head of the empire, and the tale spread fear in everyone. Old Joshua was sitting with Paola Katarina in her house, removed from the rest of the island people, and from afar they heard the shouting as chaos unfolded.

"Do you hear, Joshua? "Paola Katarina asked. "It has begun," she said softly and continued, "I've been sensing this in the air for many days now, and now the terrible feeling I had has become reality."

Joshua looked out of Paola Katarina's cabin window, listened to the faraway cries of fear and said, "The leaders of the empire want to vanquish any spark of hope humanity still holds for a life of honor, peace, and freedom. Yet the spark of hope lives in the will of our Adam. He is not like any other, he's special. He will carry on and not lose hope because hope is eternal. I believe in that strong saying that no matter how hard things get one must seek out the good. Adam knows this. Hope exists, faith exists, courage exists, we shouldn't panic over what's happening, we should focus on the things that we can do."

Paola Katarina stared at the old man. "What could we do?" she asked, the sadness in her eyes portraying what was in her heart.

"We could pray, Paola Katarina, we could pray that God remains at Adam's right side always, up until the moment of victory. He will become that victory, nothing could make him stray from that path, I believe in him—and we have our own efforts to do," Joshua said and approached the window when he noticed a familiar figure drawing near. It was Simon, with the latest news.

"The situation is grave, friends," said Simon as he entered the cabin. "The latest word from the European resistance tells of disaster," Simon continued.

The old man approached him with a warm cup of tea in his hands. "Here, Simon, sip a little and calm down, then you can tell us what the latest news from our friends in Europe is," Joshua said, taking his seat on one of the wooden chairs.

Simon sipped slowly from the hot tea, sighed softly, and turned to the woman and old man. "The news is catastrophic—no one could imagine the leaders of the empire would act in such a fashion."

Paola Katarina's eyes were already brimming with tears; she could sense what Simon was about to say and it hurt her, but Simon carried on, "Well, apparently, the empire built an army of dozens of deadly giant robots that has already destroyed a large city in the center of Europe. The empire announced worldwide to all the freedom fighters resisting it, that if they don't surrender to the empire, the empire will destroy city after city, without so much as blinking," Simon said nervously.

Joshua lowered his gaze; he understood this might mean the end of the resistance's struggle against the empire's evil rule.

Simon continued speaking, cutting this thought short, "Already some of the resistance groups had no choice but to surrender. They gave themselves up to the empire forces in order to protect the large cities from being demolished by the robot army."

Paola Katarina rose from her chair and walked to the window overlooking the sea. The wind blowing through the window caused the tears filling her eyes to flow down her cheeks unto her colorful dress. "That's it then, there's no other alternative."

"What do you mean?" Simon asked.

"I mean that since we have come to a point where evil reigns, and the only positive force that dared oppose it was forced to surrender in order to save thousands of people, then the only option remaining is the prophecy itself. Adam is our only hope," Paola Katarina said, turning to the two men in the room. "Adam carries the last reincarnation of a unique soul, which was destined to save humanity from extinction. He realizes more and more that this is his destiny, he chose to act upon it, he chose to stand up and fight, his soul will not rest until it fulfills its destiny, in his heart he carries the spark of hope for all humanity," the woman said, her face radiant. "We must concentrate all the positive power of our thoughts and all our goodwill and pray with intensity for Adam's success, just like dear Joshua said, we must do what's in our power, and the only thing in our power right now is to pray for him, to fortify his spirit, as long as we live we must keep our faith in the struggle, we can't give up. As long as we breathe, we must cling to faith and hope the way of light may triumph," Paola Katarina concluded, and it seemed her words rekindled the hope in Simon's and old Joshua's hearts.

"You're right, Paola Katarina. We won't surrender to the threat of the empire. We are still alive, and as long as we live, we will carry on with courage, hope, and faith in the way we believe in. That is why we should regroup and pray together for God to bless Adam on his way to fulfill the prophecy," Simon said in a confident voice, though in his heart, he knew that as small and hidden as the island was, they had to be wary of this great threat in the form of a new fearsome empire army. He pulled a radio from his belt and ordered his men to assemble everybody, that instead of panicking and scattering into useless worries following this news of a new threat of a giant robot army, they should assemble and unite their thoughts in something useful, in fortifying Adam's spirit and the success of his destiny which was tied to the fate of all humanity.

Chapter Seventy-Three

Adam pushed on restlessly. He could sense he was nearing the extraordinary city of Inca-Drakna and an odd excitement overtook him. He allowed no other thought to pass through his mind beside the notion that he is about to find Gim Nigma, the solution, the mysterious force that could destroy the forces of evil and wipe them off the face of the Earth once and for all. His skin tanned in the sun, his clothing slowly got torn and worn out from walking through the jungle, his heart pounded forcefully; he kept remembering Karan's words in the desert—a great will brings great achievements. Here he was, making his way toward Gim Nigma, that mysterious source of power that was buried in Mt. Victory thousands of years ago by men from another world.

For one day to come and for one man to bravely choose to find the unique solution for all suffering in the world; he felt for the first time in his life as if he was living his childhood dream. All the suffering he endured in the past and all the events and happenings led him to this place. As he marched, he occasionally paused to drink some water and eat something small, but generally, he chose to rest little and concentrate on getting closer to the mysterious city of Inca Drakna.

Suddenly, Adam stopped. He noticed the sound of the jungle's animals and birds suddenly went quiet. He held the satchel containing the Book of Light tightly to his chest and squinted his hawk eyes in concentration as he listened. A perfect silence enveloped the jungle. He turned around a few times to see if there was anything near, but nothing could be seen through the tangled green vegetation. He decided to walk on as before, but he readied himself for whatever might come his way. As he marched on, he felt a cool breeze on his face. He looked ahead and saw the jungle coming to an end. Before him lay a reddish patch of ground. He walked on and slowly giant pyramid like structures, encircled by twisting golden paths, appeared before his eyes. The breathtaking beauty revealed to him captivated Adam.

"Have I reached the city of Inca Drakna?" Adam asked himself. He advanced slowly. Still the perfect silence reigned, not a single chirp or animal shuffle to be heard. A chill passed through Adam's body; he saw, behind the huge pyramids, three tall mountains looming. "Is one of them Mt. Victory?" Adam asked himself. He stood in front of a giant stairway carved in one of the pyramids. "There must be thousands of steps between here and the top of that pyramid," Adam thought to himself.

He came closer until his feet touched the bottom of the steps and was amazed to see how tall and wide each step was. He asked himself what should he do now. Just as the question came to his mind, the Book of Light began shining brightly from inside the bag. Adam carefully drew the lit book from his satchel and laid it gently on the first step. The book opened by itself, colorful rays of light shone off the page onto the wall of the pyramid; a picture of the great pyramid appeared, and by its side, a page covered with writing that Adam couldn't read. Adam shut his eyes, calmed his body and mind, began thinking of Karan, and called out his name, "Karan, I need your help."

A few seconds later, a familiar voice rumbled through the empty city. "Adam Swandon!" Adam opened his eyes and smiled. Karan's glowing figure appeared to him, hovering above the book of Gim Nigma.

"I'm happy to see you, Karan!" Adam called joyfully. "I came to a deserted city. Is this Inca Drakna?" he asked the shining figure.

"Indeed you have reached the city of Inca Drakna," Karan said with a voice that echoed off the tops of the pyramids. A wave of joy rushed through Adam as he realized he made it to the special city. Karan continued, "This city was populated by the Inca tribe—they created this place in preparation for the day when the son of light, the pure-hearted one, shall arrive, and take Gim Nigma from

Mt. Victory." Adam's face lit up. "And I am the son of light?" Adam asked, excited.

"Yes!" Karan called, his voice echoing throughout the entire abandoned city. Adam's heart skipped a beat as Karan continued speaking, "The son of light must climb to the top of the stairs, to the top of the pyramid, reaching the crest."

Adam gazed at the staircase, then again at Karan's glowing figure. "All I have to do is climb these stairs?" Adam asked.

Karan nodded.

"And then what?" Adam inquired.

"After you climb the stairs, you will find what's next," Karan said, and his lit figure vanished at once into midair. Adam remained alone by the pyramid steps. The book of Gim Nigma closed on its own accord, the light gone. "I guess that all I have to do now is simply to do," Adam said to himself, a bit surprised by how basic and simple things actually were. He lifted the Book of Light and placed it back in his satchel, gazed up the pyramid, and began climbing up the steps. He found out at once that climbing these stairs was not an easy task; each step cost him at least five minutes of concentrated effort. The heat was oppressive, the sweat was pouring off his body, dripping into his eyes and blurring his vision; still he remained determined to climb on. Commitment to the cause and his own curiosity to see what awaited him pushed him on. He looked down and saw he came quite far from the ground already, but when he looked up, he realized that the way up was still quite long. Looking up, it seemed he hadn't come closer by a single step! Still he climbed. Suddenly to his left, a huge brick moved and fell out of the pyramid, and a large figure holding a sharp sword stepped out.

"I can't allow you to continue," the figure called loudly. Adam nearly tumbled down the stairs from the shock of seeing the figure pop out from behind the brick.

"But I must continue to the top," Adam answered stubbornly.

The large, muscular figure advanced and swung the sword. "I won't allow you to continue! I'll kill you first!" the figure threatened.

Adam backed away. "I have to continue," Adam shouted at the fearsome figure and held his little laser knife in his hand.

The muscular figure started laughing cruelly. "You think you could save yourself with this thing?"

Adam remembered that fateful day on the island of Esperanza when he held the little laser knife in one hand and in the other he held the hand of Paola Katarina, who for him represented an unwavering, unpromising faith. The figure swung the sword and brought the killing blow down on Adam, yet Adam swiftly jumped back, blocking the figure's advance with one hand and with the other aiming the little laser beam directly into the figure's eyes. It cried out with pain and dropped its sword. Thrashing about wildly and blindly, the figure lost its footing, fell off the step, and tumbled down the stairs into oblivion.

Again, a deep silence took over. Adam peered at the spot the armed figure emerged from and saw that the brick was back in its original place, as if it never moved. His breath slowly calmed. He looked at his little laser pocketknife for a long moment, grateful for having it. Then he put it back in his pocket and resumed his climb. He began repeating to himself, "As hard as this seems, I'll do it anyway. As hard as this seems, I'll do it anyway."

One stair after the other, he could feel his strength running out. He decided he must stop now, take a break, eat, and drink something. He rested his back on one of the large steps, took out the food from his pack, and laid it on the step. He realized, to his surprise, that not much food was left. He gazed up to the top of the pyramid, "The way up was still long and arduous, who knows what awaits me up there, and the food is almost gone," Adam thought to himself. He bit into the cornbread the people of Kallag'aro Chicko provided him with, when he suddenly heard footsteps approaching from behind.

He turned sharply and saw behind him a young fawn, accompanied by two squirrels, a few birds, and a child, a child of about eight years old. Adam wondered where these creatures came from, especially the child. Where were his parents, and how did he come here, so high off the ground?

He followed their gazes and saw they were staring at the food, their eyes desperately hungry. He took the piece of cornbread out of his mouth and crumbled it on the step. The birds and the squirrels began eating at once. The vegetables he had left he offered to the fawn, who devoured them hungrily. The last piece of cheese he gave to the child. The child looked into Adam's hawk eyes and spoke, "But, mister, there's nothing left for you to eat."

Adam patted the child's head. "It's all right, kid. I can't sit here and eat when I know someone else is suffering and hungry, so eat. You are more important." Adam was weak from his efforts and his hunger, yet his heart told him he was doing the right thing by feeding the hungry animals and the hungry child. He rested his head on the step and his eyes shut. He slept for only a few moments, and when he awoke, he was surprised to see the child and animals disappeared, as if the Earth swallowed them.

"Where did they go?" he asked himself, thinking for a moment he hallucinated the whole thing, but then he saw a few feathers on the step in front of him, and a few wisps of the fawn's hair. Adam concentrated his attention once more on the mission of climbing the stairs. He didn't imagine to himself at first that the climb to the top would turn out to be this difficult, this long. He looked at the sky that was turning red with the sunset. "I'll go on climbing through the night," Adam decided. He took out his pocket laser and used it to light a dry branch, so it may be used as a torch to light the darkness.

After an hour of climbing in the growing darkness, it was full night, and Adam was fatigued and hungry. His torch was about to burn out. Adam looked up, but in the darkness, he couldn't even see the top. Entirely spent, he fell on the surface of the step.

A dry cough wracked him, but his throat was too dry to swallow. His hawk eye's sought some source of light, but beside the star-speckled sky above him, there was nothing to light his way.

"Could this be the end?" he asked himself. His entire body hurt. He began weeping on the step, feeling his strength leave him, feeling death was about to claim him. "I have to get up there, I have to continue." Adam groaned with pain. "As long as I live, I'll fight," he whispered, breathing heavily. "I choose to carry on through all these difficulties. I have to focus on the positive flow, I can't let any of these happenings to influence me, to break me," Adam said, grinding his teeth angrily; his efforts to rise were futile. He was too hungry, too dehydrated. He simply remained on the big slab of stone in the dark. Suddenly, a flutter of wind blew across his face. He opened his eyes and a small gathering of birds stood beside him, holding clusters of grapes in their beaks. Bird after bird, they came close and brought the grapes to his mouth. Adam ate the fruit, quenching his thirst somewhat on their juices. Within a few minutes, he felt himself slightly recuperated. He stood up and looked at the little birds. "Thank you, kind birds, thanks for you your help." Tears filled his eyes. Once again, God has shown him he was not abandoning him. Suddenly, he heard footsteps from behind and was amazed to see the young fawn he fed earlier, with his mother now, emerge from the darkness. The mother came close to Adam, turning her full udders to him. Greatly touched, Adam realized the gazelle was offering him to drink her milk, so he may grow strong. That is what he did: he drank the milk from the gazelle's udders, and when he finished, he hugged the young fawn and his mother. "I thank you, God, and I thank you two," he cried excitedly to the star-strewn heaven.

The birds spread their wings and disappeared into the darkness, as did the young fawn and gazelle. With great excitement, Adam realized that divine providence indeed exists, and that he is cared for from above. Once again, he held up his burning torch; once again he climbed the huge steps, his blood was gushing through his veins. He felt himself so close to his destination now. He still couldn't see the top, but in his mind's eyes, he saw himself standing there already.

After many hours in which he did nothing but climb, his body gave in and he fainted. His head crashed against the step and blood came trickling down his forehead. The torch fell out of his hand and extinguished as it hit the faraway ground. Darkness enveloped him.

Adam, sprawled on the large step with blood gushing from his forehead, began dreaming. In his dream, he saw himself as he was, stuck on a step, motionless, going nowhere—not up and on, nor back down, simply immobile on the step. Then he heard the screech of a hawk, turned his gaze to a blue sky above, and on the summit of the pyramid, he saw a young child watching him with large eyes. He notices that the face of the child is his own, as a little child at the age of eight.

The child began speaking, "Why are you there?" little Adam asked him. Adam gazed at him, stunned. He is seeing himself when he was eight and talking to himself. "What do you mean?" big Adam asked.

"Why are you stuck there on the step and not going on up?" asked little Adam.

"I don't know," big Adam replied.

"Go back then," little Adam said.

"Back?" asked big Adam and continued at once, "I can't go back, there's no way back."

Big Adam said, "Why is there no way back?" little Adam asked.

"Because I burnt the bridge down," big Adam answered him.

"So you'll stay right here on this step, not going up to the place you always wanted to reach?" little Adam asked.

"I just can't reach the top," big Adam answered him.

"Why?" little Adam asked again.

"Because I'm afraid," big Adam answered.

"What are you afraid of?" little Adam asked.

"That I'll fail," big Adam answered.

"But you must know that victory is in the path you follow, not its destination," little Adam said.

"I don't understand," big Adam said.

"No one can guarantee that we will actually reach the goal we strive for, but what we do know is that as long as we are struggling to reach it we are in fact victorious. The victory is in the striving. As long as you keep trying, you must realize that only God knows it all, the beginning, the middle and the end, only God knows past, present and future. We can only influence the present, and at this moment, we have the power to act, to influence, to try and make things better. That's all you have to do—simply keep doing it. Keep looking forward. You and I, we are one, and this is the place we wished ourselves to be our entire lives. You almost didn't notice this with all your adventures and all the near-deaths, but you should realize that you are already victorious, because you never gave up. You stuck to the path—and the victory is walking the path," little Adam said.

"But I'm worried that if I go on, I'll fail, I won't make it," big Adam said

"You have nothing to worry about. Remember that the only thing that interests you is your goal, your achievement. You have no interest at all in failure. Failure is only a stage you pass through to reach your goal. The good will always win in the end, and if you happen to die before that happens, there's nothing to worry about since you'll already be dead—but you are alive, that's why you have to continue, because this is what you want, and your will shall overcome all the doubts and fears."

Big Adam shook his head. "No, I can't, I'm scared, I don't think I can go any further. I don't think I can take on the force of the entire evil empire," big Adam said. Little Adam began to cry suddenly.

"Why are you crying?" big Adam asked.

"Because you lost your faith, you lost your way, you lost your will to carry out what we always dreamt of doing," little Adam wept.

"What was it we wanted to do?" Adam asked

"We wanted to fix the world. Make it better, save it from all the evil suffocating it, we wanted to do something big that will cast a light over the world, obliterating darkness once and for all," little Adam said in tears.

Big Adam rose to his feet and looked down at little Adam, "I didn't lose my faith, I didn't lose my way, and I still wish to save the world," Adam called out loudly.

Little Adam ceased his crying, wiped his tears, and called out to big Adam, "So what are you doing there, stuck on that step in the middle of the way? Rise up and do it, rise, fight and win—rise, fight, and win!" Little Adam's eyes suddenly shone in a blinding light, and ray of light streamed from them into Adam's hawk eyes. Little Adam and big Adam stood connected by a bright ray of light.

Adam woke up.

Chapter Seventy-Four

The sun already rose. A new morning was shining over Inca Drakna. Birds chirped all around. Adam looked around and was astonished; he found himself sitting on a large step, only one step away from the top of the pyramid. A warm breeze caressed his bruised face. At once he forgot the pain, the hunger, the exhaustion. His mouth managed to express all that was in his heart. "I made it," Adam said with emotion. "All the difficulties, the doubts, against all odds I made it to the summit," Adam said, as he took the last step forward and climbed the last stair.

On the pyramid's summit, there was an odd pedestal, and on it rested a large crystal pyramid, in its center a round, transparent ball the size of a man's fist.

Adam noticed that below the crystal pyramid was a special slot, shaped like a drawer one would place something flat in.

The weather was pleasantly warm. He looked around from the top of the pyramid and realized the pyramid was actually extremely large and tall. He could see the entire city of Inca Drakna sprawled before him. He saw how beautiful it was, how majestic with its huge structures, surrounded by jungles. He turned in the direction of the three great mountains looming behind the city, slipped the pack off his shoulder, and took out the book of Gim Nigma. He laid the book on the pedestal and asked for Karan's guidance. The spiritual apparition of Karan materialized at once.

"Hello there, Adam! I see you made it to the top of the pyramid," said Karan with a satisfied smile. "I'm here because of you and all the good people that helped me along the way. I'm here because of my faith in God, who helps those who help themselves," Adam answered, and the Book of Light opened on its own accord to the center fold; both pages showed a gilded drawing of a stylized sun. "Take the book, Adam. Slide it below the key-pyramid," Karan instructed.

"Key pyramid?" Adam asked.

"Yes, Adam, this is the key that will split open Mt. Victory where Gim Nigma is buried. No one ever made it here, no one had your faith, only you had a heart pure enough to withstand the tests you've been put through, and the suffering you've been put through. The key cannot be activated without the book, and the book would have never been found without your brave decision to embark on a quest after the Book of Light," Karan said. "And now, my son, you must do what you longed to do this entire journey, you must release the mysterious force which is the answer to all the injustice in the world, unleash the power that will right all wrongs. You must free Gim Nigma," Karan called toward the excited Adam.

Adam lifted the book of light, opened it in the middle, and inserted it into the slot underneath the crystal pyramid. The moment the book slid in it glowed brightly, so brightly Adam had to step back. He looked at the sky and saw the sun was in its zenith, then a strong beam of light from the sun fell directly upon the crystal pyramid, which lit up with such a powerful glow it nearly blinded Adam completely. The globe inside the pyramid absorbed the concentrated dose of light, then a colorful beam shot out from it toward the center of the mountain standing in between two other peaks. The beam of light was so powerful that the mountain began crumbling into chunks of rock, which tumbled everywhere. The immense ray of light kept flowing from the center of the glowing pyramid. Adam's eyes grew wide at the astounding sight: the ray of light was shattering the great mountain into rubble. After some time, the ray of light faded, and silence took over. The book of light stopped glowing. Adam was rubbing his eyes, looking at the direction of what a moment ago was a huge mountain; the pillars of dust began to scatter, and Adam gazed upon the thing he searched for so long—from the broken mountain Gim Nigma was revealed, in all its might and glory.

Adam stood on the top of the pyramid looking at Gim Nigma, and an electrifying chill ran through his body. The sight of Gim Nigma was breathtaking.

The image of Gim Nigma was that of an enormous robot. Golden horns twisted out of its head, one emerged from the center of the head. It eyes were in the shape of golden rhombus. His face was elongated and metallic. From its large shoulders, sharp spikes emerged. His entire body was sculpted in metal, in the colors of blue, red, gray and black. In the center of Gim Nigma's chest was a golden emblem of the sun. Gim Nigma didn't move.

Adam, thoroughly astounded, ran his fingers through his hair. "This is Gim Nigma?" Adam asked out loud. Beside the billowing wind, there was no answer. "Gim Nigma is a huge robot," Adam said to himself, and suddenly Karan's glowing image was hovering beside him above the pyramid. "This is Gim Nigma, Adam. This is the mysterious force my people from another planet hid here in the mountains thousands of years ago, so that a day may come and the son of light, the pure-hearted one, would fulfill the prophecy and release Gim Nigma from the mountain and give his pure heart to operate Gim Nigma," said Karan loudly, his voice reverberating.

Adam looked at the enormous figure of Gim Nigma then back at Karan's glowing image. "Karan, did you say that the son of light must give Gim Nigma a heart?" Adam asked as the wind around him began blowing stronger and stronger.

"Yes, Adam, you must give Gim Nigma your heart. Gim Nigma needs a pure heart in order to work. You must combine with him, become one," Karan spoke to Adam.

Adam gazed at the huge robot excitedly. "I have to unite with Gim Nigma?" he wondered out loud. Then for a long moment, he was quiet, listening to the wind blowing around him powerfully. "I understand, Karan. I understand I must merge with this giant robot—the solution can never be fulfilled unless I combine with the robot, I realize that it is my heart that will bring Gim Nigma to life. That is how it must operate, that's how it must live," Adam said gravely.

Karan smiled with satisfaction. Adam understood what he must do. "Adam Swandon. Take the Book of Light with you and enter Gim Nigma now and embark on your voyage to the other world."

"A voyage to another world?" Adam asked.

"Yes, Adam, you and Gim Nigma together must reach the other world, the planet of Solouce-Saran, the blue planet, for only there could you learn how to use Gim Nigma and pit his strength against the forces of evil on Earth. Solouce-Saran is where Gim Nigma was created—that is why you must journey there now," Karan said.

Adam looked at Karan doubtfully. He thought that once he found Gim Nigma he could turn to fight the empire's evil forces, and now he learns he must leave on yet another expedition, to Solouce-Saran, the blue planet. Despair washed over him. "Why must I leave for another planet now? Earth is dying, humans are on the verge of extinction," Adam said in a voice that gave away his feelings.

"That is what the prophecy foretells, that once the son of light finds Gim Nigma, he will have to leave on a second voyage, to the planet of Solouce-Saran, so he may learn to use Gim Nigma's mysterious and unique power. Only then will the victory of the son of light over the forces of evil be a real, solid fact," Karan said.

Adam remembered that he set his heart to go forward no matter what; he remembered burning the bridge behind him. There was no way back; all he could do is go forward, only forward. "All right, Karan, I understand. I'll do what I must in order to save humanity from calamity, in order to bring salvation to this world. Just tell me, how do I combine with Gim Nigma?" Adam asked, his fighting spirit rising once again.

Karan said nothing; he only smiled. Before Adam had a chance to speak more, the billowing wind turned into a vortex, creating something resembling a tunnel made of flying sand and stones. Then Karan spoke, "Adam, walk through this wind tunnel, it will lead you to Gim Nigma's chest. Once you find your way in, your heart will activate Gim Nigma, who will automatically launch to outer space, it's course is set to the other world, the blue planet, Solouce-Saran."

Adam looked at the tunnel carved by wind, encircled by the rapid flow of sand and rocks. The tunnel started at the tip of the pyramid and ended at the chest of Gim Nigma, the giant robot.

"Have no fear, Adam, believe in yourself, believe in the good God, believe in your destiny," Adam murmured to himself as he walked into the tunnel, holding tightly to Gim Nigma's Book of Light. He walked forward, the glowing image of Karan following him with a gaze of trust and encouragement. As Adam drew near to the great robot's chest, he noticed the emblem of the sun unfold and open to receive Adam into it. Adam took a deep breath and entered. He was swallowed into Gim Nigma.

Adam found himself in a strangely textured cell. Everywhere there was a soft, even light. Adam was filled with a sense of pleasant warmth, of homecoming, a sense of security. The unique light all around him enveloped him in love. Gim Nigma received Adam into itself with love. Adam sat down on a sitting pad, pleasant to touch. Adam felt himself integrating with Gim Nigma's systems. He laid his hands on two rounded plaques, lit with soft, pleasant, colorful lights. Adam smiled. He reached the solution, he managed to reach the object of his efforts, and he was ready to move on. In his heart, he told himself that no matter what happens, he won't give in and he won't give up. He will carry on bravely and he will win. Outside it was silent once more, the wind stopped blowing. Karan gazed at the huge robot that held Adam in its center and said, "My dear Adam, leave on your journey with confidence, go to fulfill your destiny, have no fear. God will be with you the whole way. Believe in yourself, believe in the path you walk, and you will succeed in fulfilling your destiny. From now on, Adam, you shall be called the Son of Light. Carry on and become victorious then return to save this world as your hearts commands."

Karan's glowing figure disappeared, and in Gim Nigma's chest, Adam's Swandon's heart, the heart of the son of light, beat fiercely. The robot lifted its enormous arms up toward the endless sky; from its back, a blast of fire shot out, which launched Gim Nigma the giant robot, into space. Gim Nigma and Adam Swandon, the son of light, took off together toward their new destination, toward the blue planet, leaving behind them as they flew a long trail of light in all the colors of the rainbow. Adam Swandon, the son of light, and Gim Nigma, called out together in one voice that reverberated through the endless space, "On toward the next destination, on to Solouce-Saran!"

The End

Printed in the USA
CPSIA information can be obtained
at www.ICGtesting.com
LVHW040522181023
761328LV00058B/539